BLOOD
Sisters

Reflections

BLOOD
Sisters

Joe & Ruth Krakovsky

TATE PUBLISHING
AND ENTERPRISES, LLC

Published by Tate Publishing & Enterprises, LLC
127 E. Trade Center Terrace | Mustang, Oklahoma 73064 USA
1.888.361.9473 | www.tatepublishing.com

Tate Publishing is committed to excellence in the publishing industry. The company reflects the philosophy established by the founders, based on Psalm 68:11,
"The Lord gave the word and great was the company of those who published it."

Published in the United States of America

ISBN: 978-1-63418-392-5
Fiction / Action & Adventure
14.10.01

1

The pharaoh's general scanned the riverbank. There was no sign of the enemy. It wasn't like them to not at least have a lookout along the shoreline being as the river was the Egyptians most likely route of travel. From his perch at the front of the ship, the pilot signaled that they had arrived at their destination. With a wave of his hand, the general gave the signal to land and disembark the troops. While the helmsman leaned on the tiller to turn the ship, the rest of the crew prepared to lower the sails. All of this was accomplished in silence so as not to betray their presence to the enemy. Behind them, the other ships in the small river fleet followed their lead.

As soon as the ship ground to a halt in the shallow water of the mud flat, the first soldiers began splashing ashore with their weapons ready. By the time the general joined his troops on dry land, the first units were formed up and ready to advance. Satisfied that all was organized, he gave the signal. The troops moved out into the brush where up ahead lay their objective.

Had it not been for their war dogs and the scouts that were sent out ahead alerting them to the presence of a Nubian ambush, the Egyptian soldiers might have walked right into their trap. As it was, the Nubians had lost their element of surprise and had no other choice but to boldly launch their attack on the invading Egyptian main body.

The general's veterans met the onrush of natives with a shower of arrows and stone bullets flung from their slings. This weakened the impact of their charge and continued to do so even further as they engaged in hand-to-hand combat with the Egyptian infantry. Try as they might, these fierce warriors were no match against the combined might of the trained military men and their modern copper-edged weapons. The Nubians were adept as light skirmishers but were at a disadvantage in a stand-up fight against heavy infantry in formation, and as a result, they were driven back with a fearful slaughter. The native survivors fell back toward their village, having bought time for most of the other inhabitants to make their escape.

The general's troops followed, except for those who had stopped to claim their bloody trophies. Having experienced combat for the first time, and eager to gather up proof of their martial abilities, some of the newer soldiers briefly broke formation to cut off the hands of their slain enemies before rejoining their units. Confident in the final outcome of victory, their leader overlooked this minor infraction because he valued the importance of good morale in his troops. In this case, he would be content to leave the discipline to their direct superiors at a later date.

The natives were defeated, slaves were taken, and the village was put to the torch. The general had accomplished his mission, and there would be no further hindrance to trade arising from these bothersome villagers for some time to come.

With their prisoners in tow, the Egyptians quickly re-formed and made their way back to their ships. There was no serious attempt by the natives to impede the victors as they withdrew. A few spears were thrown, and arrows shot, but the Nubians knew what fate would befall them if they drew too close. They then limited their show of resistance to a halfhearted attempt at defiance from a distance, and the Egyptian missile troops reciprocated in kind.

The embarkation was completed without any more interference on the part of the defeated villagers. Now that the invaders were gone, they returned to salvage what they could of their homes and to seek the whereabouts of their loved ones. The dead and missing would be mourned, but life would go on as it had for generations.

Out on the River Nile, the flotilla began the journey southward. There was no need for unfurling the sails, as now the current would carry them home. The physicians tended to the wounded. The Egyptians were naturally treated first, and then the newly captured slaves. Any of the prisoners deemed to be beyond help, or not worth saving, were simply thrown overboard to feed the hungry crocodiles that inhabited these waters. Weapons were cleaned, and claims of valor were exchanged among the men. Proudly showing off their grisly trophies brought affected admiration from the more experienced men, as well as the lash from their superiors for breaking ranks to have gathered them. It was all part of an elaborate, unrehearsed ritual that soldiers throughout the ages would experience.

The River Nile teemed with life, but it could also be a treacherous source of death. Herds of seemingly gentle hippopotamus could be more dangerous than the crocodiles, and they were actually the more likely killer of man when disturbed. A sharp lookout was kept for them, and when nightfall was closing in, the ships headed for the safety of the shore where they would make camp. Only the inexperienced or the foolish would attempt to navigate the Nile in the dark.

It was during their first night in camp when tragedy struck. Being unable to sleep and feeling the need to check on the camp, the general rose from his cot only to startle a snake, which had slithered into his tent seeking warmth. He managed to kill it, but not before it sank its fangs deeply into his forearm. The venom was extremely potent, and before the sun god Ra made his appearance in the morning sky, the revered general was dead. It was with great sadness that his troops bore his body back to the land of the Egyptians.

2

The general had been loved and respected by many. He had served his pharaoh well. His funeral would be a stately one, complete with the required days of mourning, elaborate preparations of his body, and finally, the burial. No expense would be spared. Not only would he be remembered in this life down through the ages, but he would be properly prepared for the next one as well. Everything he might need in his next life would be buried with him. After all, death was not a permanent state but was merely a temporary deep sleep.

Unfortunately, this love for the general was not shared by everyone. Aside from some jealous individuals at the palace, there was also a certain slave belonging to the priest who was responsible for overseeing the preparations for the deceased before burial. She was Nubian by birth, and proud, but had lost her freedom long ago to one of the general's earliest punitive raids against her homeland to the south. She greeted the news of his painful death with elation and looked at it as long overdue retribution from her gods. These feelings of hatred she kept to herself. She thanked the gods for smiling upon her by allowing her to oversee the preparations of the general's body. Her master was a lazy and lecherous man, who found it more to his taste to entertain himself with earthly pleasures rather than to do as he was entrusted. He would have this slave see to the endless tedious details as she had been trained to do.

This Nubian woman, whom he had named Helea, had turned out to be one of his better investments. She wasn't much to look at, and she had boldly repelled his one and only attempt to have his way with her; yet for some reason, he could not bring himself to punish her. This had more to do with a nameless uneasy fear of what he believed she might be capable of rather than respect for her as a person.

As it was, she was quite useful to him in other ways. She was very intelligent for a savage, and she was eager to learn, not only the arts of mummification, but she had also learned how to read and write. Being educated was frowned upon and was a punishable offense for the commoner who dared defy those who held the power to make the laws. Therefore, even those who had the way and means to learn simply chose not to. Even many of the scribes who copied the writings of the *Book of the Dead* could not read but rather simply duplicated what was in front of them. In this master's case, although he had the means and opportunity to do so, he also chose not to learn to read and write purely out of laziness. Yet he was perceptive enough to see the advantages of having his servant know these things so that she could perform certain tasks in his stead. He in turn had powerful friends who relied upon him for this service too, so as a result, this lowly slave had the ability and the opportunity to read secret documents and correspondence. And even if caught in the act, who would suspect that a mere slave would be able to figure out the meaning of the elaborate pictorial writing that was hieroglyphics? No one could fault her for merely gazing on the curious pictures and markings.

And so it transpired that the person who probably hated the general the most was placed in charge of preparing him for his next glorious life.

Preparations started immediately, as soon as the general's body was delivered. To all outward appearances, Helea appeared to be performing her job with all the skill and outward display of reverence. But unseen, deep within her heart, her hatred burned as she quickly formulated her secretive plan. Surreptitious orders were given to other household slaves to gather the items she desired. Quickly and covertly, they began to gather these materials without question, just as they had done on many other occasions. They knew better than to oppose this woman who was believed to possess magical powers, therefore those ignorant slaves all feared her. None of them questioned what use she could possibly have for such things as lethal venoms and poisons, skin from individuals who suffered from leprosy or had died from disease, and the dung from both humans and animals. They obeyed her out of fear of the lash she so freely used on them, but most of all because of the widespread knowledge that she was a powerful witch.

It was a common belief of the Egyptians that after a period of death, a worthy person would enter a new life with their same body, and that any items buried with them would be used and cherished by them in the hereafter. For this reason, the bodies of the worthy, which usually meant the rich and powerful, were prepared for preservation by means of mummification. Before Helea began to work, she gave orders that sent all others off on various tasks, which temporarily left her alone with the corpse. She used this time to lean close to his face and whisper her oath of hatred and her promise of vengeance by the use of a powerful curse—a curse so potent that it would follow him into the hereafter, tormenting him for all eternity.

Due to the general's elevated status, the woman pretended to show her respect by overseeing and performing much of the work herself. She started the process of mummification by bathing his body in perfumed water. According to the standard practice, she then inserted hooks up through his nostrils in order to chop up and extract the bloody gray matter that was his brain. She had taken a special delight in ramming those sharp hooks into the general's skull. What was not extracted with the hooks was dissolved with a special solution prepared for the occasion, and then drained. This useless material would not be needed in the next life, so after it was removed, it was simply discarded. The cranial cavity was then rinsed, not with the usual perfumes and oils, but with sewage that had been gathered by the slaves, unbeknownst to them, for just this purpose. With a thrill of long overdue satisfaction, she poured the liquefied dung in through his nostrils.

The heart, lungs, and certain other organs were all needed in the next life, so these were removed through a careful incision and set aside. Common practice was to preserve each one separately in their own special jar until they were reclaimed by the resurrected deceased. In this case however, the organs were washed in a solution consisting of the diseased organs of those who had died, and then they were sealed in jars along with pieces of rancid and diseased flesh and feces. Although the Nubian witch did not understand the concept of disease-causing microorganisms, logic dictated to this intelligent woman that the opposite of what was most desirable would be the best thing to substitute in this case.

The body cavity was emptied and ready to be cleansed and packed with herbs and spices, but in their stead, a special sludge of feces, poisons, venoms, and all the toxic materials, and contaminated human flesh that she had accumulated, were used to pack into the hollowed opening that had been formed by the removal of his internal organs.

The standard practice was to steep the body in natrum for seventy days. Helea cut this period short, which her master often secretly did in order to save on expenses. Her diabolical intention was to carry out just enough of the traditional ritual to make certain the resurrection would take place yet would still ensure that the general suffered greatly through her revised faulty burial procedures.

After waiting impatiently for the steeping to be completed, she wrapped the corpse in clean bandages, some of which should have had powerful prayers written on them to aid and protect the individual on their journey through the netherworld. But in this case, they were inscribed with powerful curses.

For the last step in the process, the cloth-wrapped body was smeared in gum, and placed in the wooden casket in which it would be transported by procession to its final resting place.

Almost as an afterthought, she added an additional curse to a scroll, threatening anyone who disturbed this mummy or its tomb. This was to prevent anyone from inadvertently interfering with, or foiling her attempt at revenge.

> I call upon the gods of the Egyptians and those of Nubia
> To torment any who dare disturb this burial chamber or
> the occupant within
> May you be plagued by venomous creatures of the land
> May your enemies spirit away your beloved family
> May you be afflicted with disease for which no cure can
> be found
> May you suffer unspeakable pain unrelieved even upon
> death.

The woman finally had her vengeance on the man who had murdered her family and enslaved her people. Her curse would follow and haunt him into his next life. He would not enjoy his wealth, power and health when he rose again. When the time came to reclaim his body, he would find it was crippled and wracked with disease. And best of all, he would find no release from his suffering by death. She had done everything she could to ensure that he would suffer into the eternities.

All this elaborate planning was unknown to those who loved and respected the great man. A horrible death would have awaited this woman, and all who had assisted her, including her master, had they had been found out. But it seemed that this crime and terrible desecration was not to be discovered, so Helea appeared to have gotten away with it. And so, in an act of boldness, she decided to take one additional step. Just before the body was to be laid in its coffin, she switched the general's body with that of another so that the general was buried in the tomb of a common man. She was then able to have him secretly dug up, entrusting other slaves with the special mission of transporting the body to her homeland. By her reasoning, when the time came for him to reclaim his physical form, not only would he find one that's diseased and crippled, he would also be a pauper in a strange land, far from his gods, and surrounded by his hated enemies!

What was unknown to this vindictive woman was that the general's body was not taken all the way back to Nubia as she had ordered. Tired of struggling with the unwieldy mummy wrapped in a heavy Egyptian carpet and only having been provided with a sway backed old donkey to carry the tools and the heavy stone Canopic jars, the slave in charge decided that the general be taken only far enough south as was deemed safe before they entombed the body in a cave, which was found by chance.

This slave was not privy to Helea's diabolical plan, and though he feared her, he was no better a faithful servant than she was. He suspected something sinister about this secretive task, so he wanted his part to be over and done with. Besides, he had no desire to travel all the way to Nubia and risk being taken by savages. The Nubians were not his people. So after the general's body was laid to rest, he killed the two others who had helped him, leaving them where they had fallen there in the tomb. He then attempted to mark one of the walls with some of the symbols written on the scroll, but when it started to grow dark, he gave up, leaving the task unfinished. He could not read nor write, but he felt better for having tried his best to make things right. He then sealed the cave and started on his return trip home where an assassin, sent by Helea, waited en route to silence him forever.

3

And so it was that the general's body lay forgotten in his secret tomb beneath the sands. Over the centuries, the various gods came and went, along with their invading armies. Through the desert above the sleeping general, there had marched the Greeks, the Romans, the soldiers of Islam, and then the French. Each had left their mark on the ancient land, and in time, they too passed away. Only the ever shifting sands remained, blowing and drifting in the wind.

In the nineteenth century, it was now the turn of the British. Ever since the massed ranks of British infantry had stood up to and decimated Marshal Ney's charging cavalry with musket fire at Waterloo, the British star had been on the rise. Even before that, their armies and naval forces, along with those of the other European nations, had been carving up the world into "spheres of influence," which was a euphemism for conquered territories. The British were so successful that it would be said that the sun never set on the English Empire.

There was indeed certain cockiness on the part of the British themselves. Like ancient Rome, they conquered much of the known world. Like Rome, they suffered their setbacks from time to time, such as when General "Chinese" Gordon was butchered at Khartoum during the Mahdist uprising. And like Rome, they always sprang back. Driven from the field by the Mahdist armies who were descendants of those ancient Nubian warriors, and challenged elsewhere by Russian Imperial interests, the British had left the Nubian territory that was then known as the Sudan. Years later, they would eventually return in greater numbers, and with more powerful weapons. They would crush the descendants of those proud Nubian warriors who still fought with spears and shields, just as their ancestors had done over four millennium ago.

Following in the footsteps of the victorious British armies were armies of a different sort, composed of engineers, doctors, missionaries, civil servants, scientists, and businessmen, as well as thrill-seeking adventurers of various kinds.

Back in England, one of these forthcoming adventurers, Sir Arthur Billingsley, was discussing with a friend his plans for a trip to the Orient, as the Middle East was called at that time. The two English gentlemen were smoking their pipes and sipping after dinner drinks in Sir Billingsley's study. They were both men of some means; but other than that, they were quite different.

One of the men, Sir Michael Elliot, a short round gentleman with black hair streaked with gray, whose girth was probably equal to his height, seemed to roll like a ball whenever he leaned forward to pick up or put down his glass or pipe. At the moment, his hands were clasped, with thick fingers interlocked and resting on the ledge made by his ample belly. The other man was tall, lean, and already totally gray, though in a distinguished way. And he moved with the grace of a fine swordsman whose movements were quick, clean, and precise. The short, stout one spoke.

"Well, my dear friend, I admit there may be some advantages to financing such an adventure. Although chances are slim, there is always the possibility that a discovery could be made that would bring a certain notoriety to those involved, not to mention the potential for great riches. Imagine finding the tomb of some long forgotten king, untouched by grave robbers! Such a place would probably be packed full of jewels and gold. It would make one quite a wealthy man. Or add to his wealth…" he quickly amended, with a nod of his head to his friend. Sir Arthur Billingsley was already a rich man by any standards.

"I am not doing this for the money," Sir Billingsley said as he finished his drink with a gulp. He always felt uncomfortable whenever his friend made reference to his wealth. True, he was born into money and the titles that came with it. But since his beloved wife died falling from her horse years ago during a fox hunt, he felt like a man who had lost every bit of his worldly goods. Every bit of it that is, except for one precious jewel of radiant beauty.

From down the hall came the soft laughter of a feminine voice. It brought a subdued smile to Sir Billingsley's face. It was his only child, Lilly, who had grown and matured into a beautiful young woman, who not only reminded him of his late wife, but was the one thing that he truly cherished in this world. Of medium height with a slender build, she had her mother's auburn hair with glints of red that came alive like fire in the sunlight. Her thick lashed green eyes sparkled like jewels when she was happy, and Sir Billingsley strove to keep her happy, sometimes to the point of overindulgence. She had her father's open friendly smile and seemed totally unaware of her exceptional beauty. It was solely for her that Sir Billingsley cared for and hung on to his worldly possessions. Otherwise he felt that he would have abandoned it all long ago, for with his wife's passing, he had almost lost his will to live. Sometimes he lay alone at night and wondered if he had been but a poor tenant on one of the farms of his family's estate, would he still be enjoying life with Lilly's mother? He would gladly give it all up if he could have her back.

Another laugh wafted through the air like the soft tones vibrating from the taut strings of a violin. As if sitting in the balcony at the symphony, both men paused to listen.

"You are not seriously considering letting her go, are you? Trudging around the hot sands like a common soldier is not a very ladylike thing for one of noble birth to be doing. You can't really mean to allow this!" Suddenly afraid he may have said the wrong thing, or at least without the right amount of tact, he quickly added jokingly, "At least buy her a commission and a fancy uniform." Sir Michael Elliot halfheartedly chuckled as he rolled forward to retrieve his glass and then took a long slow sip as he stared at Sir Billingsley, signifying that he really desired an answer.

Sir Billingsley slowly puffed on his pipe while he thought about the matter. Other than muffled voices from down the hall, the only other sound was that of the crackling fire, which cast dancing shadows over the leather bound books lining the shelves of the room. How could he explain to his friend how he felt?

Sir Billingsley's feelings of guilt had played a part in his decision. It was partially his fault that Lilly had her heart set on this expedition. He was responsible for lighting that fire that led to her interest in ancient history and also fueled her desire to attend the university to begin with. It was he who had stimulated her yearning to find out more about the world around her. He would always remember the night shortly after his wife died, when he was sinking down into the depths of despair. Selfishly thinking only of his own pain, he lost his will to live and was about to pass the point of no return, when he heard muffled cries from a little face buried in her pillow. Maybe it was fatherly instinct, or perhaps his wife's angelic hand upon his shoulder that gave him the strength to rise up and go to his little daughter who was crying alone in her room. Wanting her mother and not understanding why she was gone, she looked up at him with those big green eyes full of tears that were pleading for an answer. Angry at God for taking his wife, and not feeling very pious at the moment, he explained death as a voyage that her mother had undertaken, much like something he had once read about of some ancient peoples' beliefs. In an attempt to calm her, he described her mother's journey as one to a far and distant land where she would see many amazing and wondrous things. His feeble efforts brought surprising results, and so it was, that the nightly ritual began in which he taught her of the wonders of the world, in similitude with her mother's ongoing journey. What developed was a bonding between him and his daughter.

In time, the seed he planted in her mind began to grow. She started to read and study on her own. Then one night, it was *she* who told *him* of the sights and wonders of a strange land while he sat and listened. This went on until the time came when he felt as though she didn't need him or his stories any longer because it was obvious that she was learning more about the world than he could teach her. Feeling a little embarrassed, he stopped going to her room for their nightly chats, under some false pretense or another. Thinking back and remembering those nights, he missed them and the closeness he had felt to her. Yes, not only would he let her go on this expedition that he was funding, but he would accompany her as well. It would be father and daughter bonding once again!

"Yes, I am letting her go," he said at last. "And *I* am going with her." The words spoken softly yet firmly and with such authority, conveyed the message to Sir Elliot that the discussion was over. In desperation, Sir Elliot did however have one more card to play.

Looking down into his glass as he swirled the caramel-colored liquid around, he asked, "What about marriage? She is what, seventeen now? I'm sure she must have many worthy suitors." *Such as my son, Richard,* he thought to himself.

"We will have plenty of time for such a wondrous occasion when we return," Sir Billingsley said with a forced smile. This was his last chance to regain that closeness with his daughter, and he was not going to let it pass by. Once she was married, another man's love and needs would necessarily have to come first.

Sir Elliot knew better than to pursue the matter. He was still thinking about it though. He would have to have a serious talk with his son. It might be prudent if Richard went along on this journey to look after the girl whom his ambitious father was planning on him taking to wife.

4

"What do you mean she is going to Egypt? She didn't mention any of this to me. Just how and when am I supposed to woo her if she is running off to Egypt?" Richard Elliot was visibly upset. He began pacing back and forth like a jackal in a cage. It was bad enough that she persisted with this nonsense of continuing her education, but now this was going too far. He blamed this unladylike behavior on her rich father who, to Richard's thinking, let her get away with too much. She wouldn't even have been allowed to attend the university, especially at her age, had her father not showered funds on that establishment of higher learning. While it was true that she had always excelled in her studies, at seventeen, she should be thinking about more practical things such as making a good marriage. Wasting time seeking an advanced education only encouraged objectionable behavior in women, such as gallivanting around the world instead of staying home and raising children!

Richard Elliot was a rather handsome man, as all the ladies would attest, and he was as unlike his father as a son could be. Tall, with black hair and sensuous, almost sleepy brown eyes, his muscular body showed no signs of taking after the elder man's portly shape, and he moved with the bearing and grace of a prince performing a waltz. His contemporaries, with a hint of jealousy, snidely called him "Wolf" behind his back. The ladies all vied for this gentleman's attentions, but to those who really knew him, he was anything *but* a gentleman. He was a man used to doing whatever it took to get his own way.

"I spoke to her father," Sir Elliot said to his son. "He has given her permission to go, and is financing the expedition. And now he says he is also going with her. I'm beginning to think he is as anxious to go on this trip as she appears to be, so I really don't think there is anything we could say that will make him reconsider."

"Well, Father, what am I to do?" If his father could not fix this, who could? Richard had the feeling that Sir Billingsley did not really like him very much, so there was no sense in speaking to him himself.

"There is only one thing that you can do. You must go with them."

"To Egypt? Why the devil would I want to go there?" This was not the quick fix answer that he wanted to hear.

"Because the one you plan on marrying is going there!"

"But it is bloody hot there and…"

Sir Elliot interrupted him. "How will it look if you don't go with her? The young lady who you supposedly love is marching around the desert, living in a tent, and enduring hardships, while you sit around back here in comfort playing cards with your friends. It is your duty to be there to protect her, from bandits, lions, and other wild animals!" *Not to mention other possible suitors!*

Orchestrating this marriage was turning out to be much more difficult than he had originally anticipated. His son was now acting like he wasn't even interested in pursuing her. "You're going! I will see to the arrangements."

It was clear that Sir Elliot had said the final word here. Though he often let his son have his own way, it was occasionally necessary for him to put his foot down.

Richard knew it was useless to argue with his father when he made a decision concerning his future, and since it was Sir Elliot who controlled the purse strings, the young man had to give in to his father's demands. Sir Elliot was a shrewd businessman and was tired of constantly having to finance his son's extravagant lifestyle and make good on his gambling debts. At twenty-five years old, it was time for the boy to become a man and fend for himself, albeit with the help of his spouse's fortune, but it would free his parent from all financial responsibility concerning his wild offspring. Sir Elliot had put a lot of thought into this, and he too was used to getting his own way.

After his father left the room, Richard swore under his breath. He supposed going through with the rituals and ceremony of marriage was worth it, considering the prize. Marrying into such money would be a blessing in itself. Once they were wed, any and all of Lilly's inheritance would legally become his. Winning Lilly was just an added bonus. She was truly beautiful, and he would be proud to show her off at social functions. No doubt she would bear him many fine children, but the smile that came to his lips was not for thought of Lilly.

It was Maggie who had just come to his mind at the thought of children. She had already bore him one child, a daughter. At least she assured him it was his. You never could be certain of these things especially since the woman involved was definitely not an innocent. One thing he *could* be sure of was that Lilly was a lady, not a woman of questionable morals.

The thought of going to Egypt for God knows how long was repulsive to him. That was certainly no place for a lady. He groaned and ran his hands through his hair. He supposed his father was right. He could use the time on this trip to convince her that her future was with him. Every other woman would jump at the chance to return his attentions. Why was it that the one woman he wished to win over was tantalizingly just out of his reach? She seemed to like him well enough and responded to his flirtations, but when he tried to talk about a potential future together, she managed to evade the subject.

What was her father thinking to allow this trip to take place? It just wasn't something she should be a part of. It was not a woman's place to travel to foreign lands, be involved in politics, science, or business. Lord knows, if you let them do that then one day, they would want to be in the military too! Such things were biologically, theologically, and sociologically wrong! A woman's place was in the home, not on safari. Some of his friends had been on safari and had told him of their adventures. That was just not his cup of tea. Tea! He decided that he wanted some and called for the butler.

5

While Sir Elliot was making his arrangements, everybody else was too. Sir Arthur Billingsley called his manservant and told him to prepare to pack his bags. He then went to his study and started writing instructions for his lawyer and accountant. He had the utmost confidence that his loyal servant would see to the rest of the household affairs as he had in the past. As he was writing, he paused for a moment and smiled as he realized that Lilly would need to go shopping to prepare for this trip.

Taking Lilly shopping was one of the things he really enjoyed doing with her. For someone born into wealth, she was very frugal when it came to spending money. It wasn't that she wanted to jealously hoard her wealth, or flaunt it as many others were wont to do. She could be quite generous with it, such as when she was little. Hearing about the plight of the poor children in the orphanage, she asked her father if they could do something for them. He made a sizable donation, which provided the much-needed food, bedding, and clothing; but it turned out what she had really wanted to do was to invite the orphans to her birthday party, to which he finally relented.

He smiled as he remembered the looks of disapproval on the faces of some of the more well-to-do guests. But it had been worth it! Lilly may not be one to worship money, but she was a woman, and she still loved to examine the finer items in the London shops. It brought him great joy to watch as she studied each article that caught her eye, admiring the material and workmanship, which made each piece unique. And when she finally did make her purchase, she would be so happy with it and would hug her father like a little girl as she thanked him. Yes, he would definitely have to take her shopping!

The man who had arranged for the trip to take place, Professor William Buller, was also busy getting everything in order. His first expedition had been at age twenty-one when he was quite young, so many years ago; the same age his nephew and traveling companion, Charles Buller, was now. He had been on many journeys since then, so he was quite experienced at this sort of thing. The one thing he was apprehensive about was the fact that they would be bringing a female along. He thought about that as he twirled the long black ends of his waxed mustache. Even though Lilly was an exceptional student of his, and Charles had taken on the role of her tutor, it didn't change the fact that traveling with a woman was thought to bring bad luck, which could only mean trouble. But since her father was paying for the whole expedition, as well as being one of the main benefactors of the university, how could he refuse? They would just have to make do as best they could. It was a good thing Charles was coming along as he could watch after her and hopefully keep her out of trouble.

When the professor first mentioned to his nephew, Charles, that Lilly and her father would be accompanying them on their trip to Egypt, he didn't know what to think. He knew how the professor felt about it, so he was a little apprehensive at first. Although he thought it strange that an educated man such as his uncle should be so superstitious, he imagined there must be a logical reason for it. Maybe women have a knack for getting into difficult situations in the field? After all, they are the weaker sex. He could just picture her getting lost or snagging her dress on thorn bushes. Maybe living in a tent and trudging about in the wilds is no place for gently bred Lilly. He could not picture her using a slit trench out in the brush as a latrine, nor bathing in a river.

Bathing in a river? Hmmm... He was surprised and felt a little embarrassed that he had dwelt on that thought for a moment, but he then smiled to himself as he pictured the comical scene of her being chased out of the river by a snake or baby hippopotamus while everyone laughed, and he had to step in to rescue her. Maybe his uncle was right, but Charles still felt quite excited about this adventure. And when his uncle mentioned that he would expect him to stay close to Lilly and watch over her, he didn't realize that he had a big smile on his face until his uncle reminded him that this was serious business.

Lilly, whom he regarded as a friend in a strictly platonic relationship, (she was, after all, above his station), had the essence of a beautiful Greek goddess, whom he never tired to gaze upon. Her beauty, combined with her seeming lack of awareness of it, had a calming effect, which made the sharing of his knowledge of the ancient world with her such a pleasurable experience. When he spoke to her of things that were his passion, she not only listened to the facts, but absorbed them in such a way that made it easy for him to open up. When tutoring her, she seemed to draw the knowledge from him in an almost mystical way. It was like she could see into his soul, and he was no longer nervous or afraid, which was unusual since he was normally awkward and extremely shy around women.

He was quite handsome in a serious, studious kind of way. Of average height, he appeared to be a little on the thin side, which caused him to appear almost gangly, but this was misleading.

Even though there was probably not an ounce of fat on him, the flesh that he did carry on his frame was pure muscle. His rather long brown hair was always neatly combed back, except for that persistent lock that always seemed to flop down into his hazel eyes to serve as a distraction whenever he really needed to concentrate. One of these days, he swore that he would just cut it all off and be done with it!

Thoughts of sharing his traveling experiences with Lilly made Charles start making his plans with an eagerness that he had never experienced before. There was so much to do, yet as he went about his business, he found that his thoughts kept drifting back to Lilly and all the time he would be spending with her. He really did enjoy telling her about history. She was such a good listener. Ever since his uncle had taken him in when his parents had died, he had grown up in a somewhat sheltered life. While other boys his age were studying in the classroom and playing sports, Charles was studying his textbooks while on archeological digs with his uncle in various lands around the world. Archeology had become his passion, and ever since he met Lilly, he had someone other than his uncle to share this passion with. When he started explaining things and teaching her, he felt so at ease, that he became quite creative in his descriptions and lessons.

Sometimes, to her amusement, he would tell her to close her eyes and relax, and as she listened to his voice, she would imagine the scenes he would be describing with such clarity, that she could almost smell the smells and hear the sounds in her mind's eye as he spoke. This was so easy for him to do because it was as if he was actually seeing her in the different settings and picturing her as the person who lived during the time he was talking about. The thought of now actually being able to physically show her these things while explaining them would be sheer joy! Oh, the magic he could work with his imagination! If he could have her sit in an actual throne room while he explained in detail what could have been going on around her there some two or three thousand years ago, she would probably start speaking Egyptian! The thought pleased him.

He then remembered who her father was, and that suddenly made him sad, for he suspected that once they returned home and her father married her off to someone rich or with a title, that would be the end of her studies at the university. But until that day came, or at least while they were on their expedition, he would teach Lilly all he knew about ancient Egypt.

At this same time, Lilly was contemplating what may be needed for this exciting venture and was mentally constructing an organized list of necessities. She knew that she would need some new clothes to wear. Common sense told her that packing for an expedition required a different sort of clothing than what she normally wore. Formal evening gowns were beautiful and fun to wear when one dined or entertained one's guests, but would they be appropriate for where she was going? She thought not but really had no idea. Some of her lighter weight summer dresses would probably do just fine, especially for such events as taking tea out in the field, but what else might she need?

Lilly decided to ask her father to take her shopping. She suspected that he enjoyed their shopping trips, for whenever she asked him, he always said yes and somehow always found the time to take her. But this time, it would be different. She would not be shopping for a fine dress, but it should be one that was suitable for where they were going. What was in style in that part of the world? A young woman should always look her best. What was the weather like? Would it be hot, dry, or rainy? Most probably hot but one could never know unless one had actually been there.

She thought about it, and then had an idea. What if she should ask if Charles could accompany them when they went shopping? He would know what she would need, and she did trust his judgment. After all, he had been abroad many times with his uncle. She would ask her father if he would permit it.

When Lilly had first asked about going shopping, as he knew she would, Sir Billingsley was ready to agree as usual. He was, however, a bit surprised when she asked about bringing Charles along. Once he got over the surprise, and yes, even a bit of jealousy, he realized that she was right, and it was the sensible thing to do. Being as he wanted the best for his daughter, he told her that as soon as she wrote out the invitation, he would have a member of the household staff deliver it to Mr. Charles Buller in person. Excited, like the school girl that she was, she ran to get her stationery and sat down to work.

True to his word, Sir Billingsley sent the envelope off with the coachman shortly after receiving it from his daughter's hand. When he saw her standing in the parlor watching through the window as the invitation went on its way, he felt satisfied that he had made the right decision.

On Wednesday, the twenty-third, at precisely nine of the clock, Charles approached the wrought iron gate in front of the Billingsley's luxurious home. He just stood there for a moment feeling out of place with a large book tucked under one arm until he looked over to his right and saw a uniformed bobby eyeing him. As if he wasn't nervous enough as it was, the bobby turned and made it obvious that he was going to keep him in his sight. Charles boldly stepped forward to open the latch and let himself in. It was as though by doing so, he was showing the policeman that he had legitimate business being there. Quickly and carefully, he latched it shut again behind him, as if to put a barrier between him and that man of the law who seemed to be on the verge of challenging him. Like a thief seeking sanctuary, he turned and walked briskly up the brick sidewalk leading across the immaculate lawn to the front door.

Looking nervously over his shoulder, he saw that the bobby had moved over and was now standing just on the other side of the gate, silently watching.

After a few anxious moments, a butler opened the door causing Charles to expel the breath he hadn't even realized he was holding. Before the man in black could speak, Charles blurted out the reason for his visit.

"My name is Charles Buller, and I have come to see Miss Billingsley." *That is not what I meant to say!* he thought, mentally kicking himself. "What I mean is, I have received an invitation from Miss Billingsley. To see her; an appointment actually."

With that, he reached into his jacket and pulled her letter out of his vest pocket presenting it as proof.

The butler abruptly reached out and plucked it from his hand. Recognizing the envelope and the handwriting, he stepped back, holding the door open for Charles to enter.

"Charles, please do come in," called Lilly from the adjoining room.

Charles entered the room and bowed as he greeted her. "Good morning, Lilly. I brought something to show you." With that announcement, he removed a statue from a side table and replaced it with a large open book riddled with pieces of torn paper, marking interesting pages he had come across.

"I have gathered the most likely sources that pertain to our upcoming dig. It's just a matter of sifting through the material to find what I need." Charles likened himself to a poor Bedouin sifting the sand through the various screens in search of pottery pieces at one of his uncle's sites. One never knew which insignificant piece might be the one to finish a puzzle or lead to a treasure.

"This book here, let me show you, was recently published in 1893. It's titled, *The Mummy: Chapters on Egyptian Funeral*

Archaeology." Charles picked up the tome and started paging through it. "I just saw something interesting which stated that the ancient Egyptians did not celebrate birth as others did but were far more interested in a proper burial."

Before Lilly could even read the information for herself, he pulled the book away in his excitement and started flipping pages again. "There was something else here that I wanted to tell you about. Do you remember what I said about the mummification process? You know, what I said about them removing the internal organs and preserving them in jars? It seems that a man must have these organs, especially the intestines, if he wishes to live again someday."

Suddenly, the sound of someone pointedly clearing their throat drew his attention.

"Excuse me, Charles, I believe you know my dear friend, Richard Elliot," Lilly said with a smile as she half turned and innocently touched Charles on his forearm.

It was then that Charles realized they were not alone in the room. Flushing in embarrassment, he looked at the handsome, cultured man sitting in the chair, legs crossed, and pipe jutting out of the corner of his mouth. With a sinking feeling, Charles wondered if this "dear friend" of hers had also received an invitation. "I don't believe we have ever been formally introduced. I'm very sorry for my rudeness. Good morning, sir."

Richard stared insolently at him for a few awkward seconds. It always annoyed him when Lilly acted so friendly toward other men. In his mind, she was being flirtatious. He would break her of that habit when she was his wife. Richard paused to puff on his pipe as though this were the excuse for his rudeness. When he concluded that this gangly, slightly disheveled man could not possibly pose a threat to his pursuit of Lilly, he exhaled the smoke and finally returned the salutation with a nod.

When Sir Billingsley joined them, the carriage was called for. Once everyone was seated, Lilly broke the ice. Up to this point, there was a slight tension in the air between the two young men that was only masked by Lilly's enthusiasm for this little outing. The daughter naturally sat next to her father while Richard and Charles sat across from them.

"Well, where do you suggest we begin?" asked Lilly, looking to Charles for guidance. Charles started to say something when Richard rudely interrupted him to suggest one of the boutiques where Lilly usually did her shopping. He only remembered the name of the establishment because his mistress, Maggie, had mentioned it more than once in her not so subtle hints that she wanted to shop there.

"Charles, were you about to say something?" asked Sir Billingsley. He had thought it rude for Richard to speak over him. Besides, he had taken a liking to his daughter's scholarly acquaintance who had exhibited favorable traits that Richard sometimes seemed to be lacking.

With a bit of shyness, Charles meekly spoke up. "I would suggest that we visit a tailor specializing in men's attire."

Before he could continue, Richard again interrupted him with a terrific snort of surprise, and he laughed out loud until Sir Billingsley silenced him with a pointed look and a slight movement of his hand. Such an act exhibited boorishness and hinted at a lack of good breeding, which Sir Billingsley knew was certainly not the case with his friend's son. Charles hadn't noticed this silent admonishment because he was looking down at the carriage floor in embarrassment, but Lilly had noticed, and she threw Richard a concerned look that silently entreated, "Please don't be mean."

Sir Billingsley did not like the idea of his daughter wearing men's clothing. Not even the suffrage marchers were bold enough to do that! But to make up for Richard's ill manners, he waited politely for further enlightenment on the subject.

Charles continued, "Although I am sure that Miss Billingsley…"

"Lilly," she interrupted, and blushed as she realized she was guilty of the same rudeness as Richard. Charles always called her by her given name when they were at school or when he was helping her with her studies. He just didn't think it appropriate to do so in front of others, especially her father.

He started over with his carefully chosen words. "Although I'm sure that Miss Lilly has many fine dresses that would serve her well at most any social engagement that she cared to honor with her presence, they would be quite impractical where we are going."

He paused, still looking meekly at the floor, and therefore did not notice the look of surprise on Lilly's face. She had never heard him pay her such a personal compliment before, other than for her school work.

Deducing that the silence was his cue to continue. He said, "If I may be so bold, sir," raising his eyes as he addressed Sir Billingsley. "I would suggest a visit to a men's tailor, one who specializes in military type uniforms, which from my experience, are quite practical for where we are going and for what we will be doing. This material will hold up better and be more comfortable, and in certain instances, it will offer her more protection as well." He then nervously looked around, seeking approval for his recommendation.

Lilly didn't know what to think. The very idea surprised yet also intrigued her. What a bold and nonconforming suggestion! And coming from Charles! The idea titillated her senses and smacked of uncommon adventure, which was naturally a lure to her.

Richard, for one, did not like the idea of this young man suggesting that she should be dressing up in men's clothing. He wanted to throw open the carriage door and shove the upstart out onto the road with his foot! What would he be suggesting next?

That she vote? Smoke cigars? Or maybe even stand upright to relieve herself?

Sir Billingsley thought about Charles's unconventional idea and his reasoning. He had no intention of allowing his daughter to dress in such a fashion, but the young man was so uncomfortable and ill at ease that he didn't want to embarrass him any further. So before Richard could protest as he sensed he was about to do, he chuckled in amusement remembering Sir Elliot's joking suggestion that Lilly should join the military and wear a uniform, and said, "Well, young man. There is no harm in looking into the matter. Now that you mention it, I seem to recall someone else suggesting a similar thing. To the tailor it is then."

The proprietor, whose acquaintances often said that he could "smell money in a crowd," did not need his large nose to tell him that these visitors to his shop carried plenty of gold coin. Their bearing and the cut of their clothes said it all.

"We are here to obtain the appropriate attire for a trip abroad, as we will be roughing it up a little, on safari you see. We will need to be outfitted accordingly."

"Certainly, sir. You do understand that I am a men's clothier and am not experienced in the making of women's dresses? Perhaps I could suggest a capable seamstress for the young lady."

"Excuse me, sir. If I may clarify, what the lady needs, what we all need," Charles said to the shopkeeper in the form of a highly recommended proposal, "is more along the lines of the standard issue common white drill, perhaps a dyed khaki or tan, possibly in the form of a split skirt for the lady." To Lilly, he added as an explanation, "Although the material may not be as soft as the exquisite fabrics you are accustomed to, it will hold up better, and won't show off the dirt as much, nor will it easily tear if the going gets rough." He knew the thought of getting dirty wouldn't discourage her and would only mean one thing to her adventurous spirit. They would be doing some serious exploring! "Of course, you may substitute the finer grade as is usually requested by officers."

The tailor looked to Sir Billingsley for confirmation of these guidelines, who gave a nod of approval. Although the father had been against the impression his daughter might make to others parading around in the desert like a common soldier, he now was feeling more comfortable with Charles's clever compromise of the divided skirt, and knowing his daughter would still be dressed as a young lady won his approval. Sir Billingsley made it clear to the tailor that he was to make the skirts to the proper length and fit as was becoming to one of her station. He was beginning to take a liking to this young man, Charles. He seemed to have a good head on his shoulders.

The tailor decided to take on the challenge of a feminine version of the military uniform. Money was money, and he suspected there was an abundance of it here.

Once she had selected her material, Lilly accompanied the tailor's young wife into another room to take her measurements. While they were gone, the tailor would service the rest of them, minus Charles, who had already made previous trips to this region and would only be purchasing a new pair of boots later in the day.

Except for some polite small talk, not much else was said while measurements were taken of Lilly's young body. She didn't have to put on a show of friendliness, for that was something that came naturally to her. It wasn't what was said but rather the open and familiar way she spoke to others that hinted of her true character. She always gave the impression of someone who truly took an interest in others, but her conversation now seemed hindered by something that was weighing on her mind. The tailor's wife felt there was something Lilly wished to say to her, so she finally asked her outright whether there were any other instructions she wished for her to convey to her husband.

"There *is* something that I wanted to ask of you, but I will understand if you decline my request," said Lilly, unsure if she should continue.

"Well, we won't know that until you ask, will we?" said the woman with a kind smile as she continued reading the numbers off the measuring tape and writing them down. Not once did she make eye contact with Lilly, but there was something about her genuinely friendly manner that encouraged Lilly to continue.

"Well, as you know, we are going out of the country, to Egypt, to do some serious exploring. My good friend Charles is the gentleman with the brown hair in the other room with my father and Richard, a good friend of our family. Charles, who has done this sort of thing before, is the one who suggested we come here to begin with. He wanted me to dress appropriately for our adventure. My father agreed to this, but I feel that his fatherly instincts may be overriding, or hindering, what Charles really had in mind for me.

"I would actually like to ask a rather large favor of you for which I will gladly pay extra," she continued, as she reached for her handbag. She opened it up and fingered the gold and silver coins, wondering how much she should offer. Too little might offend her.

The woman looked up at Lilly quizzically. "You don't remember me, do you?"

This caught Lilly off guard. She had no idea who this woman was. "I'm sorry?"

"I remember *you*, Miss Lillian. Although I have seen you off and on in the past, the first time I saw you was *years* ago. We were all quite young then. I myself was only twelve years old at that time. My little sister and I had been placed in an orphanage when our mother died of consumption. We were both very unhappy, and it seemed like we were always hungry. Then one day, things miraculously improved for us. We got a bed that we could share, and my sister got her first pair of shoes. And then suddenly, we had enough to eat, so we were no longer hungry. It was all due to a generous man who gave money to the orphanage. That man was your father.

"But the thing that I will always remember and cherish, until the day I die, was that we were invited to a little girl's birthday party. We had such a wonderful time there that day! Being older, I saw the way some of your other guests treated me and the other orphans. My sister, on the other hand, was too young and innocent to notice that. To her, that day was like a taste of heaven. She wore a smile all day long and cherished the doll that you had given to her. I still have it. My sister treasured it until the day she died. She never named it. She simply called it, the doll that Miss Lilly gave me.

"No, you keep your money, miss. I will gladly do anything you ask of me."

Lilly threw her arms around her in a heartfelt hug, and when their tears had dried, she proceeded to confide to Emma, whose name she now knew, the daring plan she wanted her newfound friend to help her with.

And so it was that the morning was spent being fitted and measured, and groped and prodded, so they would have a suitable and serviceable wardrobe for their journey far from home. After a stop for a quick midday meal, the shoppers finished off their quest for goods by picking out such necessary items as sun helmets, boots, Sam Brown belts, pistols, holsters, and ammunition.

Richard thought it was a rash decision on Sir Billingsley's part and felt he was assuredly going too far in also allowing Lilly to purchase a small pistol and holster. Good heavens! She was being equipped like one of those American Wild West gunslingers! Why couldn't she just leave the matter of protection to the men? Not that she would be capable of protecting herself even with a pistol in hand. Women were just not strong enough physically or mentally to deal with the harsher side of life. They should stick to the duties and responsibilities that were more suited to their delicate natures.

Charles, on the other hand, was not averse to Lilly being armed for added protection. He knew there would be soldiers of the Crown there to protect them, and they should be fairly safe where they were going, but one could never be too careful in such a strange and exotic land. He knew that both Sir Billingsley and Richard probably carried a small pistol in a hidden pocket of their jackets, as most English gentlemen did for protection on the London streets. After all, common sense told one that when the law was not around, the criminals came crawling out of hiding. It was important for all of them to be armed, as travelers always should be when on expedition. If necessary, he would gladly teach Lilly how to shoot.

Sir Billingsley also liked the idea of Lilly learning how use a gun. Many a fine and proper Englishwoman had acquired this skill. One could often see them plinking away at paper targets with their small caliber rifles on the greens. They also practiced archery, just like the men used to do in the days of King Henry V's reign. Only back then, it was mandatory for all men to know how to handle a bow because it was an important part of the defense of the realm. Times had changed, and now the women did it for sport. There would be no harm in Lilly knowing how to shoot. It was not something that she would have to do where they were going, but it would serve her later on in her social functions with other ladies of her class. Sir Billingsley looked forward to teaching her, as it would give him another opportunity to do something pleasurable with his offspring.

Lilly was becoming more excited about this trip every minute. Naturally, she looked forward to seeing the pyramids up close and maybe even touching and climbing on them. She would actually be physically smelling the air of Egypt and feeling the desert wind in her face and not just in her imagination as she listened hypnotically to Charles telling his stories. Even if it were dusty and hot, she told herself, she would not mind, for that was what the pharaohs and their queens had experienced as they walked the lands millenniums ago. She was so excited to have her father coming on this trip with her, and it was fitting to have Charles there to show her the sights he had so far only been able to describe.

She had been pleasantly surprised when she found that Richard had also requested to come. This was the first time he had ever shown an interest in her passion for archaeology. She was glad about that because she really did like Richard and enjoyed spending time with him. She wasn't serious about him, although she did like him very much, but sometimes she suspected he felt more for her than just a friend. He was very handsome and could be extremely charming, yet the feelings she held for him were simply those of friendship.

6

The little group of explorers traveled via steamship, by way of the Mediterranean, on their way to the ancient and mystical land of Egypt. Sir Billingsley could see that Lilly was becoming more excited and was enjoying each and every aspect of the entire experience. She never tired of pointing out the sites, that up until now, she had only read about. Ever since they had passed the mighty British Fortress at Gibraltar, she hardly spent a quiet moment in her stateroom. At first, the rough weather out in the Atlantic Ocean had made her ill; and she was confined to her room for a short time, but she rapidly found her "sea legs" and now she went there only to sleep. She could often be found topside in the presence of Charles Buller and his uncle, the professor, who were usually engaged in serious discussions of what impending wonders lay ahead. Occasionally, Sir Billingsley would join the group on deck, and they would all talk about their hopes and expectations of what they might accomplish when they reached their destination. At these times, Lilly would listen with rapt attention; and with such a sparkle of anticipation in her green eyes, her father knew that if only a fraction of what she hoped for came true, she would be completely satisfied.

Lilly had just finished her afternoon stroll on deck with Richard, which they always took sometime after their midday meal, or at least, after *her* midday meal. Richard wasn't adapting to the pitch and roll of the ship as well as the rest of them were and was therefore eating very lightly and spending much of his time in his cabin below. She thought it was sweet of him to make sure they spent this time together even though he was obviously not feeling his best. Although she enjoyed this time with him, the closer they got to their destination, the more preoccupied she became with thoughts of what lay ahead and was barely able to speak of anything else.

Richard could see that her mind was elsewhere, and it annoyed him. He was outwardly pleasant and seemingly interested in Lilly's excited prattling, but inwardly, he was beginning to regret going along with this whole thing. The constant motion under his feet was wearing on him. He hoped his health would improve once they were on solid ground again. In the meantime, he had found his own distractions to keep his mind off of his physical maladies, and as this excursion was already underway, there was no possibility of turning back now.

The couple parted company with their usual exchange of pleasantries, and they went their separate ways. Lilly sought out the two men of science on the rear deck who were deeply engrossed in studying a map and making notes.

"Hello, professor. Charles."

"Hello, Miss Lilly," the professor said as he only briefly took his eyes off of the map before him.

"Hello, Lilly," Charles replied as he lifted his gaze to note with some relief that she was alone. Richard had a way of making him feel like a dolt, and he always feared that Lilly would one day see him through Richard's eyes and find him lacking in everything that the other man had in such abundance.

"What are you two working on?" she inquired as she came up and stood next to the younger man. She eagerly leaned forward and gazed intently at the crude but artistic hand-drawn map. "Where did you get this?" she asked as she admired all the hard work somebody had so obviously put into it. Besides the usual contours and physical landmarks, there were colorful representations of life in ancient Egypt carefully inserted along the borders.

"I made it," Charles answered shyly. He was not sure what she thought of it. He wasn't much of an artist, so he had drawn it in the style of the writings he had seen in tombs and on papyrus.

"This is amazing! Why haven't I seen this before?"

"Well, I guess I just never had the opportunity to show it to you," he replied with growing pride. Unless she was just being polite, it was evident that she admired it.

The professor noticed Charles studying the contours and features of the girl's face as intently as Lilly studied the map. "Youth!" he thought to himself. *To be young and in love again.* "If you will excuse me, Lilly, there is something I need to retrieve from my stateroom. I trust Charles will keep you company until I return," he said with a polite nod to her.

"Certainly, professor. Hurry back," she called after him.

"So what were you working on?" she asked again as she continued to examine the array of carefully drawn figures. Before he could answer, she changed the subject back to the map. "You drew this all on your own?"

"Yes, it was meant as a record, a keepsake of sorts. A remembrance of all of our expeditions. Do you see the drawings along the border?" As she nodded, he continued. "Each one has some significance to the locations on the map.

"You see this one here of a queen is from the time we were excavating near the tomb of a queen, and we had a near disaster with some Bedouin camel raiders. We came off all right, but it still gave us quite a fright.

"But don't worry," he hastened to add. "We will have nothing of that sort to fear where we are going. That incident happened years ago. Things are quite different now."

She looked more closely at the sketch of the queen. "It seems that she is wearing clothing that hides nothing, almost as if it is transparent." At this, she blushed prettily. "I mean, I can see she is certainly covered by her clothing, but at the same time she gives the illusion of not being covered at all!"

"Why, that is a very astute observation! It is indeed a transparent garment. If you are going to study archeology, one needs to be observant and notice these subtle details, for each one may hold a clue or have significant meaning."

Lilly's eyes took on a dreamy quality as she said, "Oh, I can just imagine sitting on that throne in my own palace, somewhere along the great River Nile, three thousand years ago…"

As she closed her eyes out of the habit of repetition, Charles took up the narration of the images she pictured in her mind. She slowly relaxed and just concentrated on his voice; all the background noise of the ship seemed to fade away to nothingness.

Charles was staring at her intently and studying her features of which he could not help but notice were of near perfection. A sudden gust of wind came up from the starboard side causing a few stray strands of soft auburn hair to work their way from under the protection of her bonnet to tantalizingly caress her cheek. "Do you feel the desert wind blowing in from the north?"

She was becoming so attuned to him that these sessions were getting easier each time. She could actually feel the desert wind that he spoke of, and suddenly her reality was altered, and she was the one sitting on that palace throne. It was as though she had stepped into the body of this ancient Egyptian queen…as if she was actually there.

"Your king, the pharaoh, sits by your side…"

She slowly turned her head to the right and to her surprise, saw Richard, dressed as pharaoh, sitting on his throne beside her. He turned his head to her and smiled a gentle smile. It was that same smile that had captured the hearts of so many. His gaze then shifted back to the front.

"You are dressed in a manner most fitting for a queen of Egypt. On your lovely feet is a pair of soft leather sandals."

Did he say lovely? She looked down and saw her feet were encased in exquisitely fashioned gold leather sandals. She lifted a delicate foot to better admire the detailed workmanship. When she set her foot down, she could actually feel the ever present sand on the otherwise immaculate polished stone floor of the palace, beneath the sole of her shoe.

"Wrapped snugly around your body, from chest down to your ankles, is a soft linen garment trimmed in gold thread. This garment is held up by a single golden strap, which extends up and over your shoulder. A circlet of gold sits upon your regal head. It is adorned with a cobra whose glittering eyes are of jade stones, which exactly match the green of your own eyes."

Yes, she could feel the weight of it on her head.

Lilly heard his voice as if from a distance. She felt as though she were under a hypnotic spell. Suddenly, she became frightened, for she had never felt so totally helpless before. She felt she had lost the ability to control her own thoughts and actions. Charles's words flowed forth as freely as unhindered truth and were accepted by her as if by some royal decree, which made no allowances for any feelings of offense or inappropriateness. She realized that she suddenly wanted, *and needed,* to hear more. Was something pulling her from the other side? She inhaled and felt the silky soft linen material stretch tighter on her skin.

"Around your neck is a small cape that is also made of this same fine linen and extends only as far as your elbows, the ends of which are gathered and held in place by a jeweled clasp. Worn over the cape is a collar made of painted linen—colorful and costly."

As she looked down to behold her described finery, she could see her body clearly outlined beneath the sheer garments. With each breath that she took, the transparent fabric stretched and then contracted with the rise and fall of her chest. Shocked at being so exposed, she realized that she wore the very same transparent garment as the queen in the drawing! Lilly wanted to protest and cover herself, but the mesmerizing voice continued to speak and she was helpless to resist.

"Like the collar, your face is also painted. Red ocher gives your lips a deep red luster, while malachite stands out in bright green contrast around your eyes."

For some reason, she was accepting all of this as fact, and she suddenly didn't care about being so exposed and painted, for the words were describing her as something beautiful and pleasing to the eye. She felt beautiful and powerful, and she decided she liked this feeling. She liked it very much!

"Before you stands your court, with your retainers, ministers, scribes, priests, generals, and musicians…"

Lilly looked out upon the crowd and saw a childhood friend of hers, Marie, who was one of the musicians there in the front rank before the throne. They smiled at one another in recognition. She too was wearing nothing but a transparent covering that reached up to just below her breasts, which were exposed. She was gazing at the figure next to Lilly with a flirtatious, seductive look. Lilly was amused, and she looked over to see if Richard had noticed Marie's boldness. To her shock, Richard was no longer seated next to her, and in his place was a dirty cloth wrapped man-creature. She could smell the stench of it and could see decay and maggots where its dirty rags were torn, revealing exposed rotten flesh! The disgusting being turned its head to look at her. As she stared at him in frozen horror, a large black beetle scrabbled out of the empty socket where an eye should have been. Lilly gasped and stifled a scream as her eyes flew open, breaking the spell she had been a prisoner of. Immediately, she came back to reality.

"Are you all right!" the now-alarmed Charles cried.

She was breathing hard, and a tear escaped her eye. This had never happened before! "I... I...yes, I'm fine. Please excuse me. I must go now." And with that, she hurried off, almost stumbling in her haste to get away.

Confused and bewildered, she tried to make sense out of her bizarre experience. She felt afraid and embarrassed of her secret thoughts and visions. What had happened to her? Had she been hypnotized? Did Charles knowingly submit her to some type of mind control? No, Charles would never harm her in any way. What if, maybe, just maybe, it was a premonition of some kind?

Now she was just being silly. She must have simply been caught up in a vivid daydream. Still shaken, she continued on to her cabin to change for dinner.

By the time everyone had met up for their evening meal at the captain's table, Lilly had finally come back to her senses. She put the experience behind her, feeling a bit silly for allowing it to frighten her so. She glanced at Charles and then quickly away again when she saw his frown of concern directed at her. She was embarrassed for her earlier reaction and sudden flight, so she tried to avoid meeting his eye again. She would speak to him later, and they could laugh about her overreaction to her daydream, or whatever it had been.

Captain Cooper rose to greet the four of them as they approached his table. "Ah, good evening, gentlemen." He bowed charmingly to Lilly and kissed the back of her extended hand. "My Dear."

"Good evening, captain." Lilly dimpled prettily and lowered her long thick lashes shyly before raising them to meet his own sky blue gaze. He was extremely charming, and Richard was annoyed to see her responding to his flirtations.

The captain's damaged smile didn't detract from the man's sincere show of admiration for her. His good looks were marred by a white jagged scar that ran from mid cheek and continued at an angle down through his top lip, which caused one side of his mouth to pucker slightly and appear higher than the other. When he spoke, there was a noticeable empty spot where two of his teeth should have been. Lilly thought perhaps they may have been knocked out when he received his wound, but far from being repulsed by the unsightly scar, she was actually intrigued and wished she could ask him about the origin of it and hear the exciting story behind it. There had always been an adventurous streak in her only held at bay by her upbringing and of course by the fact that she was a female. Maybe she couldn't take part in the exciting stories, but she did so love to hear about them.

Captain Cooper always made sure to clean up and dress in his finest whenever they met for dinner. He also made sure that any and all of his officers who joined them at his table did so as well. But as fine as these officers appeared, they were clearly outshone by their new first mate. They had taken him on at Gibraltar to replace the previous first mate, Mr. Flynn. The unfortunate Mr. Flynn had been left ashore when he became ill with a relapse of malaria.

This new first mate was a mysterious-looking fellow—tall, with sun darkened skin, and quite handsome with his stormy blue-gray eyes, strong jutting jawbone, long jet black side-plaited hair, and with his left ear sporting a large gold hoop earring!

All other faces at the table were familiar from previous meals except this one. The captain noticed Lilly's curious glances at his man. "Please forgive my discourtesy. May I present to you, Monsieur Dumas."

A Frenchman! she thought excitedly.

The tall dashing man bowed and brushed the back of Lilly's hand with his lips. Lilly suppressed a shiver of pleasure. "I am pleased to make your acquaintance, Mademoiselle Lilly." In the

French manner, he put the emphasis on the second syllable of her name.

She smiled back shyly, not quite knowing what to make of this flamboyant character.

Observing this exchange and noting Lilly's interest in this outrageously arrayed peacock, Richard broke etiquette protocol. "Good heavens, is that an earring?" *How barbaric!* Such a thing would be unheard of back home among decent company.

"That it is, sir," he answered, unperturbed at the discourteousness of the disagreeable young man's outburst. Immediately following his response, he turned his attention back to Lilly, and in doing so, he effectively dismissed Richard as he would have any small annoyance such as a gnat.

Richard's eyes narrowed angrily as he drained his wine glass. How could he possibly win Lilly over with all of these distractions for her attention? He would have to make it a point to be extra attentive and charming during their afternoon walk tomorrow. In the meantime, didn't they have anything stronger than wine to drink? He drained a second glass and motioned impatiently for a refill.

"I find it rather dashing," said Lilly, tilting her head as she examined the adorned ear. That defused the situation as far as Monsieur Dumas was concerned. Richard could say whatever he wished. He wasn't going to respond to his gibes as long as this beautiful young woman graced the captain's table.

During the meal, Lilly casually mentioned that Charles had earlier been explaining to her the type of clothing worn by the ancient Egyptians. "It was extremely interesting," she said, as she carefully cut a bite of mutton.

"Oh? Sounds fascinating," Richard said as he raised one eyebrow sardonically.

Noticing the unpleasant tone of Richard's voice, she realized that perhaps he may be feeling left out; and so not wanting to antagonize him, she turned the subject to include him and continued on.

"Charles, did I ever tell you about how Richard and I first met?"

Charles didn't know what to think. First, she was ignoring him and avoiding eye contact, and now suddenly, she was speaking directly to him as though nothing uncomfortable or strange had occurred. That little episode earlier had disturbed him, for she had never acted so strangely before. Had he done or said something to upset her? He decided to follow her lead and see where this took them.

"No, you never told me about that," he said as he pushed the persistent lock of hair off his forehead and sipped some wine.

"When I turned sixteen, Father decided that I should acquire a gown worthy of my coming out. We had just moved back into the city from our country home when an audience was sought, and gained, with Queen Victoria. Although, I must say, at that time I was far more interested in staying in the country. I think it was more important to my father, although now I can say I am grateful for the experience. And too, I might never have met Richard. Even though our fathers were friends, he and I had never met," she said with a smile directed at him. "As you know, being presented to the Sovereign at court is a great honor. It is also considered to be the start of the social season. There was a grand celebration ball, and I must admit that I was extremely excited and quite nervous as I made my entrance. It felt like all eyes were upon me."

All masculine eyes at the table *were* upon her now.

"My gown was pure silk satin, white of course, hand embroidered with seed pearls, and trimmed in a lace so fine it was like a spider's web. It was so lovely. I felt as though I were attending my own coronation. I had just made my curtsey to Her Majesty, the Queen, and was backing away, when I glanced to my right, and there I saw Richard for the first time. He was standing in the crowd, yet he stood out," she said rather fondly.

He too remembered that moment. Richard thought about that night and about how pleased his father had been when he told him about the beautiful young woman of the House of Billingsley. His father had then informed him about his friendship with her father. Even without his sire's prodding, Richard would have gladly sought the company of this young beauty. The only difference was, with their fathers being friends, he had to be careful to treat her with gentlemanly respect. No trifling with this one.

"I danced with many partners that night, but he is the only one who made an impression on me. He was so gallant and charming."

It was difficult for her audience to believe that the individual she was speaking of so fondly was the same boorish man now sitting morosely silent and inattentive. All was quiet; no one even chewed.

Richard smiled to himself remembering the pleasant afternoons they had shared since then, and he determined to try harder to be agreeable when in her company.

For a short time, Richard *did* make a special effort to be the charming gentleman that he was capable of portraying. This was made easier by the fact that he was actually beginning to enjoy himself although all of the expedition talk bored him to no end. He had found a few souls willing to sit down and join him in a nightly game of cards. Even here on the ship, there were more than enough men who seemed eager to risk parting with their money. Ever since they had set sail, he was enjoying quite a streak of good luck with the cards. Albeit, the past couple of days his luck seemed to be changing, but even so, he was still ahead in his winnings. As it is with many gamblers, he was confident that given the time, he could turn things back around in his favor. This trip could turn out to be profitable for him after all. A full bank account and a wealthy wife would certainly make his present discomforts well worth it.

7

When the ship landed at Alexandria, they were transferred to the depot where their journey would continue by way of rail. Once again, their travel was to be powered by steam. What others took for granted brought amazement and wonder to Charles. He speculated on how long the modern world could survive without the miracle of coal power. Electricity had its limited uses, but coal, *that* was clearly the energy of modern man.

The European travelers alighted from their horse-drawn carriage at the station and simply stood together marveling at the bustle and sights around them. A group of laborers materialized out of the milling crowds, just as they had at the docks, and efficiently proceeded to unload their trunks from the accompanying wagon.

Lilly's arrival was duly noted by more than just a few random bystanders. Even in the extreme heat, she appeared like a freshly bloomed flower in a desert oasis. The reddish streaks in her rich brown hair had now been joined by sun bleached golden strands. Although proper young ladies were taught to avoid exposing their skin to the sun, Lilly loved the feel of it on hers; and as a result, her face was becoming lightly tanned. Standing there in her peach-colored summer frock amid a sea of dirty white and military issue tan, she definitely stood out in the crowd.

Over near some packing crates, Mr. Harry Brown spit out the wooden matchstick he had been savoring and gave the fellow next to him a sharp jab in the ribs. The startled gentleman looked up from the newspaper he had been engrossed in and was about to offer his companion a harsh rebuke for his painful gesture, when he too caught sight of Lilly through the crowd.

"Get a load of *that!*" Mr. Brown exclaimed, as he straightened his white drill jacket and repositioned his straw hat on his rather large head.

"How many times have I told you it's impolite to stare?" his friend with the sore ribs admonished. With that, he abruptly left his companion behind and rapidly started weaving his way through the noisome mob toward the beautiful woman.

"Hey! I saw her first!" Mr. Brown exclaimed in his distinct American accent as he took off after the usurper who was trying to move in and steal his girl.

The "usurper," wearing a slightly dusty gray bowler hat and matching suit, reached the "prize" first with his indignant companion close on his heels.

"Please excuse me if I do not follow the proper etiquette and wait to be properly introduced, but I believe it may be to our mutual benefit to dispense with the usual formalities," he said as he presented himself to the newly arrived travelers. This little speech was addressed to them all, but his eyes were continually drawn to Lilly.

"Hello there! My name is Mr. Harry Brown!" his American companion blurted out as he pushed his way up to introduce himself. At the last second, he remembered to remove his hat and perform a courteous bow.

Lilly, surprised at first by his abruptness, had to smile at his courtly bow, which seemed so out of place in this somewhat primitive foreign land. The professor was the first to respond vocally.

"How do you do? My name is Professor William Buller. May I present Sir Arthur Billingsley, his daughter Miss Lillian Billingsley, Mr. Richard Elliot, of the London House of Elliot, and my nephew, Mr. Charles Buller. We are looking to procure accommodations for travel by rail."

This was what the first man was hoping for—acceptance. "It is so nice to make your acquaintance. My name is Spencer Longstreet, of the *London Daily Telegraph*."

Ah, yes, the professor thought with satisfaction. Just as I have suspected—a reporter.

"And of course, you have already met my eager companion here," Longstreet continued, as a mischievous smile formed below his outlandish oversized handlebar moustache. He often considered himself to be witty, usually at his friend's expense.

"I am Harry Brown, of the *San Francisco Examiner*." Mr. Brown reached out to vigorously shake hands all around. He exuded a friendly enthusiasm that seemed genuine, which usually caused people to take an instant liking to him. He was a little rough around the edges, and seemed to lack the education and the air of cultured refinement of his associate, but he gave the impression of an honest, if simple, man. Lilly took an instant liking to him.

"Perhaps I can be of some assistance to you," Mr. Longstreet offered. "What is your destination, if I may be so bold to ask?"

"Our destination is Cairo," Professor Buller answered. "We would greatly appreciate any assistance you can offer." Looking around at the massive amount of people milling about, he added, "We seem to have arrived at a busy time. Things seem a bit jumbled at the moment, and I'm afraid we may have missed our opportunity to procure decent accommodations on this train. Perhaps you would be so good as to accompany me to the ticket office?" The professor was an experienced traveler and had been to Cairo multiple times, so he was indeed familiar with making his own travel arrangements. But he had decided to take the reporter up on his offer to help regardless, since there was always the distinct possibility that they might have further use for a man in his profession.

"Why, that is precisely where we are going!" exclaimed Longstreet. He could sense a story just as accurately as the professor could sense a reporter. "I suggest we hurry and make our ticket purchases. Perhaps we will be fortunate enough to be travel companions."

He directed his next comment to Lilly, offering her a tantalizing lure. "I hear they have an actual Pullman car on this train, but since accommodations are limited, I recommend we act quickly." They had all become aware of the growing milling masses of English soldiers, missionaries, and assorted other local laborers and travelers.

"Please wait for me here," the professor said as he and Spencer Longstreet snaked their way through the crowd.

"Am I correct to assume you are an American, Mr. Brown?" Lilly asked the reporter.

Answering her in an affected English accent, he asked, "How did you possibly guess that, Miss Lillian?"

She laughed at his teasing and said, "You may call me Lilly. Please tell us about yourself, and why you are here. You are a rather long way from home to simply be out for a stroll," she teased back. He seemed like such a sincerely nice man; she was glad to make his acquaintance.

"My employer has sent me out here to report on the military situation." Leaning forward slightly, he whispered, "Rumor has it that the Brits...excuse me...the British may be organizing for an offensive to take back the Sudan from the Mahdists." With that, he looked at the noisy throng around them.

Following his cue, Richard, Lilly, and her father looked about and took another closer inventory. Was it their imagination, or were there really an excessive number of soldiers present? Maybe at long last the military really was going to avenge General Gordon's death at Khartoum at the hands of the Mahdists. So far, every other attempt at this had failed. Could they finally be taking serious action now?

"The *San Francisco Examiner*, you say?" Richard was familiar with the paper, or at least the publisher.

"Why, yes, do you follow it?" he asked hopefully. He liked these people and wanted to be accepted by them. He had already shelved the idea of wooing the beautiful young woman before him. He was clearly outclassed by this one. He would have to be content with simply getting to know her.

Richard, who sometimes took a hidden delight in tormenting or mocking those of whom he felt were forgetting their station in life, suppressed the urge to do so now. He didn't think this was the time or the place to alienate someone who might be able to help them in their present situation. This being Richard's first time on foreign soil, and suffering from the heat, thirst, and hunger, he was like a fish out of water. His discomforts were beginning to make him irritable, but he bit his tongue and answered civilly, "I have had occasion to peruse it." That would have to suffice for now.

Taking Richard's answer for one of acceptance and encouragement, Harry Brown dared to inquire as to their reason for being there. After all, he *was* a reporter for one of the largest newspapers on the other side of the Atlantic. Asking questions was his business. "I hope I'm not out of place by asking what brings *you* here, especially with the threat of a war coming and all." Were they missionaries? He really didn't think so.

"Actually, we are going to be examining some Egyptian tombs!" Lilly exclaimed, like an excited child announcing a trip to the circus. "The professor and Charles Buller have experience, as they have done this before. But this time, since I am one of the professor's students and a friend of Charles, they have consented to my joining and helping them."

And quite likely, her father was footing the bill, Harry Brown mused. This was a logical enough conclusion. Ever since Napoleon had awakened the world's interest in ancient Egypt with his attempted invasion of that land, all sorts of adventurers had been flocking to the region in search of relics and buried treasure. In fact, it had become quite the business for the locals too. Sifting the sands and desecrating the tombs of their own ancestors was not uncommon practice in their own searches for artifacts to sell to the Europeans.

"That does sound exciting." Harry noticed a trickle of sweat slowly working its way down her neck and pooling in the little hollow between her collar bones. As she swatted at an annoying fly, he gave a start. How thoughtless of him to subject her to such discomfort!

"There is no reason for you to stand out here in the hot sun. Why don't we all move inside where there's shade, and I will find the professor and tell him where you are."

"Why thank you, Mr. Brown. That would be very kind of you."

As if on cue, Charles rejoined the group after having checked on the security of their luggage. "Perhaps Richard could escort you and your father inside? I should get back to keep an eye on things. I would hate for any of our belongings to mysteriously disappear. I'll rejoin you shortly." Since he had usually been the youngest one on past trips, these tasks had somehow always fallen to him by default.

As Mr. Brown went off to find the professor, Richard searched in vain for a comfortable place for Lilly to rest. All seats were occupied, so an empty crate was found and set against the wall. When she was settled, Sir Billingsley thought it an opportune time to ask Richard something that had been nagging at him.

"Richard, what do you think the odds are that warfare will brew up to the south in the Sudan?"

Richard paused for a moment, amused at the way the question was worded. The odds? Was Sir Billingsley aware that he was one to favor a game of chance? No matter. His penchant for gambling was harmless compared to some of his other recreational vices.

"I don't really think we have anything to be worried about. You see, poor Harry Brown's publisher is none other than William Randolph Hearst."

Sir Billingsley's eyes widened.

Ah, so even Sir Billingsley has heard of him! Richard could tell this by the surprised look of recognition on his face. You are not a serious card player if you don't know how to read an opponent's face when they respond to stimuli, whether it is important news, or a favorable hand of cards.

Richard continued, "For years, Mr. Hearst has been attempting to stir up trouble for the Spanish in Cuba with the use of his 'yellow press' simply to sell newspapers over there in the States." Richard felt the same distain for the British papers who crusaded for the child labor laws back in England. The passing of such laws really took a bite out of the family fortune. "That man tries to create news rather than report it. I don't think we have anything to fear from events in the Sudan. These are most likely just ordinary troop movements," he concluded, with a dismissive wave of his hand.

They moved closer to stand next to Lilly when a couple of soldiers graciously vacated their seats. A grateful "Thank you" and a smile from Lilly made the gesture well worthwhile for the men. A short while later, Harry Brown sought them out again bringing the professor and Mr. Longstreet back to rejoin them.

"Well, professor, were you successful in obtaining tickets for the Pullman car?" Lilly asked hopefully. To her father, she still seemed like such an innocent child at times. Simple things in life made her happy.

"It seems that the military has already requisitioned most of the space on this train for moving some troops."

Sir Billingsley and Richard exchanged furtive glances, but neither one spoke.

The professor continued, "However, this sort of thing is a common occurrence out here. This is not England. Space is limited when you travel by rail, so should the military decide to move a unit, well, be thankful we don't have to ride on the carriage roof like the natives." Having witnessed the outside of a train covered with people like wool on a sheep, they all found some humor in that.

"But you *were* able buy tickets?" she asked again.

"Yes, we were, Lilly. But for that, we all owe a special thanks to our newfound friend, Mr. Spencer Longstreet, of the *London Daily Telegraph.*"

Longstreet tipped his hat. "It was nothing really," he said with affected modesty.

"Nonsense. If it were not for Mr. Longstreet here, we may not even have secured tickets for this train at all. We would have been forced to wait here for an additional four hours, which is when the next one is due to arrive." Although he really was grateful, the professor was also appealing to the reporter's vanity, for it took all sorts of methods to get things done out here, and the more resources one had, the better.

"We are very grateful to you, young man," said Sir Billingsley.

"As I was saying, the military had secured several carriages, including the Pullman, for exclusive use by one of their units thereby putting space anywhere on this train at a premium. Traveling with this unit is a British general and his staff, who, naturally enough, require the best. Well it seems that our friend here, Mr. Longstreet," *who tips his hat again*, "is a personal acquaintance of the general. Mr. Longstreet explained our situation to him so the kind gentleman took it upon himself to personally make room for us to travel with them. By moving some members of his staff, he has made room for Sir Billingsley, Richard, and Lilly in the Pullman car. He has also made space for the rest of us to travel with the military personnel."

"Bravo, Mr. Longstreet," said Richard. This exclusive mode of travel was indeed a luxury.

"Why thank you, Mr. Longstreet," said Lilly. Even though she had made up her mind to endure the hardships and suffer any discomforts right along with the others, this was something that she had always wanted to do but had never found the opportunity to enjoy. This was certainly an unexpected pleasure.

Charles was still outside with the luggage. He was not taking any chances with local thieves making off with any of their belongings. There were priceless books, old manuscripts, and maps stored away in the professor's trunk, and who knew what valuables might be lying nestled in those brought by the House of Billingsley.

Charles was gazing at Lilly's trunk without even realizing it. It was like a dream come true for him to be sharing this experience with her. He was coming to look forward to every day when they could spend time together. He could see that Richard felt he had some sort of exclusive claim on her, so Charles tried to conjure up something else to do whenever the other man was around. It was hard to tell if Lilly felt anything for Richard other than friendship. She was friendly toward everyone. But Charles had heard some unflattering things about the other man that he hoped were untrue, but that he suspected were more than likely accurate. Charles felt protective of his friend and didn't want to see her hurt or ill used by anyone.

As he continued to daydream in the hot sun, he pictured her as she was when she was visualizing herself as the Egyptian queen. She had looked so lovely with her eyes closed and her long dark lashes fanning against her cheeks. Her soft full lips had been curved slightly upward at the corners in a mysterious smile. Tendrils of rich curls around her face had framed it like an exquisite painting...

Charles was startled out of his reverie by the voices of the chattering locals, soldiers, and railroad workers. He realized the porters had approached him and were waiting to load the trunks onto the train.

"Yes, go on, take them!" he yelled with a wave of his hand. Immediately he was embarrassed, for he never liked to be rude to anyone. But his real embarrassment came from the sudden stirrings of unfamiliar feelings he had just been experiencing for Lilly in his imaginings.

The fact that she was a beautiful woman was no surprise to him, but what had been unexpected was that he seemed to be seeing her not as simply a friend; but for the first time, he looked upon her as a desirable woman. The fact that the object of this desire was Lilly surprised him, and he fought to cleanse his mind of such thoughts. But the harder he tried, the more his mind rebelled.

Leading his newfound friends out onto the busy loading platform, Mr. Longstreet proudly showed them to the Pullman car. Although the station was packed with people as were most of the inhabited areas in that part of the world, the masses magically parted for them as if Moses himself led the way. Perhaps this was a result of the way Sir Billingsley and Richard carried themselves with such an air of omnipotence, or maybe it was their obviously expensive clothing that smacked of wealth, and therefore, most likely, power. Instinct warned the common people that it would be wise to give these gentlemen a wide berth. Of course, Lilly's presence may have had something to do with it too. One does not go about bumping and jostling such a fine jewel of an English lady as one might do to shoppers competing for the best bargain in a bazaar.

As people stepped aside to let them pass through, Lilly saw the Pullman car for the first time. Its once dark "Pullman green" paint was now fading due to long exposure to the harsh desert sun and wind driven sands. As Lilly examined the craftsmanship of the carpenters' and ironworkers' skilled hands, she could picture it as the fine specimen it had once been. To her, it still retained just enough of its original grandeur to give off an aura of lofty dignity.

Mr. Longstreet couldn't help but notice her admiring the railcar. "Am I to believe that this is actually your first ride on a Pullman?" he asked.

"Why, yes it is indeed. As a matter of fact, this is my first ride by rail at all, Mr. Longstreet," she said with excited anticipation as she continued to peruse the outside of the car.

As he led her over to the stairs, he caught a faint pleasing scent emanating from her hair. She smelled much better, even in these circumstances, than many women he was acquainted with did in their everyday lives.

Eager hands materialized to assist her as she climbed the metal stairs at the rear of the car. Once on the train, they all made their introductions to their hosts and were shown to their seats.

A few cars back Charles sat down next to a burley sergeant who kindly moved some of his personal gear to make room for him. After an exchange of pleasantries, Charles could think of nothing more to say. His mind was elsewhere at the moment. He was still disturbed at the realization that he might be feeling more for Lilly than he had believed. Were his feelings ever revealed to her, it could create a very uncomfortable presence in their friendship. He would just have to suppress his growing attraction for her and carry on as though nothing had changed.

Charles glanced over to see how the professor was faring. He seemed to be involved in a deep discussion with the lieutenant he was seated next to. That was just like him, always taking favorable advantage of any given situation to learn something useful that he would store away in that index file of his brain, to be retrieved when needed at some future date. He knew he should be doing the same, but the only thing on his mind right now was Lilly, and he wondered how she was getting along.

An excited Lilly took her seat, along with her father, Richard, and the general in one of the coach compartments. They let her choose her seat, and naturally, she sat by the window where she could get a better view of the world around her.

General Jeffery Mackenzie, a jolly white-haired old gentleman, with large white sideburns and moustache, sat directly across from her. Faithfully married to his wife for going on fifty years, he still allowed himself to indulge in innocent flirtations from time to time with attractive young women whom he viewed more as the daughters he had never been blessed with.

"So tell me, general, are you related to Sir Alexander Campbell Mackenzie?" she asked hopefully.

"Are you speaking of the great Scottish composer?"

"Yes," she replied sitting on the edge of her seat. "I just adore his work."

Her father smiled, remembering the times when he took his daughter to the opera. Even at a young age, she focused on the stage with rapt attention, and more than once she had come away from a performance with tears in her eyes.

As a little girl, she had seemed older and more mature than her years. The passing of her mother had caused her to feel emotional pain at a young age that many girls are spared until they are much older and better able to cope with it. He thought this tragedy in her life may be one reason for the more restless side of her nature. At times, she seemed to be resentful of the limitations set upon her for simply having been born female. At these times, it wasn't uncommon to see her jumping astride her horse and racing across the fields at breakneck speed, replacing her feelings of frustration and sadness with feelings of euphoria, excitement, and a feeling of being liberated from the constraints put upon her by others. At these times, he feared for her safely; but he had come to realize this was her way of coping, and it did appear to ease her mind and lessen her sorrow for a time.

"No, I am no relation to the composer, miss, although I am asked that question quite often. I *am*, however, related to Alexander Mackenzie, the Canadian statesman."

"Oh yes, the editor of a Liberal newspaper, a member of parliament, premier," Richard said, attempting to impress Lilly with his knowledge. "I believe it was he, who declined the honor of knighthood? And more than once, I have heard." *What a foolish thing to have done*, thought Richard.

Sir Billingsley felt that Richard's comment bordered on impudence, and so thought it best to redirect the conversation. He asked General Mackenzie about how he came to make the military his career.

"It seems I was born with the soul of a soldier." With a bit of nostalgia as he remembered, the general continued, "My earliest memories are of playing with the painted lead guardsmen soldiers in my father's study. I always loved playing in there," he said as he shifted his gaze to Lilly and smiled, "because my father, who was also a general, had captured arms and banners mounted on the walls. As I played, I often wondered what it would be like to be victorious on the battlefield and take such trophies of my own."

"And did you?" Lilly asked, thinking it was very likely, seeing as he had attained the rank of general.

The military man sat back into his seat, prepared to entertain his audience with stories of valor, humor, and even horror.

And so although the ride was physically uncomfortable at times and the soot-filled air occasionally made its way in through the windows, they settled in for an enjoyable time of listening to and exchanging stories. Time flew by and eventually, the professor, Charles, Mr. Brown, and of course, Mr. Longstreet, were summoned to join them, and they were all escorted to the small dining area where they enjoyed a rather delicious snack and refreshing drinks.

As soon as they were finishing with the refreshments and began conversing about various subjects of no interest to him,

Richard was contemplating about whether it would be too impolite to excuse himself and return to his seat for a nap. Deciding it would be imprudent to leave the others until Lilly made the first move, he forced a polite smile and pretended to listen to the prosaic conversation.

Thoroughly enjoying an unusual beverage set before her, Lilly emptied half of her glass of the frothy, sweet drink. She no sooner set her glass down when she had to suppress a rather large bubble of air that made its way up from her stomach and attempted to make its way past her lips. In great embarrassment, she brought her handkerchief to her lips, and exclaimed, "Oh my!"

Amid the shielded smiles around the table, Lilly sat blushing, at a loss for words. Coming to her rescue, a handsome young private graciously provided an explanation for her momentary lack of couth. "Please forgive me. I neglected to warn you that could happen. This drink is called Root Beer. You see, after the brew is made, it ferments, causing gas to form. Should a freshly opened bottle be poured too quickly, the gas escapes causing it to form foam, which will overflow the glass. Should one consume the drink too quickly, some unwitting embarrassment may ensue."

Lilly felt a little better on hearing this was a common consequence of drinking this refreshment, and she decided it would be wiser to take her time and sip the remaining liquid more slowly.

When the train finally reached Cairo, they proceeded to find accommodations in a finer hotel as was used by the upper classes of British travelers. They would enjoy one night's rest on solid ground before continuing on to Giza the following day. While everyone else was settling into the hotel, the professor went out on his own to make some last minute arrangements.

Before long, it was time for the evening meal, so Lilly met her father, Richard, and Charles in the lobby. Mr. Brown and

Mr. Longstreet had both been invited to join them, but Mr. Longstreet had already accepted an invitation to dine with his friend, General Mackenzie. "He is probably pursuing a hot story," Mr. Brown had said, feeling a little put out for not having been included by Longstreet. He decided to graciously accept Lilly's proffered invitation.

"Where is the professor?" Lilly asked Charles. "Shouldn't we wait for him?"

"He should have been here by now. If he was detained, there's no telling how long he might be. It's just as well we go ahead with our meal. I am sure he will join us when he can."

"But what if something has happened to him?" she asked. "Aren't you the least bit concerned?"

Charles knew his uncle, and his uncle knew Cairo. If he were detained, it would be for a good reason. "I'm sure there were some last minute preparations to be addressed, and they are most likely not the kind that could have been taken care of long distance, through mail packets. Sometimes one has to meet face to face in order to hash out the money matters, in much the same manner that some Roman might have done two thousand years ago," he assured her.

As they sat down at their table, he continued, "I remember one time I did stay up all night worrying about him, only to find that he had simply called upon an old friend of his. They had sat up until all hours of the night imbibing heavily in spirits until they both blacked out. There we were the next morning, heading out into the desert on camelback. My uncle, deathly ill with a hangover, and I, eyes heavy from my lack of sleep. It's a wonder we managed to keep our seats on our jarring ride!"

They all laughed, even Richard, who could relate to such excesses.

"Oh, Charles, I can't imagine the professor becoming drunk! Surely, you made that up for our amusement!" exclaimed Lilly.

"I'm afraid he is telling the truth, though I am not proud to be admitting it," the professor said as he strolled up to their table. From his ruffled appearance, it was evident he had been in a hurry to change for dinner.

"Why, professor, I'm so glad you could join us." She felt better now that she could see that no harm had come to him.

The professor sat down next to her and leaned in to impart some news. "I have been made privy to some exciting information." Glancing around the table, he continued, "It involves all of us." That got everyone's attention. He continued in not much more above a whisper, for effect. "Mr. Brown, I trust you will keep what you are about to hear to yourself?"

"Oh, by all means. Yes indeed, you can count on me," he said, also leaning in closer.

Charles immediately thought to warn his uncle about trusting a newspaper man to keep a secret, when he suddenly realized that his uncle probably knew exactly what he was doing. He most likely wanted to appear to let something "slip," knowing Mr. Brown would relay the information through the post. The professor knew this was a sure fire way to get publicity, and therefore possible financial backing for his expeditions. His uncle was a very clever man!

The professor continued, "A certain associate of mine, a captain in the Lincolnshire Regiment, has sent me a cable containing news of an unexpected discovery. It seems that while digging some fortifications, his troops stumbled upon a tomb of sorts. From what I understand of his message, we have our own little code you see. The tomb appears to have been previously undisturbed."

"Why, that means…"

"Yes, Charles, it appears to be an ancient, and until now undiscovered, mummy's tomb! This would mean, of course, a change in our travel plans—a detour, so to speak."

All at the table, exchanged glances of excitement. Then all heads turned as one to look at Sir Billingsley.

Without even asking, he knew what they waited for. It was Lilly who finally spoke. Her single word was delivered in the form of a plea. "Father?"

Her father was silent as he looked into his daughter's beseeching eyes. At last, he sighed and asked, "Just where is this tomb that you speak of?"

"It is located a ways to the south, about halfway between Aswan and Korosko," said the professor, trying to stifle his own feelings of hopeful anticipation.

Sir Billingsley again looked at Lilly, who exclaimed, "Oh, Father, imagine that! An undiscovered tomb! We would be the very first to explore it!"

Richard spoke up, "What's so special about this tomb? Wouldn't it just be some nobody buried out in the desert?" He knew enough about the subject to realize that if the person laid to rest was one of importance, then he would have been buried in a tomb in the Valley of the Kings.

"That is the mystery. I don't yet know what it is, but my partner intimated there *is* something special about this tomb."

"It perhaps contains a treasure?" Richard asked hopefully. Charles and Lilly exchanged hopeful looks.

"We can't be sure until we investigate. All I know is, this is not an ordinary find."

Lilly added. "It *is* possible that a treasure could be in an undisturbed tomb. Charles told me that the ancient Egyptians strongly believed in a resurrection of the dead. That is why they buried gold, jewelry, and precious stones with them, so they could wear or use them again someday. Tell Father, Charles."

Charles's excitement was apparent. He could only imagine what they might find. "Yes, Lilly is correct in that. They did commonly bury treasure with the body along with many other more common items. Tombs have been found to contain furniture, tools, weapons, and even food and seeds. Granted, one may not wish to partake of any two-thousand-year-old food discovered in a tomb, but the seeds are another story. Do you know that some of these very same seeds were planted and they actually sprouted?"

"That *is* amazing!" Lilly replied as she looked directly into his eyes. Charles, for an instant was pulled into those green pools and could do nothing but gaze back at her. Just as two magnets have no choice or will of their own when the two sides are attracted to one another, Charles felt momentarily helpless before this force of nature. Suddenly breaking the spell, she looked away, leaving him feeling flustered and confused. To cover his brief embarrassment, he continued speaking while looking at no one in particular. "Apparently, the conditions in these tombs actually aid in preserving the seeds without any special preparation."

Richard had noticed the look that passed between Lilly and Charles, and he sneered mockingly as if to discredit the knowledge Charles was sharing. This upstart was obviously attempting to win Lilly's favor by trying to impress her with some half-baked tale.

The professor noticed Richard's slight, and he jumped to his nephew's defense, adding, "This is true. Unfortunately, I found this out the hard way. I myself came upon some such seeds on one of my expeditions, and I decided the best way to study them was to plant them."

"What happened, professor? Did they grow?" Lilly asked.

"I'm sorry to say that shortly after sprouting, the plants all wilted and died."

"Oh, how awful!" she exclaimed, knowing how this had probably saddened him.

"Yes, it was very unfortunate. Here I had seeds, perfectly preserved for two thousand years, and what happens? In a matter of a few weeks, I manage to destroy them."

"He left town on business and forgot about needing to water them," Charles added with a fond smile.

Everyone sat in silence for a moment, until realizing the irony of the story, they all burst into laughter.

After some thought, Sir Billingsley asked, "I still don't understand why this particular tomb is special?"

The professor took a drink from his glass and continued, "In all honesty, according to our code, the words 'different' and 'special' could be construed as one and the same. So this find may just be different, meaning, out of the ordinary. However, my friend, Captain Peter Lewis, has a somewhat limited knowledge of these things and therefore relies on my expertise."

"So Captain Lewis is a fellow archeologist?" asked Lilly, who thought she understood.

"Well, no, not exactly. I would classify him as more of a businessman."

"I thought you said he was a soldier," Richard said, suspiciously.

Sir Billingsley was one who was used to dealing in facts, especially when it came to making important decisions. He was beginning to feel like the professor was attempting to hide something. "Professor, please explain yourself. You sound as though you are speaking in riddles."

"Well, you see…" the professor said carefully, "Captain Lewis has made a business of dealing in objects of antiquity."

"Ah, a grave robber!" exclaimed Richard. He leaned back with a self-satisfied smirk.

"Yes, in a sense, this is somewhat true. The captain is what some might refer to as a grave robber, of sorts. He does indeed, on occasion, take possession of the valuables he finds and has sometimes called on me to identify pieces for him," he admitted sheepishly. "However, I have been successful in persuading him to donate certain items to various museums for the benefit of his fellow man," he added with self-justification. "One hand washes the other, so to speak. It is the price we sometimes must pay," he added, probably more to reassure himself.

The professor continued, "He does not, as far as I am aware, deal in the shadier aspects of this business, which is the thievery and selling of the actual mummy itself. The unfortunate thing is, over the centuries, many a mummy has been shipped and sold for use by apothecaries. There are many who swear that ground up mummies make effective drugs for what ails you, whether taken internally or applied to open wounds."

A look of disgust crossed Lilly's face. Charles had heard of this practice before, but this was the first time the others had ever heard of such an outlandish thing.

"This practice was started in the Middle Ages and became quite popular."

"I say! You don't really expect us to believe that," said Richard, as though his intelligence had been insulted.

The professor nodded. "I assure you I am speaking the truth. Throughout the ages, there have been other instances of people using their fellow man as medicine. Some scholars believe the Greeks sacrificed slaves, as well as criminals, for medical purposes. In some circles, it is rumored that the Arabs made use of the elderly. After certain treatments, which caused the death of the person involved, the body would be aged in honey, like a fine wine, for as long as one hundred years before use."

Another story! thought Mr. Brown. Boy, this was getting better all the time. He recalled the sensation of one of his articles about the snake oil salesman selling tonic that he claimed would cure all manner of diseases. The public had loved it. That story had ended with the unscrupulous fellow hanging at the end of a rope. Too bad he hadn't had a cure for *that!*

The professor let his words sink in before continuing. "As in the case of the mummies, what some unprincipled individuals began doing was manufacture their own for the trade. They would take the bodies of dead slaves and mummify them so as to give the appearance of an authentic ancient mummy. When even this failed to supply enough to meet the black market demands, they began using the bodies of the sick and even those who had died of plague, or any other unfortunate they happened upon. It was only then that the authorities started to crack down on the trade, for it seems that the use of this diseased flesh may have had unintended consequences."

Leaning forward, the professor added in a hushed tone, "There are some who think this practice may have led to some of the outbreaks of plague through the ages however this is merely speculation and has never been confirmed."

Charles added, "It is rumored that the practice of grinding up mummies for medicinal use continues even today."

"So this makes it extremely important for us to preserve as many as we possibly can," the professor said before finishing off his drink in one large gulp. Embarrassed by his breach of manners in female company, he started to say something, in effect to apologize for his lack of couth, but he was cut off by Sir Billingsley.

Although he found this information interesting, Sir Billingsley was becoming frustrated by the evasion of a direct answer to his question, so he asked one more time. "Professor, I hesitate to commit to this change of plans without knowing why this particular discovery is so much more desirable than another might be at our original destination?"

"I'm sorry I can't be more specific. Captain Lewis does not have the proficiency to know why this find is unique, but he has seen enough of such things to realize there is something intriguingly different about this one. And so, before he allows anyone to disturb it any further, he recommends we come to examine it. Judging from his request, I must admit I have become very curious. To continue on our original course, we can only *hope* to discover a find such as this. Here, the difficult task of discovery has already been accomplished. This is a sure thing. All we need do is alter our course and enjoy the task of exploring what has already been found. Someday, such mummies, any mummies, will become very few and far between."

Charles could now clearly see the reasoning behind sharing this information in the presence of a reporter. Should they make a substantial find, it would be recorded for the entire world to see. Many an investor had been found, or had found them, in just this way.

"There is one more point I should like to stress. Should we decide to proceed on this new little venture, I shall need to beg your discretion in keeping the purpose of it to ourselves," he said as he turned to look pointedly at Mr. Brown.

Lilly's eyes lit up. *A secret adventure!*

"Europeans, who are interested in documenting and recovering these rare pieces of antiquity, have a most difficult time acquiring the proper license to dig from the Egyptian government. This can only be obtained at a certain time of the year. The locals, on the other hand, are allowed to dig wherever and whenever they please. As a result, the items they recover are not properly cataloged, for their places of origin are kept secret in the hope that additional items will eventually be found there. Recovering these items is not done for scholarly research but is strictly for monetary gain. They care nothing for uncovering the details of their own past history, but rather, their sole purpose is to rob their own dead!"

The professor was clearly becoming emotional about the matter. It truly angered him when he thought about past experiences, of being denied permits to excavate by some corrupt Egyptian official, and then stepping outside only to be confronted by some barefoot street urchin offering to sell him a rare artifact. Especially when said artifact was handled roughly and as a consequence, has had engravings rubbed or scratched off through carelessness. He paused to calm down and collect himself.

He could see from Sir Billingsley's demeanor that he was looking less apprehensive and more interested, so he continued with the point he was trying to make.

"As you may have guessed, I do not have a permit for this particular dig. However, since this dig is technically a part of the construction of a military fortification, such a license is unnecessary. Even so, discretion on our part will help to avoid any discrepancies from arising."

The professor had made a very convincing argument. There was not one among them who wasn't intrigued. It all sounded legal, or so they hoped, but that remaining niggling doubt only served to make it seem all the more enticing.

After Lilly had retired for the night, the professor noted Sir Billingsley's concerned expression and strove to put his mind to rest. "Captain Lewis is there with his command building a fort, so there is no need to worry about the safety of this operation. We will be under the protection of an entire unit of trained military personnel. Things have been quiet in the Sudan for some time now, so I don't foresee any danger from that quarter."

Sir Billingsley felt comfortable in trusting the professor's word so he asked, "What about our transportation? Even if we did go, how would we find a means of travel at this late date?"

The professor looked away in embarrassment as he admitted, "I took the liberty to make inquiries, not to be presumptuous, but only in an effort to be prepared for any eventuality. There is a small flotilla moving supplies upriver for the troops that has a military escort. Thanks to a recommendation from our new friend, General Mackenzie, we have been invited to travel in their company."

Sir Billingsley reflected on all he had been told so far. This would indeed be the chance of a lifetime for Lilly. He didn't believe the professor would do anything to put any of them in peril, and who would have a better knowledge of the military situation here than General Mackenzie? He looked at Richard questioningly who immediately spoke up.

"I'm sure none of us will be in any danger whatsoever. Besides the soldiers that the professor assures us will be present. We will have our pistols. My vote is to go." Then he added, "Think of how happy this would make Lilly." Richard, however, was thinking more about the priceless treasures he might find.

Sir Billingsley's resolve was weakening. They had already come this far. Why not continue on a little farther and give Lilly this extraordinary opportunity that many archaeologists only dream about? Sir Billingsley was in no hurry to get back to England only to see his daughter married and starting a new life without him. Throwing his hands up in a gesture of surrender, he asked, "When does this flotilla set sail?"

"Tomorrow morning at ten," the professor answered, trying to suppress an urge to clap his hands with glee.

"I'm packing too," said Mr. Brown. "That is, if you think they can find room for me, Professor Buller?" He was inviting himself along, but Sir Billingsley didn't mind. He knew Mr. Brown was doing precisely what the professor wanted him to do, and that was to be a witness as they made their great find.

After saying a polite good night to the others, Sir Billingsley hurried off to impart the news to Lilly. Even if she was sleeping, which he doubted, he would wake her just to be the first to see the look on her face when he told her where they were going.

8

Thanks to General Mackenzie's recommendation and Sir Billingsley's title, passage with the convoy was secured. They all met up on the docks where there was much activity and confusion as the vessels were loaded with supplies. Everyone was eager to get under way, but since this was a military convoy, it was out of their hands.

"Mr. Brown! Are you joining us?" asked Lilly, with a pleased look on her face.

"Why, yes. I…our fellow traveling companions have kindly consented to my coming along. I hope you don't mind." He wasn't sure how she would feel about him inviting himself.

"Not at all! We will be very happy to have you."

When Mr. Brown had informed Mr. Longstreet of his plans to accompany the Billingsley's, he had neglected to mention the newly discovered tomb and its significance. By the same token, Mr. Longstreet never told Mr. Brown about the latest military developments taking place in the nation of Ethiopia to the east. So while Mr. Brown would be traveling with Lilly to the south, Mr. Longstreet would be heading east with General Mackenzie and his men. Each of them was pursuing a story they were afraid to disclose to the other for fear of having it snatched out from under them.

The officers of her Majesty's Lincolnshire 10th Regiment of Foot were understandably pleased to have such an attractive Englishwoman joining them, and introductions were made all around.

Lilly smiled at the three gentlemen officers standing before her. They were introduced as Captain Wilson, and Lieutenants Steward and Fleming. All wore the same brown high top service boots, with khaki colored strips of cloth wrapped around their legs from ankles to just below the knees. They were all dressed in the same khaki breeches and jackets, with brown leather belt, holster, and supporting straps over their shoulders. Regulation swords hung on their left sides, slightly behind their holsters. Silver trim and gold buttons of rank stood out on the shoulder straps. Around each of their necks was draped the lanyard that was attached to their pistols. In addition, each wore a silk scarf, which was the only thing that varied in color between them. The captain wore a white one, Lieutenant Steward, blue, while Lieutenant Fleming's was green. Perched atop their heads were their regulation sun helmets.

Lilly extended her dainty, white-gloved hand to the captain, and the two lieutenants both "smartened up a bit," as their sergeant-major would say, as they anticipated shaking hands with the young lady. She favored each one with a dimpled smile and a show of even, white teeth. "Please, call me Lilly," she said out of habit.

Her father watched with amusement, the almost comical attempt by the young officers to make a good first impression on his daughter.

"Will all of you fine gentlemen be traveling with us?" Lilly asked as she twirled her silk sunshade on her shoulder.

"Lieutenant Steward and I will be traveling with this shipment of goods, Miss Lilly," Captain Wilson replied. "Lieutenant

Fleming and his platoon will follow at a later date with another convoy, but I won't bore your pretty head with the details."

"I assure you I wouldn't be bored, Captain Wilson," Lilly said, hoping to hear more. But she could see that his mind was already preoccupied with all that must be done before their departure. At times she found it frustrating when men assumed that just because she was a woman, she wasn't interested, or wasn't capable of understanding what went on in the world of men. Sometimes she thought if she had been born a male, she would have been able to outsmart them all; but because she was a female, she would never have the opportunity to be taken seriously.

Another soldier approached and stood a short distance away. Lilly wasn't sure if he was waiting to be properly introduced, or if he was merely wanting to report to the captain. Since he was standing a little to the rear of the captain and out of his line of sight, he remained unnoticed.

Being a rather large man, very tall, with a full beard and large white mustache beneath a prominent Roman nose, and friendly brown eyes with permanent crow's feet etched into the outer corners, he reminded her of her late, dear Uncle John back home. He wore the same white helmet as the other officers but by the number of large white stripes on the sleeve of his immaculate uniform, Lilly deduced that he must be an enlisted man of some importance. Their eyes briefly met, but then he shyly looked away. Lilly decided to dispense with the proper etiquette and simply introduced herself to "Uncle John."

"And who is *this* handsome giant of a man?" she asked with a big smile as she walked past the officers. Turning slightly and speaking over her shoulder to the captain, she asked, "He *is* friendly, isn't he? Or must I approach this one with caution?" This teasing made the big man appear a little uncomfortable.

"Ah, sergeant major, I didn't realize you were there. Miss Lilly Billingsley, this is Sergeant Major MacDonald, and yes, I assure you, he is quite tame." The officers all found some humor in the big man's obvious nervousness, for that was something he totally lacked when under fire. Knowing firsthand how cool he was and how his courage provided the substance, which held the command together when other men wanted to break down or run, and now seeing him so helpless and distressed facing a helpless little woman, was a great source of amusement to the men.

"Pleased to meet you, ma'am." He bowed slightly, but with such stiffness, he reminded Lilly of one of the wooden figures on the ornamental Cuckoo clock she had once seen in a merchant's shop. Each time the Cuckoo announced the hour, the two figures, one male and one female, would exit the small doors and meet in the middle front of the clock, where the stiff wooden man would bow to the woman before they returned to enter their assigned doors again.

"Everyone just calls me Lilly."

He took her hand and surprisingly planted a soft shaky kiss on the back of it while turning red to the roots of his hair. "There, you see," he said shyly, "you are still in possession of all of your fingers."

Lilly, momentarily bewildered, looked at her hand with fingers spread and suddenly burst out laughing. "Fortunately for me, the captain was being truthful about your nature!" At this, Lilly walked over next to him and slipped her arm through his.

"Perhaps the sergeant major here could escort me safely to my accommodations?" She tilted her head up to favor him with a smile. "With the captain's permission of course," she added looking to Captain Wilson for his consent.

Though the sergeant major did have other duties, the captain relented. He was enjoying the sight of one of his bravest men being reduced to jelly like a confused, raw recruit, so it amused him to grant her request. The sergeant-major was a good foot and a half taller than she, which only added to the comical effect. Sir Billingsley was beginning to think that all his worry over her safety had been for naught. She, all of them, would be in good hands here.

The other soldiers were no less pleased to learn that the lovely lady would be traveling with them for a time. During the course of the day, Lilly made her rounds of the small ship and had spoken to almost everyone on board. Having no regard for a person's financial status or rank in life, she treated each and every individual with kindness and respect. Even if she hadn't been a well-bred, attractive female, every man who made her acquaintance on that craft would have still treated her with polite courtesy.

Sergeant Major MacDonald was feeling more at ease in her presence, as Lilly had a charm about her that made everyone feel comfortable. Whenever he had some time to spare, he proudly led his young charge around the deck as if she were his daughter accompanying him on a Sunday stroll back in Trafalgar Square.

Lilly was surprised to learn that this flotilla of ships was also carrying some camp followers. Ever since days of old, camp followers had accompanied armies, sometimes living on the fringes of the camps, sometimes with them, performing such chores as cooking and laundry as they sought to eke out a living. On occasion, soldiers would take these individuals as their wives and raise families with them. In an army where the enlistment requirement was for twelve years or more, this was an acceptable practice.

Sergeant Major MacDonald had introduced her to Private O'Hare who had his wife, Stana, as well as their two young sons, John, six years old, and Will, four, traveling with him. Lilly couldn't imagine what it would be like to raise a family while having to live like gypsies, not knowing from one day to the next where you may be called upon to go in order to keep your family together.

"I was married once," the sergeant major confided to Lilly, as they watched the little boys playing soldiers. "My wife contracted cholera and died while I was on campaign. We had a daughter whom I tried to raise by myself, but the frontier is no place to raise a daughter without a mother. So I sent her back home to Scotland, to relatives. She is about your age," he said with a touch of loneliness in his voice.

"Oh, how terribly sad! That must have been so painful for you!" she exclaimed sympathetically.

"Yes, it was a very difficult time. But my wife is in a better place now, and my daughter has had a much better upbringing than I could have provided for her." He cleared his throat with a muffled "harrumph," and said, "Well, I must be getting back to business, young miss. I look forward to dining with you this evening."

Before he could take his leave, Lilly suddenly reached up to hug him. Startled and pleasantly surprised, he hugged her back in a fatherly embrace, blinking back tears of gratitude. After surreptitiously wiping his eyes with the back of his hand, he quickly strode away to attend to his duties.

The first day's journey was uneventful, and everyone just took the opportunity to become acquainted. Even Richard was happy to find some men who promised to indulge him in a game of cards later that night.

Their first evening meal was as formal an occasion as the circumstances would permit. Everyone was in a festive mood, and they entertained each other with stories throughout the meal. The fact that Lilly found their stories so entertaining only encouraged them to try to think of even wilder and more amusing tales. These of course were not the types of experiences mentioned in the military dispatches, which were sent up the chain of command to proclaim deeds of valor achieved by the troops. Captain Wilson had just finished sharing a humorous story about one of these comical exploits, when Lieutenant Steward chimed in. "And we mustn't forget the time when our own Sergeant Major

MacDonald single-handedly took on that fierce man-eating beast." All the military men roared with laughter, except of course the burly sergeant major.

"They don't really have man-eating beasts out here, do they?" Lilly questioned with exaggerated fear, playing along with them.

"This one, miss, was as vicious and mean as the devil. Some even swore that he was Satan himself! But our sergeant major was not intimidated by this devil's black reputation. He had his duty to Queen and country, and by God, he was going to get the pack on that camel's back if it killed him!" The men guffawed loudly. Even the professor and the rest of Lilly's party were starting to grin in anticipation.

"That camel was so ornery it bit him on the arm as he was struggling with some rigging. Then, adding insult to injury, it spit at him, hitting him right smack square in his face! They are known to do that you know." Everyone was laughing now, and even the sergeant major was finding it difficult to keep his stern expression.

"What in heaven's name did he do?" she asked with a wink at the huge red-faced man sitting across from her.

"Why, without the least hesitation, he retaliated in kind! He spit a wad of tobacco in its eye and then bit it on the lip!" The men all roared.

"Make fun all you want to, gentlemen," said Lilly, when things began to quiet down, "but if there is danger about, *especially* ill-mannered camels,"—there was more laughter—"I for one shall find safety and refuge in the very large shadow of our dear sergeant major. I only hope that his teeth are kept sharp, and his tobacco tin is full." Now even the sergeant major joined in on the laughter.

"Now if you will excuse me, gentlemen, I would like to take a short stroll along the deck before retiring." They all rose as one as she left the table. The remaining gentlemen presented their pipes and cigars and settled back to enjoy an after dinner drink and a smoke.

Lilly slowly sauntered along the deck, enjoying the slight breeze, a welcome relief from the unrelenting heat of the day. Someone aboard one of the other river craft began strumming a soft melody on his stringed instrument. The beautiful music floated across the waters to caress the darkness surrounding Lilly's boat. She was standing by the railing, enjoying the beautiful desert stars when she heard it. Everything was so wonderful and beautiful. She felt so happy and content. She loved this feeling of newness, of meeting new people and experiencing new things every day, this feeling of freedom from the mundane routine of everyday life back at home. She took a deep breath of night air and unconsciously started to hum along with the music.

Caught up in the moment, she began softly singing the words. She stopped abruptly as she heard footsteps behind her. Her father joined her at the railing and with a fond smile, he entreated, "Please don't stop." *Dear God, she was so much like her mother!*

Lilly returned his smile, and turning back to look into the darkness and with her father's arm around her, she took up the melody once again. Except for the rhythmic "putt-putt" of the ship's engine, the distant music, and her lovely voice, all became still as each and every shipborne soul was reminded of loved ones, their homes, and all that they held dear. Even Richard and his partners lowered their cards and listened to the soft voice seeming to come from the night air itself. When the music finally stopped and she finished her song, the sound of applause rang out from the ships of the flotilla. Somewhat embarrassed now, and thankful for the cover of darkness, her father escorted her to her berth.

9

The next morning, Lilly searched for Richard in hopes of spending some time with him. She thought perhaps she may have been so preoccupied with her own pursuits, that he may be feeling neglected. When she found him, he seemed rather tired and irritable; and when she suggested a walk up on deck, he declined. When he realized he had hurt her feelings, he quickly apologized, blaming his shortness on the fact that he was not feeling well and wished to retire. Lilly couldn't help being concerned because she knew that many early explorers to the African interior were struck down with sickness. Not even their horses and pack animals were immune to the diseases which ravished their ranks. So few explorers survived in the interior of Africa, it was referred to as the Dark Continent. She graciously forgave him and urged him to go and lie down, for he must take care of himself. She would never forgive herself if anything happened to him. This trip had been her idea, and she felt responsible for his safety and well-being. She told him she would check on him later and left to continue her rounds.

Lilly was personally greeted by each and every soul on board. Some even waved from the other vessels, and she responded with a friendly greeting. She came across Charles checking on some of their supplies that by necessity were stored out in the open on deck. He had been taught early on the importance of protecting and taking care of their equipment. The last thing they wanted was to find that some precious item had been stolen or damaged through negligence. Where and how could one replace a lost item in a foreign land far from civilization?

"Good morning, Charles."

"Good morning. How are you holding up in this heat? It seems to get hotter with every passing day," he said, trying to push his uncooperative damp hair out of his eyes. "The scenery is beautiful though, don't you think?" Lately, every day was a beautiful day for Charles.

"The scenery is lovely! And I do agree about the heat. There doesn't seem to be any relief from it until the sun goes down in the evening, and even then I'm not certain it is any cooler below deck.

"Charles," she added, "I'm concerned about Richard."

"What is wrong?" Charles asked apprehensively. He didn't care for the fellow and therefore was not happy about discussing him with someone who he knew *did* care.

"I'm afraid the poor man is feeling under the weather. I encouraged him to go get some rest, but I'm worried about him. I sincerely hope he has not contracted one of those horrible African diseases."

Charles didn't like to see her upset and wanted to put her mind at ease, for he knew Richard's problem was most likely self-inflicted, brought on by staying up drinking and gambling all night. "Don't fret, Lilly, I'm sure he'll be fine. He most likely just had trouble sleeping or ate something that didn't agree with him," he said, thinking this would make her feel better. Seeking to change the topic, he informed her that her father had been searching for her with a request to meet him on the rear deck.

She left Charles to his job, curious as to why her father wished to see her. She encountered Mr. Brown along the way, and since being inquisitive was an integral part of his job description, he naturally chose to accompany her.

They found her father waiting at the far end of the ship. Sir Billingsley had been meaning to do this for some time and thought that now was the perfect opportunity. Having obtained the captain's permission to proceed, he had been anxiously waiting for Lilly to receive his message and join him.

Lilly noticed her new pistol and some ammunition lying on a large supply box. A thrill of excitement shot through her at the thought that she may actually be doing some shooting. She didn't know if she would like it or not, but she was certainly excited to give it a try. She always looked at life as one big learning experience, and she made sure to take every available opportunity to make the best of, and enjoy, every minute.

Mr. Brown, noting the display of pistol and ammunition, stood back and chewed on his match stick as he watched Sir Billingsley explain to Lilly exactly how the pistol operated. The reporter noticed how the girl watched intently as her father placed a cartridge into the cylinder. After he had illustrated the basics of handling, loading, and aiming the weapon, he fired at a log that was lazily floating by. The shot was much louder than Lilly had anticipated, and she jumped involuntarily, startled into closing her eyes. The loud report drew the attention of the crew. When they saw the older man pass the pistol to his daughter, they all stopped what they were doing to watch and see what happened.

With her ears still ringing, Lilly proceeded to load the cartridges into the cylinder as she had seen her father do. Mr. Brown could see she had paid close attention to detail. She would have made a good news reporter. But of course, that would never happen. *A woman reporter?*

Prepared and determined, she approached the ship's railing gripping the pistol tightly with both hands. She raised it up in front of her at arm's length aiming at another log, slowly squeezed the trigger as her father had said, and fired. Her pistol exploded and to her surprise, smoke and flame shot out the end of the barrel almost causing her to drop it into the water. The unexpected recoil drove her hands, still griping the gun in a death grip, up above her head as she stumbled back into her father's arms. Everyone watching laughed, including Lilly. Then she strutted back to the railing, cocked the pistol, and taking careful aim, fired again. This time, she was ready for the recoil and had braced herself. She was rewarded by a small splash marking the spot where the lead ball clearly struck the log at the waterline. Exclamations of admiration filled the air.

"She is quite the Annie Oakley," commented Mr. Brown.

While Lilly searched the water for another target, the sergeant major approached and offered her some cotton to protect her ears from the deafening noise. As she was occupied with this, the men on the ship off their port side threw in a piece of wood attached to a long rope.

Presented with a suitable target, Lilly continued practicing her marksmanship while her father and the crew offered guidance and encouragement. Captain Wilson was very impressed with her skill. Almost every shot hit the wood, so the men rigged up an even smaller target for her. Lilly was enjoying herself immensely. Time after time, she aimed at the smaller target and got great satisfaction in seeing pieces of it being whittled away by bullets. Everyone watching was also enjoying themselves, and even a few bets were made on the accuracy of some of her shots.

Admiring the success she was having with the pistol, the captain had the sergeant major procure a standard issue rifle for him. Standing tall and speaking as he had to countless recruits over the years, Sergeant Major MacDonald projected his voice with authority, "This, Miss Lilly, is a Lee-Metford rifle. It has a caliber of .303 inch and has a ten-cartridge magazine, but I am only loading five," he said as he inserted the cartridges one at a time, pushing them down through the open bolt in the top and into the magazine. "And it fires a smokeless cordite powder," he added with an amused twinkle in his eye. Working the bolt to chamber a round, the sergeant major demonstrated the proper way to shoulder the weapon and aim. Without firing, he passed the weapon to Lilly and took up a position to her side, standing parade ground erect with his cane tucked snugly under his arm.

Mimicking his firing stance, she tried to get the feel of this new weapon. As she wasn't as strong as the sergeant major and her arms didn't have as long of a reach, the heavy cumbersome rifle had a tendency for the barrel to dip downward. It took her a minute to find the right grip and balance to be able to take aim. "Careful, luv, hold the butt in tight," he cautioned as a forewarning of the powerful kick from the recoil. There was silence as she pulled it back tighter against her shoulder and began to slowly squeeze the trigger. She could feel the small lever give way ever so slightly until the sudden deafening explosion rang out. Although she had thought she was prepared for the recoil, the power of it startled her, and the sharp pain in her shoulder almost brought her to her knees. As it was, she staggered back a few steps before she regained her balance and thought to check on whether she had hit her target. Her right ear was clogged and ringing loudly, and her shoulder would surely sport a bruise, but a triumphant smile lit up her face as she was informed of how close her bullet had come to striking the bobbing wood. There were some cheers and a few exchanges of money, including Richard, who had been curious about all the noise and had come up to see what it was about.

With a little effort, and to the sergeant major's surprise, she determinedly worked the bolt and chambered a new round. Raising the rifle to her shoulder once more, she braced herself against the powerful kick and this time clearly hit her target. The men cheered as she handed the rifle back to the sergeant major. "I'm afraid I'll not be able to handle this one much longer, sergeant major. It is quite heavy, and the recoil has bruised my shoulder. I'll stick to firing my pistol for now."

"That was very impressive, miss." Turning to face the watching men, he continued in his parade ground voice, "I only wish it were that easy to teach the men how *not* to waste Her Majesty's ammunition!" The men all laughed and slapped each other on the back, each one thinking that he was referring to everybody else, with the exception of themselves.

Wishing to join in on the fun and innocent flirtation, Captain Wilson addressed Lilly. "It's clear you have a keen eye for marksmanship."

She blushed, but she was having fun being the center of attention. Turning to address her father, he continued, "If I may, sir, I have a little surprise for your daughter."

"By all means, captain," answered her father with a permissive nod. He was pleased to see her so happy, and this made him happy also.

The captain offered her his hand, which she accepted, and he led her up a small flight of stairs to an overhang on the upper deck. A murmur rippled through the ranks as all realized where he was leading her. More money quickly exchanged hands among the men. Richard didn't know what was about to take place, but he put his money on the girl.

Unfastening some straps, the captain threw back a canvas cover and said, "This is a Maxim machinegun." As the sergeant major assisted him in readying the intimidating weapon, the captain explained how it worked. After placing the end of the cloth belt holding the shiny brass cartridge in the breach, slamming down the cover, and pulling back on the charging handle, he then demonstrated the correct firing position. Instead of squeezing the trigger, as Lilly expected, he stepped aside to allow her to take up a position behind the gun. There was no need for her to load the weapon herself. It wasn't as if she would ever have a need to do that. Noting her apprehensive expression and hesitation, he added, "Do not fear, my dear. You will feel no recoil with this machinegun, as it is the recoil itself, which does the job of chambering the next bullet."

Lilly wiped her damp palms on the front of her skirt. The combination of nervous excitement and the extreme heat of the day was taking its toll. Her sweat dampened hair clung to the back of her neck, and her skin glistened with a sheen of light perspiration. She put her discomfort aside and grasped the handles as she had seen him do.

Leaning over her right shoulder, he spoke calmly into her ear. "Look through that tiny hole in the rear sight and line it up with the top of the front sight and with your target." He then respectfully stepped back.

She aimed carefully at a random chunk of driftwood and fired. Instead of one loud bang, the gun vibrated as it simultaneously fired off several bullets before she even knew what had happened. Small geysers erupted all around the chosen target. Everyone loudly praised her attempt. Lilly stopped firing and sat frozen as if stunned into immobility. Still gripping the handles, she turned her wondering eyes to the captain; and in a voice sounding pleasantly surprised, exclaimed, "I rather enjoyed that!"

Her face was beaming with joy, so the captain, without even needing to ask if she would like to try it a second time, positioned himself behind her. Again looking over her shoulder, he coached her. "Get the feel of the gun. Handle it for a minute to get used to the weight of it. You are in control of it. Do not let it take control of you. *Never* allow it to get away from you. You are the master of this weapon, and it is up to you to guide it and tell it what you want it to do. Think about how it operates, and only squeeze off two or three rounds at a time. Focus on your target, and don't let yourself be distracted by anything else around you. Allow the weapon to become an extension of yourself."

His voice had a calming effect on her. This reminded her of her sessions with Charles. She could visualize everything she was being told, and suddenly she was feeling very confident, and not at all threatened by this powerful machine.

"Keep watching the fall of the shot. You will see the splashes made by the bullets. Simply walk those splashes onto your target." He touched her lightly on the back of the arm. "Now go ahead and try again."

She fired again, spraying the area around her target, but this time the impact of the bullets made a tighter group. The captain reached around her, placing a hand on each of her forearms. He gently moved them from side to side. "Adjust your fire with smooth motions. Focus. Relax your body in between bursts of fire, but never take your eyes off of your objective."

Lilly fired another short burst, keeping sight of the little spatters of water as she triumphantly guided the pattern of the bullets until pieces of driftwood were flying everywhere. Everyone roared their approval. Lilly exultantly finished off the belt of ammunition on what remained of the bullet-riddled target.

Thereafter, for a portion of each and every day, it became a common sight to see Lilly at the deck railing with her pistol, plinking away at various objects in the river.

Despite the lack of modern conveniences, Lilly had never been happier in her life. Each day was filled with getting to know her fellow shipmates, learning new things, and embracing this lifestyle she was growing to love. Like a curious child, she wandered the ship taking time to speak to everyone, and learning as much as possible about them.

Charles had been so busy with his uncle lately, studying and planning the details of this unexpected detour, that she hadn't had many opportunities to spend time with him since they boarded the ship. Richard was also making himself scarce, and when she *was* with him, he appeared somewhat withdrawn and acted almost surly at times. She was afraid he might be regretting his decision to come along with them, but there was nothing he could do about it now. She felt bad for him but she was determined not to allow his attitude to ruin her trip.

Her first order of business for the day was to pay a visit to the ship's small galley in a quest for some sweets for the O'Hare boys, and while there, she ended up peeling some potatoes as she chatted with the cook. She then worked her way down to visit the engine room, stopping along the way to deliver her pilfered sweets to the two boys.

From there, she made her way up to the Maxim. As she was observing the gun crew cleaning the weapon, her father caught up with her. He found her squatting down listening intently as an enlisted man was explaining the rudiments of the gun's operation.

"Hello, Father!" she exclaimed as she stood up. "These nice fellows were just explaining to me how the cam utilizes the recoil to operate the gun. It's so very fascinating."

"Is that grease on your face?" her father asked with surprise. "And I see that you have some on your dress too. I think you had better go clean up before dinner."

"Yes, Father." She kissed him amiably on the cheek and went off to do as he said.

One of the soldiers spoke up, "We're terribly sorry, sir. Miss Lilly was just so…"

Sir Billingsley cut off the apology with a good natured wave of his hand. "I know how persuasive my daughter can be, men. I thank you for taking the time to satisfy her curiosity. Please carry on, and don't give it another thought."

This wasn't the first time Lilly had ruined a dress, and from the looks of things, it would not be the last. He smiled as he recalled an incident long ago when she was quite young. The family had just come home from Christmas services and were entertaining some distinguished guests. Lilly and some of the other children had sneaked into the coal bin while wearing their finest holiday clothes. Imitating Welsh coal miners, they had been trying to break up the pieces of coal with a hammer and had ended up covered in black dust. That was the image that flashed through his mind just minutes ago when his now grown daughter had looked up at him with black smudges on her face and dress. He shook his head in amused exasperation, knowing he wouldn't have her any other way.

The following morning as Lilly prepared to dress for the day, she viewed the growing pile of soiled, stained, and torn dresses. This environment certainly was not conducive to the type of clothing that had been suitable for living in London society. She had taken to changing into a fresh frock by midafternoon since the clothing she put on in the morning was soiled and moisture stained by then. She had begun to wear only her chemise and one petticoat beneath her dresses, but even that felt suffocating after only a couple of hours. The men had it so much better with their lightweight material that wicked the perspiration away from their bodies and seemed so much more comfortable in this climate. She sighed in resignation. Then suddenly, a mischievous glint sparked in her eye as her gaze rested upon her second, as yet unopened, trunk.

Charles came to call on Lilly the first thing in the morning, for there was something he needed to discuss with her. He was glad to have an excuse to see her because he had been so preoccupied lately he missed being able to spend time with her. Expecting her to emerge from her berth at any moment, he sat patiently waiting for her to appear.

He heard her door opening and as he looked up to greet her, his jaw dropped, and not one word was spoken for a full minute. He was speechless to see that in lieu of one of her usual colorful dresses, she wore the clothing that had been specially purchased and tailored for the expedition. He wasn't shocked by the fact that she was attired in the outfit that was meant to be worn when they entered the field, but rather it was the nature of the clothing itself. In place of the split skirt dress he had suggested, and had also assumed had been made for her, she was wearing riding breeches and a button-down shirt! Men's clothes! In place of her impractical women's boots, made of silk, with toes of shiny patent leather, she had on ankle high men's boots made of rough unpolished leather. Perched on her head was a white cork sun helmet, which was very practical for working in the hot sun. Although it was a man's hat, it looked extremely becoming on her. The white rim of the helmet created the effect of a halo around her angelic face. He didn't know what to think. Although she looked absolutely stunning, he inwardly cringed when he imagined the negative reaction this outfit may elicit from her father. Such men of substance were usually rigidly conservative. He feared her father would surely blame this on him.

"I'm glad you are here, Charles. You can be the first to tell me what you think of my safari outfit," she said, as she walked out with a confidence she wasn't entirely feeling.

She was still getting used to this new mode of dress. When she had first donned the masculine breeches, she was amazed at the freedom of movement they afforded her. She had never experienced such comfort when wearing her cumbersome skirts and underclothing. She felt so exposed and almost indecent, yet she was completely covered by material. Donning the shirt had helped somewhat, as it covered the curves of her hips and buttocks, and the boots served to cover her slim ankles. Plopping the helmet on her head, she had checked her reflection, twisting and craning her head and body, trying to view the whole effect in her small hand mirror. *There,* she had thought, *I am clothed from head to toe, so how can anyone possibly disapprove?* It was at this point that she had thrown open her door, only to find Charles waiting for her. She certainly hadn't expected to meet up with anyone so soon.

Charles didn't know what to say. Of course he liked it! Rags would look good on her. "I think you look smashing!" he blurted out with honest enthusiasm.

As soon as the words were out of his mouth, he wished he could take them back. What if she should quote him to her father? It was too late now to make a retraction. She was all smiles and seemed to be enjoying her new look.

Seating herself next to him, she said, laughing, "I'm at a loss as to the correct method to wearing these." She held up the roll of khaki strips of cloth. "Can you show me how they are worn?" She was referring to the puttees that many troops wore in place of leather leggings.

At first, Charles didn't know how to respond. True, he had been there when she shopped for her clothing, but this definitely was not the outfit Sir Billingsley and the tailor had agreed upon. Had they made a change that Charles was not aware of? He didn't want to be rude and ask her outright if her father knew about this unconventional fashion choice.

"Ah, well, why, yes of course," he finally managed to say, as he laid his folder on the chair and knelt down in front of her. "If I may..." He reached for her small booted foot and placed it carefully on his thigh. Lilly watched him begin to tightly wrap the roll of cloth, starting at her ankle and working it around and up her calf and ending just below her knee. Instead of paying attention to detail as she normally did, she found that she had not even been fully listening to his verbal instruction. She had been gazing at the errant lock of hair that kept falling down over his eyes. Each time he pushed it back, it stubbornly slid back to lie across his forehead. She had to fight the urge to reach out and gently brush it back into place. He was indeed quite a handsome man. How had she never noticed this before?

As Charles slowly bound the cloth around her leg, he couldn't help but marvel at the shapely curve of her calf. He found himself wondering how soft her skin might feel underneath. Pulling the cloth snugly, he realized he was loath for this moment to end. Unable to stretch his pleasurable task out any longer, he started to work the loose end of the wrapping under itself to make it snug and secure.

Lilly felt a bit strange as Charles worked the cloth slowly up her leg. She had never allowed any man, other than a doctor, to handle her in such a way. She didn't even allow Richard to touch her, other than to give her a chaste little peck of a kiss on the cheek. Now here she was letting a man who was not even her husband, touch her in a way she would never had condoned had she been clad in a proper dress. Perhaps your outer appearance also affected your behavior in some way. She would need to make certain to continue to conduct herself like a lady regardless of what she chose to wear.

"And then you just tuck it in like so," he said as he finished. "If not wrapped properly, the whole binding may come unraveled as one moves about." Her boot still rested on his thigh, and she abruptly pulled her foot away and pretended to examine his handy work. They were both feeling embarrassed and self-conscious.

In an attempt to diffuse the sudden awkwardness between them, she began to bind her other leg with the second roll. "Please let me know if I am doing it correctly," she said, as she slowly wrapped the material using her already wrapped leg as a guide. This time, he talked her through it without touching her at all; and by the time she was done, they were again laughing with each other.

"Were you waiting for me this morning? Was there something you wanted to see me about?" she asked, as though the uncomfortable moment had never happened.

Charles, still somewhat flustered, was suddenly in fear of behaving like a clumsy fool. He had never had this problem around Lilly before, and he hoped it was only temporary. "Oh, it was nothing important. I was hoping perhaps you would accompany me to breakfast," he suggested. "But I can wait here for you to change."

"Change?" she asked, somewhat confused.

"Why, yes. Well, I just assumed you were going to change back into your regular clothes before going in to break your fast."

"No, Charles." She smiled. "I have decided that from now, until we return to civilization, these will be my regular clothes. There's no sense in spoiling all of my dresses, not to mention roasting like a trussed Christmas goose in this abominable heat! I have made up my mind!"

Seeing her determined expression, he knew better than to argue, and it was with great apprehension that he escorted her through the ship.

Everyone was more than a little surprised to see Lilly strolling about in her "safari outfit," as she called it. She received many compliments on how well she wore it, by which they really inferred that it looked much more flattering on her than it did on any of them. A couple of the men even stopped her to make suggestions as to the proper way of wearing certain items. Even the cook brought her some tea to rinse her sun helmet with in order to give it a more subdued, tanned look, rather than its natural bright shiny white. "You won't present such a prominent target that way, lassie," he said as he transformed her head gear into that of a seasoned soldier. It was as though she had been unanimously elected to serve as their mascot, and they all wanted a hand in molding her to look the part.

Sir Billingsley, Professor Buller, and Richard were busy having a discussion concerning the added costs of extending the expedition. Even though the professor knew that money was no object to Sir Billingsley where Lilly was concerned, he still desired to be up-front with the man financing this extension, for it entailed both additional time and money. He had included

Richard in the consultation strictly as a courtesy. None of the added financial burden would be falling on him, but the trip would go much smoother with the cooperation of everyone involved. The professor had traveled with difficult companions in the past, so he strove to make everyone feel included and asked for their input and suggestions. So far, this had been a successful strategy with Richard, seeming to nourish his ego by making him feel a part of the decision-making process.

On conclusion of their meeting, the three men set off to join the others in the dining area. As they came upon Charles standing in a small cluster of men, all three stopped in their tracks when they realized that one of these men was actually Lilly in a man's uniform! Richard's initial shock turned to anger and embarrassment at the sight of Lilly clad as a man. He fought back the urge to grab her roughly by the arm and forcibly drag her to change into decent clothing. His hands were shaking, and he clenched his jaw, biting back the harsh words she sorely deserved to hear. Looking to Sir Billingsley to take his daughter in hand, he saw with satisfaction the shock and anger, which mirrored his own.

Sir Billingsley excused himself as he pulled Lilly aside to speak to her privately. His first reaction was to scold her and order her to go change into one of her usual dresses that covered her from instep to neck, lest she arouse indecent lustful feelings in these men, who had most likely not been in the company of a female for some months now. They argued back and forth for quite some time, with Lilly attempting to explain to her father the reasons for her unusual choice, and why it shouldn't be deemed indecent when she was more covered up than when she was wearing some of her lower cut gowns. Her father's ire slowly dwindled until it was nothing stronger than exasperated disapproval.

Seeing this change in Sir Billingsley's demeanor, Richard stalked off in angry frustration. He swore that if he were successful in making her his wife, her days of manipulating men to get her own way would be over!

Lilly could sense her father's resolve weakening as she presented her case, until at last, in a halfhearted surrender, he gave his consent, allowing her to continue to dress in this more practical fashion, but only until this dig was concluded, and they were on their way home again.

Observing Sir Billingsley's acceptance of her attire, both the professor and Charles felt it prudent to keep any objections they may have to themselves. She had rejoined the group of waiting men who would probably all be willing to give their lives to protect her. There was such joy on her face that her father automatically responded with a smile as if by reflex. This in turn, caused her smile to widen even more.

10

The following day, the convoy of ships prepared to make an unscheduled stop. They had received word by way of a messenger that the local magistrate had need of military assistance. A band of Bedouin raiders had made off with some cattle, and all that was needed was a show of strength to drive them off. The magistrate sent a request for a small unit of soldiers to come ashore and deploy as a blocking force not far from the river. The bandits had been tracked and were being followed, but the trackers weren't strong enough, or numerous enough, to challenge them. A simple show of power by Her Majesty's soldiers would be enough to make the thieves abandon the cattle and disappear into the desert. It was an easy enough task, and it would give the men a chance to practice their martial skills.

All other passengers were ordered to remain with the ships. They would be allowed to stretch their legs ashore but were warned to stay close to the flotilla. Making the best of this opportunity, Lilly, her father, Richard, and Charles went for a short walk along the riverbank. Mr. Brown soon joined them, and Charles entertained them by identifying some of the more unusual plants, and pointing out some strange species of birds in the trees overhead. Taking time to stop and admire the beauty of it, one could not help but notice that the Nile gave birth to an abundance of life amid the harsh desert.

The soldiers had been away on their assigned mission for a few hours when the individuals who had been left behind heard scattered gun shots off in the distance. One of the soldiers on the shore reassured them that it sounded like the friendly fire of his comrades, and that there was no need to worry. The troops must have found their objective, which meant that they would be returning very soon.

This soldier was a very young private who was a new recruit to the service. There was a quavering nervousness in his voice, and Lilly noticed that he carried his rifle in his hands, rather than slung over his shoulder.

She suddenly regretted not strapping on her own belt and holster this morning. It wasn't that she desired to shoot at anybody, or at any living thing for that matter, but rather the thought of having added protection at hand would make her feel safer.

Suddenly, they heard a louder gunshot. This one was obviously closer than the original shots had been. Very close. They all exchanged looks of surprised alarm. None of them were sure what to make of it. Then there was another loud report, immediately followed by a second, then a third. As each successive gunshot sounded nearer, the various camp followers began to panic. The inexperienced young soldier ran by with a terrified look on his face shouting for everyone to return to their vessels.

"Move to the ships!" shouted Sir Billingsley. He was a man of few words, but when he spoke, people listened. Charles immediately grabbed Lilly by the arm, yanking her from her chair, and started running her toward the water with Mr. Brown right behind them. The remainder of the group followed close on their heels.

People were screaming and running around in confusion, abandoning everything and scrambling to reach the apparent safety of the boats. Finally, a couple of the more seasoned soldiers who had been left behind to guard the cargo, attempted to restore some semblance of order and managed to guide the frightened passengers onto their respective vessels.

Once on board, Lilly and the others quickly made their way to the rear of the ship, instinctively trying to put the greatest distance possible between themselves and the shore. Sir Billingsley shouted for Charles and the professor to take Lilly below, as he and Richard dashed off to retrieve the pistols stashed away in their berths. Mr. Brown didn't know what to do, other than observe. Only by witnessing the events unfolding around him, and distancing himself by seeing things through a reporter's impartial viewpoint for reporting's sake, could he manage to control his own rising panic.

Refusing to retire to the safety of her cabin, Lilly scanned the shore for clues as to what had been the cause of the abrupt desertion of the shoreline. She finally caught sight of the same soldier who had assured them there was nothing to be concerned about just a short time earlier. He was uneasily eyeing the thick vegetation while yelling loudly for an unseen comrade to respond to his shouts. The other soldier suddenly stumbled out of the brush, falling in his haste to break through the grasping branches and vines. As soon as he hit the ground, he was up and running again all the while glancing over his shoulder with a look of terror distorting his features. Reaching the first soldier, he frantically motioned to the ships, obviously terrified of what he had seen.

A disturbance in the area where the frightened man had just appeared from caught their attention. As they froze in trepidation, a huge reptile burst through the brush, immediately honing in on and bearing down on the two men. They both fired their rifles at the enormous beast, but even though some of their bullets flew wide in their panic, they both managed to hit it more than once. The massive creature never even slowed down. They fired again, but to no avail.

Lilly could see the two men were attempting to hold their ground in order to destroy the crocodile with the huge jaws and gnashing teeth, when to her horror another monster appeared, and right behind that one, several more! She was amazed at how fast they were able to move on land. The young private fired again, and the first croc finally just dropped in its tracks. As he chambered another round, Lilly noticed that the second soldier was in dire need to reload his weapon. In his frantic haste to do so, he fumbled while trying to open and extract the rounds from his ammunition pouch. His hands shook violently as he attempted to insert one of the bullets into his rifle, so that he ended up dropping most of them on the ground. With no time to pick up or replace the cartridges, that marvelous, high tech, ten shot, smokeless powder Lee-Metford rifle, became nothing more than a primitive club, and an extremely ineffective one at that.

Captain Wilson and his men had successfully driven off the raiders and were celebrating their easy victory when they heard distant gunfire coming from the direction of their ships. "Sergeant major, assemble the men!" commanded the captain.

"Fall in! Assemble on me and be quick about it!" bellowed Sergeant Major MacDonald.

The troops lost no time snapping into formation. The almost picnic-like atmosphere had vanished in an instant, to be replaced by a sense of urgency derived from the helplessness of not being there to defend their families and friends. The men did what they were trained to do in emergency situations. They would trust in and follow their commanding officers automatically and unquestioningly, with the faith that their leaders would make the right decisions. Making sure all his men were accounted for, the captain moved them out at a brisk trot.

All the other ships were anchored to the starboard side of Lilly's, so she was afforded a clear view of the nightmare unfolding on land. To be a helpless witness to the two men's terrible impending fate made her feel physically ill. "Dear, Lord, please help them!" she prayed over and over again.

Looking around in despair, she could see Lieutenant Steward on a neighboring boat directing the fire of the sentries who were shooting at the attacking crocs from the safety their ships. Unfortunately, Lilly's vessel was in their line of fire, blocking any chance for a clear shot at the fast moving beasts, and causing their efforts to be mostly in vain.

Shots and screams of terror filled the air, yet one voice stood out that immediately grabbed their attention. It was the voice of a hysterical mother frantically screaming for her children. Fearing the worst, Stana ran to the railing searching for her babies.

Lilly looked at Charles and yelled, "Charles, the boys!"

Charles turned to Mr. Brown. "Go below and see if the boys are on board. The professor and I will look for them up here. Lilly, stay here and let us know immediately if anybody finds them."

Motivated by the urgency of the situation, Mr. Brown raced below frantically searching in, under, and on top of every single potential hiding place. He passed Sir Billingsley and Richard along the way. "Did you see two small boys anywhere about?" he questioned. When they answered in the negative, he rushed off to continue with his quest, determined that if they were somewhere below, he would find them.

Charles and the professor had both worked their way forward from opposite sides. Meeting at the bow, a look of discouragement clearly showed on their faces. They both stood there, looking around wondering where the children could be. Charles suddenly threw his leg over the side of the ship with the intention of jumping down to continue his search on land. It was at that instant when he heard the professor call his name.

"Charles! I see them! The boys are there on the other ship!" Sure enough, he too clearly saw them clutched in the arms of a soldier. They had gotten separated from their mother and had been swept up onto a different boat. Charles's relief was short lived as he realized there were still men ashore fighting for their lives.

Lilly could see the boys were safe, and now she frantically searched for some evidence of the two soldiers being rescued. Was there nobody who could help them?

Suddenly, she looked up and saw the covered Maxim machinegun. Without a second thought, she ran up the stairs and started clawing and tearing at the protective tarp. Finally, throwing the cover clear of the gun, she was relieved to see a fresh box of ammunition lying beside it. Recalling the loading procedure she had closely observed the captain follow, she opened the breach as he had done and inserted the heavy belt of ammunition. She could feel the adrenalin surging through her all the way to her fingertips. Slamming the breach shut, she somehow found the strength to pull back on the charging handle and let it snap forward to chamber the first round. Everything was accomplished so quickly and efficiently, it seemed almost as though she had done this type of thing countless times before. Gripping the handles firmly, she focused on aiming down the sights and blocking all else from her mind. All her senses were attuned to one thing, and one thing only, and that was stopping the terrifying scene being played out on the shoreline. Concentrating on her chosen target, Lilly took a deep cleansing breath, and squeezed off the first round.

Just at that moment, Charles and the professor reached the rail and watched in amazement as that first burst from the Maxim marched across the ground closer and closer until it caught one charging beast in the right shoulder area, forcing it to drop. The impact of several of the bullets had shattered bone and torn ligaments.

Feeling more confident now, she carefully traversed the gun and fired another short burst at a frightening looking crocodile whose mouth was wide open as it tried to snap its jaws on one of the men. Both soldiers had fired their last bullet and had not had the chance to reload. Using their rifle butts as clubs, they were attempting to drive the attacking crocs back in order to make a dash for safety, but the massive reptiles were too frenzied now by the smell of blood coming from the dead and injured animals. The young skinny private stumbled and fell as he was backing away, and a beast snapped its jaws, trapping the screaming man's leg in its vise-like mouth. As the crocodile began its death roll, which would probably result in tearing off the man's limb, Lilly carefully adjusted her aim and fired more rounds that caught the beast in the chest area, causing it to release the hold it had on the bleeding appendage. The splattering of the fierce animal's flesh and blood was a clear indication she was right on target, so she squeezed the trigger yet again, finishing it off.

Swinging the barrel to a fresh target, she walked the rounds onto another huge reptile that was honing in on its victims. When she had killed that one, a crocodile directly behind it stopped to feed on the carcass. This gave the uninjured soldier the opportunity to help his bleeding comrade to his feet and half drag him toward the safety of the nearest ship. "Go help them!" she screamed over her shoulder, hoping someone would hear her.

When Sir Billingsley and Richard appeared with pistols drawn preparing to do whatever they could to assist, they heard the Maxim above them hammering away at the monsters on the riverbank. They glanced up, but were unable to get a good view of the soldier firing the machinegun. Then they exchanged glances as they both realized at the same moment that Lilly was nowhere in sight.

Charles had moved forward to help the soldiers climb aboard. Mr. Brown having heard the professor yelling that the boys were safe, had come up from below and stood transfixed by the whole scene. He was so intent on trying to take everything in that he jumped when Sir Billingsley grasped his shoulder and yelled, "Where is Lilly?"

The reporter really had no recollection of where she was. "Perhaps she got frightened and went down below," he suggested hopefully.

"I'll go down and check on her, sir," Richard volunteered gratefully, anxious to put himself out of harm's way. He turned and ran below deck to comfort Lilly, and hopefully earn some points with her for doing so.

Charles was assisting the injured man up over the side of the ship. Someone had knocked the gangplank askew, so it wasn't stable enough to walk on. He had just pulled him to safety, when he saw another croc stealthily crawling up behind the soldier who was waiting to be helped aboard. Its massive jaws started snapping in anticipation, and a loud hissing sound issued from its throat. The helpless people witnessing this nightmarish sight were screaming, the Maxim was roaring, and the frightening reptiles were splashing, adding to the din.

Charles reached down in a desperate attempt to save the other man. Grabbing firmly onto his arms, he pulled with all his might. His muscles strained, and he squeezed his eyes shut for fear of seeing the poor soul wrenched from his arms and pulled to his death. Amid the machinegun fire, the dangling soldier screamed, and Charles felt the warm splatter on his face of what he knew must be blood. Somehow, he managed to pull the terrified man up and over the side, and the two of them fell to the deck. Charles couldn't believe his eyes when he saw that he had succeeded in literally, snatching someone from the jaws of death. When he could stand, he got up shakily and looked into the river where he saw the croc floating with its brains blown out.

He was so drained of energy it was surprising that his trembling legs could hold him up. Since the professor and the military doctor were tending to wounds and all were presently out of harm's way, he looked up to give the soldier at the Maxim the all clear. Charles was dumbfounded by the sight of Lilly sitting where one of the soldiers should have been. Her sun helmet had fallen off, and the bright hot sun beat down on her exposed head, causing the red and gold streaks to shine like burnished brass.

All of a sudden, his physical weakness was forgotten, and he ran across the deck and up the stairs to her side. "Are you all right?" he asked.

He felt ridiculous as soon as the words were spoken since *she* was the reason *they* were all right. She barely heard him through the loud incessant ringing in her ears. She nodded her head slightly as though in a daze and proceeded to release her grip, prying her hands free of the gun as though her skin had been glued to the metal.

Having seen Charles race past them, Mr. Brown and Sir Billingsley followed him. They couldn't believe it had been Lilly manning this weapon the whole time and not some experienced military man. Recognizing that she must be in shock, her father put his arm around her supportively and helped her to stand. She walked away from him without acknowledging his presence.

Richard came up the stairs just as she was coming down, and she brushed by him as though she didn't even see him. She continued to the area where the two soldiers were still being treated to check on their injuries. She had to see their condition for herself. Now that the urgent situation was over, she realized that she could have accidentally shot the very people she had been trying to save. She thanked God none of their wounds had been caused by her bullets.

Sir Billingsley asked if she was all right, and she indicated she would like to go lie down. As he attempted to put his arm around her to help her to her cabin, she put up one hand and shook her head as though rejecting his offer, and she quickly walked off alone. Along the way, she had to stop to empty her churning stomach over the railing and into the river. Wiping her mouth with her shirt sleeve, she was oblivious to everything as she finally reached the solitude of her room where she laid down in her bed. The raw emotions she had been holding back let loose like a dam, and she broke down and sobbed.

As the returning British column had drawn closer to the shooting, they could differentiate between the sound of rifle fire, which had increased in tempo, and the sound of the Maxim, which had replaced it. The captain, with a look of concern to the sergeant major, had exclaimed, "The Maxim!" The situation had to be serious, but there had been no soldier left behind with the expertise to use that massive gun. That ominous sound caused them to pick up their speed even more. The only problem was, in order to keep their command intact, they were forced to move at the pace of the slowest man.

"Sergeant major," the captain shouted, "I will race ahead with the two fastest men. You follow with the rest as quickly as you can."

Two men were ordered to join the captain, and the three of them broke into a dead run. There was too much at stake to waste time getting there. Whatever the threat was, they knew that as long as that Maxim kept firing, there was hope.

As the three men neared their destination, all gun fire stopped. They slowed down, approaching the area warily. Upon seeing the few remaining crocodiles feeding on their own dead, they instantly deduced what all the shooting had been for. The Maxim sat silent except for the steam, which was still hissing from its water jacket. After quickly scanning the riverbank, the captain sent one of the men back to warn the rest of the command to approach with caution, while he and the remaining soldier made their way toward the recently stabilized gangplank and climbed aboard unnoticed by the now sated beasts.

From Lilly's father, and the others who were witness to the events, Captain Wilson learned what had transpired in his absence. He kept returning to the fact that it was Lilly who had taken charge of the Maxim. Now he was thankful he had taught her how to shoot, but how in the world would he explain *this* in the military dispatches?

Needless to say, word spread like wild fire, and everyone talked about how Lilly had turned out to be quite the heroine. For years afterward, soldiers would tell the story of "Lock and Load Lilly," as they had jokingly dubbed her. She would brush off their compliments and good-natured teasing, but not because she was embarrassed, or even being modest. The truth was, the whole incident was not something she took pride in. Although she was thankful no one had been killed, the thought of having taking the life of God's creatures greatly disturbed her. She felt different, almost violated, for having been forced to kill.

After a couple of days, she seemed to be back to the same old Lilly and had resumed her previous routine of making her daily rounds of the ship. Everyone was glad to see her returning to her normal self again and putting the traumatic event behind her. But Charles, who probably knew her better than anybody else, with the exception of her own father, sensed a change in her that went deeper than the persona she presented to others. There was a sadness behind her winning smile, and a new look of maturity in her emerald eyes. Lilly had lost that touch of childlike innocence, and literally, overnight, had stepped into the serious, sometimes frightening, world of adulthood. Not only did she seem wiser and more mature, but Charles noticed that she was now never without her pistol strapped to her side.

11

Several stops were made on their way up the Nile, mainly for trade purposes with the locals. This time it would be in Aswan. Instead of landing on the riverbank, this time they were stopping at a real town, which sported an actual dock. Richard, for one, could hardly wait to get ashore. It would be so nice to have his feet on solid ground again without the threat of being eaten by local creatures!

For the first time since she had started wearing her new tailored clothes, Lilly had consented to wear one of her dresses. Her father thought it more fitting attire for her to be seen in a populated town. Charles, who was in the middle of a conversation with Mr. Brown, was pleasantly surprised to see her dressed up and decided a little teasing was in order. "Showing the flag, are we?" he asked.

"Why, I think the young lady is dressed quite appropriately for the occasion. Are you suggesting this is but a show of gunboat diplomacy strength?" Mr. Brown inquired with a note of friendly banter. "I think you look simply stunning, Milady," he added, supporting the compliment with an exaggerated courtly bow.

"Thank you, kind sir. You may rise." She stifled a smile as she turned to Charles. "As for you, Mr. Buller, apparently you have forgotten the proper manner of greeting a fashionable young lady. As a means of allowing you to make amends for your breach of etiquette, I shall grant you special permission to escort me into town," she said with an upturned nose, as though speaking to one beneath her.

"At your Majesty's service!" He humored her by clicking his heels together dramatically before bowing. "My sincerest apologies, Mililly, er, I mean, Milady." Breaking character, they all laughed at their silliness.

Captain Wilson decided to accompany Lilly and the others into town while Sergeant Major MacDonald and the rest of the men took care of necessary but mundane details. Once the crew finished their assigned chores, they would be allowed to go ashore and let off some steam of their own.

The first stop was the hotel where they all secured lodgings for the night. Lilly was eager to enjoy the luxury of a real bath, but once she had finished with that, she was pestering Richard to take her sightseeing in the town.

Richard willingly agreed to her request. He was thoroughly sick and tired of life on the river. His luck with cards had never returned, and it seemed like every time he played now, he ended up losing. He was hoping while they were out, he might find a bank in order to cash a draft. "Even if you should find a bank, good luck trying to get them to give you gold sovereigns for what appears to them to be nothing but a worthless piece of paper," the captain had told him.

The rest of the group would also be joining them since there was really nothing else to do, and more importantly, there was safety in numbers. Mr. Brown excused himself from their company in order to send off a dispatch to his employer. After all, that was the reason for inviting himself along on this adventure.

The rest of them started off in the direction of the bazaar down a crude hot and dusty road. Lilly tried to take it all in by continually turning her head from one side to the other and craning her neck on tiptoe in an effort to see over and around the milling natives. The professor in front of her, and the captain behind, were both simultaneously trying to point out things of interest.

The professor turned his head to yell above the noise of the marketplace, "Do you notice how everyone looks to be arguing with one another?" Now that he mentioned it, she did notice. "What they are doing is haggling over prices."

"Haggling?" she asked, puzzled.

"That, Lilly, is the acceptable way to do business here. To offer to pay the seller's first asking price is a disappointment to the seller, and you will have cheated him out of the enjoyment of negotiating the sale."

"Why don't they simply mark the prices like some merchants do in England?" she asked.

"Yes, why waste everyone's time?" added Richard. Now that he was actually here, he decided the less time he had to spend in this hot, smelly, dirty bazaar, the better.

"That would take all the sport out of buying and selling," added the captain.

"That is true, and I might add that both the buyer and the seller have the satisfaction of feeling they have gotten the better end of the deal," said Charles.

"What a peculiar custom!" mused Lilly aloud.

In addition to the exotic foods and animals offered for sale, there were clothing, jewelry, pottery, spices, weapons, and just about anything else one might desire. Some rather old-looking pottery and vases caught the professor's attention. The seller assured him they came from a tomb of some long forgotten king. At another stall, the captain stopped to examine some fine handmade daggers in jeweled sheathes. Spotting a rather wealthy-looking character with some weights, whom Richard took to be a money changer, he stopped to attempt a business transaction. Sir Billingsley decided to stay with the professor. Once the professor finished what he was doing, Sir Billingsley was going to ask for his assistance with purchasing some scented soaps and perfumes for Lilly. He thought her supply may be running low since now their expedition was taking longer than they had originally planned. Charles, by design or default, stuck close to Lilly.

A colorful, soft, silk scarf caught her eye at one of the booths, and she stopped to take a closer look at it. "I think I would like to get this for my friend Marie. I'm certain she would like it. What do you think, Charles?" she asked as she held it up to seductively cover part of her face, the way she noticed some of the local women were wearing them.

Charles smiled shyly and thought it looked rather flattering on her. "Yes, it's quite nice," he responded.

Anticipating a bit of fun, Lilly turned to face the seller and proceeded to "haggle."

The seller, being much older than Lilly, saw her chance for making a good profit off of this naive foreigner. She knew precisely what Lilly was asking, even though she understood not a word of English; and she answered in her own tongue, which sounded as foreign to Lilly as her language had sounded to the woman.

The transaction took some minutes with much theatrics and exaggerated gesturing on the part of both seller and buyer.

Charles's uncle had offered him many words of wisdom over the years, one of the most important being to never get involved when two women were having an argument. In this case, although he was naturally biased, he was content to just stand back in amusement and observe.

Finally, the transaction complete, Lilly held the scarf up triumphantly waving the fine material in Charles's face. "What fun, and what a beautiful scarf! I think Marie will love it! Let's go find something else to purchase."

Charles shook his head and looked at her with an indulgent grin.

They had only walked a short way down the crowded street before they heard a loud commotion down one of the side alleys. Unable to resist satisfying her curiosity, Lilly linked her arm in his and practically pulled him down the street after her. He really didn't mind going with her to investigate. As a matter of fact, he felt he would let her pull him just about anywhere she wanted as long as their arms were entwined.

A small crowd had gathered around an Arab standing on a small platform off in a corner who seemed to be telling the crowd something about the tall black man standing next to him. The man was very dark skinned and muscular, looking like one of the savages from the jungles of the African interior. Lilly remembered seeing some photographs of Zulu warriors from South Africa. Maybe he was one of them. He was certainly fierce looking. She and Charles pushed their way through the spectators in order to get a better look. As they drew closer to the platform, Lilly was shocked to see a thick rope looped around the African's neck. "Charles, is this a slave auction?" she asked in disbelief.

"I do believe it is just that," he answered in surprise.

"I thought the practice was outlawed."

"It is. The Crown views slavery as piracy, therefore the practice carries the death penalty. But remember where we are, or more importantly, where we are not."

She hugged his arm closer to her and worked her way through the stifling, reeking people until they were very near the front. Now they could see that the slave also wore shackles around his ankles, which were attached by a chain to smaller irons locked around his wrists. One by one, potential buyers stepped onto the platform to more closely examine the slave. They poked and prodded him humiliatingly while they laughed and joked.

Looking away from the poor man in embarrassment, Lilly noticed another African native standing off to the side. This one was female. She too had a rope around her neck; the end of which was tightly tied around the platform's end post. Sadly, she too wore the heavy metal shackles around her wrists and ankles. Turning to Charles, she said urgently, "Oh my God! We must do something!"

Charles led her back the way they had come. He knew slavery was common practice in some areas of the world, but he also knew this knowledge alone would not stop Lilly from feeling passionately about what she had just witnessed. They would find the others, and maybe together they could convince her there was nothing she could do to stop it.

They successfully rounded up Richard, the professor, and her father but were unable to locate the captain. A distressed Lilly explained what was going on as they hurried back to the auction. She still couldn't comprehend how such an atrocity could be taking place in this day and age.

"I'm afraid this type of thing happens far too often out here," said the professor. "One African tribe in the interior will raid the village of another, taking prisoners, who are then traded for goods to Arab slave traders. These poor souls are ripped from their homes and sold in the manner you have just seen, to any who have the means to pay for them. Sadly, there are those who value human life only as a commodity to be used for making money."

Lilly, in her innocence, had really believed such a practice was a thing of the distant past, so Charles added, "It wasn't until as recently as a few years ago when our Christian country along with that of the Germans gained control of the area known as the Sultanate of Zanzibar making it into protectorates, that the open trading of slaves by Muslim Arabs was finally brought to an end. More African slaves passed through Zanzibar on their way to other Muslim countries than anywhere else in the world."

Charles was getting under Richard's skin. He was always throwing historical facts around trying to impress Lilly with his useless knowledge of things long dead. And now he was doing the same thing with religion. Well, he too had attended the university.

"There are some who think those Christian missionaries spreading the word of Christ to poor heathens are no better than the papist Jesuits who tortured and burned those they considered heretics," Richard said with some smugness in his tone. "One must also consider the Christian African nation of Ethiopia, which even today still openly practices slavery."

The professor took umbrage to Richard's comment. Not for his own sake, but for his nephew's. He would have loved to point out that the English sweatshops, such as the ones owned by the House of Elliott, employed women and children to manufacture goods at unlivable wages and under deplorable working conditions, which made them not much different from the abusive slave owners.

"But can't we do *something* to help these poor people here and now?" Lilly entreated impatiently. She cast a desperate look at her father, as a girl who believes that her father has the strength and power to make everything right again.

The savage black man was no longer in sight. The young African girl seemed to be the object of everyone's attention now. A line was forming to one side of the platform as each potential buyer was allowed to approach and examine the proffered human merchandise one at a time. The majority of these men were obviously too poor to be able to afford to spend their little bit of money on something as frivolous as a slave, but the trader had learned that wealthy men sometimes sent one of their servants to make this type of purchase for them.

Lilly found it much easier to make her way to the front now that so many had joined the line to await their turn. She could see the girl clearly now. She had very dark skin, which appeared to have been coated with some sort of oil to make it shine. She wore a piece of cloth wrapped around her hips but was otherwise naked from the waist up. Regardless of her state of undress in front of a mass of men with greedy lustful eyes, she stood straight and aloof, her black eyes looking steadily over their heads with an almost regal bearing. At the moment, there was a rather unclean Arab with soiled clothes, who was forcing the slave's lips back with his dirty fingers in order to examine her strong white teeth.

"Oh, Father! Please do something!" Lilly pleaded tearfully.

It appeared to Sir Billingsley that the young slave could have been about Lilly's age. He saw his daughter standing before him as she had many years ago begging him to help the poor children at the orphanage.

The next man in line approached the dark-skinned girl and laughing to his friends, began pinching her exposed breasts. Conversing with the seller, he made it clear that he wanted him to remove the remainder of her clothing.

Turning to the professor, Sir Billingsley abruptly ordered, "Buy her!"

"You can't be serious!" exclaimed Richard. "That would only be supporting this kind of behavior. And it *is* against the law!"

"Well, it appears the law is nowhere about," said the professor as he loudly cast a bid in the local dialect.

There was a murmur in the crowd as they became aware of the apparently well to do Englishman prematurely casting his bid. At first, the auctioneer wasn't sure if he was serious. Decorum had been broken by submitting a bid before the official auction had even begun. Looking around, it was clear there were probably no potential buyers in this lowly group. Many of them were only here out of boredom and curiosity. Hoping for a good sale, he decided to carry on with the bidding. Giving a secret signal to his partners in the crowd, they cried out bogus bids, driving the price up until they received a second signal telling them to stop. This practice was very profitable at times like this when an obviously wealthy individual was so openly anxious to buy. The shifty auctioneer had learned to read facial expressions in order to avoid going too far and losing a sale, and these particular buyers weren't difficult to read at all.

Without moving her head an inch, the slave girl shifted her gaze and locked her eyes on Lilly's. She had never seen such a fair-skinned woman before, as Lilly had never seen such beautiful dark skin.

The bidding apparently over, the professor held out his hand to Sir Billingsley and said, "Three sovereigns and two shillings please."

The professor paid the sum, and the seller unlocked the shackles and led the young woman over to Lilly by the end of her rope. There were angry murmurs coming from the disgruntled men who had been cheated out of their turn to inspect the half-naked woman. The seller hastily disappeared through a previously unnoticed panel in the wall, and two burly Arabs with sharply honed scimitars now stood guarding the entrance. Little by little, the crowd broke up and moved off to find some other form of entertainment.

The two women just stood looking at each other for a few moments. The color of their skin and the texture of their hair was so different from what they each knew. Lilly's auburn hair was long, smooth, and shiny while the other's was short, black, and frizzy. Lilly's nose was narrow, and the other young woman's was broader and flatter. Both were about the same height and build except that the slave was more muscular, and she appeared to be a little undernourished. She looked to be healthy enough apart from the bruises and rope burns that marked her smooth inky skin. Dressed only in the rag tied about her hips, dirty, and barefoot, she had probably been abused since the day she had been taken from her home. There was a proud yet mistrustful look in her eyes in place of the fear that Lilly had expected to see there. Lilly smiled and then carefully loosened and removed the rope from around the long slim neck. "My name is Lilly," she said as she pointed to herself. She then took the newly purchased silk scarf from the pocket of her skirt and wrapped it around the girl's bare chest, tying it in place. "Come," she said gently as she motioned for her to follow. The auction crowd had already dissipated into the bustle of everyday life as the little group left the alley.

The slave was unsure of what lay ahead for her. These strangers seemed unthreatening enough, and the white woman had given her the strange colorful covering that felt as soft as the skin of a newborn baby. She resisted the urge to run away, for intuition told her she was probably better off with these people than she would be with any of the others back in that alley.

All she had known since she was cruelly snatched from her home and family was the lash and abuse. She thought it wiser to stay with these people for now. She was such a long way from home, and should she be taken again, fate may not be so kind a second time. So rather than run, she decided to stick closely to the white woman in the center of this small tribe of men. She felt safer here among these strange people than she had for a long while.

One of the two younger men kept looking at her in a way that made her skin crawl. She was beginning to think he was one that should not be trusted. It would probably be smart to keep her distance from him. He now began speaking to the woman whom she assumed was her new owner.

"So what do you plan on doing with your newly acquired slave?" Richard teased, as they walked back to the hotel.

"She is *not* my slave," Lilly answered defensively.

"You *did* buy her," he pointed out logically. "That would make her your property."

"Lilly only did that to help her," Charles added. He thought Richard was being purposely mean spirited.

Seeing Lilly's annoyed look, and not wishing to take a chance on angering her father, Richard changed his approach. Pretending admiration for what he deemed was a foolish action to have taken, he said, "I know that, and I think it was a very noble gesture. I was simply wondering what on earth you were going to do with her now?"

She hadn't really thought that far ahead. "I'm not certain. I suppose we could just set her free."

"That would not be possible here, Lilly," said the professor. "I suggest we wait for the right time and place to perform that chivalrous act. The poor girl would not have a chance of surviving here. She would only end up back on the auction block or possibly even somewhere worse. Might I suggest we clean her up some and offer her nourishment while we figure out the best solution?"

As they neared their hotel, they met up with Captain Wilson who was returning from taking care of some urgent business. "I'm so sorry I had to leave you on such short notice. There was a telegram that needed my immediate attention." Noticing Lilly's strange new companion, the captain asked, "And what have we here?"

"This is…well, I don't know her name," replied Lilly awkwardly.

"This is Lilly's most recent purchase, captain," Richard added. "Would you happen to know of anyone willing to take her off our hands?" Seeing Lilly's angry glare, Richard chuckled in an attempt to make it seem as though he had been joking.

The captain looked the newcomer over with a practiced eye, more with curiosity than compassion. He had commanded enough Sudanese troops to have gained respect for them and their people. This one looked to be a fine representation of their strength and proud bearing.

The young captive could tell these people were discussing her, but she had no idea what was being said. Maybe they were still debating her fate. This new man, with his fancy clothes and weapons, was clearly a person of some importance. Were they trying to sell her to him?

The professor explained to the captain the circumstances surrounding their acquisition of the native. This whole matter of the capturing and selling of slaves was something with which the captain was all too familiar. Rather than pursue the matter, which would only delay them on their journey, he simply nodded his acceptance of the situation and then turned to lead them back to their lodgings.

When they reached the hotel, they immediately encountered a problem when the proprietor balked at allowing the dirty African to enter either the dining area or the small room, which had been procured for the sole use of the English woman. He finally agreed to let the slave sleep outside of the young lady's door, but after a substantial amount of additional money had been slipped into the greedy man's hand, he consented to her staying in the room as long as no problems resulted from it. That being settled, they all parted company as each went off to attend to their own business.

After ordering hot water for a bath, Lilly led the young woman up to her room. "Now we can get you cleaned up," she said with forced cheerfulness, even though the poor girl had no idea what was being said. Now that they were in an enclosed room, Lilly noticed a strong unpleasant odor emanating from the girl. Lilly supervised the hotel servants as they brought up the hot water buckets and poured them into the tub. The servants kept sneaking curious looks at the savage crouched in the corner stuffing her mouth with fresh fruit.

Watching all this activity from the safety of her corner, the girl began feeling a little apprehensive. She was confused. Her new owner had been kind in saving her from those disgusting Arabs and then bringing her here to her shelter and even feeding her. But she didn't understand what these others were doing.

"That should be enough hot water. Thank you," Lilly said as she tested the temperature with her hand. Lilly's back was to the young woman as she held her fingers up to smell the fragrant oils she had added to the bath water. It was so thoughtful of her father to have purchased them for her.

The confused woman watching Lilly wondered why she was tasting the water. She was puzzled and was becoming even more alarmed at this strange behavior.

Lilly dismissed the help and turned her attention to the wary-looking girl who was staring at her intently. "Come," Lilly gestured toward the bath. Black eyes glanced at the steaming tub and then settled back on Lilly. This did not look good. First they fed her, and now they wanted to put her in that strange-looking, steaming pot. Suddenly she knew! They wanted to cook her, so they could eat her! They were cannibals!

Lilly took a hold of her arm, thinking to urge the girl to get into the water. Yanking her arm from Lilly's grasp, she pressed herself tighter into her corner.

"What on earth is the matter with you?" Lilly exclaimed, bewildered by this response to her kindness. She tried to speak slowly and calmly to the uncooperative young woman in hopes to gain her trust, but from her unwavering tense and wary demeanor, this approach clearly did not seem to be working.

Trying to think of how to make her understand that she meant no harm, Lilly calmly walked over to the tub. Keeping one eye on the crouched figure, she undressed. Unable to throw all modesty aside, she kept on her chemise and bloomers and stepped into the tub. She made an exaggerated show of washing her body, which had the immediate effect of calming the other woman down, and she could see comprehension dawning in the dark watching eyes. It had all become clear now. These white-skinned people bathed in containers indoors, and with their clothes on! Why they should go through all this trouble when there were rivers and streams to wash and swim in was beyond crazy. The calmed native walked over, and without removing her cloth coverings, climbed into the tub with Lilly.

"Oh, my." Lilly laughed. "You are supposed to take your clothing off when you bathe, but I imagine you are just following my example. Well, at least we've made a start of things."

The small tub wasn't meant for two, so soapy water spilled over onto the floor. Sitting facing each other, Lilly grinned at the expressionless face sitting across from her. Starting to feel self-conscious, she wondered what she should do next.

Suddenly, she heard the sound of a series of large bubbles breaking the surface around her bathing companion like an exploding underwater volcano. Lilly gasped and sprang to her feet, her eyes huge with surprise. The offending young woman just looked at her in stoic, confused innocence, until it occurred to her what it was that had startled her new owner.

There she stood, water pouring off of her soaked hair and clothing, with one hand covering her mouth and eyes opened wide. The native girl looked up at Lilly, and without batting a lash, let loose with another major eruption. Lilly squealed and frantically hopped the rest of the way out of the tub. As she did so, she saw the gleam of white teeth as a smile spread across the face of the offender still sitting in the water. As quickly as the smile had appeared, it was gone again, but a trace of amusement still glinted in the bright dark eyes.

At first, Lilly smiled back, but then she started laughing as the thought of the comical scene replayed in her mind. Reaching for her towel, she said, "I think bath time is over for me." After Lilly made it understood that clothes needed to be removed before washing one's self, the bath was successfully completed.

As Lilly changed into dry underclothes, she realized the crude clothing the other girl had been wearing needed to be replaced with clean, more appropriate garments. "We had better find something for you to wear." Lilly briefly harbored the idea of outfitting her in one of her own dresses, but the thought passed as being not only impractical, but the idea also seemed ludicrous. Not even *she* enjoyed wearing these clothes in this climate, and she also thought that the vision of this proud, savage-looking native in a frilly English dress would somehow be humiliating and demeaning for her. It would probably be best to get her some clothes as the Egyptians wore, which were loose fitting and cooler. Her mind decided she sent a servant off to find the requested items.

As they waited, Lilly again smiled at the now serious, clean, and better smelling girl. Her heart ached at the sight of the welts and scars that marred the otherwise smooth skin of her back. She pulled a light blanket off of the bed and wrapped it around the poor girl's shoulders. Her smile received no friendly response in return, and it seemed like the previous lighthearted moment in the tub might never have happened. There was a scratching at the door as three servants arrived to clean the room, and a moment later, a fourth one appeared with the new clothes packed in a bundle. The slave girl put on her new clothes as the servants bustled around the room cleaning and disposing of the dirty bath water.

When the girl had finished dressing, Lilly was admiring the huge improvement in her appearance, when the dark intelligent eyes suddenly hardened at something across the room. The girl pushed past her and grabbed a hold of one of the servant's arms. As Lilly wondered what to make of it, the startled servant tried to wrestle free of the slave's grip calling for her friends to help her. Before they could intervene, the "savage" roughly yanked the bundle of wet towels from her arms, and they all watched in shock as a piece of Lilly's expensive jewelry tumbled out onto the floor. Everyone started talking and yelling at once, causing the proprietor to arrive at their door to investigate the commotion. Everybody froze except Lilly, who bent down to retrieve her necklace.

Immediately, the thieving servant began wailing incoherently, and the other servants scurried away like mice deserting a sinking ship. The proprietor seized her roughly, half dragging the frightened criminal down the stairs. Everything had happened so fast that it took a minute for Lilly to comprehend what had just taken place.

"Thank you!" she said gratefully to the slave girl. She pointed to herself and said, "My name is Lilly." When she received no response, she again pointed to herself and repeated, "Lilly." And then again more slowly, "Lil-ly."

Finally, she was rewarded by a look of comprehension. "Li Li," the girl parroted as she pointed to Lilly. Then to her surprise, the girl then pointed to herself and said something that sounded like, "Ba La."

"Bala?" When she received no further attempt at communication, Lilly said, "I guess Bala it is then. What a pretty name."

That afternoon, Charles appeared at their lodgings with an elderly Arab. Introducing himself to Lilly, the man explained that in his younger years, he had been a merchant who had by necessity become fluent in many dialects as he traveled the camel caravan routes throughout the Sudan. As a favor to their mutual friend the professor, he consented to stop by the hotel to try and converse with the African slave in an effort to find out something about her. After several unsuccessful attempts to communicate, they came to the conclusion that she must surely be a long way from home. Nevertheless, the Arab assured them he would try to find someone who could speak her native tongue; and if successful, he would return with them at a later date. In the meantime, they would have to get by as best they could using crude sign language and pantomime.

Before he left, Lilly had one more question for him. Since he was a local, she thought he surely must be familiar with the area's laws. "One of the staff from this establishment, a servant, attempted to steal my necklace. Thanks to Bala here, the theft was discovered in time. I was just wondering what has become of her—the one who tried to rob me?" Lilly imagined the guilty woman was probably sitting in a jail cell somewhere, and that perhaps she could be set free. No real harm had been done after all, and she had surely learned her lesson by now.

"Do not concern yourself any longer, miss. Justice is swift in these matters, and I am sure the criminal has already been dealt with."

"But what has happened to her? Is she in jail?"

The Arab looked at her quizzically. "Surely, you know the penalty for theft?"

When Lilly answered with a shake of her head, he continued, "Considering the seriousness of the crime," *meaning stealing from a well-to-do foreigner* "the usual punishment is to cut off the offending hand."

Lilly was horrified! What other atrocities would she discover were practiced in this strange and barbaric land!

12

The next morning, the travelers gathered their belongings and returned to their ship. It had been decided for Bala to accompany them until they could discover her origins and then perhaps she could be set free among her own people. They hadn't been able to find anyone who spoke her language, so the assumption was that she was most likely from somewhere farther south, or even possibly from the interior of Africa. They all agreed on one thing. She would not survive long if left behind.

Lilly was happy that the girl was going with them. Maybe they would be able to get her back to her people, and at least she would be safe until then.

The only one who wasn't so pleased about the arrangement was Richard. Whenever he was around Lilly now, he could feel those liquid black eyes boring into him. He didn't even need to see them. He could sense the hostile malevolence directed toward him that made the hair on the back of his neck stand up. He felt the sooner they got rid of this evil creature, the better he would like it. She followed Lilly about like a faithful dog. A dog that looked like it would love to sink its teeth into his throat.

Captain Wilson approached the professor as soon as he boarded the ship. "Good day, professor. I'm glad to see everyone is ready to go. We really need to set sail as soon as possible."

"Is there a problem?" The professor hoped not. It would be a shame to have unforeseen complications change their plans after having come this far.

"Nothing to be alarmed about. I have just received word that we are to proceed farther south after dropping your party off. The other convoy that is following us with the second platoon will join up with us there. The Mahdists are making demonstrations to the south, and so we are to make a show of doing the same. It is nothing to be disturbed about, just a bit of tit for tat."

Lilly had just stepped aboard with Bala when they were greeted by the O'Hare boys, John and Will. "Hello, Miss Lilly!" John yelled with a wave. Will was right alongside of his big brother, smiling and waving wildly.

"Mind your manners!" warned their mother. She smiled at Lilly apologetically as the boys ran over to see if Lilly had anything for them.

John, being the older, removed his cap and bowed slightly. "Good day, Miss Lilly," he said, trying to remember his father's instructions. Young Will simply continued to grin, while shifting from one foot to the other. After Lilly presented them both with a piece of wrapped taffy, the boys looked curiously at the black-skinned woman standing slightly behind her.

"John and Will, this is Bala."

The boys just stared open mouthed at Bala until suddenly remembering his manners, John said, "Pleased to meet you." They had seen black-skinned people before, but this was certainly the first time they had ever been introduced to one. Will continued to stare, as Bala looked soberly back at the fascinated boys.

Noticing her frizzy black hair, John asked in all innocence, "Is she a Fuzzy-Wuzzy?"

"What?" Lilly asked in surprise.

"Is Bala a Fuzzy-Wuzzy?" he asked again with a trace of fear in his voice.

"Come now, lads, mind your manners," Sergeant Major MacDonald scolded as he strolled up nonchalantly to greet his favorite people.

The big man ruffled the boy's hair affectionately and acknowledged Bala with an ever so slight nod. He had already heard about the manner in which Lilly had acquired her. He then scowled ferociously at the boys, who responded with giggles, for they knew he was only pretending to be angry with them.

"Run along now, men!" he commanded with an exaggerated military bearing. As she fondly watched them run off, Lilly looked up at the gentle giant of a man and inquired, "Sergeant major, what did John mean when he asked if Bala was a Fuzzy-Wuzzy?"

"No doubt it is because of the texture of the young lady's hair. Those of the Mahdists, who are known as the Dervish, have long frizzy hair similar to your young friend here, hence the name. Although the name hints of mockery, it was given as a simple obvious description, for we British have nothing but respect for the fighting abilities of those tribesmen. It was for this reason Rudyard Kipling paid homage to them in one of his poems.

"Do you recall the Barrack-Room Ballads?" he continued. "They were a series of poems about the British fighting man and events surrounding him. There is one about the Sudan Expeditionary Force and its ill-fated march to relieve General Gordon at Khartoum. It is simply entitled, *Fuzzy-Wuzzy*."

The sergeant major looked off into the distance as he repeated, almost with reverence, the words he had committed to memory so long ago.

"So 'ere's to you, Fuzzy-Wuzzy,
At your 'ome in the Soudan:
You're a pore benighted 'eathen
But a first-class fightin' man;

An 'ere's to you, Fuzzy-Wuzzy,
With your 'ayrick 'ead of 'air–
You big black boundin' beggar–
For you broke a British square!"

He then hesitated as if reflecting on some profound thought, or a remembrance of some great event in his past, before continuing.

"You see, one of the most effective defensive infantry formations is the square. That is when the soldiers form close order ranks of three or four rows deep, in the form of a hollow square. With fixed bayonets and volley fire to greet an adversary from any direction, there is nothing short of cannon fire that can break through those ranks. The British infantry square was the deciding factor at the Duke of Wellington's great victory over Napoleon at Waterloo. Yet time and again, it was those brave warriors of the Sudan, the Fuzzy-Wuzzy, who repeatedly attacked the British squares, and even succeeded in breaking through more than one!"

Remembering the sights and sounds of a battle long ago, the smell of smoke, the stickiness of warm blood, the sight of charging, screaming, ferocious savages, and the fear that reduced a young soldier into a helpless, sobbing child, the sergeant major looked tenderly at the innocent girl standing before him.

"I must get back to work now. If you will excuse me, young lady, I will bid you a good day." He then strutted away in almost as much haste as had the boys.

Shortly after they set sail again, Captain Wilson assembled everyone on deck for a little ceremony. "I would like to take this opportunity to thank you, Miss Lillian Billingsley, for your part in the rescue of two of Her Majesty's soldiers." He paused to indicate the pair standing to his left, one of them leaning on crutches. Every one of your shipmates, to a man, has contributed money toward a special gift as a token of appreciation. And I might add admiration, for your bravery."

With that said, the captain folded back a cloth to unveil a shining silver dagger lying on a bed of black velvet. He extended the gift to her almost reverently, and she accepted it with gentle grace and humility. It was an extraordinarily beautiful piece of craftsmanship. She slid the blade from its protective sheath and smiled when she saw that it was engraved with crocodiles and palm trees.

"Whenever you look upon it, may you always remember the friends you have made here in the 10th Regiment of Foot." Every man present let loose with a loud cheer, which was echoed by the men across the water on the other ships.

Lilly, face flushed with pleasure and embarrassment, turned the dagger over in her hands as she examined it. It was such a lovely gift.

Bala, who was standing close behind her looked at it suspiciously. Was this man trying to buy her with this fine gift? She wished she could understand what was being said. Bala felt safer with Lilly, but if she was being sold again, there would be no choice, and she would have to go with this man.

"It is indeed exquisite, captain!" Turning to face the men, Lilly thanked them by holding the dagger above her head and throwing a kiss to them all. Bala sensed from Lilly's actions that this gift was not the payment she had feared and relief washed over her. She was safe for now, until she could find a means of escape to rejoin her people.

Sir Billingsley beamed with pleasure. His daughter was turning into quite a woman. She made a father proud, and she would one day make someone an admirable wife. He used to think Richard would be a good match for her, but lately, he had been having some doubts about that union.

He was even beginning to regret allowing him to come along with them to begin with. The captain had found it necessary to bring Richard's recent questionable behavior to Sir Billingsley's attention. It seems the young man had taken his fondness for gambling a bit too far, and having lost a substantial amount of money, he may have turned to some disreputable sources for an advance of funds. Even though the captain had seemed apologetic for bringing up the subject, he had been adamant that these types of dealings would bring nothing but trouble, not only to Richard, but possibly to anyone associated with him.

When evening came, they anchored in shallow water close to shore. Sentries were posted, meals eaten, and as the crew performed the last of their daily chores, the night finally closed in upon them.

Charles had just finished checking on their supplies and taking his twice daily inventory. Feeling too restless to retire for the night, he decided to see if the others were still up so he could maybe join them for a while.

He walked toward the fantail, passing under the overhang on which the Maxim gun was mounted and paused to gaze up at it. Though it was silent and still under its canvas cover, Charles couldn't help feeling in awe of the fearful destructive potential that it was capable of. After having witnessed the extreme devastating power of it firsthand, he dreaded the thought of what it could do to man. True, it was used out here against backward tribesmen, but only as a great equalizer. By impressing the natives with its destructive power, they could sue for peace and avoid further bloodshed. Now, on the other hand, should modern European nations utilize it to war against other modern European nations, the slaughter would literally bleed the nations of their manhood. He sincerely hoped it would never come to that.

"Charles, I'm so happy you could join us!" Lilly said as he stepped out of the darkness and into the lantern light. Lilly was once again dressed in khaki, and Bala, still dressed Egyptian fashion, crouched on the deck nearby. Every one in their group was present and sitting on makeshift seats made up of crates and rolled netting and talking companionably in the cozy ring of light. Even Richard had forgone his card game after Sir Billingsley had expressed his concern over his financial dealings. Not that he was giving up on winning his money back. He just thought he should make a show of mending his ways until the focus was off of him, and he could continue his chosen lifestyle in peace.

"Here, have a seat, next to me." Mr. Brown scooted over on the large crate he was sitting on. He rather liked Charles. He was much friendlier than the superior acting Richard, who was sometimes snobbishly disagreeable.

"Thank you, Mr. Brown. So catch me up. What is the topic of tonight's discussion?" One never knew with a group as diverse as theirs.

"Miss Lilly here has been telling us about an interesting book she has been reading. It's the story of a doctor who assembles a man out of an assortment of human body parts and then brings him to life with the application of electricity. It sounds quite fascinating."

"Frankenstein?" Charles asked.

"Yes, Charles, have you read it too?" she asked hopefully.

"Yes, I have, and yes, Mr. Brown, I also find it to be fascinating."

"Such a thing would, of course, be impossible." said Richard, feeling that old familiar jealousy creeping back in. Apparently, Charles had yet another thing in common with Lilly. "Bringing a body back to life by passing an electrical current through it? Preposterous!"

The professor, who had so far been content to sit back and just listen to the young people's conversation, was nettled by Richard's know-it-all attitude. "I don't really think such a concept is so outlandish. I know of quite a few scientists, even some at our own university, who believe that by applying just the right amount of electricity, a corpse could possibly be brought back to life."

Richard wasn't so easily convinced. "Do you mean to say that simply by passing a current through dead tissue, it will miraculously spring to life?"

"Nothing is that simple. Science is much more complex. There are a multitude of things that could affect the outcome of any scientific experiment. I am simply stating that in the right circumstances, and with extensive research and experimentation, there are those who believe the reanimation of life is possible."

"So you are, in effect, saying that in the future it may be possible to bring the dead back to life!" The man must be daft to think they would believe such a thing.

The professor, ignoring Richard's remark, continued with his dissertation, "Over one hundred years ago, scientists were performing experiments with electricity on dissected animals. They found that muscle tissue responded when an electric current was applied to it. Perhaps you may have heard the term, 'galvanized into action?' Galvanism is the act of bringing dead matter to life with electricity. Some think that even Charles Darwin may have attempted it."

Lilly was spellbound by the professor's words. Richard was still skeptical and folded his arms across his chest in a gesture of derision. "Even if electricity could make a muscle move, that doesn't mean the brain will start thinking and a heart will start beating," Richard challenged. "And one cannot take organs and limbs from one body and attach them to another, as the doctor in the story did. It is just that—a story. A fable created out of someone's vivid imagination."

"The book may be fiction, Richard," corrected the professor, "but it is man's vivid imagination, which brings about the discoveries that skeptics and nonbelievers originally believed were impossible. A closed-minded individual would be incapable of ever making such a discovery."

Richard smarted at the veiled barb.

The professor, for one, was growing tired and thought to bring the evening to a close with one of his favorite stories. "Did you know there are accounts of heads remaining alive for moments after being severed by the guillotine?"

"Why, I have heard of that too!" Of all the people there, it was Richard who was now supporting him. The guillotine was one of the many dark things that fascinated him.

As he began to snuff out his pipe and knock out the ashes, the professor continued, "Many years ago, I knew of one old professor who had firsthand knowledge of these guillotined heads. He once saw a man beheaded over in France. They still use the guillotine there, you know. According to the story, no sooner had the blade made its fatal cut when he immediately approached the basket containing the severed head. He noticed at once that the eyes and lips were still moving. Because the executed man was a pauper, and this professor was a respected man of science, he was granted permission to retrieve it. This he did by scooping it up and placing it in a box of ice in order to preserve it. He took the head back to his laboratory and basing his experiment on data collected over many years, he attached electrodes to the neck, in a manner very similar to what Dr. Frankenstein did. As he applied the measured charge, the eyes suddenly and unexpectedly popped open. And as if that in itself was not shocking enough, the head then spoke!"

"What did it say?" Lilly asked.

The head said, "Sacrebleu, zat hurt!"

They all laughed, even Richard.

"From that day on, whenever the old professor grew lonely, he would take that head out of the crate of ice, give it a jolt, stick a lit pipe in its mouth, and converse with it for hours on end. They got on so well, they ultimately became the best of friends."

Lilly was glad to see that even Richard had to smile at the thought of a bodiless head, chatting away while puffing on a pipe.

Seeing that they all enjoyed his little story, the professor bid them all good night and retired.

"*Frankenstein* sounds like a remarkable story," said Mr. Brown. "I will definitely have to read it myself someday."

"Do you know what else is remarkable about that story?" asked Charles.

"And what would that be, Mr. Buller?" Sir Billingsley asked.

"Incredibly, the story was written, not by a learned man of science, but by a woman named Mary Shelley. She wrote it for entertainment while vacationing with her family and friends back in 1818. That was a mere three years after Waterloo! Just think of all the progress that has been made in science and medicine since then. She wrote of impossible things back then that people now believe might become quite possible one day in the future."

"Mary Shelley must have been a truly extraordinary woman!" added Lilly.

Lilly wasn't aware of it, but people were coming to the same conclusion about her.

13

That night, Lilly had a strange dream. Both she and Bala were digging through a dirt wall. They weren't using any tools, but they clawed at the earth with their bare hands. Only suddenly, the dirt had turned into a huge mound of coal. And they weren't in Egypt, but back home in England, in her father's coal bin. Both she and Bala were wearing their finest gowns. They were filthy from head to toe, and they knew that Mother would be upset because there were guests due to arrive at any minute. Lilly heard a voice calling her name, but strangely, it seemed to be coming from inside the mound itself.

"Hurry, Bala, dig faster!" Lilly cried, digging frantically.

"Lilly!" called the voice again, and this time she recognized the voice of her father, and she knew he was calling for help.

Her eyes snapped open, and she just lay there waiting for the pounding of her heart to return to normal. The dream had seemed so real. Then she noticed the sound and felt the vibrations of the ship's engine and realized they were moving. They must have fired up the engine again in the early hours while she was still fast asleep. The soothing putt-putt of the engine helped to calm her even more, and she pushed the disturbing dream from her mind.

Hearing the sound of rushing water, she sprang to her feet to look out the port hole, almost stepping on Bala who had been fast asleep on the floor. Bala had made it clear, without speaking one word of English, that she would sleep nowhere except on the rug beside Lilly's bed. Lilly opened the porthole and was treated to the sight of frothing rushing rapids just up ahead. "Oh my, I wonder how we will get our ships over that?"

She quickly pulled on her khaki's and leggings, strapped on her Sam Brown belt and holster, and clapped the sun helmet on her head. Up on deck, the bright sunshine promised another hot yet glorious day. Lilly, with the ever present Bala at her side, looked anxiously at the treacherous waters ahead. From the corner of her eye, she saw the sergeant major approaching.

"Sergeant major, how are we to continue up river? The water seems so rough, and I can see boulders sticking up even from here."

"What you see before you are the rapids known as the 1st Cataract. There are also others farther upstream. For some reason, the river is very shallow in these parts, and the rushing water never seems to succeed in eroding away the stones beneath the surface. It's almost as though the river bottom is sprouting forth from the depths beneath. Under normal circumstances, travelers would go ashore and proceed by caravan some miles upstream, where they would then find other ships waiting for them to continue on their way. However, in this case, our mission is to take our ships with us, so we will have a slight delay while we lighten their load and maneuver them over the rapids. Even as we speak, preparations are being made over on both banks of the river."

Sure enough, there were hundreds of people who seemed to have materialized out of nowhere, some of whom, along with their various beasts of burden, were lining up and pulling on long ropes. Others were helping the soldiers transfer supplies and equipment ashore where it was being loaded onto the backs of camels and donkeys.

Captain Wilson was ordering the gunners to dismantle the Maxim and set it up atop the bluffs overlooking the river when Charles appeared with exciting news. There had been some previous excavation of these very same bluffs harboring the tombs of Mekhu and Sebui. So as long as they had to go ashore anyway, they were going to take some time to explore them. This would be Lilly's very first hands on exploration!

As they approached the entrance of the tomb, it appeared to be just a nondescript mud brick or stone wall on the face of the bluff. Upon closer examination, however, it became apparent why this had become a site of interest. Ancient writings in the manner of the Egyptians covered both walls of the entrance. Inside was a dim passageway, which opened up to a room where they found huge pillars engraved with what appeared to be men with animal heads, some of which were sitting on chairs or thrones. On the heads of these man-beasts rested what could be described as ancient Egyptian headdress or crowns.

The whole edifice was constructed of stone blocks, cut and pieced together so precisely that from a distance it appeared to have been formed from one solid mass. Lilly ran her hand slowly across the blocks, her fingertips probing the tight seams, as if searching for a flaw in the smooth stone. She found it amazing that after all these centuries, the blocks still fit together so tightly. She could just imagine what it must have been like when it was made—each huge block being painstakingly cut and transported by a multitude of slaves and workers. Every piece having to be the same dimensions as the blocks before it, and nothing less than perfect was acceptable. The surface would have been sanded and polished by hand until it was as smooth as glass.

Lilly closed her eyes. She saw herself, as an Egyptian princess overseeing the laboring masses. She could see her reflection looking back at her in the shiny stone. She could even discern the glowing green eyes of the cobra on her golden crown, which so well matched the color of her own eyes as to make it appear eerily as though both sets of eyes actually belonged to her. The princess looked around at the walls, which radiated with bright beautiful colors. As she tilted her head back a little, she could feel her heavy crown begin to slip.

"Come on, let's see what else is in here," urged Richard, bringing her back to the present with a start. Maybe if he was lucky, he would stumble onto some hidden treasure that had eluded everyone else over the centuries. Lilly touched the brim of her helmet, which had slipped back on her head, as if to reassure herself that it was not indeed a crown.

They entered a long hallway, which extended back into the hillside. Even before the torches and lamps were lit, Lilly felt a shiver of pleasant anticipation. Even though others had been there before her, she felt privileged to walk down these passages of time. To capture a faded glimpse of this majestic bygone age was to her, the same feeling of peace and reverence she felt when she entered a magnificent cathedral. It was a whole mind, body, and spiritual experience.

"Is this him?" Lilly whispered, looking up at a figure carved into the wall.

"Yes, my dear, that it is," answered the professor. "He is bidding you welcome to his home," he teased.

"Or warning you away," quipped Richard.

Lilly smiled, but Charles was annoyed. Richard always seemed to have something negative to say about everything. "Go ahead, Lilly," urged Charles. "You can be our guide. Tell us your observations and conclusions about what you see."

"Oh, all right. Do you see these figures, Father? The ones that are larger than the others but have the heads of animals? They are no doubt some of the various gods who help and guide the ancient Egyptians through life, and also aid them on their voyage in the hereafter." She paused to study them more closely.

"I recognize this one with the body of a man and the head of a hawk. He is named Horus, a special protector of the pharaoh."

Mr. Brown was listening with interest. He noticed the African slave also seemed to be listening closely, and he wondered if she could understand any of what was being said. Richard was examining every inch of the walls with his fingers, most likely hoping to find some small niche in the stone that would cause the wall to magically slide open to expose a room full of gold. Mr. Brown smirked and turned his attention back to Lilly.

"These other figures are probably bakers preparing bread, and over here," pointing to another section, she said, "these men are making wine or ale. The Egyptians often portrayed simple acts from everyday life on the walls of their tombs, so some are obvious as to what they stand for.

"The reason I concluded that this figure was the owner of this tomb was because, for one thing, it is much larger than the others, which signifies importance. He doesn't appear to be a god. These walls tell the story of his life, and this picture most likely represents a particular important feat, in this case a possible military victory. You see how all of these smaller figures appear to be fleeing and are being trampled underneath the wheels of his chariot, while being attacked by war dogs. They are the enemy. And over here, observe the captured enemy, bound as slaves. That is a clear indication of a victory."

They walked on, studying the walls. Anything of value had long since been hauled away, leaving only these empty halls and passageways, which merely hinted of a past greatness. Lilly spoke sadly, to no one in particular. "It's such a terrible shame."

"What is, Lilly?" Charles seemed more attentive to her than to his surroundings.

"These paintings. Some are fading, no doubt by the touch of hand prints over the years, while others up higher and on the ceiling have become obscured by the soot of torches. Someday I fear they will all be gone completely."

It was just like her to notice such details.

"Charles, I was wondering how those ancient peoples illuminated the chambers and passageways underground while working in and painting them? Surely, they would not have used torches that produced this filthy soot and would burn up the precious air needed to breathe."

Mr. Brown was amazed at her insight. That thought would never have occurred to him, and he was a man who had to think fast on his feet!

As the professor wandered off on his own, Charles explained, "They actually did it with strategically placed mirrors. Those supposedly backward people, positioned mirrors throughout the interiors, which lit them up as bright as day!"

"That's incredible and ingenious! It amazes me when I think of all the miraculous things that were accomplished thousands of years ago, that today, even with our modern tools we would be hard pressed to imitate. Perhaps to them, *we* would be considered to be the more primitive and unenlightened peoples. I think there is much to be learned from the past."

"If they were so intelligent," asked Richard, "why would they build such monuments to themselves to preserve their bodies and treasures, and not think somebody would come along after they were buried and steal everything?"

The professor rejoined them and attempted to explain. "Although some of the tombs, such as the Great Pyramids, are in plain view for all to see, there were many others that were hidden. Of the ones that were not concealed, the contents were guarded and protected in various ways. Of course, the original owners believed that their greatness in life would be respected by following generations. Just as they were revered and unopposed in life, they undoubtedly thought that their bodies and their belongings would still be respected once they were in the grave. This was obviously not always the case. There were some tombs that were looted and desecrated even back then. Notice the writing on that far wall."

They all looked to where he was pointing. One section had some sort of writing on it in plain white paint, part of which looked much like English. Unlike the carefully drawn hieroglyphics in a variety of colors, someone had painted graffiti during a previous visit.

"It appears to be Greek," said Charles, "though I don't know what it says."

"Very good, my boy, it is indeed. And I assure you it was written long before any of us were born," he said. "It is ancient Greek. I've seen this same type of Greek and Roman writing in other previously opened tombs." To Lilly, he added, "For all we know, Alexander the Great himself could have walked these very halls centuries ago."

Richard thought the professor was doing a lot of explaining without actually answering his question. Trying to get him back on track, he commented, "It seems that every society has their share of lower classes that lack respect for their betters and cannot be trusted. Those who are not ambitious enough to make their own fortunes are always willing to take from those of us who are."

This was ironic, coming from a man who was very comfortable living off of his father's money. "The fear of discipline is the key to respect," he said, remembering how his grandfather had made good use of the threat of debtor's prison to secure all that was owed to him. He was quite a successful businessman.

"It wasn't only the poor and needy who robbed their dead pharaohs of their treasures," corrected the professor. "Although the poor would certainly have a need for the treasures that lay within the tombs, it was sometimes those who were already rich and driven by pure greed that would rob the defenseless dead. Remember, it was believed those items would actually be needed in the afterlife; so in a sense, robbing the dead was as serious an offence as stealing from the living."

"Do you mean that even the rich pharaohs robbed graves?" asked Lilly in surprise.

"Yes, my dear. Such a thing was actually quite common during periods of strife, such as civil war. It was at these times of crises when those in power felt that their immediate needs in this life were of far greater importance than of those in the next. It seems that throughout the ages, man has not truly evolved when it comes to human desires such as greed, lust, and a myriad of other sins."

This didn't make sense to Lilly, so repeating Richard's earlier question, she asked, "But, professor, why then would they even bother burying their earthly goods with them, knowing from their own transgressions that others would most likely do the same to them?"

"Their religion and beliefs were of the utmost importance to them. They devoutly believed in the afterlife, so they tried to come up with ways to foil any attempts at desecration and thievery. No doubt there originally were guards patrolling around the various sites of importance. Also, the entrances to some tombs were hidden, disguised, or even had traps and pitfalls built into them meant to maim and even kill the unwary. The Egyptians were also known throughout the ancient world as masters in the art of preparing powerful poisons, some of which were devised to punish those who dared to violate the sanctity of their resting place. And another fact we must not overlook is that they believed in their religion as strongly as we believe in ours. They called upon their gods to protect their bodies and treasures until they rose again. This was done through various spells, incantations, and of course, curses."

"Curses?" Richard asked. Now this was something that sparked his interest. "What kind of curses?"

"The curses were put in place when the tombs were sealed. Just how effective they were, we don't know. For so long, we did not even know they existed because the writings of the

Egyptians was a dead language for centuries. It was only with the discovery of the Rosetta Stone that modern man was able to begin interpreting these writings. Once archeologists were able to translate the hieroglyphics in the tombs, they found that some of them were protected by powerful curses."

Reading the doubt on Richard's face, the professor added, "Those curses were powerful to the ones who put them there, and to those who believed in them. The man who first translated this ancient writing was a brilliant man by the name of Jean-Francois Champollion. Even though the picture writing of the ancients has been with us all this time, many scholars before Jean-Francois refused to study them. You see, the drawings were considered to be holy, or mystic, and so they were feared. Indeed, it was rumored that when he finally succeeded in decoding the writings, he fell into a trance and saw visions of the pharaohs mentioned in his translations. Of course, if one has no knowledge of the curse and some misfortune befalls them, it is simply thought to be accidental and not the retribution of some long dead priest and his god."

"What exactly do these curses entail?" Richard's morbid curiosity was aroused.

The professor recalled some that he himself had translated. "One in particular that I remember warned that whomever disturbed the body or the contents of a certain resting place would rouse the wrath of a certain deity, and their necks would be snapped like a chicken.

"Others have spoken of horrible death by fire, devastating floods, and the destruction of homes. There have been all manner of threats and warnings. Not all of them were protected by curses mind you, only those that held people of importance, which also usually contained many items worth stealing.

"All of these translations I am speaking of were found in tombs that had long ago been emptied of their contents. Just as we have no knowledge of the identity of the original thieves, we also have no idea of how effective these curses may have been. Did the gods punish the defilers and trespassers? There is no way to know for sure."

For a moment, nobody spoke. The wavering torchlight casting shadows on the walls had taken on a more ominous atmosphere. They were standing in the final resting place of a person who no doubt thought their body and belongings would be respected and left in peace. Stealing the personal belongings one needed in the afterlife was bad enough, but to rob the spirit of the mummified body that was needed for resurrection was a most heinous crime, worse than murder itself. Lilly thought it was no wonder the Egyptians did all in their power to protect themselves, even going so far as to put a curse on those who used not only their possessions for monetary purposes, but their physical bodies as well. Here in the tomb, one could almost imagine that such a thing as a curse could be real. Even Sir Billingsley briefly wondered if he had somehow unwittingly put Lilly in danger.

"Are curses real? There's no way of knowing for certain, but it does make for very interesting stories," the professor said with a glint of amusement in his eyes.

That seemed to break the spell. After all, it was the nineteenth century!

Their exploring was continued with forced lightheartedness. No one wanted to admit they had gotten caught up in the eerie talk. If they secretly wondered whether this particular place had a curse on it, none of them spoke up to ask. The fact that they were simply admiring and studying the tomb gave them at least some sense of security. However, once they stepped back out into the sunshine, whatever fear or doubt they may have had, evaporated like the morning dew in the brilliance of the glaring sun.

14

It took several days for the small army of laborers and animals to move the cumbersome ships up past the 1st Cataract. Sometimes the water was a little deeper, which made progress easier. At other times, it seemed they would never succeed in getting past a certain shallow spot.

This slow progress suited Lilly just fine, and she kept herself occupied by spending more time exploring, as well as making herself useful wherever she could. Idling away the time in her tent was not an option. She was determined to use this time fully, whether it was helping out the cook, studying her surroundings, or teaching Bala English.

Bala was also trying to teach Lilly her language, so they were finding it a little easier to communicate, plus it was fun to learn a new language only the two of them could understand. What they couldn't communicate through words, they managed to get their meaning across using gestures and pantomime. Sometimes it seemed as though Bala knew what Lilly wanted without even being told. And whatever Lilly wanted, Bala willingly did.

Truthfully, she knew that without Lilly's protection, she could, and most likely would, be living in horrendous conditions and suffering unspeakable abuse. This was the main reason she stuck close to Lilly whenever possible. Bala felt uncomfortable without her nearby, and there was no one else she trusted. She knew Lilly was special to just about everyone there, and being as she belonged to her, the others seemed to respect this fact and treated her kindly too. Would they still treat her kindly if her protector wasn't around? She had no intention on finding that out. She also had no intention of causing her owner to be displeased with her. This was the best place to be for the time being.

Even though Bala couldn't understand what these people said to one another, she was observant enough to know that the eyes spoke volumes. She could see a father's love for his daughter in the eyes of the tall silent one. There was another kind of love in the eyes of the older man with hair on his face who everyone seemed to go to for advice or council. His love was just that— the love the village elder doled out to all of the children equally. Then there was the love of that one whom she now recognized consisted more of a sense of possession rather than a true love of man for woman. The flashes of love in his eyes were lustful. His hooded eyes hinted of a darkness hidden in the soul. And then there was the love in the eyes of the one called Charles. It was funny how quickly she had learned *his* name. In the way that Charles and Lilly looked at each other, Bala could see feelings of contentment, happiness, and in Charles's eyes even a kindling of passion. And Lilly's eyes spoke of kindness, sincerity, and trust. It was apparent that she had not yet learned there are some who should not be trusted.

At the moment, Lilly was pacing, impatiently awaiting the return of her father and Richard from their trek in search of game for the cook pot. She had heard recent shots, and so she anticipated their appearance at any time now. A few soldiers had accompanied them for safety's sake, but it was her father who loved the hunt and would be excited to be able to repay everyone's kindness by providing fresh meat for all.

Sir Billingsley slowly approached the antelope-like dying beast. In appearance, it reminded him of deer back home. Such a thing of beauty should not be made to suffer so. It suddenly let out an agonizing bellow before it lay it's head on the ground, its eyes rolling wildly. Private Beck and Richard stood on either side of Sir Billingsley. Together, the three of them watched as the animal's life drained away along with its blood, into the dirt.

Outwardly, Sir Billingsley appeared calm, but inside he was smoldering with anger. To allow anything to die such a drawn out horrible death was unnecessarily cruel and heartless. The humane thing would have been to end the animal's pain by allowing the porter to kill it quickly, but Richard had insisted the bullets had done a thorough enough job. Not only was Lilly's father saddened for the animal, he was also upset to have witnessed this disturbing side of his friend's son. What type of person could callously watch the painful suffering of a living being as though they enjoyed it? To kill for food was one thing; to kill for the sheer enjoyment of seeing an animal die in agony was despicable.

Lilly greeted them as they strolled into camp, all dusty and sweat stained. Richard had a triumphant smile on his face, pleased with himself for a successful hunt. Her father was quiet but still managed a smile for his daughter.

"You got one! I knew you would!" she exclaimed, linking her arms through theirs. "Oh, everyone will be so happy! I just know they will enjoy their meal tonight."

"You have Richard to thank for that, my dear."

Indeed, it had been *Richard* who had shot the animal, taking the jump on Sir Billingsley's intended target. But his unsportsmanlike conduct on the hunt, and his cruelly prolonging the suffering of the beast would be details that Lilly need never know.

Charles had been on his way to find Lilly. He was excited about a piece of pottery he had found with Greek letters inscribed on it. When he saw the three of them walking by with their arms linked and with Richard and Lilly so happy, he instantly lost all the enthusiasm that had been bubbling within him just moments before. They were so wrapped up in each other, they didn't even notice him. He continued watching until they disappeared into the crowd of workers. Charles stared at the pottery without even really seeing it before casting it aside as if it were trash. He then turned and stomped off in the opposite direction, suddenly angry at the world.

Charles and the professor were kept busy over the next few days as they lent a hand with the placing of the pulleys and tackle, which made moving the ships so much easier. The professor understood the concept of leverage, so by his calculations, they were able to figure out the most efficient way of making the best possible use of their meager resources.

Charles had plenty of time to think while he was helping his uncle. Lilly was always on his mind lately. He was glad he hadn't said any harsh words to her on the day of the hunt because he would have just ended up having to apologize for whatever foolish thing he had unthinkingly uttered. He had let Richard get under his skin once again, but still, he was Lilly's friend. Whether they were more than just friends was none of Charles's concern. In a few more days, they would be past this river obstacle and he could concentrate once more on what they were here for.

Lilly was oblivious to the ever changing moods of the men in her life. She was too focused on her physical surroundings and new experiences to worry about if one of her traveling companions was in an off mood. This trip was not just an adventure and a learning experience, but it had turned out to be a daily source of enjoyment for her. The things she had taken for granted such as a fine meal served on china while seated at a table in a luxurious setting, was quite the opposite of eating an entire meal off of a tin plate, with a wooden spoon, while sitting on a rock. But she loved it! It was as if "roughing it" taught her to better appreciate her blessings, and just as importantly, this simple lifestyle served to cleanse her soul. Being out among nature made her feel so much closer to God than she had ever felt even in the finest man-made cathedral.

The day finally came when the last vessel was clear of the rapids and in deep water once again. After the supplies were reloaded and the laborers were compensated, the workers disappeared off into the desert from whence they came. Proceeding upriver, the flotilla traveled all that day and the next until toward evening of the second day they reached their destination and settled down to spend their last night on shipboard.

15

Lilly awoke early the next morning to find their escort from the garrison had arrived. Bala assisted her in preparing for the day ahead. Even though she had grown up with people waiting on her, she still felt uncomfortable about Bala taking on the role of her servant. She felt guilty, mainly due to the way in which they had "acquired" her services. Bala was not a servant by choice, but she seemed to be content in her present situation; so for that reason, Lilly didn't try to push her into a less subservient role. She considered the native more of a companion than a personal maid, but it was difficult to figure out if Bala returned those feelings of friendship. She seemed dedicated to Lilly, but there was a part of her that remained aloof and distant, which prevented them from becoming true friends.

Lilly watched as soldiers from the column joined in with those of the flotilla to transfer the supplies and luggage to the backs of camels. One particular camel was giving some soldiers a rough time, and Lilly had to smile as she wondered if that was the sergeant major's old nemesis. She would have to tease him about whether there were any telltale bite mark scars on the camel's lip. She would miss Sergeant Major MacDonald. She had grown very fond of the gentle giant, and he in turn was quite fond of her.

She was still a little puzzled about their last conversation. He had stood stiffly, with hands clasped behind his back. His reed cane, another symbol of his authority, was tucked under his left arm. Lilly had slipped her arm under his and squeezed it tight. "I will always remember you and the kindness you showed me, sergeant major." He had been trying to appear stern, but she could tell this was just a cover used to mask his emotions. The more he tried to hide it, the harder she tried to break through his protective shell.

"Will I ever see you again?" she asked. "Perhaps you will be our escort back north when we return home." That produced a faint glimmer of a smile.

"This morning, I was remembering our preparations for this trip. My father, Richard, and Charles took me shopping. Father was going to take me to one of my usual establishments for some lightweight dresses, but Charles suggested we go to a men's tailor to purchase a feminine version of these fine clothes I have on now. I'm afraid I was very naughty and took it upon myself to persuade the tailor's wife to outfit me in the same attire as the men. I am now so glad I did that. Just imagine how uncomfortable I would be trying to cross a sand dune bogged down by a skirt. And wearing a sun bonnet adorned with flowers while trekking through the desert? Why, I would have birds nesting on my head!"

That produced a bigger grin. This child was a breath of fresh air in his life of rigid rules and regulations. He would miss her tremendously. He couldn't help but be concerned about her naivety and trusting nature though. The sergeant major believed Charles would always look out for her, and that his feelings ran deeper than either he or Lilly realized. But it was Lilly's trust in Richard that was most concerning. Sometimes it took someone from the outside looking in to be able to see objectively, and the sergeant major did not like what he saw in Richard.

"Allow me to give you some words of advice, my dear. I do not feel justified to comment as a father figure, being as I have not raised my own daughter. What I have been is a soldier for most of my life, so my advice is of a military nature. Even so, I think it can be translated into civilian terms that pertain to your own life experience."

The seriousness of his tone almost made the smile fade from her face for she knew that he was speaking from his heart, and she respected him greatly.

Although she was his sole audience, he cleared his throat as though in preparation to address his men. "Expect the unexpected, young miss. Napoleon said something to the effect that no plan survives intact after the first five minutes of the engagement. Keep your eyes open, and be ready to change or modify your plans at any given moment. Take advantage of any situation which presents itself.

"Lead by example. Ask nothing of your men that you are not willing to do yourself." As an aside, he added, "I imagine the same applies to marriage and family."

He then took up where he had left off. "Be brave, and have faith in your men, or in your case, your man.

"And last of all, know your men, and what they are capable of. Most need to be molded into soldiers. This requires discipline. Everything is to be done 'by the book.' After much hard work, most become fine soldiers. But if after all of your efforts to feed, clothe, arm, and train your men, you know in your heart you still have serious doubts about their capabilities, it is best not to commit them to battle, for they will see after their own welfare and ultimately let you down, which will mean your own personal ruin. Follow your instincts, and heed your inner voice. If you are experiencing misgivings about someone or something, do not be afraid to change your course."

Lilly let his words sink in. Most of it made sense, but she wasn't sure what he was actually getting at. She would have to think more about it, for she knew that sooner or later, it would all become clear.

The officer in charge of escorting them was Lieutenant John Prescott, who despite his youthful appearance was already a veteran of many small skirmishes that frequently broke out on the fringes of the empire. His cheek bore the scar of a saber cut about an inch below his left eye. Lilly thought the scar gave his otherwise boyish face a certain look of maturity. He had, under his command, a mixed force of Anglo-Egyptian infantry who were, no doubt, capable fighting men like himself.

Lieutenant Prescott estimated they would reach the garrison in a day or two, depending on how well Lilly could keep up. He expected they would need to make room for her on one of the camels before long. Their destination was along an old caravan route, which was by no means an easy trek. He sighed in resignation at having been assigned to conduct a rich, pampered female across this rough terrain, and he really doubted she would be able to handle the march. The sight of her dressed in trousers made him snicker in amusement. He didn't think it would be long before this pretty little flower began to wither in the harshness of the desert.

Bala had high hopes that they would continue traveling south. By her reckoning, her homelands lay in that direction, and their travels were taking them southeast into the sparse desert. But her land was lush with vegetation, which meant her home was still a long distance away. She considered slipping away and trying to make it on her own but decided against that idea. She could probably survive in the jungle, but alone in the desert, she might be recaptured by desert raiders. No, it would be safer to stay yet awhile longer with this one called Lilly.

Richard was becoming more and more upset with each step he took. It was bad enough to be out in the middle of nowhere having to do without all the creature comforts he was accustomed to, but at least on the ship he had had a few basic luxuries. Here in the desert he had none, and now he was going to be expected to live in a tent like some nomad. This was certainly not what he imagined it would be like. He was used to staying in the finest hotels when he traveled, and being obsequiously waited on hand and foot.

The oppressive heat of the day coupled with the filthy flies, not to mention the unusually cold nights, were all things that kept him from experiencing any enjoyment whatsoever. He missed his comfortable bed, getting together with his friends, and having servants catering to his every need. And he missed Maggie. How had he ever let his father talk him into this? The only thing keeping him going at all was the hope of some sort of compensation for all of his misery. There had better be some treasure to be found at the end of all this! Either that or he would have to depend solely upon winning over Lilly and her fortune.

Charles noticed Lilly was having no trouble at all in keeping up with the caravan. In fact, Richard and Mr. Brown looked more like they were experiencing difficulty with their depleting energy than she was. She was becoming more excited the closer they got to their objective. This adventure would have been unheard of for a woman at the beginning of the century. Most people still believed a female's place was in the home, but more opportunities were opening up to women all the time. *Besides, those people didn't know Lilly*, Charles thought with a grin.

After walking for most of the day, they had just rounded a low lying sand dune when they first sighted the garrison. At first appearance it didn't look to be much of a fort. As they drew closer they could see the outlying walls which seemed to still be in the process of being erected. Observed from a distance they didn't seem high enough to even contain a herd of goats, let alone repel an enemy. Passing through the opening that would one day be gated, Lilly could see the wall appeared to be composed of loose stone and mortared with clay bricks, which were actually being made on site and were scattered about everywhere drying in the sun. She wondered if these bricks were made in the same manner as those fashioned by the Jews long ago when they slaved under the Pharaoh?

The caravan route led right into the main entrance and up to a well. The purpose of building the fort around the well was twofold. This allowed them to be able to control trade, and more importantly, they could effectively deny the only local source of water to those deemed hostile to the Crown.

Other than the unfinished walls, there wasn't much more as yet in the way of buildings. Most of the troops were quartered in tents erected on the low foundations of their future building sites. After the outer walls were completed, the construction would then continue on the barracks, stables, and various other internal structures.

A group of white-clad Egyptian soldiers were marching in the hot sun, as the individual putting them through their paces kept up a seemingly never ending stream of verbal abuse in their native language.

Approaching the dusty, sweating travelers was a group of officers, whom Lilly surmised must be their reception committee. The professor's friend, Captain Peter Lewis, was among them—a short, rather stout gentleman. His upper lip sported the thin mustache that seemed to be the style favored by the military men in this part of the Empire. Recognizing his old friend, he greeted him with a quick and heavy handshake, followed by an enthusiastic slap on the back.

"It's jolly good to see you again, professor. I do believe your cushy command back at the university suits you rather well. You seem not to have aged at all."

"Nor have you, captain. I must say this work suits you well, defending Her Majesty's interests out here around the local watering hole!"

"Ha!" Captain Lewis laughed. "Someone needs to make the sacrifice, so why not one of Her Majesty's most distinguished fighting men?

"And, Charles," he continued, "how long has it been? Five years? What a fine young man you have become in spite of your rogue relation! I just hope you have not acquired too many of your uncle's unseemly vices."

Charles chuckled. He fondly remembered the antics of Captain Lewis and his uncle, some of which they no doubt thought he wasn't privy to.

Introductions were made all around. Sir Billingsley caught a look of interest in the eyes of the second in command, Lieutenant Jeffery Miles, as he greeted Lilly. He decided he had better keep a watch on this one. His daughter was much too guileless in certain matters, and here they were in the middle of the desert with no one but himself to protect her virtue.

That was one detail he had completely overlooked when making his preparations for this journey. He was regretting not having employed a female chaperone to accompany them. It was just not possible for him to watch over her all of the time. The professor was one who could be trusted to see to Lilly's safety and welfare, but as far as Richard's reliability in this matter, well, it appeared he would need to be watched as carefully as the next man. Living in such close quarters afforded Sir Billingsley the opportunity to really get to know this young man who apparently had a more than a passing interest in his daughter. And Richard's weaknesses in character had gradually begun to surface as their living conditions had become more challenging.

Of course, Charles would look after her, but he was also a young man, and no doubt could be tempted like any other young man would be. Yet Sir Billingsley perceived in him a genuine devotion to her. And at least now there was Bala.

Sir Billingsley saw how she went to great lengths to take care of Lilly. He knew his daughter considered her to be more of a companion, partly because she was lonely for female company, and partly because he knew his daughter. Just as she would never have expected an orphan, whom she had invited to the manor, to serve her, she must surely feel the same for the young African girl.

Yet Bala *did* wait on her, and she did it as the most faithful and efficient servant one could ever hope to find. The only reason she acted as such was because she evidently wanted it that way. What she did for Lilly however, she declined to do for others. Sir Billingsley recalled an amusing incident when Bala had gathered up her own and Lilly's dishes after a meal on the ship, and Richard tried to foist his own on her as well. Not only did she pointedly ignore his offered plate, but without speaking a word, she had stared him down until he had placed it back on the table in embarrassment. Apparently, Bala was as headstrong in character as his Lilly. No doubt she would look out for his daughter as best as she could.

Bala was standing in the background, assumed by Captain Lewis and his men to be Lilly's personal servant. Lilly knew by now that Bala felt the most comfortable remaining unnoticed, so she didn't want to draw attention to her by correcting this false assumption.

Mr. Brown finally caught up to the others, huffing and puffing. He had a harder time keeping up with the pace of the march and had dropped back toward the rear some time ago. He now introduced himself to Captain Lewis and his men. The captain knew right away why the professor had brought him along and did not blame him one bit. He himself wished there had been a reporter present the time his men were involved in a skirmish with hostile Arabs. He fancied his name would look rather well in print.

Like many other units in this region, this one was made up of the reformed Egyptian Army, which was led by British officers and some enlisted men, most of whom were sergeants. It was their job to rebuild the old Egyptian Army that had been repeatedly beaten in combat against the Mahdist armies in the Sudan. Instead of the Lee-Metford, these soldiers all carried a different type of rifle, which mounted an old-fashioned-looking, socket-type bayonet. Sir Billingsley had some misgivings about them not being a British unit such as the Grenadier Guards, or at least of the same caliber of those fine military men they had left behind on the flotilla.

While their tents were being set up, Lilly noticed some native troops performing a strange chore. Taking a few steps closer to get a better look, she asked Lieutenant Jeffery Miles what they were doing.

The lieutenant was more than eager to answer the attractive young lady's questions. "Those men are washing their clothes," he informed her.

"What, with sand instead of water?" She stepped closer but still couldn't make sense of what she was seeing. Sure enough, in place of water, they were scrubbing their clothes with sand!

Lieutenant Miles offered an explanation for what to him was a normal everyday occurrence. "Water is a precious commodity here in the arid desert. Even though we have a well, wells can go dry, so we need to conserve our water for drinking. During times of plenty, such as when it rains, we need to use it to increase the production of our bricks. But when the water levels run low, we must sometimes resort to rationing. But don't you worry, miss, I guarantee you will not go thirsty."

Normally, such a topic would cause him to yawn in boredom, but having sparked her interest, and thereby capturing her undivided attention, he was willing to pretend a regard for the mundane that he didn't feel.

"As for the laundering chore, it's a common necessity out here. You see, salt and grime build up in the material. By briskly rubbing the clothes with the fine grainy sand, these substances are broken loose from the cloth. Of course, it can wreak havoc on certain fabrics, but for the more durable materials such as our uniforms are made of, this process works just fine."

It occurred to Lilly that she would need to clean some of her own clothing soon. She thought back to when she had helped Stana O'Hare do some laundry on the ship. Stana no doubt thought it was strange when Lilly had been so pleased with herself to have learned to do something so basic. But Lilly had grown up in circumstances where she never had the need to learn this chore. She imagined how surprised Stana would be now if Lilly taught *her* how to do laundry, and *without* water!

Their attention was suddenly diverted by a rather loud series of reprimands spilling forth from the man who was drilling the soldiers in the hot sun. While Lieutenant Miles dismissed the scene as just another part of his everyday routine, it stirred Lilly's curiosity.

"That's just some of the troops practicing their drills," he offered. He wondered if she was just being polite, or if she really was this interested in such prosaic occurrences.

Lilly wandered off in that direction, and the lieutenant had to quick step to catch up with her. Regardless of whether or not she was being sincere, he was glad to have an excuse to spend more time at her side.

"Drilling, miss, is a very important part of soldiering. A military unit marches, lives, and fights as a unit."

She was being very attentive hanging on his every word, so he continued, "Individually, the unit is just a rabble, subject to the whims and desires of each individual at will. Together, they are a formidable strength of one mind, motivated and led by their officers. Discipline is the key, as a general cannot easily control a rabble. Such a unit would be nothing more than an undisciplined assemblage of individuals who feel free to come and go as they please. In times of victory, their numbers would swell as men would join in the hopes of war booty and looting. In times of defeat, their numbers would dwindle as they started to lose heart, and they ended up deserting in order to make their way home. By instilling discipline, this unruly mass of humanity is transformed into a cohesive military unit, which can better be controlled on the battlefield."

He could hardly believe he still had her full attention!

"Years ago, the standard firearm of Her Majesty's troops was the Brown Bess flintlock musket. It fired a large caliber lead shot and was not very accurate. Do you know that sometimes troops actually turned their faces away from the 'flash in the pan' when firing? Imagine that, not even aiming while firing!" *He really had her attention now!* "But by firing in volleys at close range, they could not miss, and the damage from so much lead shot at that short of a distance was devastating. It was the key to the Duke of Wellington's great victory at Waterloo."

"Yes, but it wasn't just the volley fire alone. It was volley fire *while in square formation*," she corrected him with an innocent smile.

Her answer surprised him. Evidently, there was more to this girl than he thought. At first meeting, he had taken her for simply a rich girl playing at roughing it, while toting her personal servant around in order to be indulged and pampered. Now he wasn't so sure. She seemed to be sincerely genuine, unaffected, and intelligent.

The drill leader was unused to having outsiders watch him work, so as a result, he and his trainees began making more and more mistakes. He yelled once again, raising his cane menacingly to his bungling men.

A look of comprehension crossed Lilly's face. "And the way the general ensures his troops stay in formation in order to deliver the said volley fire successfully, is by constant practicing and marching about as a unit!" She looked pleased to have figured this out with her own logic.

"Exactly!" he exclaimed. She surely was a quick study.

Watching the men closely, Lilly stood up straighter, eyes forward and arms at her side. "Is this correct, lieutenant?" she asked out of the corner of her mouth.

He took full advantage of the excuse to look her over closely. She was a fine-looking woman, even dressed as she was.

"That's it. Shoulders back, hands closed and by your side. That's better." He tried not to stare as her shirt pulled tightly across her chest.

Lieutenant Miles signaled for the instructor to stop, and he led Lilly to the rear of the column. He then nodded for the exercise to continue. The soldier in charge yelled a command for the men to re-form their lines and come rigidly to attention. Although his voice was still loud, the drill master now spoke more clearly and slowly as he shouted his commands. His men could now understand him better and were afforded more time to react to each instruction. Lilly learned things quickly, and with her memory for detail, she was doing a fine job. Now that a slower pace had been set for the newcomer, the men were shaping up and were able to follow his orders more efficiently. This relieved some of the pressure from the instructor. It was nerve-racking to have the lieutenant's full attention focused on his motley crew of men. He also wanted to make certain this lady friend of Lieutenant Miles looked good as she attempted to follow along. And so it was with relief that he saw she was indeed making progress.

Lieutenant Miles was amazed at how quickly she had learned the drill. Her participation had even put these misfits on their toes. They were not about to let themselves be out marched by a mere woman!

Lilly felt proud of being able to keep up with the maneuvers, but she felt sorry for the soldiers who had been practicing for such a long time in the intense heat. Sweat was dripping off of brows and soaking through their clothing. She quickly glanced at the man next to her, but when he noticed her look, it threw him off, causing him to misstep. She felt terrible that because of her the soldier had made a mistake, so before his blunder could be noted, Lilly purposely fumbled into the man on her other side. The chain reaction caused the neat military formation to gradually transform into a milling swarm.

The instructor threw up his hands in despair. Lieutenant Miles was amused, and Lilly apologized to everyone around her and especially to the leader of the drill.

"I am so sorry for that awful muck up. I think this horrible heat is making me light-headed. Would it be possible for us to pause for a quick refreshing taste of water? I would like to give it one more try after a brief respite. You are such a fine master of drill!"

This caused a flush of pleasure, and he called the unit to attention, dismissing them for a water break.

"You are an amazing woman, Miss Lilly!" complimented Lieutenant Miles. You could put most recruits to shame," he added as they walked toward the well. "Oh, and for the record, I know what you did."

"And what is it you think I have done, lieutenant?" she asked, smiling sweetly up at him.

"That unfortunate 'mistake' you made to cover up for your neighbor's error, not to mention your timely request for a water break for which the men will be forever grateful to you."

And they were very grateful indeed. By the time she reached the well, the men from the drilling detail had already crowded around it. The mass of men parted as Lilly and the lieutenant approached. As parched as they all were, the men had not yet tasted the cool refreshing moisture. Instead, the man Lilly had helped offered her the first cup. As she accepted and sipped the cool liquid, she saw every man's eyes were on her, and their smiling faces beamed an unmistakable "thank you." She returned the cup with thanks and walked back with Lieutenant Miles to await her lesson.

Bala watched Lilly mimicking the movements of the fighting men. She knew from her own people that it would have been much easier to stay together as a group if they had been chanting or singing. In a way, Lilly was like herself. Bala was always a headstrong, determined girl, who had insisted on playing warrior with her older brother. That seemed so long ago, but that characteristic had never changed. Only now she was a headstrong, determined woman.

Then she noticed the man they called Mister Brown, the one with the head covering of straw, observing Lilly. Maybe he was some kind of medicine man, for he was always making symbols on those little pieces of stiff white cloth. She assumed he must be there for Lilly's spiritual protection since he seemed to spend a lot of time watching her, and making more symbols. Bala's curiosity was peaked. She wished she could get a look at what he was doing.

Once the newcomer's tents were set up, they all gathered together in the early evening for a much-needed impromptu meal. The topic of conversation was naturally centered around the events highlighting their first day there.

"I hope you and your colleagues find your accommodations to your satisfaction," said the captain, as he passed the salt cellar to Lilly.

"Thank you, Captain Lewis," Lilly murmured as she shook out a sprinkling of salt onto the meat on her plate. She preferred it a little on the salty side as it made the bland food a little more palatable. She passed the salt cellar on to her father and accepted the pepper pot in turn.

"Our accommodations are quite adequate thank you," Sir Billingsley answered for all of them. "I hope our presence is not intruding on your command."

"Not at all," the captain lied convincingly. "Please let me know if there is anything else I can do to make your stay here more pleasant," he said with a nod to his guests. With any luck, his "guests" wouldn't be staying for very long. Imagine, bringing a delicate genteel young lady to a primitive place such as this. Whatever would the poor girl do without all of the modern conveniences she was used to? Why, he imagined the first time she had to plant her dainty bottom upon a splinter-filled wooden seat to do nature's business, or discovered a snake in her tent, she would be ready to run back to the comfort of her home where she belonged.

Lilly was in the process of relating how she had spent her day. "Lieutenant Miles was kind enough to escort me around the fort."

"Your daughter is very inquisitive, Sir Billingsley. It was difficult to keep up with her," said the lieutenant.

Sir Billingsley smiled at his daughter fondly.

Lilly began by telling them about how the lieutenant had allowed her to drill with some of his troops.

"And how did she do?" Charles couldn't help asking. He was sure he already knew the answer, but he took a certain pride in hearing Lilly being praised by others.

"Why, she did just fine," the lieutenant answered somewhat condescendingly. *Considering she's a woman.* This wasn't spoken, but his tone implied it.

Charles detected a subtle hint of mockery in his voice, but before he could say anything, Lilly spoke up, "Why, do you really think so, Lieutenant Miles?" Lilly smiled sweetly and lowered her lashes demurely. Charles hid his grin behind a slice of bread. He knew Lilly was toying with the man. The unsuspecting lieutenant had no idea what he had started.

"Did I march about as well as the men in that little group did?" she asked with exaggerated innocence.

He cleared his throat uncomfortably and answered. "You did a fine job," he repeated, "but military matters are hardly the domain of a lovely young woman such as yourself."

His attempt at flattery fell flat. "Ah, but you see, Lieutenant Miles, *this* young woman does more than just sit around and embroider, or paint with water colors, without a thought in her lovely young head! At times, my friends and I hold some quite serious discussions."

After a pause, her tone changed ever so slightly when she realized he still seemed to be humoring her, rather than really listening. Was he one who viewed a woman's role in the world as being nothing more than a man's property, or one of those who approved of using violence against the suffrage marchers? Maybe it *was* a man's world, but one day soon that would change. She was sure of it!

"Some of our most lively discussions have been about Marshal Sebastien de Vauban, the great military engineer who served the 'Sun King.'"

"That would be the French King, Louis XIV," interjected the professor. He took great pride in his students who excelled, even when he knew it was in something he had nothing to do with teaching them.

"Yes, thank you, professor. As I was saying, Vauban was the king's chief engineer. As such, it was he who was responsible for building the fortifications that ringed the French frontiers. These fortifications were laid out in such a way as to dominate the terrain and also incorporate it in such a way as to be almost impregnable to assault. The layout of the walls often resembled a star pattern, which allowed for no blind spots where enemy soldiers could hide. He set the pattern that was studied and imitated for one hundred years.

"He was an expert in the construction of these nearly impregnable fortresses and a master at siege warfare." Turning to Captain Lewis as if seeking confirmation, she touched her finger thoughtfully to her lip and said, "Please correct me if I'm wrong, but I do believe he conducted over fifty successful sieges during his career."

The captain wasn't certain one way or another, but he nodded knowingly.

Addressing Lieutenant Miles once again, she said, "My friends and I would discuss the layout of some of his most famous fortresses, and we also on occasion would even paint them with our water colors."

She emphasized her point by saying, "I know building materials are at a premium out here, captain, but if it were possible to incorporate flanking bastions in the outer walls, such as in Vauban's standard star fort, with the points of the bastions at an angle somewhere between seventy-five and ninety degrees, or if you could at least construct a redoubt, your garrison would have a much better chance at withstanding an enemy attack."

The captain was pleasantly surprised at Lilly's intelligence, and the articulate way she got her point across was admirable. He knew she was probably accurate on all counts. "You are quite right, my dear, but it is as you pointed out. Our building materials are not as plentiful here as they would be in a place as bountiful as the French frontier. I do admire your opinions as well as your insight," he said, with more respect than he had shown earlier.

Since Lilly appeared to know a good deal more about fortifications than any of the military men present, Charles had an amusing thought. It seemed that some of these seasoned soldiers could benefit by spending some time with Lilly painting with water colors.

Lieutenant Miles, wishing to switch to something he knew more about, addressed Lilly. "I see you are carrying a gun, young miss. If you like, I would gladly give you instruction on the proper way to use it."

Richard, who was feeling irritated to begin with, for he had quickly grown tired of swatting flies off of his food, answered shortly, "I assure you Lilly does not need anyone's help with that." Richard wouldn't admit even to himself that he was experiencing a flash of jealousy over the attention she was receiving.

Lieutenant Miles was annoyed at Richard, whom at first sight he had decided he did not like, for butting into his conversation with the young lady.

"Well, it seems I may have underestimated you!" he said to Lilly with an indulgent, somewhat condescending smile.

Lilly looked down at her plate in an attempt to hide her irritation. It was clear she still wasn't being taken seriously here and was simply being humored like a small child being told, "My, you are getting to be a big girl now, aren't you?" She neither smiled nor commented but only played with the food on her plate with her fork. Unseen, under the table, her other hand unconsciously rested on her pistol.

Later that evening, she came across Lieutenant Miles with Sergeant Wright examining the contents of some crates that had been delivered to the fort.

Her first instinct was to pretend as though she hadn't seen them and go off in another direction, but then she remembered the lieutenant's kindness in showing her around and explaining things to her earlier, so she decided to forgive his patronizing attitude during their meal and give him a chance to redeem himself.

"Greetings, Lieutenant Miles, Sergeant Wright."

"Hello, Miss Lilly," Lieutenant Miles responded with a grin. He was always happy to see her beautiful face.

Sergeant Wright merely nodded politely.

"What have we here?" she asked, as she walked up and looked into one of the open crates. Inside was row upon row of brand new Lee-Metford rifles. "Oh my goodness!" Her eyes lit up as she impulsively reached in to touch one.

"Wait!" Lieutenant Miles warned as he grabbed her reaching hand. "They are still covered in grease," he said, turning red with embarrassment. He released her hand after holding onto it for a few seconds longer than was needed. He looked away, avoiding her gaze as he turned and picked up a grease-free rifle.

"This one is clean," he said as he offered it to her. "Be careful now! It's not loaded, but it should still be handled with caution!"

Sergeant Wright was watching all of this with amusement, waiting to see what happened next. He sensed the lieutenant had a thing for this girl.

Lilly took the rifle and with a mischievous grin, said, "If you would like, I could give you some pointers on the proper way to use this."

Standing erect and reciting from memory, Lilly tried her best to sound like her old friend, Sergeant Major MacDonald. "This, Lieutenant Miles, is a Lee-Metford rifle. It has a caliber of .303 inch and a ten-cartridge magazine, but I am only loading five," she said as she snapped open the bolt and pretended to insert the cartridges one at a time, pushing them down through the open bolt in the top and into the magazine. "It fires a smokeless cordite powder," she added with a twinkle in her eye. Working the bolt and pretending to chamber a round, she demonstrated the proper way to shoulder the weapon and aim. Without firing, she handed the weapon to Lieutenant Miles and took up a position to his side. Snatching up a cleaning rod and tucking it under her arm as she had so often seen her beloved sergeant major do with his cane, she stood waiting.

At first, both men stared at her in surprise, but then Lieutenant Miles laughed heartily; and raising the rifle to his shoulder, he aimed at some imaginary target off in the distance.

"Careful, Luv, hold the butt in tight," she said with the most masculine voice she could manage.

He pretended to focus and squeezed the trigger.

She squinted to look off into the distance and said, "Very good shooting!"

Sergeant Wright guffawed loudly, and Lieutenant Miles chuckled as he said to Lilly, "Point well taken, miss. Point well taken. I apologize for underestimating you and your skills."

Lilly could tell that this time his compliment was sincerely given.

16

All visitors were up early the next morning, ready and waiting to get started. Captain Lewis found himself wishing that his men would display the same eagerness to greet the morning as these civilians did. He was anxious to get over to the tomb. Even though he had bought his commission, it had turned out to be a lucrative investment. If things turned out as he hoped, he might still be able to return to England as a man of means. The glory and honor of a brilliant military career seemed to have escaped him, but he had other irons in the fire, which could make his dream of retiring a wealthy man come true.

Everyone was understandably excited. Lilly had dressed hurriedly that morning, not bothering to take the extra time to wrap her legs in puttees. The sooner they got started, the better. She made an attempt to leave Bala behind at the camp, but still not having enough common language between them, she found it difficult to explain that she was not going far and would be coming back. Bala seemed determined to stay close to her, especially in this new place where the people didn't seem as friendly as those they had recently left behind. Lilly finally relented and promised the professor she would make sure Bala didn't disrupt their work in any way.

A few soldiers accompanied Captain Lewis as he led the professor and the others to the burial site. They didn't have far to go, as it was actually just outside a section of the fortification's walls. All work had been temporarily suspended at this spot, and a constant guard was posted, protecting the captain's find as well as in defense of the unfinished portion of that wall.

The tomb entrance was nothing more than a small natural cave opening in a shallow ravine that had been walled up long ago with clay, mud, and rocks and then covered with sand. After withstanding nature's test of time, this wall had crumbled under the repeated blows of the soldiers' picks.

Armed with a lantern and his service sword, the captain led the way into his latest find. Behind him was his friend and business partner, Professor Buller. Richard followed next under the pretense of ensuring the way was clear for Lilly. Lilly followed behind him with Charles very close beside her due to the narrowness of the entrance. In one hand, he carried his lantern, as they all did, except for Lilly and Bala. His other hand protectively held onto Lilly's arm. Climbing over the rubble, she stumbled, and Charles quickly grabbed her tightly around the waist holding her firmly. She looked at him for a couple of seconds with only inches separating their faces, and for just that instant, he shared her breath. She smiled a silent thank you and turned her head away in anticipation of the wonders she might shortly see as soon as her eyes grew accustomed to the dim light.

Charles released his hold on her and watched as she moved ahead. He was caught off guard by the strength of his feelings as he had held her so close, and when she had turned her face to his, it was everything he could do to keep from kissing her soft lips. Suddenly remembering why they were there, he continued following the others.

Bala, close behind, had observed this interaction wondering how these two could be so blind? She shook her head, muttering to herself as she thought that these people were not observant enough to follow an elephant through a mud flat.

Bala was stepping over the debris that had caused Lilly to lose her footing when she was startled to feel a firm hand grasp her arm. Her first instinct was to angrily snatch it away. Glancing over her shoulder with a hostile glare, she saw the one who was Lilly's father had grabbed her but only to steady her, and from the look in his eyes, his actions were clearly paternal. Bala instantly formed her opinion of this man. She knew she need never fear anything from him, and hereafter he would have her respect as though he were an elder of her own tribe.

The inside of the cave was dark and cool. "Watch out! Don't step on that," cautioned Captain Lewis as he pointed with his sword tip to something on the floor.

"Why this is most peculiar!" exclaimed the professor.

"What is it?" asked Lilly as she hurried over to those who were gathering around the discovery.

"It appears to be the remains of some poor individual who may have been left here when the tomb was sealed," said the professor. He stooped down for a closer look. "My guess would be that this person died a violent death, as there appears to be a sizable fracture in his skull."

"Maybe he was a grave robber," Richard offered.

"Well, we won't know anything for certain until we get a chance to examine everything thoroughly," answered the professor as he gazed thoughtfully at the remains. This was the first time he had ever seen such a thing.

"There's another body over here by the wall," said the captain.

The professor frowned in bewilderment and went over to investigate. After satisfying a morbid curiosity for what ancient dead bodies looked like, the rest of them followed.

Crumpled in the dirt was another set of human remains. On the wall above where the skeleton lay were symbols and markings, but these writings looked to be incomplete. The professor made his unofficial deduction.

"From all appearances, it looks as though this person may have been a scribe in the process of marking the walls when he met his demise. I suspect he had not even finished this task before he met his untimely death."

The professor noticed there was no evidence of any scrolls lying around. Someone had perhaps taken them after they had murdered these two, or possibly they may even have been removed more recently. His eyes rested briefly on the captain.

"I would venture to say, these unfortunate individuals were killed in order to silence them from revealing some sort of information about this tomb." The professor began thinking aloud, which was something he frequently did to sort out puzzling information. "Now, why would someone go through all the trouble to transport a body to such an out of the way place, and then take such drastic steps to ensure that it remain undiscovered? Hmmm, this is very unusual. Grave robbing was punishable by death, but this doesn't seem to be the kind of tomb that would attract thieves. Something was being protected, but it certainly doesn't look like there is anything of value here. Of course, we need to do more extensive exploring, but there is definitely something intriguing about this place."

Bala didn't know what the people were talking about, but she reasoned it had to do with the dead men. She didn't like the looks of this place. It reeked of death and evil. A shiver ran down her back, making her want to run away. Something was not right here.

Glancing around the seemingly bare cavern, the professor inquired, "This tomb did contain a mummy, did it not?"

The captain nodded and led everyone over to a darkened section of the cold room. Propped against the stone wall was an intact being wrapped in dingy cloth from head to toe.

Even though Lilly knew what to expect, the sight of the mummy in this eerie setting scared her. Her pupils dilated with fear, and her whole body trembled. She had to fight the urge to run telling herself over and over there was nothing here that could possibly harm her. She received little reassurance from Bala's frightened expression, but Charles didn't seem to be alarmed, and that helped to calm her somewhat.

Bala couldn't remember ever having such a violent physical reaction to her fear. Gooseflesh was raised over her whole body, and even though she was cold, she had broken out in a sweat. Her knees felt wobbly and weak, and her heart was pounding erratically. When she had been captured, she had been afraid; but those men had been flesh and blood, and she knew what she was dealing with. This "thing" emanated a suffocating malevolence that tainted the air with a heaviness so stifling it was an effort just to draw a deep breath.

She wasn't normally fearful of the dead for she had seen enough of them in her time and had even helped to bury them. She had seen one woman die in childbirth, and another mangled by wild beasts. There was a warrior who died of his putrefied wounds, and a small child who had succumbed to disease. Seeing and handling those bodies did not bother her other than the fact that she may have cared about them. But this one was different. Those other corpses on the ground were dried and shriveled as would be expected, but this one still had bulk to it, as if it had somehow escaped the natural ravages of time. It was as though the gods had chosen not to claim this one's body for some reason. Bala's eyes darted around the room searching for any real or imaginary potential threats that may be lurking in the shadows.

"Why isn't he in a coffin?" Lilly whispered nervously.

"Yes," echoed Richard, "Why isn't he?" It was one thing to pilfer from some random individual tightly sealed in a box, but this fellow looked uncannily as though he was watching over his burial vault. Even though there were no apparent signs of valuables, there was still a chance something could be buried or somehow hidden. That was his hope anyway. He would hate to find out this expedition had been an enormous waste of his time. Richard wasn't superstitious or even easily spooked, but he didn't relish the thought of ransacking this tomb while this formidable creature looked on.

Charles swept back the hair from his forehead, and shaking his head in bewilderment, said, "It was the custom for people to keep a mummified family member until such time when they could afford to give them a proper burial. But that usually meant storing it somewhere in their home, not in a secret cave hundreds of miles away from anywhere. This just doesn't make any sense."

Sir Billingsley now understood why the captain's original message had stated this tomb was unusual.

"I will need to translate these wall writings, as well as examine our friend here. Maybe I can uncover some clue as to who he is, or was," said the professor.

The captain sent one of his men for more lanterns, and the group moved around examining whatever caught their eye. "Please don't touch anything," warned the professor.

Considering the sparseness of the tomb, that warning seemed unnecessary until he added, "If you do find something, where you find it may in itself be of import. One small, seemingly insignificant detail, may lead to other more substantial discoveries."

As everyone spread out to look around on their own, the professor quietly asked Captain Lewis if anything had previously been tampered with or removed. The captain knew what was suspected of him, and he admitted to removing some papyrus scrolls to his quarters for "safekeeping." His first thought had actually been to sell the scrolls to a dealer, but not having the skills to determine their worth and now knowing that his friend was suspicious of his duplicity, he decided it would be best to give them up. "I'll show them to you later," he promised.

Upon receiving the extra lanterns, they got down to work. "First things first," the professor said as he examined what was left of the first two corpses. "I don't think there is any value here other than the tale these remains may tell us of these individuals' fates. I think we can carefully and safely remove them for now to get them out of our way.

"Charles, I will put you in charge of this task, and Lilly, if you would be so kind as to assist him? Please pack and record each piece with great care. You never know if any small item or bone might turn out to be an important piece to solving a much bigger puzzle in the future. Handle everything as little as possible. We must be meticulous in categorizing and preserving all we find."

"I can check around for any hidden niches or loose stones," volunteered Richard. If there was anything of value to be found, he was determined to be the one to uncover it.

"That would be fine, but if you find anything, please don't disturb the area. Let me know about it immediately," the professor cautioned. At least this was something the young man seemed enthusiastic about, and so he would be sure to do a thorough search. So far, the professor wasn't impressed by Lilly's gentleman friend.

"Sir Billingsley, would you like to lend a hand to Charles and Lilly?" He sensed the father would enjoy working with his daughter, and from his look of pleasure at the assignment, the professor knew he had made the right call.

"And, Mr. Brown, why don't you do what you do best. Please take careful notes as to what transpires here. We may have to refer back to a specific event, or need to remember the chronological order of the said events."

Satisfied he had an important role to play, Mr. Harry Brown was eager to start doing his part.

Addressing everyone, the professor said, "Now let's all get to work, shall we?"

Lilly was less fearful now that she was absorbed in doing something with her father and Charles. This in turn caused Bala to calm down enough to slowly wander around, although she never once turned her back on the cloth wrapped figure in the corner. Feeling braver now since no one else appeared to be frightened, she scolded herself for showing her weakness in front of the others. She saw a few large stone jars and simple tools scattered about. As her eyes grew more accustomed to the dim light and shadows, she spied something lying against the far wall. Stealthily creeping closer, she leaned forward to get a better look. It looked like some sort of a small stature.

She remembered having seen such a thing before. The old medicine woman in her village had used molded likenesses similar to this one as she worked her magic, conjuring up spirits. Whether good spirits or evil, all depended on the particular totem used and the reason for needing such assistance from the spirit world. When she was quite young, Bala had once found such a figure, and thinking it was something to play with, she had amused herself with it for hours. The old woman had scared Bala half to death when she ran at the little girl screaming threats and curses while chasing her with a stick. The old woman recovered the totem and warned her to never touch such a figure again, or misfortune would follow her throughout her life.

Bala stood up and quickly backed away from the crudely made form. As she stumbled over a protruding rock, Lilly looked up and noticed her distress.

"What is it, Bala?" she asked, concerned about this strange behavior.

She hurried over and knelt down to see what Bala was pointing at. "Charles! Professor! Come take a look at what Bala has found," she called. As Lilly reached out to touch it, Bala leaped forward with a yell and pulled her away. "Bala! What on earth?" Lilly exclaimed. Bala flung her arm in front of Lilly to keep her from touching the relic as she chattered away.

"All right, Bala, I'll stay away. Come," she urged, "we can stand over here." And she led Bala a few more feet away from it.

In the wavering light, the professor reached down to gently pry the small statue loose from the rubble. An extremely large black insect emitting an ominous hissing sound skittered out from under it and headed straight for Lilly, running right up the inseam of her trouser leg. She let out a shrill scream and jumped around frantically in an attempt to expel whatever it was that was crawling up her leg. Was it her imagination, or was it biting and pinching her tender skin?

Charles immediately began trying to ineffectually brush the outside of her trousers with his bare hands. With Lilly in a state of panic, and the clinging object refusing to let go as it moved higher up her leg, Charles had no choice but to throw inhibitions aside.

Bala was just as determined to help Lilly as he was. Getting a firm grip with both hands at the top of her inner thigh so the intruder could go no higher, Bala motioned for Charles to help. He placed his hands under Bala's and gave one mighty sweep downward as he firmly slid his hands down her leg, knocking the creature loose and into the dirt. The second it hit the floor, he stomped on it with the heel of his boot and ground it from side to side, before lifting his foot.

Left unmoving, and oozing greenish, yellow fluid and matter, was the biggest cockroach Lilly had ever seen. She shuddered in disgust, knowing she would never forget the horrible feeling of that thing crawling on her bare flesh. She had learned the hard way, the important function of those time-consuming puttees, and she vowed to never be so foolish as to go without them again. Shakily, she hugged Charles thankfully, and then a surprised Bala.

It took some time for her to calm down, but once everyone was satisfied that Lilly wasn't hurt and she was able to reassure them that even though she was still shaken up a bit she still wished to continue, the mysterious relic once again became the center of attention.

It was a small deteriorated clay figure that had broken off from its base. The features of its face were still discernible, even though parts of it were crumbling away. Bala was unable to relax until the little statue was finally safely tucked away and securely sealed into a small wooden box.

Everyone went back to their assigned tasks, stopping only to wolf down a quick noon day meal. The captain eventually needed to attend to his military duties, but he made sure to leave Sergeant Wright and two others of his men behind to help out and also to report any new developments that might occur during his absence.

Charles occasionally glanced around at everyone hard at work. He looked at Lilly working so intently across from him. She appeared to have recovered from her little scare and was enjoying herself once more. His eyes lingered upon her for longer than was proper. His face reddened when he thought of how he had so boldly grasped her thigh and slid his hands down her leg. He longed to reach out and touch her again.

As he looked away, he locked eyes with Bala who had been observing him watching Lilly. He was embarrassed to have been caught, for he was sure that his thoughts had been written all over his face. He knew the native girl didn't speak English, but she was always in the background watching, and he got the feeling she knew things about them all that no one else was aware of. It was a good thing she didn't speak English because there was no telling what she might say. Charles tried to concentrate on his work in an attempt to forget about those knowing eyes boring into him.

When they had finished up working on the first skeletal remains, Charles and his helpers began on the dead scribe. Every piece was gently packed in padded empty supply, ammunition, and rifle crates, which the captain had ready at hand.

The professor, with Richard acting as his secretary, was struggling to translate the obscure wall writings. He didn't usually have such difficulty as he was now experiencing. "Richard, please read back what you have so far."

Richard read from his notes. *"Forever warrior Pharaohs I conquer."*

"I just don't understand this. Charles, can you help me out here for a moment?"

Charles made sure that Lilly and her father were able to keep working on their own and went over to see what the professor needed. "What is it, uncle?"

"I'm having some trouble in making sense of these jumbled writings. Richard, read that again exactly as I have translated it to you."

Richard took special care to read it exactly in the same order as the professor had dictated them. *"Forever warrior Pharaohs I conquer."*

The professor frowned. "There are other things written here that are also confusing and out of the ordinary from the typical prayers and safe passages. There is mention of curses and stumbling blocks. This will be much more intricate and time-consuming than I originally hoped. I'm not complaining, mind you. In fact, it is just the opposite. I am actually looking forward to the challenge, and any input you have to offer would be appreciated."

Charles thought about some of the difficulties they had in the past with trying to understand the writings of the ancients. "Are you reading them in the right direction? Perhaps you need to read them from right to left, or horizontally instead of vertically?" As soon as he said it, he felt like he had insulted his uncle's intelligence by suggesting he may have made such a simple mistake.

If the professor felt insulted, he didn't show it; after all, he was asking for help. "Judging from the color of the ink, if red signifies the topic, and black, the text, then I am reading this in the right direction. But that is when it gets confusing."

"What do you mean?"

"Well, you see, when it is read in reverse, it makes more sense, only it sounds more like a threat than a prayer."

"Conquer I Pharaohs warrior forever." But why would someone wish to conquer pharaoh's warrior, and forever?"

"Could it be due to mistakes made by the original scribe?" Charles remembered other errors they had come across in the past that were probably due to the fact that some of these scribes could not actually read the figures—they merely copied the symbols.

"That thought did cross my mind. Also, the lighting is rather poor in here, as is my eyesight. But something tells me there is much more to this than a simple explanation can satisfy." The professor was clearly becoming tired and frustrated.

Finally, they agreed to pack everything up and come back for a fresh start the next day. Professor Buller had another reason for wanting to stop working. He was very anxious to examine those scrolls the captain had secreted away. Hopefully, they would provide some answers.

After their evening meal, Captain Lewis took the professor to his shelter. The professor had an uneasy feeling that his friend and associate had intended to keep the scrolls for his own monetary gain. As he examined the fragile, deteriorating parchment, he realized these were different from anything he had ever seen before. "We will have to show these to the others."

"Absolutely not!" exclaimed the captain.

"I'm afraid we have no choice. These scrolls are unique. I need Charles to help with the translation, and even Lilly can be of some service. The sooner I can translate them, the sooner we can determine what sets this tomb apart from the others we have seen."

The captain still looked dubious, so he added, "The more heads we have working on this, the faster we can unravel the mystery, and these scrolls may hold the key to discovering if there is indeed any hidden treasures. As this burial site was previously undisturbed, the chances are favorable that it holds more than just rotting bodies."

After weighing all the facts, the captain finally relented, albeit reluctantly. "Very well, I will agree for you to consult with the others; however, I don't feel entirely comfortable about this decision. I trust you will keep their involvement to a necessary minimum."

"Yes, of course, you will not regret this."

Later that evening, the others were informed about the need to translate the scrolls before continuing the dig in earnest. The professor expressed his concern to Sir Billingsley since he was the sole source of income for the project, and they were looking at yet another delay.

"After making a cursory translation of part of the scroll, I believe what was transcribed to the walls was either in error, or else it was intentionally altered. For what purpose, I couldn't say, but whatever information they hold will necessarily determine our next move."

"What might that be?" asked Lilly.

"I am hoping that the scrolls will give us a hint as to whether we need to look more closely at the mummy, or whether we should even bother to search for any additional items of value. If nothing else, I hope to discover the mystery surrounding the circumstances of this particular burial.

"Sir Billingsley, I leave the final decision to you. You have already been very generous, and I don't wish to take advantage of your kindness. With that said, I will give you some time to think things over before we either proceed, or prepare to return home."

The professor was in his tent going over a few things with Charles when Sir Billingsley stopped by.

"I was hoping to speak to you for a moment, professor."

"By all means, sir, please come in. Charles, will you give us a moment?"

"Certainly, uncle." He carefully closed the old book that lay on the table before him and presented the visitor with the chair he had just vacated.

It was clear Sir Billingsley was waiting until they were alone before he proceeded, and the professor used the opportunity to offer him a drink.

"Would you care for a glass of brandy?" he asked.

"Yes, thank you. You are most kind."

Sir Billingsley swirled the brandy around in his glass and took a sip. Then looking thoughtful, he asked, "In your honest opinion as a gentleman, is this enterprise worth pursuing?"

"From my viewpoint as a scientist and researcher, I would say yes, it *is* worth pursuing."

The other man nodded. He already knew that he would let them continue on for as long as it was worthwhile. Besides, he really was enjoying this time with his daughter, and he wasn't looking forward to returning home where she would again become wrapped up in her own life and friends. At times, he selfishly fancied this expedition continuing on for years. Such a thing was not unheard of.

"There is one more concern I have, professor. Do you think we have anything to fear from the Mahdists?"

"Captain Lewis has assured me the frontier has been peaceful for some time now. We are far enough in to hear of any developments occurring, and there is no safer place for us to be than with our very own military unit to protect us."

Content that all was well, Sir Billingsley raised his glass to offer a toast. "Well then, here's to continuing our journey of discovery." The professor grinned widely and raised his glass in response.

17

The professor, Charles, and Lilly were too excited to wait for morning to begin working on the translation. Even though the sun had already set, they decided to work by lantern light under the front flap of professor and Charles's tent. The professor chose this place for easy access to the various reference books in his trunk. A large table borrowed from the mess tent provided them with a spacious working surface. Scattered across this table were the scrolls, reference books, writing paper, pens and ink, and a local map. The captain and Mr. Brown finally arrived, and all their attention was on the professor as he began to scrutinize the scrolls in the uncertain light.

"Ah, we are most fortunate! What we have here are actually two different types of manuscripts," he announced as he adjusted his glasses. "Here we have the scrolls made of papyrus, but we also have inscriptions, which are made upon a type of parchment paper."

"Is there some significance to that?" inquired Mr. Brown.

"Indeed there is!" said the professor. "This picture writing on the papyrus is what is known as hieroglyphics. It is written in ink with a reed brush and can be read right to left, or left to right, depending on the individual who writes it. This is used exclusively on religious documents, such as the *Book of the Dead.*"

"The *Book of the Dead* would contain the prayers," added Lilly for Mr. Brown's benefit.

Charles took up the explanation. "These other documents are used more often by clerks, merchants, and officials. They are covered with a different type of writing known as hieratic. Hieratic always reads from right to left, is more cursive, and has more ligatures." For everyone's clarity, he added, "Ligatures are formed when some letters, or in this case symbols, run together as though they were one letter or word instead of two. Hieratic also has some signs, which are unique to it that hieroglyphics lack."

"So what we might find on these secondary documents are additional instructions, possibly directed to those tasked with preparing this particular tomb," said the professor.

All was quiet as he studied a few lines of the papyrus. "Well it's no wonder I had difficulty with the translation from the walls!" he suddenly exclaimed, startling those who had been watching so intently. "It may have been just as you suggested, Charles. The scribe evidently was unable to read the words he was copying. It looks as though he was careless and may have substituted incorrect words. This was most likely done through force of habit through repetition, rather than intentionally."

"He may also have been working under duress," offered Captain Lewis.

"There may be a lot of truth in that theory, captain. Especially if he had any idea of what his attacker had in store for him. If he suspected his life was in danger, he could have been more focused on how he might make good his escape rather than the task at hand."

Lilly was happy to see her father and Richard stepping out of the dark night to join them. She was anxious for them both to enjoy themselves, but more so for her father. After all, his gold had made this wonderful experience possible, and she would hate to think she had talked him into something he now regretted.

Other than Lilly, no one else seemed to notice the latecomers' arrival. Everyone was too absorbed in the enigmatic story being pieced together before their eyes.

The professor turned to his young protégé and asked, "Charles, considering that the scribe was commissioned to copy the contents of these scrolls, do you notice anything peculiar about them?"

Charles compared some of the hieroglyphics to others he found in one of his reference books. "Various things are normally written, such as chapters from the *Book of the Dead*, events from a man's life, or even prayers to the gods to have mercy on his soul." He compared the documents again. "What I don't understand is that those particular things are not what is written *here*." Looking puzzled, he said, "If I'm reading these symbols correctly, some of them are not intended to be prayers at all. Instead, these writings speak of curses!"

"Exactly! For this poor soul to be buried in such a Spartan grave, one would expect him to be nothing more than a nondescript peasant. Yet someone took an inordinate amount of time and effort to bury him, as they would have someone of importance. They took steps to ensure this fellow's resurrection, yet they still turned around and cursed the poor chap. Take for instance, the *shabti*."

There was a look of confusion on some of the faces surrounding the table. Before he could continue, Lilly interjected to explain. "The shabti are little figures made of wood, clay, or stone that are buried with the deceased, such as the one we found earlier. They are usually inscribed with a prayer stating something to the effect of in the afterlife the shabti will be resurrected along with its master in order to perform such things as manual labor. These lowly tasks are not, of course, what any high born Egyptian expects to have to do for themselves in their version of heaven."

"Thank you for that accurate explanation, my dear. You can be proud of your daughter, Sir Billingsley."

He was.

"As I was saying," he continued, "take for example the shabti. There was only one found in this tomb, being that rather nasty looking statue Bala discovered." He glanced at the girl crouched indiscriminately in the shadows of the canvas and walked over to a storage box. He carefully removed the small, plain clay figure and laid it gently on the table. There were pieces missing, which had long since fallen off, some of which had probably crumbled to dust.

Everyone leaned closer to examine the object that had caused Bala to make such a dramatic scene. It didn't appear imposing or threatening in any way, yet none of them except the professor reached out to touch it. The statue's arms were folded across its chest, and in one hand, it was holding a flail of some sort.

The man of science held the lantern closer and said, "There is an inscription here, which I can barely make out." He blew gently on the obscure message to clear the loose particles of debris from the creases and held it under a magnifying glass. "In essence, it says this shabti has been tasked with arising from its slumber, and forever tormenting the deceased in the afterlife. Charles, your eyes are younger than mine. See what you can make of this."

Charles took possession of the figure. "You are correct, professor. It also indicates the deceased is to labor as a slave in the Nubian fields for eternity or be beaten until he obeys."

"That seems rather odd," said Mr. Brown, speaking the words they all were thinking.

The professor was systematically trying to sort and make sense of the confusing fragments of information. "Since there is no coffin, I would surmise that some of the lines of hieroglyphics on the walls are a substitute for coffin text." He looked pointedly at Lilly as her cue to clarify this bit of information for the others.

Interpreting his look correctly, Lilly explained, "Coffin text is usually written on the inside of the coffin so that the dead individual can read them. They are powerful prayers offering guidance and assistance to them as they travel the subterranean underworld, which is filled with traps and evil beings who might ensnare one, causing them to suffer a second death."

"And?" the professor urged her to continue, for there was more to add. She looked back at him blankly, so he turned to his nephew to complete the explanation.

Charles jumped in eagerly. "They also usually contain spells for the person to use so they do not have to do certain things, such as manual labor, in the afterlife." He and Lilly grinned at each other. They were really enjoying working together on something they were both so passionate about.

"That is correct. But I have a feeling that those helpful prayers and spells may have been withheld in this case. Someone, for some reason, went through much trouble and preparation to ensure this fellow would be miserable in his afterlife."

He continued, lost in thought, and was clearly thinking aloud again. "I suspect this person was probably one of rank who somehow lost favor and was therefore condemned. Why else would he be treated as such? What could he have done to deserve such a fate? So the question we must ask ourselves is why would anybody want to curse someone, yet at the same time ensure that they rose again in immortality, which is normally a time of bliss? And if they did expect them to rise again, they usually made additional preparations for them in the next life by burying items of value or of normal everyday use to them. There may be a clue hidden here in these very curses."

Everyone stood mulling over his words. The dark night surrounding them was becoming chilly, but none of them seemed to notice. The lantern light cast their black shadows upon the canvas wall where the flickering light made them appear to move as separate living beings. The professor, engrossed in the documents spread out on the table, looked up. "Why, this just keeps getting stranger!

"It looks like the usual Egyptian gods who are petitioned to damn this person in the hereafter are to be joined by some alien gods as well! Though I'm not exactly sure of just what race they may be associated with, I don't think they were from the north or east, but probably from the south. My guess would be the Sudan, or as it was known back then, Nubia. Also, these curses are not only called down upon the head of *this* poor individual but additionally on any others who disturb his final resting place or its contents."

"Hah! What do we have to fear of curses, especially of some long forgotten fictional gods?" asked Richard.

The professor paused and stared at Richard just long enough to make him feel uncomfortable.

"Maybe their gods were real or at least real to them," offered Lilly.

"Are you suggesting that these ancient gods and their curses are real then?"

Charles intervened, "Do you recall the story of the Syrian noble cured of leprosy by the Prophet Elisha? As he was preparing to return home, he asked for a load of earth to be carried on two mules. Why do you suppose he asked for that?" Charles asked Lilly.

"Is this pertinent to my question?" asked Richard. He wished these people would just answer a simple question with a simple answer for once, without all these elusive references and stories!

"Only those who listen may learn," the professor muttered under his breath as he continued working.

Lilly answered Charles, "He felt he needed the soil so he could pray to the Lord on it!"

Charles nodded. "That's right. In ancient times, one would revere the local god of the land. Being Christians, we trust in our Lord and need not fear. However, I have always found it curious that certain passages in the Good Book speak of alien nations fearing the God of Israel, while still firmly believing in their own."

"Exactly!" exclaimed the professor. "And there are many other passages that speak of witches, sorcerers, and others who dabble in the black arts. And what was the Lord's attitude toward such individuals, Richard?"

"He wanted them put to death," he answered.

"That was true and even specifically stated at times. But the point I would like to make here is that the Great Jehovah specifically instructed his chosen people not to seek their council, and most certainly not to serve them. Therefore, *their existence was not denied, but rather they were simply warned not to follow them!*"

"So then, the answer to my question is, curses are real and are something we should fear?" Richard asked mockingly. "Well then, we better beware of *this* little fellow," he said laughing, as he picked up the statue.

Suddenly, an agonizing scream rent the air, followed immediately by a commotion over in the direction of the mess tent. The captain took off running, and everyone turned as one to stare at the shabti still in Richard's hand. He hastily put it down as though it had burned his fingers, and they all hurried over to find out the source of the disturbance.

They got there just in time to see a man writhing in pain being carried out of the mess tent on a stretcher. In preparing for the following morning's meal, one of the cook's helpers had been stung by a scorpion. That in itself was not uncommon in the area where they were stationed. What was unusual was that he had been stung several times as he tried to escape. Witnesses told the captain that the aggressive, fast moving creature had actually pursued the frantic victim, flinging itself at him as he ran away and sinking its painful stinger into his flesh over and over again.

More yelling was coming from inside the tent, and a few more men came spilling out, pushing one another in their haste to escape. Captain Lewis strode over and entered the deserted shelter, and just as abruptly stepped back out again calling for assistance. It was being overrun by scorpions! The officers and sergeants immediately started barking out orders and directing men with shovels and torches to counterattack the desert invaders.

Everyone else was encouraged to retire for the night to try and get some rest, allowing the soldiers to tend to the extermination unimpeded without having the civilians underfoot. Needless to say, it was an uneasy night for all, and bedding was checked for uninvited "guests" more than once throughout the long sleepless night.

18

The morning meal was understandably late and consisted of only some stale bread, dried beef, and tea. Upon investigation, there was discovered to be a huge cavity beneath the ground of the mess tent site, which hosted a massive nest of scorpions. Hot tar was poured into the opening, and as an extra precaution, the whole facility was relocated, but still the agitated cook and workers refused to carry out their duties until extra men were detailed to stand by as guards. Once the food was ready, most of the men chose to collect their rations and hurry off to eat elsewhere. It was a difficult situation, and things would not get back to normal until everyone, including the men in charge, sufficiently recovered their wits.

Only the one unfortunate man had been stung, and he had suffered terribly throughout the night before succumbing to the potent venom just before dawn. As his blanket-wrapped body was carried away for burial, Lilly bowed her head and made the sign of the cross as she said a prayer for his soul.

Suddenly, a small movement caught the attention of one of the litter bearers. It was a scorpion working its way up the handle of the shovel that he carried in his free hand. Frightened for his own life, he unthinkingly let go of both the shovel and his corner of the litter at the same time. He screamed as shrilly as a scared little girl and thoroughly stomped on and crushed the scorpion into the sand as the lifeless body of the soldier rolled off of the stretcher and out of the blanket. Lilly had a clear enough view of the macabre scene to see that the dead man was one of the soldiers that had earlier worked with them in the tomb.

The professor and the others decided to eat their meal in his tent where they had their temporary work space set up. Bala didn't know what was planned for the day, but she followed Lilly's lead, determined to stay close to her. A couple of men brought the sparse breakfast over to the work tent for the captain and his guests where chairs were set up and the food passed out. The bread, which was served as a part of every meal, had burned in the oven when the scorpions had made their appearance, so they all had to make due with stale and hardened loaves from two days before. The cooks were making a fresh batch, but it wouldn't be ready until the noon day meal. Lilly offered some to Bala, but she declined it, and both Charles and the professor politely passed on it also. Richard made short work of a whole loaf himself, and the captain, wanting to make sure there was enough to go around, passed his portion on to Lilly who nibbled at it politely. The others made due with some dried beef and hot tea.

Not much was said during the meal other than an attempt at small talk on the part of the captain, as he tried to take everyone's minds off of the recent upset by asking about life back home in England. Even Bala could see that everyone was nervous and distracted.

Lilly was eager to get back to the work at hand. The sooner they finished, the sooner they could all go home. It was strange to realize that she suddenly thought that way, and she wondered if anyone else felt as she did?

"Are you all right, Lilly?" Her father could tell that something was bothering her.

"Oh, I don't know. It has been a long trip. Perhaps I'm just tired."

"Would you like to go lie down for a while?"

"No, I will be all right." It would be difficult to sleep right now with the thought of scorpions crawling on her. She ate more of her bread and sipped at her tea before she laid the remainder of the loaf on her plate with a sigh. "I'm afraid I don't have much of an appetite this morning."

"I do apologize for this crude fare," said the captain. He didn't mind for himself and his men, but a woman was more accustomed to better accommodations than this.

"Oh, no, it's not that, captain. I'm just not feeling very hungry this morning," Lilly said apologetically. In fact, she had thought the bread had a strange aftertaste to it, but she didn't want to be rude and tell him that.

Ah, Captain Lewis thought. *It's just as I suspected. The little lady was not cut out for this tough life.* He did have to give her credit however. It was quite an achievement for her to have gotten this far.

A private came by to collect the plates, and everyone started to get back to the work at hand. As he walked away, Lilly smiled to see him stop to let his dog gobble up the remaining bread and scraps.

The events of the night before faded in their minds and were pushed aside by the excitement of the project at hand, and the original excitement of their archeological discovery slowly reestablished itself in their psyche. More of the scrolls were translated, and some sections were being copied by Lilly and her father under the supervision of Charles. The captain wasn't comfortable with it, but the professor assured him that it was being used strictly for academic purposes. After all, it wasn't a treasure map; and even if it was, there was nothing any one of them could do with it. It was not as if they could be sneaking around looking for valuables in this part of the desert without someone here finding out about it.

Lilly and her father were in the middle of working on their assigned portion of the scrolls when she grew quiet and pensive. This was unusual for her, as she was ordinarily either explaining things to him or asking questions about something. Now she sat deep in thought, running her finger lightly over the cryptic symbols when she asked, "Father, do you think it's somehow possible that I have some Egyptian blood?"

At first, her father thought she was joking; and he almost laughed, but when he saw her sober expression, he realized she was serious. He assured her that as far as he knew, they descended from English stock. They probably had Welsh, Danish, and even some German blood in their veins, but as for Egyptian, it was very unlikely. "Why do you ask?"

"I was just wondering. I sometimes feel such an affinity to the Egyptian culture, especially of times past. This ancient civilization and its people are so different from ours, yet they seem strangely familiar and comfortable to me. It was always fascinating listening to Charles telling me his stories of the Egypt of old. When he talks of their life as it was, I feel a kinship to those people. Listening to him, I feel I am there in the moment, seeing, and even feeling what he is saying, and I think, 'I've heard this before. I've seen this before!' I sometimes wonder if perhaps I was an Egyptian princess in a past life."

She gave a start as she realized everyone had stopped working and was looking at her. She smiled in embarrassment. "Oh, don't mind me. I'm just daydreaming and being silly." She laughed self-consciously.

Her father and Charles exchanged looks. Her father's raised brows said, "Is this your doing?" While Charles's look exuded a puzzled innocence, he didn't entirely feel.

The professor announced their need to revisit the tomb to study the walls again. Now that the translations were becoming clearer, it would be easier to compare the text on the walls with that of the scrolls to determine any discrepancies between the two. They gathered up selected parchments, books, and lanterns and Captain Lewis sent for some men to serve as their escort.

As they walked, Richard thought to have a little fun with Charles. "I say, Charles, do you really think there is a curse on this tomb?"

"I don't know," he answered uncomfortably. "These burial vaults usually have some such warnings, the sole intent being to frighten intruders away."

"You mean intruders such as we are?"

"No. No, certainly not us. We are scientists, scholars."

"But aren't we stealing from and desecrating graves in the name of science?" He smirked in amusement as Charles opened his mouth to speak, and nothing came out.

"Oh, Richard, stop teasing Charles," scolded Lilly stepping in between them as a buffer.

Richard grinned at Charles's agitation and dropped back a little. "I meant no harm, Lilly. But if we *have* been cursed, I believe we only have Charles to blame. Regardless of your good intentions and what lofty title you pin on yourself, the crime remains the same."

One of the Egyptian soldiers accompanying them was able to understand English fairly well. His father had been a merchant and knew the value of learning the language and teaching it to his sons. This particular son had been rounded up and pressed into the army. This was one of those times when knowing the language had its advantages. Had he not understood what the white men were saying, he might never have learned of this curse. The first chance he got, he would alert the others. The foreigners may scoff at the Egyptian's belief in curses, but these unbelievers had no idea what sinister and powerful forces they were dealing with.

The professor stood back and studied portions of the wall that had not yet been copied. In one outstretched hand, he held a sheet of the transcribed writings and in the other, a translation from the parchment. He read aloud the curse of damnation, which was interwoven into the prayers and supplications to the gods. Charles was sitting at the professor's feet, recording his words, which echoed hollowly in the cave-like chamber.

Lilly listened intently as she focused on the professor's words. *Is this similar to what had transpired so long ago?* she wondered. She imagined the professor as an ancient priest damning the occupant of this tomb, while the scribe at his feet, in this case Charles, recorded his words, which would then be transposed to the crypt walls.

The professor's voice was clearly heard by all who surrounded him in curiosity.

> I call upon the gods of the Egyptians and those of Nubia
>> To torment any who dare disturb this burial chamber or
> the occupant within
>> May you be plagued by venomous creatures of the land
>> May your enemies spirit away your beloved family
>> May you be afflicted with disease for which no cure can
> be found
>> May you suffer unspeakable pain unrelieved even upon
> death.

Just then, a moan issued from one of the soldiers who began rubbing his stomach, and he started muttering something about not feeling well. He leaned against the wall as beads of sweat broke out on his forehead. At first, the others thought he might be joking in an attempt to ridicule the predictions of the curse, but it didn't take long to realize he was serious. He cried out and doubled over in pain, dropping his lantern; and then without waiting for permission, he stumbled out into the sunshine.

The captain immediately sent one of his men out after him.

Richard sidled up next to Charles and whispered teasingly, "It must be the curse!"

Charles pointedly ignored him and returned to his work. Richard then uttered an oath as he wrapped his arms around his own stomach. Charles glared at him and hissed, "Enough, Richard! You are really not amusing anyone!"

"I'm afraid I really don't feel very well," Richard replied, breathing heavily.

Everyone looked over at Richard who now had both hands firmly clenched over his midsection. Before anyone could respond, he had dropped to his knees, moaning, "Oh God. Oh God, help me."

"Father, I am not feeling very well either," Lilly admitted reluctantly.

"Quickly, everyone outside!" cried the professor as he herded everyone with his outstretched arms.

Unused to having others ordering him about, the captain hesitated at first, but then he decided it would be best to do as instructed. He signaled for the remaining soldiers to help Richard to the infirmary and to gather everything up before meeting outside in the fresh air. Some of them couldn't help but to secretly entertain the idea that this could possibly be the work of the curse, and wonder was it too late to escape it now? Had the damage already been done to the extent that they were all now doomed? Seeing everyone's agitation and fear, the professor made an attempt to restore calm.

"I am sure everyone is wondering why I had you vacate the tomb in such a hurry. I assure you it has nothing to do with any ancient curse. Although it is true that some of us are feeling ill," he glanced over at Lilly who was sitting on a large rock looking pale and her father hovering anxiously over her, "I'm sure there is a logical explanation for what has occurred. There may be some rancid air in there, perhaps some gas permeating from an underground cavity, such as the one from whence our scorpion invaders had their nest. But until we find out for sure, I thought it safest to evacuate."

Satisfied with the professor's scientific explanation, which did much to calm any anxieties, except of course Bala's, who could only guess at what was taking place as she hovered in the background unnoticed, they all settled down to take stock of their situation in order to plan their next course of action.

"Captain, do you have a physician here under your command?" asked the professor.

"No, I'm afraid we do not. Our barber serves most of our medical needs, with some assistance from the cook and drummer."

"In that case, captain, the first thing I would like to do is examine all those afflicted with this latest bout of sickness if you don't mind. It would be best to know exactly what we are dealing with before we continue on with our work."

19

Lilly was admitted to the infirmary along with Richard and four of the military men. Although the professor was not a medical doctor, everyone would be looking to him for answers, especially Lilly's father. He was extremely worried about his daughter's health out here in the middle of nowhere.

Bala had her own reasons for being greatly concerned. She didn't know what would happen if Lilly was no longer around to protect her. Would she be sold to another? She was determined not to let that happen again. She would run away and take her chances in the desert rather than be subjected to any more abuse from men. She had been taught from childhood that the role of the woman in her tribal society was strictly one of subservience, but the rebel in her always had a problem conforming, and she had often wondered what would happen to her when it was her time to take a mate.

It was actually this rebellious nature, which led to her being captured to begin with. She had been warned to avoid the area around the falls, but they were so beautiful, and the pool at the foot was the perfect place to swim when she was supposed to be working. In the past, several young women had been abducted from that area; but being the headstrong girl that she was, Bala thought she was careful and could take care of herself.

It had also been her rebellious spirit, which had caused her to be passed on from one unsatisfied owner to another until she ended up with Lilly. But her strong character was also her saving grace and had enabled her to survive up to this point. She should have been born a man. She thought she would have made a fine warrior. As for now, however, she would necessarily assume the role of servant. Even though Lilly was kind to her, when the opportune time presented itself, Bala was determined to strike out on her own.

The stricken patients in the makeshift infirmary seemed to each be suffering from different afflictions. They all had various rashes and diarrhea, but one was complaining of numbness in his hands and feet while another was having bouts of excessive vomiting. A third man suffered from severe insomnia.

The professor examined Lilly and Richard first. Lilly had a slight upset stomach, but other than that, she only had a light rash. Richard had a more severe rash made worse by his incessant scratching, abdominal pain, and spells of sweating and chills.

"Have you any idea what the problem could be?" asked Sir Billingsley.

"I originally suspected it could be a case of food poisoning, but the symptoms are not consistent from one patient to the next, so I need to find out what the afflicted have in common before I can determine what made them all sick. In the meantime, I suggest these men be confined here, just in case whatever they have is contagious.

"Lilly, I think you can go back to your tent and just lie down and rest for a while." He didn't want to alarm her father by suggesting she might be suffering from the same illness as the others. Fortunately, her symptoms were mild compared to theirs. "Richard, I recommend you remain here until you are feeling better unless you would be more comfortable elsewhere, although here, there is always someone on duty who can tend to your needs. In the meantime, I will look into this matter further."

When they were alone, the professor asked the captain who out of everyone had spent the most time in the tomb up to this point.

"Why that would be me, of course!" he replied.

"And are you experiencing any of the symptoms displayed by those who are feeling unwell?"

"Actually, I am in fine fettle," the captain answered proudly.

"Excellent! In that case, I was wondering if you would assist me in a little experiment as I would like to get back to work as soon as possible. What I need is for you to return and spend an hour or two confined in the tomb. Take one man in with you and have two more standing by outside. Have these men rotate their time inside with you so that you are the one getting the most exposure. If there is any problem with the air in there, these other men can ensure you are brought out safely. Mind you, this is merely a precaution. I firmly believe the air is not tainted, however this will serve to reassure the others, especially your men, some of whom may be superstitious about returning. If they see their commanding officer is willing to forge ahead with this project, they in turn will be more apt to cooperate."

The professor let those words sink in before he continued. "Once I can prove without a doubt the air is not the source of our problem, we can at least get back to work."

The captain had no qualms about carrying out this plan, and he started off at once. He spent the allotted time there and even went so far as to eat his meal in the tomb. As he suffered no ill effects, all were satisfied that bad air was not the source of their problems, and the professor deemed it safe to continue with their project in the morning.

Late the next morning, Lilly started feeling much better and could not bear to spend another moment confined to her tent. If she hoped to get any sleep that night, and more importantly, if she wanted her father to allow her to participate, she had to get up and about to assure him she was no longer ill. She and Bala wandered over to the professor's and found Charles, her father, and Richard, who was also feeling somewhat better, already there in the process of examining some stone jars they had recovered from the cave.

"These are," the professor was explaining, "the Canopic jars for our mummified friend. As you know, they contain the various internal organs of the deceased. These items were normally buried with the dead because they would be needed when they were resurrected, so the presence of these jars is no surprise. What I don't understand is why this fellow is lacking a suitable coffin. Normally, this omission would lead to the conclusion that this particular person was of lowly birth, yet his organs are stored in the ornately beautiful jars usually reserved for those of some means.

"There are also inscriptions here on the side, but what is unusual is the markings are crudely made and are of the bare minimum. It's as if these containers were brought here separately and were hastily engraved shortly before use. I am hoping they will shed some light on this enigma."

The professor studied them for quite some time before he started translating the inscriptions. "I see there is a reference here to 'The General.' Other than that, however, I see no mention of his actual given name anywhere.

Charles glanced at Lilly and grinned. *A general!* That sounded promising.

Lilly was absently scratching the neck of the camp dog. He was a hunter, a medium-sized, mangy-looking critter that was very effective at helping to keep the rodents at bay. He normally shied away from most people but had taken a great liking to Lilly.

Bala took no interest in the dog herself, but she thought Lilly's affection for the animal was pure and innocent like that of a child. They love everything and everybody until life's cruel experiences teach them otherwise.

As she stroked the dog's head, he began to whimper for no apparent reason. She leaned in closer to see what could be the matter, when he suddenly sprang to his feet and let out an awful howl. Falling backward off the rock she was sitting on, Lilly was too startled to move at first. The dog, which only seconds before, had been inches from her face, was snarling viciously and snapping randomly at the air with its bared teeth. Bala grabbed Lilly, pulling her back away from the sharp fangs. Charles and the professor placed themselves protectively between the crazed animal and the women while they all watched with surprised fascination this unaccountable transformation before them. Lieutenant Miles drew his service revolver fully intending to settle the matter once and for all.

"No, wait!" cried the professor. "Everyone just stand clear! Don't shoot unless he attacks!"

A circle quickly formed around the strange spectacle, consisting of soldiers with fixed bayonets standing ready to impale the frenzied animal should it advance on any of them. The dog was slobbering and continued to snap at the air, as if fighting some unseen specter. Catching sight of the stone container the professor had been examining, the dog's fur raised straight up, forming a ridge along the length of its back and neck. Lowering his head, he slammed it into the heavy jar over and over again like a crazed ram locked in combat.

With a final blow that should have knocked him senseless, he finally managed to tip the jar over onto its side. Pouncing on it with his teeth bared, the maddened dog began biting feverishly at the lid. As everyone watched in disbelief, he continued to attack it so viciously that his mouth was bloody from the effort. Finally gaining a firm grip with its bloodied teeth, the dog shook his head violently from side to side and somehow managed to pop the lid off. A barely detectable mist wafted from within the opened container and with that, the poor creature instantly dropped to the ground, thrashing and slavering, until mercifully it lay motionless in death.

"What the devil just happened?!" exclaimed Richard. Everyone was just as stunned by the scene as he was. "And what was that mist?"

The professor considered for a moment before he answered, "We don't know what exactly was sealed in there, or how it may have decomposed. The way it was shaken about, and allowing for any change in temperature or humidity between the time it was sealed and when it was opened, may account for the release of some sort of gas or mist."

The man seemed to have a logical answer for everything, but Richard was beginning to think he was just full of wind half the time. There were too many coincidences of late, and he was starting to dwell more and more on the thought of a curse. Too many strange things were happening.

The professor moved nearer to the lifeless animal. As he did so, Lieutenant Miles motioned for two soldiers to cover him. They moved cautiously, gently but firmly pinning the animal down with the tips of their bayonets, as if they expected it to miraculously spring back to life.

"The poor cur is dead," announced the professor. "I would like to examine it. Lieutenant, I would be grateful for help from your men to transport the carcass to the small shelter outside of the medical tent. Make sure the men wear gloves. I will be following shortly."

He then stood the jar back upright and looked cautiously inside. Tipping it, in order to cast light on the contents, he could discern a dark mass. The object was shriveled and blackened, yet it glistened with a film of moisture. Borrowing a bayonet from one of the soldiers, he attempted to pry it loose from the bottom of the container. He was then able to spill the contents out onto a section of old newspaper. The shriveled mass was unidentifiable in its current state.

After a brief inspection, the professor picked up the edges of the newspaper and carefully transferred it back into the jar, replacing the lid as securely as he could. He suggested the other jars remain sealed until he had access to his laboratory in England. He had come across Canopic jars in the past, but this was the first time he had ever seen a dog go mad trying to open one. Was there something inside, which made the animal crazed, maybe in the manner of how catnip affects a cat? Somehow he had to convince Captain Lewis to commit the remaining jars into his care.

Later that day, Charles assisted his uncle as he autopsied the dead canine. "There are some symptoms that suggest the animal suffered from hydrophobia."

"Rabies," interjected Charles, when he saw the confused look on the captain's face.

"However, the accelerated advance of the disease to its final stages and ultimate death suggest something other than that." The professor was stymied.

After some consideration, the captain said, "Well, until we know what it was that actually killed this animal, we will say it was rabies. I don't need any more rumors spreading around camp of curses and what not. I have the morale of my men to think of."

"Very well, we will abide by your decision," said the professor. He realized that he must placate his friend, but as far as discovering the real reason for the strange phenomena, this matter was not over until he found an answer.

20

The following morning, there was little change in the condition of the men in the infirmary, but four more enlisted men had fallen ill overnight. Again, all had various random symptoms, such as rashes, itching, headaches, and nausea. A couple of them had even started foaming at the mouth and seeing things that weren't actually there. For everyone's safety, as well as their own, the demented men had to be tied to their beds.

Richard was feeling better, and Lilly, despite a nagging headache and occasional bouts of dizziness, was otherwise back to normal and was even able to eat some of the bread she had stashed away in her tent so that she wouldn't have to waste time with eating a proper breakfast.

Richard was in an unusually animated mood. He was so talkative and full of energy the others were exchanging puzzled glances. Something just didn't seem to be quite right with him.

Charles pulled his uncle aside and whispered, "I have a feeling something is very wrong with Richard." He knew it wasn't polite to talk about the man's character, seeing as he was a close friend of the Billingsley's; but after having been the butt of far too many of the disagreeable fellow's jibes and torments, Charles no longer felt he owed him any loyalty.

The professor had noted the odd behavior also, but he didn't think it was his place to comment on it. But since Charles broached the subject first, he agreed with him by saying, "He is talking excessively, which is out of character for the normally subdued man that he is. He is also very energetic, but not in a natural way. It is a most unnatural, almost manic energy, as though he has been drugged. I think it wouldn't hurt to keep an eye on him being that there have been so many other strange occurrences lately."

As they made their way over to the tomb, Richard walked between Lilly and Charles, talking incessantly all the way there. Charles had since stopped listening to his ramblings, and he noticed how the Egyptian soldiers were staring at their passing group. A few of them were whispering amongst themselves, which made him a little uneasy. Did they blame the visitors for whatever was afflicting their fellow soldiers?

Bala followed a few steps behind, carrying a chair and some supplies. She wanted to keep watch on this one called Richard who was acting so oddly.

Once they were back in the cave, everyone picked up where they had left off. The professor had only resumed work for a short time before he stopped and stroked his mustache with a look of confusion. He checked the scrolls again and shook his head.

"What's wrong?" asked Charles. It was unlike his uncle to have such a hard time deciphering these types of writings.

"I believe only certain portions of the parchment were transcribed here. The question in my mind is whether or not it was intentional that whole sections were omitted. As you know, those portions of the *Book of the Dead* that usually grace the walls of tombs were more than simply decorations. They were essential instructions for the deceased in his journey through the underworld. Without their assistance, his progress could be impeded, if not outright halted altogether. So with that in mind, why would someone deliberately wish to hinder the progress of this particular man?"

"What if, whoever cursed him, didn't want him to proceed on his journey?" offered Richard. Then, in a moment of sudden enlightenment, he blurted out, "What if what they really intended was for him to rise from the dead and live again here in *this* life instead of in the next world?"

As they pondered that thought, and even wondered if perhaps Richard was right, an interruption from outside broke their concentration. A soldier arrived to urgently summon the professor to the infirmary, and he and Captain Lewis rushed out, leaving the others to their assigned tasks.

As the two men drew nearer to the sick bay, they could hear yelling and banging coming from within the canvas tent. One of the soldiers was thrashing about in the throes of convulsions while the barber and two of his assistants were trying to hold the man down. His eyes were rolled to the back of his head so that only the whites were visible.

"I thought you said he was all right this morning," said the alarmed captain. There was a look of fear on the faces of the barber and his assistants. It was obvious to them this was no ordinary illness. Only the effects of a curse could cause so much bad luck and bizarre occurrences in such a short amount of time. These strange illnesses were just one more thing to confirm their suspicions.

"I only said I observed no change in the condition of these men. As of now, it appears this one is suffering from epilepsy, or possibly even tetanus. Observe how he is in the midst of convulsions. His eyes are reversed into his head, and saliva is draining from his mouth."

"Yes, yes, I can see that!" the captain snapped irritably. "What I want to know is what is causing it." He glanced at the other patients and saw them all wide-eyed and nervous as they watched the painful-looking spasms overtaking their friend. Along with their concern for him was the unspoken fear of who among them might be next.

Lilly's increasing headache pain was preventing her from focusing, so Richard took over the job she had been doing leaving her free to wander about on her own. Charles took this opportunity to keep an eye on Richard, whose pupils were dilated and who was still hyperactively having trouble sitting still.

Lilly usually enjoyed working closely with Charles, but today she felt restlessness in herself. She leaned her aching forehead against the coolness of the stone and tuning out all else, just listened to the murmur of Charles's voice in the background. She wandered idly along the perimeter of the cavern and as he spoke she slowly let her hand brush over the painted signs and lettering, pausing now and then to let her finger tips trace the writings. *Could it have been one of my ancestors who actually painted these?* she wondered. For all she knew, it could have even been one of them who put the curse on this mummy for some wrong done countless ages ago.

She closed her eyes and allowed her mind to drift as Charles had taught her. Unbeknownst to either of them, Lilly would sometimes actually fall into a deep trance as he described for her in detail, things of the past. She did so now as she imagined herself as a high priestess in ancient Egypt standing before the wrapped mummy, cursing him for something he had done to betray her. Was this actually a memory, or was it simply the planting of autosuggestion caused by her falling into a state of hypnosis? Whatever it was, it felt very real to her.

She wondered what this person had done in his life to deserve this punishment. What if he rose again as part of the curse, but without a resurrected body? Imagine his torment at not being able to reclaim his previous physical form! Would his soul then have to take possession of another human vessel, or would he be forced to remain in this decaying state? Would he try to seek revenge against the descendants of those who had turned his glorious resurrection into an eternal hell on earth? Would he kill them or possibly try to claim their body for his own tormented soul to occupy, like some demon from *The Bible?* Lilly became aware that she was now standing before the mummified manifestation of her thoughts.

A wave of anxiety took hold of her as darkness seemed to close in, and she was finding it difficult to catch her breath. This was unlike anything she had ever experienced. Someday in the future, when such things were known and studied, it would probably be labeled as a panic attack. But at that moment, all Lilly knew was that it was a suffocating fear—a terrifying premonition of her impending death. Not even her encounter with the crocodiles had scared her so. She was so paralyzed with fear she could not move or even cry out so that all she could do was stare transfixed at the gauze wrapped, being in front of her. A deep chill ran through her and she shivered violently as if icy fingers had caressed the back of her neck.

The flame in the lantern flickered eerily. Were her eyes playing tricks on her in the darkness, or was that actually an opening in the bandages over its eyes? How could no one have noticed that before? She stood frozen to the spot still unable to move. The flame flickered again, causing Lilly to gasp as she imagined she could see a reflecting light in that slit. Was that the life light of living open eyes—eyes that were staring directly at her? A wave of light-headedness came over the terrified girl as she thought she detected a slight movement of its facial muscles being flexed, forcing the bandages farther apart so as to be able to see her better. Another chill ran through her whole being as her body responded physically to her deathly fear.

Her mind told her this was impossible, yet she was here seeing it with her own eyes! Yes, she was certain now that the head had moved slightly! Then as she stared in transfixed terror, the right arm jerked and began working to struggle free of the bandages that had held the appendage folded across its chest. Lilly labored to keep breathing, but she still could not move a muscle or utter a sound. Finally, the arm tore free of the bandages, and the mummy slowly extended its hand to her. Lilly wanted to flee from this horror, but it was as if something was forcefully holding her in place. The bandaged hand was now so close to her face; she could smell a sickening musty odor emanating from it. Unable to turn her head away, she felt the fingers brush against her cheek; and shaking uncontrollably from head to toe, she felt something warm run down her leg.

Perhaps it was this that broke her free of the spell, which had held her in its clutches, and she let out a shrill scream and stumbled backward. Drawing her pistol, she fired several shots in rapid succession into the mummy's chest, the impact of the slugs knocking it back against the wall. Suddenly, somebody grabbed her firmly and pulled her past the others who were standing in confusion, with hands clapped over their ringing ears. Her pistol still dangled from her now weakened hand. Once outside, all strength drained out of her, and she sank limply to the ground.

Bala had been watching Lilly's strange behavior, and so she was able to pull her out before the others even realized what had happened.

"It's alive! It touched me! Oh God, it's alive! Did you see it? It looked at me, and it touched me!" Lilly babbled frantically.

Unable to understand the words, Bala just stared at her with a wary look. *Crazy white woman!*

Charles came up and cautiously eased the pistol from her trembling hand. "What happened in there?" he asked. When she didn't respond, he grabbed her shoulders and shook her, forcing her to come to her senses enough to focus on his words. "Lilly! What happened?" he asked again more loudly and firmly.

Lilly stared at him confused as to how he could ask such a question. "Didn't you see it? The mummy! It came to life. I saw it move, and it looked at me. It touched me here on the cheek!" She pointed to her cheek on which Charles noticed a small patch of a red bumpy rash.

Sergeant Wright emerged from the entrance, holstering his sidearm. He had been among the first to respond to the gunshots and had rushed to investigate. "I found nothing threatening," he reported with just a touch of a sneer. "What I *did* see was a perfectly good mummy with bullet holes in him, which the captain won't be happy about, to say the least."

Charles looked at Lilly with concern. She saw the look and insisted, "I know what I saw! It moved! It even touched me!"

"If that poor bloke was alive, he's certainly dead now," the sergeant said with a grin, pleased with himself for being so witty.

"I know what I saw," she said again quietly as she looked pleadingly into Charles's eyes.

Captain Lewis and the professor had heard the gunshots and came running up. "Sergeant, report!" the captain barked.

"Sir, it seems the young miss here felt threatened by the mummy...so she shot it."

The captain, looking furious, ran in to assess the damage.

Charles hastily tried to offer an explanation to his speechless uncle. "We were all working. It was dark, and Lilly thought she saw something." He wanted to defend her without making her, *or himself*, sound crazy.

"Charles," she entreated. She could tell he didn't believe her.

Captain Lewis reappeared, his jaw clenched in rage. "This is inconceivable! How could any sane person feel threatened by something that has been dead for over two thousand years? That mummy is now practically worthless, full of bullet holes as it is!"

She appealed to her father. "Father, I saw it move. It touched me here on the cheek," she said, pointing again to the spot.

He could plainly see a red blotch where she indicated, yet he knew the sudden appearance of a rash did not mean that a mummy had come to life and touched her.

Knowing none of them believed her, she buried her face in her hands and began to sob.

Sir Billingsley's heart broke at his daughter's tears. Then he noticed the wet stain on the inside of her pant legs. He put his arm around her for support and led her away.

Captain Lewis was still angry, but from the stern look Sir Billingsley had thrown him, he knew this was *not* a man to antagonize. Regardless of any financial loss Lilly may have caused by her actions, a person of his stature could be a dangerous man to have as a political enemy back home. He bit his tongue saying nothing more until father and daughter were out of earshot. Then stalking up to the professor, he said, "Things are getting out of hand here. My financial future is at stake, not to mention I risk losing control of my command. I realize now that I made a mistake in allowing you to bring these people here."

When the professor made as though to speak, the captain raised his hand, indicating that he wasn't yet finished. "I would like them to leave as soon as possible. There is a patrol leaving tomorrow for a mission to scout to the south however I will arrange for them to first escort your party back to the river before continuing on with their assigned mission. A ship is due to put in tomorrow. Another ship is expected in a week, but I prefer to not wait that long. Under the circumstances, it would be best if this little excursion was brought to an immediate end."

The professor considered the ramifications to the expedition and his research, but he knew he would have to convince Sir Billingsley it was in their best interest to leave. Seeing the state Lilly was in, he didn't think it would be difficult to encourage them to return home.

"I understand, my friend, and I offer my sincerest apologies." He paused for effect before he continued. "May I make a suggestion?"

He took the captain's silence for permission to continue.

"Why not send the damaged mummy and the other artifacts back with us? Who other than I can you trust to ensure safe delivery of such goods back to England? And you know you will of course be reimbursed for all your troubles. We can make the usual arrangements. What do you say?"

Captain Lewis thought about it and said, "Yes, I think it would be best to send the items back with your group. They won't do me any good out here; however, *you* will not be going with them."

The professor looked surprised.

"And neither is Charles," the captain continued. "I need the two of you here for now."

Before the professor could respond, he explained, "You have unfinished business here. There is still the matter of solving the riddle of our discovery and determining if there is any hidden treasure. But most importantly, I need you to figure out what is wrong with my men. I have soldiers whom are ill with some bizarre affliction, and a dog that mysteriously went mad for no obvious reason. I know if anyone can find out what is going on here, it is you, and I will not watch my command fall apart because of some old wives' tale of curses and mummies."

The professor knew it was no good arguing with him. Besides, he had won his concession to maintain possession of all they had found so far, so rather than argue with him, he started strategizing. Maybe he could solve these puzzles in time to catch the next ship going north. That way, he could catch up to the others in Cairo before they set sail for England. He was sure that with the proper instructions, Sir Billingsley and Lilly could ensure the artifacts would be taken care of and safely transported.

"Very well then, I have much preparation to see to. If you will excuse me, captain, I need to get busy."

21

After the scene she had caused, Lilly felt guilty and embarrassed. She knew she was the sole reason they were being prematurely evicted from the camp, and knowing this, she didn't have the heart to put up much of a protest when she heard they were being sent home. She simply retired to her tent, refusing to see or speak to anyone.

Her concerned father felt it was best this way. This trip had taken a definite turn for the worse. And now it wasn't just a matter of her physical health but her mental health as well. There had been many moments that he would cherish for the rest of his life, but he had to agree with the professor's recommendation that it was time to begin the long journey home.

Richard was quiet and withdrawn, which was an odd contrast from his previous day's animated energy. He was happy to be leaving, yet he didn't show it any way. His movements were sluggish and his words slow and deliberate, as though his tongue was too big for his mouth. But since he insisted he was feeling fine, there was nothing else to do but keep an eye on him.

Mr. Brown decided to stay behind with the professor and Charles. He knew this is where the real story was, and he was able to sell the captain on the idea that some good might yet come of all this.

Eventually, the question came up as to what they should do about Bala. Since they were unable to communicate with her properly, they took it upon themselves to decide the matter for her. Taking her back with them seemed the more sensible thing to do. They assumed she would not want to be left behind at the fort therefore they decided to keep her with them.

A long wooden box was quickly constructed from the fort's precious lumber supply to transport the mummy. The other items were packed as best they could manage at such short notice, and some items, such as the Canopic jars, were simply being hung over the backs of camels with ropes. There would be enough time back in Cairo to repack everything properly for the remainder of the trip to England. It was a somber party that thanked Captain Lewis for his hospitality and bid farewell to the professor, Charles, and Mr. Brown. They then set out on their journey under the protection of a young English lieutenant by the name of Archibald Hunter, and the men of his command.

Archibald Hunter was one of several sons of a Protestant missionary. Like his older brothers, he had had one of two choices. He could either join his father in serving God, or he would join the army and serve the Queen. All his brothers chose to serve Her Majesty by enlisting in the army, except for one who chose the navy. Archibald had planned on following his father in his vocation but changed his mind after only one year in the seminary. Regardless of his reasons for the change, Archibald Hunter was a fine officer.

The troops he led were all Egyptian, with the exception of his sergeant and a corporal. Lieutenant Hunter had the greatest faith in his men, and even though he trained them hard, he treated them with respect, so that they reciprocated that respect and would follow him anywhere. Lilly didn't realize it, but she was in extremely good hands with her escort.

She wondered why she had never seen Lieutenant Hunter before, and when she questioned him about it, he stated that he had been on duty out in the field. But from what Lilly had observed, there seemed to be very little going on at the fort. Most work seemed to be of the nature of busywork designed to keep the troops occupied and out of trouble. The fortifications were being constructed, but in a leisurely manner, so what was so important that this young man had to be kept in the field? Come to think of it, she had not seen much of Lieutenant John Prescott either. This fact made Lilly all the more curious, and she was determined to pry more information out of Lieutenant Hunter before they parted company. In her mind, she pictured the men on a dangerous secret mission sneaking off to fight a war in the desert.

Back at the fort, Charles gazed forlornly out into the distance, watching the little caravan until they were out of sight. When he first heard they would be leaving, he pretended to himself that it didn't affect him one way or the other. But now that they were gone, or more precisely, now that Lilly was gone, his heart felt heavy in his chest, and he really missed her. As he went about his duties, he tried to erase her from his thoughts; but try as he might, he couldn't get her off his mind. He thought of her smile, her voice, and the smell of her hair and skin.

He would miss that twinkle in her green eyes when she would tease him in an attempt to get him to smile. She was the only person to see past his serious side and could get him to relax enough to be able to joke and laugh with her.

Then he remembered that time on the boat when he helped to wrap her puttees and how differently he suddenly felt about her. At first, he had tried to resist such thoughts by telling himself that she was not his and never could be. But after that, every time he looked at her, he knew his feelings had irreversibly altered, and he could never go back to thinking of her as just a friend. He knew this was something he would have to keep hidden if he wanted to continue spending time with her. Fortunately for him, they were on an expedition where proper manners and the usual protocol did not always apply.

As he looked again into the now empty desert, his thoughts drifted to the crocodile attack and how she had fired the Maxim with such determination, spraying death even though he knew she did not want to kill. And then he frowned as he recalled the look of helplessness in her eyes when she imagined she saw the mummy move and how he had failed to believe her, even though she had needed his support. The thought that he had let her down was like a physical pain in his chest. He wished he would have looked into her eyes and had the strength and conviction to say he believed her and supported her no matter what. Right then and there, he vowed that if ever given another chance, he would never fail her again.

His uncle could see the conflict on the young man's face. The professor was not only a scholar; he was also a man of wisdom. While still a young man, when others his age were distracted by the temptations and vices of the world, he stayed true to his studies. Arranging his priorities, the professor studied when he should have been studying, worked when he should have been working, and only played when he had any rare free time. He had the discipline necessary to arrange his life and not be led astray by its many distractions. His father had instilled in him the belief that a successful existence was obtained by the building blocks of life. First things first. This was meant to strengthen character and also serve to keep him out of trouble.

But as fate would have it, while on one of his early expeditions, he met and fell in love with the beautiful young daughter of an Englishman of Her Majesty's Foreign Service. After a whirlwind courtship, they made plans to marry, and the professor had never been happier in his life. Unfortunately, he had to temporarily return to England while she stayed on with her father, only to die of typhus a month later. For all his wisdom and self-discipline, he never saw *that* coming. Learning from life's lessons, which differ from those in academia, was emotionally painful. But from this, he learned to never again put something off in the belief that he had the luxury of a tomorrow.

It was obvious that Charles's heart lay with the woman who had disappeared into the distance. Looking at his nephew, whom he loved as his own son, he said, "Come along, Charles. We have much work to do if you hope to be able to catch up with her."

Charles was startled and a little embarrassed. Was it so obvious? Then he realized the true meaning of his uncle's words. If a man as wise as his uncle should say such a thing, then maybe Lilly wasn't out of his reach after all! The unthinkable idea that she could one day be his might not be so impossible! Charles got back to work with renewed energy and a reenergized optimism.

22

Bala was steadily learning English. Lilly had the patience to work with her every day, and the native girl went along with it, making it a point to conceal her real progress. The sooner these people realized she could understand their language, the sooner somebody would be ordering her around to do their chores. As it was now, everyone was content to let her follow Lilly around, acting as her personal servant. This suited Bala just fine. She felt she at least owed Lilly that much for what little bit of freedom she did have. This was much better than having to slave for everyone. Also, if she stuck close to Lilly, it would be less likely that some man might try to force himself on her.

It soon became obvious to Bala that they were taking the items from the cave back to the river, and this made her uneasy. Something told her they would be better off leaving it all behind, but her main concern was traveling farther away from her homeland. If she were to escape and make it home, it would have to be soon, before they put even more distance between her and her people. She needed to act now and take the first opportunity presented to her.

Part of being Lilly's servant was to carry her personal items, which included a full water bottle. The first time the travelers stopped for a rest, Bala conveyed to Lilly that she needed to relieve herself behind a sand dune. None thought it odd to see her leaving with the container of water still strapped to her side. Once she was out of their sight, she quickened her pace and made her bid for freedom.

No one noticed when she didn't return right away. She was always in the background following Lilly and so wasn't usually acknowledged by anybody else. Lilly was starting to wonder where Bala was but as yet wasn't really concerned when she didn't see her right away. Deciding she better take advantage of the rest stop and actually use it to rest, she spotted a bit of shade behind the three-sided canopy the soldiers had hastily erected for the officers. She lay on her side, growing drowsy in the heat, when she heard Lieutenant Hunter speaking in hushed tones from the other side of the canvas wall.

"All Captain Lewis seems to care about is treasure hunting when he should be soldiering, but stealing from his own troops is going too far!"

Whomever he was speaking to, whispered, "I heard it was Lieutenant Miles who gave him orders to substitute some of the troop's rations. Wheat, rye, and other grains were sold for a profit, and those of a poorer quality were distributed to the men."

"I was approached to take part in this despicable scheme but I refused," said Lieutenant Hunter. "Apparently, Miles and Wright have no reservations about stealing from their troops since most of them are Egyptians, but I for one cannot in good conscience do that, and neither could Lieutenant Prescott. That is why we were sent out on patrol indefinitely for no real purpose other than to keep us out of the way so we didn't witness what was going on."

Lilly was shocked by what she had inadvertently overheard. She rose quietly and tried to walk away unnoticed, but glancing back, she saw Lieutenant Hunter had stepped out from the shelter and was watching her thoughtfully.

Ten minutes later, orders were given to prepare to move out.

"Wait! Wait for Bala!" cried Lilly.

"What? Where is she?" asked Lieutenant Hunter with some surprise.

"Behind the sand dune. She…she went to relieve herself," she informed him, blushing with embarrassment.

The lieutenant set off to search behind the dune, and Lilly hurried to catch up with him. "I was wondering, miss, if you may have overheard a conversation not meant for your ears?"

Lilly turned redder and nodded. "I am sorry. I didn't mean to eavesdrop. I was just resting in the shade of the tarp."

"I trust you can be discreet about what you heard?"

"Oh, of course! And I trust you can forgive me?" she asked with a little smile. "I do so admire you for your loyalty to your men, and I'm sure they appreciate your integrity and devotion to them."

Finally giving in with an answering smile, he nodded his acknowledgment of her compliment.

Reaching the far side of the dune, there was no sign of Bala anywhere. "She's gone," the lieutenant announced unnecessarily.

"Gone? But we must find her. She may have gotten lost."

Was this girl really so naïve? The tracks were right there in the sand for her to see. The lieutenant gave her a look that said Bala had left of her own free will and why couldn't Lilly understand that… But understand it she did as soon as she had spoken the words. She suddenly realized that the native girl just wanted to go home. Of course, she was not happy being a servant or a slave, any more than Lilly would be. And now that she was gone, she wasn't ever coming back. It was something Lilly had known would happen sooner or later. She just didn't expect it to be so soon, and she didn't even get to say good-bye.

Lieutenant Hunter decided to send some men after the slave. For all he knew, she may have owed Lilly time still not served, much like an indentured servant. The desert was a harsh place to survive in. He might even be saving her life by bringing her back, though he really believed the young savage could survive on the moon if need be. With mixed feelings, he sent two men out with instructions to find her and bring her back. It should be easy enough to follow her footprints in the sand, and she didn't have much of a head start. In the meantime, the rest of them would continue their trek to the river.

Bala maintained a steady pace in hopes of taking full advantage of her head start. The sand dunes were unfamiliar terrain to her, but by blind reckoning based on the position of the sun, she kept going south. She reasoned if she veered to the west soon, she would reach the river by nightfall where the vegetation could provide both food and shelter.

She had gone quite a distance when she noticed many footprints in the sand crossing her path. From the looks of it, there were quite a few men heading northwest toward the river. This discovery caused somewhat of a dilemma. Should she attempt to determine the identity of the ones who made the tracks, or should she continue on? If the tracks were made by migrants rather than a war party, there would be no danger to Lilly. But regardless of who had made them, whether they were warriors or herders, there was definitely a danger that Bala herself could be taken again. She already knew firsthand what it meant to be forced into slavery, and she doubted Lilly could survive such a life.

Remembering Lilly's kindness to her, and at the same time hating herself for not simply hurrying along her path to freedom, Bala climbed one of the nearest dunes for a look around. From her vantage point, she saw the footprints led off behind other dunes in the distance. Where they went or who made them, she couldn't tell from where she was, so she decided to relocate to a higher point in order to see better.

Glancing back, she saw two soldiers following her. She was actually relieved to see them. Surely, they would notice the trail made by persons unknown and feel obligated to investigate them, rather than pursue her. She would then be free to continue unmolested, and if there was a threat to Lilly, they would deal with it and keep her safe. Bala thanked the gods for this good fortune, and she was able to continue on her way with a clear conscience.

As she made her way through the endless sand, Bala kept looking back over her shoulder. Her pursuers must surely have discovered the tracks by now. Still, she would have to be careful when she headed toward the river. If whoever was in the area were driven in her direction by the soldiers, there could be a danger of running headlong into them.

Hopefully, they would not be a threat to Lilly's group, and they would either simply interact with them to trade, or they would just continue on their way. On the other hand, if they were hostile, the soldiers would drive them off. And if in their rush to get the travelers to safety, they forgot all about tracking down a runaway slave, so much the better. All things considered, Bala figured she was most likely going to get away after all.

Maintaining her lead, she was making pretty good time and should definitely be at the river before nightfall. Stopping to look back, she was surprised to see the soldiers were still following her and had even gained ground since the last time she had spotted them. When they saw her stop, they yelled and started jogging, which caused her to turn and run.

Lieutenant Hunter was noticing signs of vegetation, a sure indication they were drawing closer to the Nile. He had been able to convince Lilly that her servant would be returned to her shortly, which made him feel better to have cheered her up. His men were seasoned veterans, so he was confident they would have no trouble in finding the native. It was just a matter of when. Hopefully, it would be before the ship to Cairo arrived. Her improved spirits were reflected in the girl's lively pace and her renewed talkative manner.

She caught up to Sergeant Sweeney, whose silence and morose expression Lilly took as a challenge. She had been trying to elicit a friendly response from him off and on since they had started this march, when finally to her surprise he addressed her directly.

"I see you have been busy working on Captain Lewis's latest project," he stated seriously.

"Why, Sergeant Sweeney, if I didn't know better, I would say from your tone you don't approve."

He looked sidelong at her in a way in which one would size up an opponent. He chose his words carefully. "I simply question the morality of disturbing the graves of those who have gone before us."

Lilly suddenly realized that maybe his sour attitude toward her, and this additional mission of acting as her escort, was due to his distaste for their project, and not because he didn't like her. "Do you disapprove of archeology?" she asked.

"Is that what you call it? Giving it a fancy name is like painting a pretty face on an ugly picture. It looks better but is still ugly underneath."

"Perhaps you aren't familiar with what legitimate archeologists do! We search for artifacts in order to place them in museums where they can be studied and admired by future generations."

"Ahh, yes, thank you for clarifying that," the sergeant responded with some sarcasm. "So if someone with the esteemed title of archeologist claimed that digging up the grave of your grandparents, or even your mother or father, would be of great benefit to future generations, I assume then you would be willing to comply?"

That stunned her into silence. She had never thought about it that way. She imagined someone disturbing her mother's grave, and her pretty smile faded from her face.

The sergeant wished he had not said anything on the subject. He spent far too much time out here in the desert and not enough in the presence of polite society to remember the proprieties he had been raised with.

"I am sorry," he apologized. "I realize you have good intentions, and you are really only doing this for what you believe to be the right reasons." He was trying to think fast on how to salvage the uncomfortable situation. It was a good thing this was not a military action because he had certainly made a proper mess of things!

When Lilly didn't respond to accept his apology, he decided it might be best to smooth things over by telling her the true reason behind his attitude. "I am sure you know that there are unscrupulous scoundrels who are only interested in finding and stealing articles of worth, whereas you are studying the past in the hopes of benefiting the future. I am not so narrow-minded that I cannot see there is a difference."

He paused and let out a deep sigh as he made up his mind to continue with an explanation. "There is a reason I was so unforgivably rude to you, and I extend my sincerest apologies. You see, my dear grandmother was laid to rest with all the pomp and ceremony befitting her as our beloved family matriarch. She was a grand old lady and was loved by all," he said with genuine pride. Just the memory of her made him smile, which caused Lilly to smile in return. "So you can imagine our horror when we discovered that grave robbers had dug up her final resting place and stolen her body away from all of us who found it comforting to visit her there. This was most likely done by those simply out to make money by selling bodies to medical facilities to be carved up and dissected like rats. This atrocity is *also* performed in the name of medical advancement and the benefit of future generations. Do you see the similarities? Maybe now you can understand why I said the things I did?"

Lilly felt his pain and sympathized with him completely. What a heart-wrenching story! "I'm so sorry, sergeant," she said as she laid her hand gently on his arm. That simple innocent show of sympathy touched him deeply.

As they continued walking and carrying on their conversation, the sergeant sought to change the subject.

"I am curious, miss, how it is you ended up at this particular destination. Was it at the request of Captain Lewis?"

"Why, yes it was. He and Professor Buller are old acquaintances and business partners. They have worked together in the past, so he was kind enough to consent for the professor to bring us along."

At your own expense, I'm sure, thought the sergeant cynically. What he wanted to reveal to her, but couldn't, was that he considered Captain Lewis to be no better than those lowlifes who had defiled his grandmother's grave. If the captain would dedicate himself to soldiering instead of spending his time scheming for ways to make money, the morale in the unit would be much higher and their combat efficiency much greater. But how do you say something like that without sounding like a disloyal mutineer?

"Well, the river is just up ahead," he said. "I'm sure the men will have found your lost companion by now, and they can join up with us there. If you will excuse me, I have some things to attend to." He touched his fingers to the brim of his helmet as a sort of modified military salute/tip of the hat, and quickened his pace.

Lilly dropped back watching him as he moved ahead. All of what they talked about flashed through her head like one who remembers the various parts of a storybook as they flip through the pages. Was he correct? Were they doing something terribly wrong in the name of right?

She suddenly became aware of the camel bearing the coffin lumbering up beside her. What had they done? This too had been a living breathing person, and they had just come along and taken his belongings and stolen…yes, stolen, not only his worldly possessions, but also his physical body! She looked over at the long wooden box and a feeling of foreboding crept over her making her lose her breath and stop in her tracks.

"Are you feeling all right, dear?" Her father came up on her other side, and the spell was broken as fast as it had come upon her.

"Yes, I'm fine. It must be the heat," she lied. Her father was worried enough about her without her adding to it by crying out that she was afraid of the mummy seeking retribution for their thoughtless acts. Lowering her gaze to the ground, she forced a smile and continued walking along, being careful not to overtake the laden camel.

As they weaved their way through the ever increasing vegetation, one of the soldiers dropped to his knees and began retching and vomiting. Sergeant Sweeney and another man stopped to assist him, and the lieutenant halted the unit as the sick man was seen to. Two other men had also become ill since starting the march, and they were already bringing up the rear of the column. Lilly noticed uneasy looks being exchanged between some of the Egyptian soldiers.

Those looks quickly turned to expressions of shock and fear as the air was filled with the sound of war cries, and chaos ensued. Springing up from behind bushes and out of depressions in the ground, a mad horde of screaming spear- and sword-wielding natives materialized out of seemingly nowhere. Clad in white clothing with patches of color forming a curious design, they were dark skinned, with their frizzy long black hair done up in what Rudyard Kipling had described as "haystacks." "Fuzzy-Wuzzies!" Lilly screamed when it became obvious to her who they were.

After she screamed her warning, the lieutenant's men rapidly deployed to defend themselves. Shots rang out, and many a white clad warrior fell before the deadly barrage of bullets. But the well-thought-out ambush had been sprung as intended, and before the soldiers could get off many more shots, the terrifying native warriors were swarming among them, slashing and hacking wildly. Not having had time to affix bayonets, the soldiers were at a disadvantage in defending against the spear thrusts.

Lilly's father had his pistol drawn, and shoving Lilly behind him, he dropped a warrior with a well-placed shot, hitting the man in the heart. Aiming at another charging figure, he fired again; but just at that moment, his intended target shifted his huge round rhino hide shield to the front. To his surprise, Sir Billingsley saw the small caliber lead bullet deflected by the primitive shield. The fierce native continued charging on with his huge sword held high. With no time to lose, Sir Billingsley took a more careful aim and fired again. The impact of the bullet snapped the man's unprotected head back, throwing up a splash of blood; and with his momentum still propelling him forward, he landed in the dust at Lilly's feet.

Lilly screamed in horror. Shooting at crocodiles at a distance was one thing. Firing at a human being at close range and seeing the damage from the impact of the bullets was another. Everything seemed to be happening in a blur, and she didn't know what to do. She never even thought to draw her own pistol.

Two soldiers moved up and stood their ground alongside her father. They were all that stood between Lilly and the attacking madmen. All three of them fired at the same time, and each managed to hit their targets, but one of the injured bloodlust-crazed warriors did not drop like the others but continued his charge. He managed to sink his broad-tipped spear into the soldier on her father's left hand side. Just as the spear made contact, the impaled soldier managed to fire another round at such close range it left a powder burn on the warrior's tunic. They both went down simultaneously, grimacing from the pain they had inflicted on one another.

A warrior with a firearm ran out of the bush shooting at the remaining soldier on Sir Billingsley's right. It was a wild shot fired from waist level, but it still managed to hit the Egyptian squarely in the forehead, killing him instantly. Sir Billingsley then got off a shot of his own that hit the attacker in the chest.

Lilly could see Lieutenant Hunter was still alive and fighting for his life. All around them soldiers were going down beneath thrusting spears and slashing swords. The lieutenant stood his ground, defiantly firing his pistol at every warrior closing in on him. Finally out of bullets, he deftly drew his sword. His calm and calculated demeanor gave her a glimmer of hope, but that hope was soon snuffed out as a spear thrust from behind him protruded out through the front of his chest. His face registered the shock, and he looked down at the exposed bloody spear tip in disbelief. He then looked over at Lilly in silent supplication before falling forward with blood gushing from his mouth.

Her father was now her sole protector, and Lilly watched in terror as a spearman quickly lunged, thrusting his spear into Sir Billingsley's neck. Her father fired his last shot into the face of his attacker and then dropped helplessly to his knees. Lilly screamed and frantically tried to reach him as he clenched the side of his neck, the blood seeping out between his fingers. He fell to the ground, unable to help his daughter as two warriors grabbed her. One of them was tearing at her clothing, and Lilly fought furiously to get away. She was afraid for what lay in store for her, but mostly, she was fighting for her father. He had lost his life trying to save her, and she would not let his death be in vain. She would do whatever she could to save herself. She screamed again, hoping somebody would hear her, and she clawed at the eyes of her assailants. Angry at her for fighting them, they hit her repeatedly with their fists until mercifully, all went dark.

Bala heard gun shots in the far distance. The soldiers must be doing the shooting, but what were they shooting at? They were probably defending themselves, but again, against what or whom? Well, whatever they were doing was no longer her problem; she was on her way home. They were armed and could certainly take care of themselves.

As she hurried along, she tried to push away the nagging gut feeling that something was terribly wrong. Had she heeded this inner warning before, she never would have been abducted to begin with. Now she was feeling it again, and again she was ignoring the premonition that something was threatening Lilly. She felt strongly that she should forgo her chance to escape and head back to check on the girl's safety. But as quickly as this thought entered her mind, she shut it out again. Those were not her people, and this was not her problem.

Looking back, Bala could see the soldiers were no longer pursuing her. They had changed course and were heading in the direction of the shooting at a brisk trot. Relieved, she lengthened her stride toward freedom.

Except for a few of the older warriors and hunters, most of her tribe had never even ventured beyond the borders of their land. She thought about her homecoming and the stories she would tell of her adventures. She imagined the look of wonder and envy on everyone's faces, especially the men, as she told of her capture at the hands of the slave traders and all her other ordeals. She tried not to think about the beatings and deprivations she had endured and the final humiliation of being displayed on the auction block. When she thought of that, she remembered the white woman whose family had rescued her from a life of pain and despair and how one of the first things this woman had done was cover her nakedness with the beautiful cloth of soft material. And then she thought of the bath and how she believed they were going to cook her, and how Lilly had jumped out of the tub when Bala made bubbles in the water.

Now that the memories had started, Bala could no longer block them out. Lilly had been the first to show her any kindness since she had been captured, and she was also the only person who cared to even learn her name. There was one time by the fire when Bala was cold, and Lilly had scooted over and shared her blanket. And the time in the cave when she looked deep into the eyes of Lilly's father and saw compassion and respect in a place where she least expected it.

Bala suddenly stopped running and just stared off into the distance where she estimated her home to be. The look of longing on her face turned to one of exasperation, and then determination, as she turned to start running back the way she had come from. She needed to be fast in order to be able to intercept the soldiers who had been trailing her.

Osman Abu Kru was very pleased with himself. He was on a mission to reconnoiter along the bank of the river and to then head to the fort where the Egyptians were building around the well. Once there, he was to await the arrival of his commander, Ahmed Mohamed, and his men. When they joined forces, they would be strong enough to attack the fort. Only then, would they withdraw back to the Sudan. This unexpected ambush of an enemy force had been a complete success. Mohamed should be very pleased with this minor victory, and especially his captive. White slaves were uncommon enough to be very profitable if you were lucky enough to capture one. Mohamed should be very pleased indeed!

Lilly regained consciousness as her face bumped hard against something solid. Something was preventing her from breathing deeply, so she turned her head to the side, seeking more air. She saw with dismay that she was tied to the back of a camel, and the reason she had trouble breathing was because she was on her stomach. All around her, the war party was quickly salvaging anything of value from the dead soldiers. She strained to look around but was unable to see her father. There didn't appear to be any survivors from her group and all she could hear were a few words of command in a foreign tongue, and the sound of someone laughing. Why were they laughing? She tried lifting her head far enough to see where it was coming from just in time to see two natives dragging Richard from behind the brush, holding him up by his arms. His legs were limp beneath him, and she saw the strange senseless laughter was coming from him.

"Richard!" she uttered hoarsely.

He looked at her with glazed eyes but didn't seem to comprehend who she was. One warrior stepped over to him, slapped him hard across the face, and yelled gibberish at him, which only made Richard start sobbing and laughing at the same time.

"Please don't hurt me! Let me go! Please don't hurt me!" he blubbered hysterically. "You have *her*." He pointed at Lilly. "Just take her, and leave me alone! Oh God, please don't hurt me!"

With a look of disgust, the warrior said something to the other two, and they shoved the hysterical man to the ground where he lay, crying and moaning with his face in the sand.

Another warrior approached the chief and handed him Lilly's dagger, the beautiful gift from her friends of the 10th Regiment of Foot. She recognized it as he pulled it from the sheath. The warrior then pointed in her direction, indicating she was the one the dagger had been taken off of. The chief strode over and grabbing her by the hair, yanked her head back to get a good look at her face. His hard black eyes glared at her menacingly, and he cracked a huge smile, which showed off what remained of his crooked yellow and blackened teeth. He said something unintelligible, and then shouting a command to his men, he slammed her head down hard against the side of the camel, causing her to lose consciousness again.

The two soldiers stopped when they saw Bala trying to catch up with them, but once they met up, no one spoke a word. One was a native Egyptian private with some knowledge of the English language, and the other was a British sergeant who had been demoted for a falling out with Lieutenant Miles, and so had found himself reassigned to Lieutenant Hunter's command. The three of them were prepared for the worst, but each decided to join together to take advantage of what little manpower they had left. One black, one brown, and one white—they traveled three abreast, with Bala indicating which way to go to keep them on track in the featureless desert. Once they reached the scrubland, Bala held up her hand to slow them down, and they began to move more cautiously. Assuming the point position, she led the way, using her native tracking skills to search for telltale signs of the presence of humans or evidence of a skirmish.

Eventually, they came upon many tracks. Some were prints of bare feet, and some were booted. They slowly moved ahead where they could hear the sounds of someone in distress. Creeping forward, they discovered the ambush site when they almost stumbled onto the mutilated body of a soldier half concealed under a shrub. Without a word, the soldiers silently attached their bayonets to their rifles. As they came closer to where the sound was coming from, they could discern it was a man crying. There were bodies of slain soldiers scattered about, but there was no sign of who had killed them. Obviously, the enemy survivors had carried off their own dead and wounded.

Bala reached down to pick up a short piece of a broken spear shaft with the spearhead still attached to it. From the way she handled it, the soldiers could tell that she expected to have to use it.

They found a sobbing Richard kneeling over the prone body of Sir Billingsley. As Bala and the British soldier moved in to determine his condition, the Egyptian stood guard with his rifle leveled, ready for action.

"What happened, mate? Are you all right?" the British soldier whispered. He knelt beside Richard, laying his hand on the distressed man's shoulder in an attempt to comfort him.

Bala knelt down by Sir Billingsley, placing her hand on his chest. She was startled when his chest suddenly heaved as he gasped for breath. Her first impression had been that he surely must be dead.

As no response was forthcoming from Richard, the soldier laid his rifle down to better examine Sir Billingsley. "We need to stop the bleeding," he said to Bala.

Between understanding some of what he said and reading his body language, Bala knew what she needed to do. Still unresponsive, Richard watched as Bala gathered up leaves, and taking some powder from a small bag, which was concealed under her robe, she sprinkled it onto the gaping neck wound and covered it with the leaves. She then pressed her hands down on it, applying a steady pressure. The wounded man moaned weakly. To her, it sounded like he was trying to say, "Lilly."

Richard began to recover somewhat, and he scooted closer. He was as shocked as everyone else by the fact that the man was still alive despite his devastating injury.

"They've taken Lilly," Richard croaked. He didn't even recognize his own voice. It sounded hoarse and raspy, and not at all like his normal voice.

Bala reached over and grabbed one of Richard's hands, trying to forcibly place it directly over the compress on the bleeding gash. When he appeared not to understand her intention, she did the same with the other. He then understood what she wanted him to do. "You want me to keep my hands here? Very well then, I can do that! I can do that!" In a pitiful attempt to seek some redemption for his previous acts of cowardice, he was more than willing to cooperate.

"I am Corporal Smith, and this is Private Bey. Do you know who did this?" the British soldier asked Richard. He already had his suspicions but needed to have them confirmed.

"They were wild savages. But not like her," he said as he nodded toward Bala. "Some were dark like her, but some of them were lighter skinned, like Egyptians."

"What were they wearing? How were they dressed?"

"They were dressed in white." That didn't help. Everyone in Egypt wore white clothing.

Corporal Smith tried again. "Were there any distinctive markings?"

Richard thought back to hiding in the brush and watching the savages slaughtering everyone in his view. He remembered seeing flashes of color. "Yes! I remember now. They had colored square patches of black, yellow, and red."

The two military men exchanged concerned looks for they knew what this meant. The Mahdists from the Sudan were at war again.

"Do you know how many there were, and which direction they went?"

"The soldiers killed some, but there were just too many. I tried to protect Lilly, but they overpowered me, and they took her." Richard began to cry again.

"And how is it you survived?" asked Corporal Smith, trying to conceal his contempt. To be the only survivor of a massive massacre and without even a scratch on him, it was obvious how he had survived. The sniveling coward!

"Think hard, man! How many were there?" Private Bey asked again, trying to avoid another breakdown. A sniveling coward was of more use to them than a weeping incoherent fool.

"I can't be sure. Fifty, a hundred. I think they split up though. Most of them went off in the direction of the fort, and the others took Lilly south along the river."

Corporal Smith said to Richard, "You stay here and tend to his wound while we take a look around."

"You won't leave me, will you?" Richard whimpered, looking frightened with tears welling up again.

The corporal threw him a look of disgust, and the two soldiers walked away to scout around the area for survivors.

Bala was tearing a piece of cloth from a dead soldier's shirt to use as a bandage and merely glanced up as the two men moved off slowly with their weapons ready. She could sense their nervousness and wondered what they planned to do?

Once they were out of earshot, Private Bey asked, "What do you think we should do?"

"I'm not sure yet. I do know we are in a bad spot. The Mahdists are at war, and from the looks of it, we are now behind enemy lines. There is also a war party between us and the fort. We have no supplies for a long trek through the desert, and they will surely have more warriors along the river watching for ships coming from the north. Trying to make it back to the fort seems to be our best option."

"What about them?" questioned Bey, dipping his head in the direction of the two bending over the injured man.

"I don't know," he answered with frustrated anger. His conscience was eating away at him as he realized the urge to save his own hide was overriding his duty to try to save the others. The native girl could fend for herself. It was easy to rationalize that. The wounded man would only slow them down, and he would most likely die soon anyway, especially if he were moved. How he had survived this long was a mystery in itself. The Englishman could accompany them if he could keep up. And then there was Lilly, who unfortunately was beyond saving. It was a shame too, for she seemed like such a nice girl, and he hated to think of the horrors awaiting her.

She had reminded him of his younger sister who had foolishly gone off across the seas to America with that no good Irishman. He had warned her that it was dangerous, and they would be on their own. He remembered standing at the dock and how she looked up at him with tender tears and said that she loved him dearly and would always remember how he took her to see the colorful soldiers and their decorated horses marching with the Queen. He pictured her in her home on the American frontier, hopefully happy with the brave choices she had made. Then he imagined that happiness being shattered by a Red Indian raid and his sister being carried off into the desert. Would anyone take it upon themselves to look for and rescue her?

He and Bey looked over at Richard who was still applying pressure to Sir Billingsley's neck. Corporal Smith didn't even realize he had made the decision until he actually opened his mouth to speak. "You stay here and continue to tend to his wound, young man. I really doubt whomever did this will be returning. We are going after the ones who took Miss Lilly." Corporal Smith looked to Private Bey, who regardless of his look of surprise, nodded in agreement with this decision.

Richard was frightened to be left behind, but he was even more afraid to go after and confront the savages who perpetrated this slaughter. And the corporal was right. There was no reason for any of the savages to return to the area, so this was most likely the safest place to be right now.

They provided Richard with a full canteen and moved Sir Billingsley under some bushes for concealment and shade. As Corporal Smith grabbed his rifle and rose to his feet, Bala rose too as if to say, "You are not leaving without me!" She knew they were going to find Lilly, and she wasn't going to let them leave her behind. They noticed she had found another broken spear shaft and had strapped it to the shorter piece with a leather thong, making quite a decent makeshift spear. The three of them moved out with Bala once again setting the pace.

23

Lilly woke up trying to recall where she was. She knew she was in a tent, but it wasn't her tent, and she didn't recognize anything in it. When she tried to sit up, she realized her ankles were bound, and her wrists were tied tightly together in front of her. Her clothes were torn, and every inch of her body ached. Then she remembered the attack and being abducted by the war party and her father being struck down and killed and Richard begging for his life while forsaking hers. Richard hadn't even tried to save her, and his life had been spared, while her father was only fighting to keep her safe and was killed for his noble effort.

As she lay on the hard ground trussed up like an animal, gradually her sadness turned to anger. She had trusted that Richard cared enough about her to help her when she needed it, but then when it mattered the most, he hadn't even tried. She knew now that she couldn't depend on others to look after her. It was up to her to take care of herself. Maybe if she had put up a fight to begin with, her father would still be alive. She would take care of herself from now on, and she vowed that no one would ever be hurt trying to defend her again while she just stood passively by without lifting a finger. Richard had taught her one thing by his cowardice. It made her determined to never hesitate to stand up and fight for herself and for others.

Being in this situation, she also now knew how Bala must have felt. To be abused and humiliated, losing all you had, and to be ripped away from your friends and family. Lilly could now understand that look of defiance and hatred that sometimes kindled in Bala's eyes. The resentment for those who can hurt you and not give a second thought to all the pain and suffering they have caused. Somehow she was going to get out of this, and with that thought, Lilly felt stronger and more determined than ever before in her life. "I will survive!" she repeated over and over to herself.

It seemed like hours later when the tent flap was thrown open, and a wickedly grinning savage brought in a wooden bowl. He squatted down and plopped it on the ground in front of her. The bowl contained bits and pieces of food, but it didn't resemble anything she had ever eaten before. There were some beans and bits of rice that she recognized, but whatever the other scraps were, she didn't even want to guess. Her stomach churned unpleasantly, but she was not going to let him know how repulsed she was. Thinking once more of Bala, and how brave she must have been throughout her whole ordeal, she managed to move her numb fingers enough to scoop up some of the food and shove the mess into her mouth. Munching on the contents, her stomach lurched once again, but she stoically chewed as though it was something she was used to eating, all the while glaring at the amused warrior. She tried not to think about what she was eating. When the native didn't get the reaction he was hoping for from her, he muttered something to himself and left.

Knowing she needed to keep up her strength, Lilly forced herself to finish her unappetizing meal and then shoving the empty bowl aside, she took stock of her situation. Somehow she had to escape. She would wait until late in the night, biting through the cords binding her wrists if she had to. She envisioned creeping through the camp, sneaking up on the sleeping warriors and killing them one by one. Although unrealistic, the thought pleased her considering what they did to her and her father, the lieutenant, and all of the men of his command.

She thought again about Richard's betrayal, her father, and everyone else who lost their lives on this day. She would have died trying to protect Richard and thought he would have done the same. If Charles had been there, he would have given his life for her. Or would he? This morning, she knew the answer was yes. But now her whole world had turned upside down, and she didn't know anything for a certainty. Well, actually there was one thing she was sure of. She would get away, or die trying.

Richard's hands and arms ached from the strain of holding a steady pressure on the compress. How the older man had survived such a deep penetration to his neck was nothing short of a miracle. As his muscles trembled begging for respite, he unconsciously began relaxing his grip little by little. To his surprise, he saw the flow of blood was slowing down. The powder the savage girl had applied seemed to be helping to stop the worst of the bleeding. He wondered what it consisted of and where he could get more.

Scanning his surroundings, he noticed the mummy lying on the ground. Before stealing the coffin-bearing camel, the ropes had been cut, and the wooden casket had burst open when it hit the ground tumbling the contents into the dirt. Racking his brain, he tried to remember what had been said about using mummies as medicine. He wished he had paid more attention to the professor's ramblings. His mind was a little foggy, and he was having trouble concentrating, but he remembered something about grinding mummies into powder. At least he thought that's what they did. Grinding them up into powder would make sense since a powder is what the girl had used.

Acting quickly in the fading light, he scrambled to find anything of which could be put to use. After the raid, there wasn't much left in the way of useful items. The only tool he had was a small dull pocket knife that the natives had overlooked when searching him. He knelt beside the mummy and began cutting away the bandages. Some ripped rather easily while others clumped together, being held fast by some sort of binding agent. Getting down to what he figured must be the dried skin of its hand, he cut and scraped away little pieces of blackened flesh. When he had gathered a small amount of this material, he began to grind it between two stones. Not having much luck making a powder, he added a little water; and using some of the mummy's bandages for good measure, he packed this concoction into Sir Billingsley's open wound.

Richard sat and waited expectantly, wondering how long it would take for his potion to work. It was getting dark, and he looked around nervously. Now that he had nothing to do, he was starting to become afraid again, and he desperately wanted Sir Billingsley to wake up. Maybe then he wouldn't be so scared and feel so alone.

Besides being frightened, he was beginning to feel a painful hunger gnawing at his stomach. Searching around, he found a few pieces of discarded bread scattered around; but on closer inspection, he saw why it had been left behind. Besides dirt, there was mold growing on it, so he threw it down and continued looking. Unable to find anything else halfway edible, and with darkness closing in on him fast, he finally decided to just eat around the mold. Retrieving those small pieces, and another larger one he found in the last vestige of light, he settled down next to the wounded man and began to nibble at his rank meal.

Bala and her two companions traveled in silence, reading the ground and their surroundings like the professor read the walls of tombs. Most of the tracks they were following were made by man, some by camel. They could not distinguish any that were made by a woman, or more specifically Lilly, and they were all clearly made by bare feet. Even if Lilly were without her boots, she had that distinctive walk with her toes pointed straight forward, and these prints were all large and pointed slightly outward. Of course, there was a chance the men and camels could have obliterated Lilly's impressions with their own, so Bala continually looked behind her in order to read them from another angle. She knew that by observing the same track at different angles, the sunlight may show details, which were not at first apparent; but if Lilly was with them, she was probably being carried. The prints and fresh camel dung were easy enough to follow, and she knew where they were headed. It was imperative to overtake them before they joined up with more of their tribe.

The sun was sinking behind the dunes when the native girl and the two soldiers closed in on their prey. Bala went first, silently creeping through the bushes as she was taught at a young age. Only once did she glance back with an angry glare when Corporal Smith carelessly let his rifle butt bump his canteen. That look had the same effect as a sergeant major's severe dressing down. After a few more steps, she stopped and pointed up ahead.

The Mahdists had set up camp amidst a grove of trees surrounded by bushes. There were a number of tents and shelters of various sizes scattered about, making it difficult to get an accurate count of the inhabitants.

Corporal Smith looked at Private Bey, who simply nodded in return, but before they could move, Bala grasped Smith's arm in a firm grip. He looked at her somewhat startled and annoyed. His initial feeling of resentment at her affront quickly subsided as he saw how intently she was studying the layout of the camp. He then realized it would be best not to make any rash moves until they assessed the situation and figured out just what, and how many, they were up against. It occurred to him that she was attempting to count the enemy, something he himself should have done, and he cursed himself for being so careless.

They watched as one dark-skinned man walked away from the center of the camp, stopping to speak to a sentry who was partially hidden from view. Then he returned to where some other warriors were gathered and started preparing a meal.

Well, that was at least one sentry they had not been aware of. It was a good thing they had heeded Bala's warning and just observed for a while. A small fire was lit, which gave off little smoke, and a short time later, the smell of the food cooking filled the air. In all, so far, they had counted thirteen men.

Bala sensed her companions were eager to attack, probably in the hope of catching the natives off guard as they ate. She saw Corporal Smith nod at the camp and point with his bayonet as if to say, "Let's go," but before he could rise, Bala grabbed his arm again in a gesture of restraint. He understood this to mean that he should wait, but for what? If they were going to do this, they might just as well get on with it while they had the advantage of the element of surprise. Frustrated at being ordered about by a woman, especially since this was his profession, the soldier swore to himself; but for some reason, he still obeyed.

As they continued observing the meal preparation, two more men joined those at the fire, which brought the count to fifteen. Then three of them walked off in different directions, which could mean they were relieving other sentries. That would put their numbers at eighteen warriors. Bala's attention was caught by one in particular who had gathered up scraps of food from out of the used bowls and was taking them into a tent. Were they feeding a prisoner?

It had taken some time and patience, but Bala managed to determine the location of the hidden sentries, and her companions positioned themselves close to two of them on opposite sides of the camp. After the second soldier was in place, she slowly and silently slithered off into the brush, hugging the ground like a large sleek snake. She moved her spear along underneath her as though it were an extension of her own body. Her only garment was a dirty piece of cloth tied around her middle and wrapped through her legs like a babies' nappy, with a small knife stuck in the folds.

Creeping around stealthily was second nature to the girl. She ever so slowly moved across the ground, keeping in the shadows and sliding into and out of the natural depressions. She had learned to track and move about undetected from her older brother, never dreaming she would ever have the chance to put her lessons to the test in such a dangerous situation. Her brother's friends thought it was amusing when she was taught such manly skills, and they had even admired and encouraged her. But that was when she was very young.

As she grew older and began to mature, these same friends began to frown on her unwomanly behavior, for they thought she should now concentrate on learning the feminine things necessary for her to someday minister to one of them. The thought of forced submission to a mate now angered her, for it reminded her of her captivity as a slave. Even though a woman's sole role in life was to serve her man and bear his children, Bala felt the stirrings of rebellion within her.

Well then, maybe her future lay not with her people! That bold thought shocked her, but this was a revelation that surprisingly was not revolting to her. On the contrary, it instantly worked to motivate her. There was suddenly no longer any fear as she moved deeper into the enemy camp. There was only a feeling of exhilaration at having discovered that her life had taken a new direction; one she would never have guessed. Bala was not only going to rescue the one person who she now realized she cared very much about, but she was also just beginning her new life's journey!

Lilly lay in the dark futilely gnawing on the cord wrapped tightly around her wrists. She had been working at it for quite some time when she detected movement just outside of the tent. She didn't move a muscle as she strained her ears for sounds of a human presence. For one brief moment, she thought of the mummy, but she just as quickly pushed that thought from her mind. That was not real; *this* was real. She could feel air movement and heard the faint sound of the tent flap slowly being pulled open. Lilly's breath quickened. She was lying on her side with her back to the entrance, so she pretended to sleep as she listened to the sound of someone quietly crawling into the shelter. She wished she knew how to fight but if nothing else, she would bite and scratch their eyes out.

"Lilly," she heard a familiar voice whisper. She knew immediately who that voice belonged to, and she looked over her shoulder in disbelief and relief. This wasn't a dream! This really was her faithful friend, Bala! She was filthy dirty, almost naked, and had twigs, dirt and leaves entangled in her curly hair. She looked a fright, but Lilly thought she had never seen anything so beautiful! Bala placed a hand over Lilly's mouth in a clear sign for silence. She then used her small knife to cut the captive free of her bonds. Motioning for her to follow, Bala slid out of the tent on her belly.

Staying close behind, Lilly tried to follow her example. The movements were painstakingly slow, far too slow for Lilly's liking. Now that she was free, she just wanted to jump up and run to safety. But even she knew that rash actions at this point would be fatal to them both. By staying close to the ground, she realized she could still see everything around her even though it was the middle of the night. Then it occurred to her that just the opposite might be true, and that anyone standing up would most likely not be able to see *her*. The only thing Lilly could discern of her rescuer was the soles of her feet just inches from her face.

As they crawled along, Lilly contemplated shedding her clothes too, but then decided it would be a silly thing to do being as lily-white as she was. Lilly white! That thought amused her and helped to calm her somewhat. She needed to keep her wits if she hoped to escape, and it appeared they just might get away undetected.

Bala had a plan. She just hoped Lilly was following her lead and didn't panic. Up ahead of them was a large thorn bush. If they could make it there, they would be safe. By hugging the ground, they would be able to crawl under the intertwined branches of long, wicked barbs. Even in the dark, they could worm their way under them without making a sound, and be hidden by the thick growth. Only a few more feet and they would be on their way to freedom!

They were a good distance from the tent and were beginning to believe they would get away with their bold escape when one of the natives appeared out of nowhere walking directly toward them. The two girls lay motionless, hoping not to be seen. Just as he was about to pass them by, something caught his eye in the moonlight. Bending slightly forward for a better look, he unknowingly presented Bala with a clear target. She drove her spear upward with all her strength, driving the tip up into his belly and under his ribcage. Instead of quietly felling him as she had hoped, he let out a strangled scream and staggered back, dropping the rifle he was carrying.

Taking the scream as a signal, the two soldiers opened fire, killing the sentries nearest to them. Chambering new rounds, they moved forward into the confused camp, firing as they advanced.

The man Bala had impaled was unbelievably still on his feet. Jumping up, she lunged forward with her small knife and drove it deep into his throat. He grabbed her wrist in a death grip as he struggled for air, and then with a gurgle, blood spewed from his mouth, and he finally fell over. Bala released her grip on the knife as she broke free from the dying warrior. She stood staring in disbelief at the first human being she had ever killed, and then she looked in stunned fascination at her forearms, which were bathed in his warm blood. Hearing the soldiers' gunshots forced her to overcome her shock and jerked her back to life. There was no time to waste; they must fight for their lives.

She knelt down and drew a sword from the sheath, which was still suspended from the dead man's neck. Lilly lay watching as if trapped in a nightmare as Bala swung the sword in an upward arc at a sleep-groggy warrior who was heading straight for them. The slash disemboweled him, and he tumbled over, nearly landing on Lilly's legs as his entrails burst free from his stomach and into the dirt. Towering over her like some dark Angel of Death, Bala held the sword poised high, ready to fend off any more attackers.

Another native materialized and began to swing and hack at Bala with his own sword. Not knowing the intricacies of sword play, the girl was relying on her speed and agility to dodge the majority of the blows, but it was just a matter of time before he would succeed in landing one on her.

Forcing her paralyzed limbs into motion from an overwhelming desire to save her friend, Lilly crawled over and snatched up the rifle belonging to the fallen warrior. With great relief, she saw it was a Lee-Metford. Working the bolt with stiff and clumsy fingers, she managed to chamber a round. In her mind, she pictured her Sergeant Major MacDonald with his cane tucked under his arm. "Steady, Luv. That's it. Work the bolt with a clean sharp action." She shouldered the weapon and took careful aim. "Remember to tuck the butt tight into your shoulder." Lilly pulled the stock a little more firmly against her shoulder and squeezed the trigger. The explosive force pushed the rifle butt deep into her shoulder, making her clench her teeth in pain.

Bursting free of the end of the barrel and followed by the flash and loud thunderclap, the spinning bullet traveled the short distance to its target in a matter of milliseconds. The bullet's impact point was true, and it bored a small hole into the chest of Bala's attacker, penetrating his flesh and hitting the breastbone, continuing on through his spinal column, and deforming into a tumbling slug of copper and lead. It then exited the warrior's back, tearing a hole ten times the size of the entry wound. In a matter of a brief second or two after she had pulled the trigger, the man lay dead on the ground.

Bala looked in shocked surprise at the dead warrior, and then at a pale and trembling Lilly. They had spilled blood for one another, which meant that they were now and forever bound to each other. Bala swung her weapon up in a ready position above her head and let out a hair raising war cry, and Lilly, caught up in the moment, lifted her rifle in the air and let out an answering yell of her own. With adrenalin pumping, they moved forward side by side alertly looking for another opponent. They would fight together, and if God so willed it, die together amidst the war camp of the Mahdists.

The firefight that followed was short and violent. Bala knew from the sounds of gun fire that the soldiers were still fighting, and that their only hope to survive lay in a quick and complete victory. She reached the front of a tent just as someone was emerging with a rifle. She swung her sword down viciously, nearly decapitating the man, and blood sprayed over her face and body without her even being aware of it this time.

Lilly, following a few steps behind her, suddenly remembered these were the people who had killed her dear father, and a storm of rage welled up inside of her, washing away her fear. Bala was pulling her blade from the dead man's body when Lilly coolly walked past her. With rifle raised and without missing a step, she shot a warrior who was advancing on them. Working the bolt, she chambered a new round. She had no idea how many bullets were left, but she prayed there would be enough to finish this battle.

The two girls were on the outer edge of the camp, and both Bey and Smith were advancing from opposite directions. This gave the encampment the impression they were surrounded, and the rapid fire of the rifles suggested a superior force was closing in.

Though it was only four against many, the four had the element of surprise on their side, and the sight of the blood smeared almost naked, black demon alongside of the wild-eyed, bloody white woman was a terrifying sight in itself. Some thought this white woman had worked some powerful magic and had summoned this demon to help to exact her revenge.

Private Bey and Corporal Smith were working their way toward each other, killing all who had the misfortune to cross their paths. Smith had just killed two more men when an unseen third raced up from the side and lunged at him with a spear. Smith saw it at the last second and tried to deflect it with the barrel of his rifle, but the effort was too late, and the spear tip sank deep into his leg. He groaned in pain but managed to raise the barrel to the native's face and pull the trigger. The impaled soldier then fell to the ground still alive but with the broken spear tip still stuck fast in his thigh.

Bala let out a wild scream and started slashing at a warrior armed with a sword. Driven by self-preservation as well as for vengeance, the two women gave the appearance of a deadly pair. The enemy swung his sword at Bala, which landed with a bone jarring clang on her own. The impact made her stagger backward, and as she did so, Lilly stepped forward and fired point blank. This time, her opponent was the one who staggered back, and Bala leapt forward chopping off his arm with a single blow. As the man fell back screaming with blood spurting out of his stump, Bala snatched up the severed appendage and held it high above her head. She let out a savage yell, waving both the severed arm and her sword. Although they were normally fearless, the sight of this maniacal sight was too much for the superstitious warriors.

The few who were still left turned to run off into the brush where most were cut down by the soldiers.

After the last shot was fired, everyone just stopped to listen. One injured man moaned, and Bala sent him to meet his maker with a powerful chop from her blade. After the recent chaos, the sudden silence felt quite surreal.

They found Corporal Smith groaning in pain, holding his bleeding leg. Since they had no other options, Private Bey took the chance of probing the wound and pulling the spear tip out. He was relieved to find it had missed any major arteries, however it was still a very serious wound, and the man could barely walk.

Bala looked hard at Lilly for the first time. The usually pristine English girl was completely disheveled, dirty, and almost unrecognizable, with blood smeared over her clothes and face. Her hair was a tangled mess, and the light from the fire caused the reddish glints to give the appearance of a ring of fire around her head. At first, Bala smiled, and then the smile turned to laughter as she pointed at Lilly. Lilly in turn, took in Bala's ungodly appearance and joined in.

Suddenly in the middle of her laughter, Lilly choked up and started crying as the whole experience finally hit her. She had killed these men without a thought. What was wrong with her? Who had she become?

After some minutes of self-indulgence, she finally remembered that it was these very men who had massacred her friends and family, and they most certainly would have killed her and these three brave souls who had risked their lives to save her. This was something that had to be done, and she thanked them for rescuing her from the clutches of the godless Mahdists.

"I assure you they are not godless, miss," said Private Bey. "In fact, it is just the opposite. It is true that it is not *your* God they are fighting for, but they are driven to war for religious reasons, and that is what makes them such fanatics."

"We need to go back now for your father and Richard," said Corporal Smith, looking weak and pale. "But we should probably wait until morning. We could all use a good rest."

"My father? But my father is dead!" she said, as tears again sprang to her eyes.

"I assure you, miss, the last time we saw him he was injured but still unmistakably alive," the corporal answered. But he decided not to upset her any more by telling her the dire condition the poor man was in when they had left him.

24

Charles and the professor were being kept very busy. They had hoped to solve the mystery of the illness spreading through the fort in time to rejoin the others, but certain events were making this difficult to accomplish. More and more men were falling sick, and some of them were even showing signs of mental derangement. The personality changes of these individuals caused rumors of the curse and even of demonic possession to run rampant among the more superstitious. With so much misfortune afflicting so many, it seemed to only confirm their suspicions, and speculation swept through the camp like a contagious disease.

Charles was working in the infirmary when yet another soldier was brought in. The man could barely walk, so an orderly needed to help him into a bed. When the orderly slipped off the man's boots and socks, he immediately recoiled in horror when three blackened toes from the left foot fell to the floor. All of the toes on his other foot were still intact but were black and rotted to the bone. The stomach churning stench of putrid flesh was overwhelming, but mercifully, the semiconscious soldier appeared to have no feeling left in his feet.

This sickening sight made Charles think of mummified flesh. How could this have advanced to such an extent without a person seeking medical care before now? An uneasy feeling passed through him as the thought of the mummy's curse pushed itself to the forefront of his mind once again. Only by remembering his duty to control his rising panic was he able to keep his fear from taking over. He calmed the orderly, so they could finish getting the man settled, and only then did he send someone to fetch his uncle.

When the professor arrived, Charles gently folded back the sheet, hesitating before revealing the damaged feet. He noticed additional black spots on them that weren't there a short time before. The sight and smell was truly a shock even for a seasoned veteran like the professor who had been witness to some gruesome injuries and illnesses over his long career. Ignoring the overpowering odor, he knelt down for a closer look.

"I believe what we are seeing is a very advanced case of dry gangrene. It's quite a revolting sight to see for the first time, especially if one is unprepared for it." He glanced up at his nephew who was looking rather pale and sickly himself. What his uncle didn't say was that he wondered what had brought on the disease and why it was so far advanced? Surely, the man would have raised the issue sooner, rather than waiting for the condition to reach the point where his toes were rotting off!

Now that Charles was back in the presence of his practical thinking uncle, he too began thinking more clearly. He wondered if perhaps this could all be attributed to something such as a case of mass food poisoning. But then why would it only be affecting the lower ranking soldiers and not the officers, the professor, and himself? Were they not all eating the same food prepared in the same place and made by the same people? If anyone should be cursed, it surely would have been the individuals who had actually invaded the tomb, yet it was they who seemed to have escaped this illness. There had to be another explanation!

The professor desperately wanted to get back to his original research, but this crisis was taking up more and more of his time.

This was something he could not put off or ignore, for even the captain's "medical man," the barber, had succumbed. The poor man was hallucinating, which put everyone on edge whenever he started screaming about scorpions crawling on him. No matter how many times it happened, everyone still responded as if it were a real sighting. The recent infestation was still too fresh in their minds.

There was good reason for the captain to be relying on the professor to fulfill the role of a doctor for his command. The professor was the most highly educated individual present, and he also had some medical background. Anyone exploring the world at this time had to either be trained for medical emergencies, or they made sure to travel with someone experienced in the medical field. Even a small wound so far from civilization could become fatal without proper treatment. So over his lifetime the professor had accumulated as much medical knowledge as possible through studies and through his life experiences. This knowledge had served him well and had even saved some lives that otherwise may have been lost unnecessarily.

Covering the unsightly appendages, he looked solemnly at his nephew. "I'm afraid there is no choice as time is of the essence here. If we are to save this fellow's life, I'm afraid we have to amputate his foot. Possibly even both of them."

Charles was taken aback by that. His uncle had no training for something as complex and invasive as this! The thought of major surgery here in the middle of the desert was not something any of them were prepared for. Charles's anxiety was clearly visible, so the professor added, "Don't worry, we have all of the necessary tools right here." With a wave of his arm, he indicated a black medical bag and a large chest in the corner. Then he added, "Oh, and one more thing, I shall be needing *you* to assist me."

The professor immediately started getting everything ready, sending word to the captain about what needed to be done. This was something that had to be carried out without delay before the infection spread, plus he was concerned that if he did not act soon, he may lose heart. An amputation was a huge undertaking, and although he had assisted in a similar operation once before, taking on the actual role of surgeon was a daunting task.

Captain Lewis, Lieutenant Miles, and Sergeant Wright arrived to check out the damaged foot. One brief glance removed any doubt about the professor's recommendation, and he was given permission to proceed. A few men were assigned to assist, and as soon as the first bucket of hot water was brought in, the professor had everyone scrub their hands thoroughly with lye soap.

"Now those of you who have just washed your hands, keep them clean. Do not touch anything unless I tell you to. Keep your hands firmly on the table unless I instruct you to move them. And for heaven's sake, do not scratch your nose, ass, or anything else!"

Sergeant Wright stood by with a bottle of chloroform and a clean cloth. His instructions were simple. Should the man regain consciousness and begin to struggle against the ropes, which held him to the bed, the sergeant was to pour some of the liquid onto the cloth and hold it over the patient's nose and mouth until he relaxed and slept again.

Most of the other assistants were there merely to fetch things or help restrain the man if he stirred from his deep sleep.

After cleaning and disinfecting the surgical instruments, the professor laid them out on a clean table and began to operate. Tying a tourniquet around the leg, he put one of the soldiers in charge of controlling it. He then selected a razor sharp scalpel. Taking a deep cleansing breath, he let it out and began to cut.

Almost immediately, the patient began to stir. "Sergeant!" was all the professor had to say before the chloroform was readministered, and the patient relaxed. He continued to cut while Charles soaked up the growing puddles of blood with towels. Working quickly and efficiently, he cut into flesh and severed the tendons and veins, finally reaching the bone at which point he switched to the bone saw. When the jagged teeth began rasping and grating against the bone, one of the helpers vomited on the floor. Without looking up from his gruesome task, the professor yelled for him to leave. This was taking longer than he had anticipated, and he was disheartened to see that the infection had spread farther than he had thought. At last, the foot fell to the floor, but even then his work was not yet done.

"Bring me that iron," the professor bellowed. A private entered carrying a red hot iron fresh from the fire. Not wasting any time, for he wanted to be done with this business as much as anybody, he held the glowing iron firmly to the wound. A sizzling sound and a smoky stench wafted from the site. The smell, combined with the thick smoke, threatened to sicken them all. Working quickly before the man could regain consciousness, he finished cauterizing the stump hoping to stop the worst of the bleeding.

"Where is that sheep's stomach?"

"What do you need that for?" Charles asked.

"To stitch over the stump to seal it."

"Won't that cause infection?" Charles normally didn't question his uncle, but this seemed barbaric and unsanitary.

"We can only use the methods and tools we have on hand here. When you don't have the correct tools, you are forced to improvise," he said with a slight note of irritation. "Would you prefer I use hot tar? That is one method used in the past."

They could all feel the tension in the air as the professor worked the needle and thread through the bladder and the patient's skin. It was so quiet they could hear the sound of the thread sliding through the flesh.

Charles realized that his uncle had been under a lot of stress lately and was probably fatigued as well.

The exhausted professor snipped the final thread and dropped his aching arms to his side. "He is in God's hands now," he said as he stepped back from the table, wiping his brow.

"Sergeant, have the men transfer the patient back to his bed." Sergeant Wright nodded and moved to do as he was bid.

"One more thing, sergeant! Please have the men dispose of the infected foot by burning it, along with some of the worst of these bloody towels. The rest we can sterilize by boiling in water for an hour." He offered Charles an apologetic smile for his earlier behavior, and in turn, Charles smiled back in understanding, making all well between them once again.

Back in his tent, the professor dug through his books until he found the one he was looking for. This wasn't one he had planned to bring on this trip but, he had grabbed it at the last minute since Egypt was so full of history. Now he was glad he had included it. He started idly thumbing through the pages trying to recall what he had read on the ship as they sailed from England. It was a section on witch hunts and the burnings at the stake that had followed. Now if he could just find that chapter.

Ah, yes, there it is. It seems that people always thought they had a legitimate reason for their witch hunts. In this chapter, these incidents were attributed to outbreaks of sickness, which in this instance was caused by ergot—a fungus that attacked grains. When this contaminated grain was consumed in foods such as bread, people became ill not only in their body but sometimes also in their minds. They would even hallucinate, which, although the professor didn't know it, was due to the LSD component lysergic acid that was created by the fungus.

People in Medieval times naturally equated these hallucinations with demonic possession, which in their thinking, was usually brought about by witches casting their evil spells. And so it was that some poor old lonely widow, or spinster, living alone and scratching out an existence on the edge of town or out in the woods, would be singled out simply because she practiced herbal healing, or was maybe "different," or a loner, and was therefore persecuted in the most terrible way. These defenseless women were not the only victims of this persecution. Jews and Gypsies were also targeted by the populace. Lacking any recourse to the law, these poor unfortunates were made to suffer, often only so their property could be "legally" confiscated.

Having found what he was looking for, the professor went to join his nephew at the mess tent. Charles had been doing some detective work of his own in trying to discover if there was a connection between these illnesses and the possibility of food contamination.

He was excited to relay to his uncle what he had discovered. "I'm sorry to tell you that your friend the captain is quite the industrious, albeit somewhat shady, businessman! Besides his other money-making side ventures, it appears it's not beneath him to cheat his own men. You see, while he has the commissary service deliver choice foods for his own consumption and those of select men of his command, the rest of the soldiers have to make do with whatever can be purchased with reduced funds. These men are left eating whatever the cooks can buy with the limited amount of money they are given to work with. My suspicions are that the captain may be pocketing the unspent funds as a personal profit."

All the pieces of the puzzle were quickly falling into place. It had been right in front of them all along! "Then it makes perfect sense why we, who share the captain's table, have not been adversely affected!" exclaimed the professor. "The remaining men may be consuming bread made with tainted grains caused by fungus and come to think of it, I recall that even Lilly and Richard may have eaten the substandard bread when the mess tent was infested with scorpions and had to be moved. There are cases throughout history of people suffering the ill effects of just such contamination. Sometimes it manifests itself as physiological problems, while at other times, they are affected psychologically.

And oddly enough, some individuals are not affected in any way at all. Even animals have been known to suffer after eating such poisons hence the mad dog we believed was rabid. It's all making sense now—Richard's strange behavior and the incident with Lilly shooting at the mummy! She must have been hallucinating!"

They decided it would be best to report their discovery to Captain Lewis immediately. The professor had to decide how to tell his friend that he himself was the cause of the devastation sweeping through his camp.

They found him reading a dispatch while tracing his finger on a map. He acknowledged them by holding up his hand for them to wait. Mr. Brown entered the tent and stood to the side out of the way. He had an uncanny way of showing up at the right, or according to some, the wrong times, and then fading into the background hoping not to be noticed before he could learn something of interest. Lieutenant Miles, Captain Lewis, and Sergeant Wright held a brief discussion in hushed tones before beckoning for the professor and Charles to join them. "Mr. Brown, you may as well be a part of this," Captain Lewis added.

"I have just received a message, which is somewhat disturbing, to say the least," he informed them as he unrolled a larger map of the African continent. Squinting at the fine print, he found what he was looking for and marked the spot with his fingertip. "A rather large Italian Army has been destroyed by the Abyssinians at Adowa in Ethiopia, which has upset the military balance in the region. The High Command has reason to believe the Mahdists may attempt offensive operations on this front. I have therefore been ordered to abandon this post and head north to join up with another unit of Her Majesty's troops."

"Lilly!" exclaimed a concerned Charles.

"No need to fear for your friends. They have a fine escort and are no doubt safely on their way back down the river as we speak. They will also be crossing paths with other British troops who are moving south to take possession of this fort and others on the frontier. There are at least two columns marching in this direction from the north that I know of, as well as gunboats that are making their way up the river."

This revelation calmed Charles tremendously.

"When do you plan on leaving?" asked the professor. He was hoping he could concentrate on the tomb now that the other enigma had been solved. There was just the matter of informing the captain of their findings, and then they would be free to pursue their original reason for being here.

"I'm afraid we must *all* set out first thing tomorrow morning. Once we have joined with the other troops, I will make arrangements for you to be escorted to the river where you can board a ship north."

"Captain Lewis, may we have a word with you privately?" asked the professor.

The captain had a multitude of things to get done in a very short time, and his lack of a response made it obvious he didn't want to be bothered with trivial matters.

"It's important, and it *is* of a military matter."

The captain looked up when he detected urgency in the professor's tone. Addressing his men, he said, "Gentlemen, will you please give us a moment?"

Sergeant Wright and Lieutenant Miles saluted and left immediately. The captain stared pointedly at Mr. Brown to let him know that he was included in the request.

"Yes, of course! Well, I have something I need to do anyway," Mr. Brown said as he hurried out. He decided to catch up with Lieutenant Miles to get a little more background information on the overall military situation in these parts.

"Well, gentlemen?" asked Captain Lewis, thinking this had better not be a waste of his time.

Professor Buller cleared his throat and began, "We believe we have discovered what has been making your men sick. After careful investigation, my nephew and I agree that it is the quality of wheat, or more specifically, the lack of quality that has been substituted for the supply earmarked for the men's rations."

A look of surprise crossed the captain's face. This was something only known of by a very few select people. Who could have opened their mouth? The only ones who knew were Wright, Hunter, Prescott, and Miles. It couldn't have been Miles, for this was his idea, and certainly not Wright. It must have been Hunter or Prescott!

"What do you mean it's the wheat?" he asked in an attempt to stall for time so he could think. Obviously, they had somehow found him out. The only thing for him to do to save face was argue that it wasn't the grain but something else, and so he was not responsible for this unfortunate debacle.

"I have examined the grain thoroughly, captain. There is no doubt it *is* of an inferior grade. I have come to the conclusion that it is contaminated with ergot, a type of mold. This mold causes an unusual sickness, the likes of which stump even the most knowledgeable men of medicine. Not everyone who consumes it becomes ill, but for the ones who do get sick, it can be fatal."

A phrase from the curse inadvertently flashed through the professor's mind, "May you be afflicted with disease for which no cure can be found." *What is wrong with me*, he thought, pushing the words from his head. I must stay focused!

"The mold growing on the wheat gives off chemicals in its life cycle, much like Pasteur's penicillin. The great difference is these chemicals are not antibiotics but rather toxins, hallucinogens, and others as yet unknown. Although people have suspected these molds to be poisonous throughout history, there were outbreaks of contamination, which were blamed on other causes namely witchcraft. In such cases, it would be easy for the uneducated to believe that a person or even an animal could be driven mad by spells conjured by witches and sorcerers."

The captain looked relieved. "So this wasn't the result of a curse after all!" But then it hit him. If the curse wasn't the culprit, then it was he who had poisoned his own troops. A wave of shame swept over him.

"May I make a suggestion?" asked the professor.

"By all means, please do." If there was a way to salvage this, he was open to suggestions, especially from an educated individual like this man.

"The grain must be burned immediately. We cannot take it back up north, and I do not know of any other way to eradicate this mold other than by burning it."

The captain realized his friend was right. They did not want to take the contaminated grain back to Egypt with them as doing so could be catastrophic. Additionally, he did not relish the idea of his actions being discovered. As soon as a quartermaster saw that grain, they would know it was of poor quality. He also knew that he could not keep feeding it to his men. Too much damage had already been done. Maybe burning it was the answer. He could then say he had ordered all grain destroyed in order to keep it from falling into the hands of the enemy, and he wouldn't have to reveal the poor quality of the grain he had purchased, or his shameful secret. Burning it would very conveniently cover up any evidence of his deplorable conduct.

But then he thought about all the damage that had been done to his unit in the short amount of time they had been eating it. There was definitely some powerful poison there, and he grinned as he realized it would be a shame to let it all go to waste.

"Yes, professor, you are quite right. The grain should be destroyed," the captain said. But he was thinking, *yes it should be burned, but it won't be.* Leaving it behind would make a nice little gift for the hungry Mahdists.

25

The captain was cursing himself for sending both Lieutenants Hunter and Prescott out on assignments. Now that the situation demanded their presence, two of his best officers and their men were out in the desert.

He had just received word by a dispatch rider that the Italian General de Bormida was killed, and his army had been wiped out by the Abyssinians at Adowa in Ethiopia. The Mahdists would surely take heart from this news and once again launch incursions in the north, if not organize an outright invasion. Preparations for just such an eventuality were underway by the British for their own counteroffensive into the Sudan.

When Lieutenant Prescott and his men finally returned, the captain updated them on the grain situation with instructions concerning their urgent orders to abandon the fort. Prescott's men would be acting as vanguard, and all must be ready to leave at dawn. There was still no sign of Lieutenant Hunter returning from escorting the Billingsley's to the river, so the weary dispatch rider was sent on to inform him of where he and his men were to meet up with everyone.

The sentry on the wall watched the messenger galloping off with more than a twinge of envy. He fantasized what it would be like to ride across the land with the wind in his face, bearing important dispatches and bypassing unimportant minor sentries such as himself without even acknowledging their existence. How exciting to be the one personally reporting to famous commanders, delivering crucial documents, which could mean the difference between life and death for many, and in the end sharing in choice rations once the mission was successfully completed. That would certainly beat the monotony of standing out in the hot sun staring out into this endless expanse of nothingness hour after hour, day after day, and month after month.

Flying across the desert on his tired steed, the messenger wasn't thinking of the honor and the glory of his important mission. His legs and back were aching from the constant riding. He had barely eaten in two days, and relieving himself was a never-ending ordeal since he had picked up a case of dysentery a while back. He received no sympathy or respect from those he risked his life to report to. And the news he delivered was not usually favorable. Being the bearer of bad news was never a good thing for the messenger. Sometimes he envied the life of the lowly foot soldiers. At least there was an end to their day when the infantryman could finally have a meal and bed down for the night. A cavalryman's day was not considered over until his mount was fed and properly cared for.

These thoughts of self-pity were forgotten when a rifle shot sounded from off to his left. The bullet passed by so closely he could hear it whiz through the air. It was immediately followed by another, which slammed through the muscle of his calf and into the hide of his horse. The animal whinnied in pain but obediently continued running, never breaking his stride. The injured man leaned forward, shouting encouragement to his mount, when another bullet hit the rider in the chest. Slowly, he slid from the saddle to the ground, causing his confused and injured horse to run off aimlessly.

After spending one sleepless night alone with Sir Billingsley, Richard decided they should try to make it back to the fort on their own. He was terrified after hearing gunfire in the distance. The soldiers had not returned for him as they had promised, and even if they did come back, what good would two men and a woman be in protecting him against a whole tribe out for blood? He would be much safer making his way to the fort where there would be food, drink, and armed soldiers.

Thankfully, the old man seemed to be doing better. His bleeding had stopped completely, and he even seemed a little stronger, although he did appear to be somewhat out of sorts and unaware of their dire circumstances. Evidently, Richard's treatment was working. He went over to the mummy and scraped off more of its flesh and bandages to use later on when he changed the injured man's dressing.

Searching the surrounding bushes, he found more bread, a piece of jerky, and another canteen that still contained some water. He was starving, so he didn't bother to even look at the bread this time. When he had eaten some of it, he fed the remainder to Sir Billingsley, dipping it in the water and feeding it to him like a baby. This was all they had, and it would have to do for now.

Richard removed the crude compress to find that although it was no longer bleeding, it smelled like something rotten, and it was beginning to ooze thick yellowish pus. Trying not to gag, he quickly repacked it. Then he got another idea. Removing the shirt from a dead soldier, he tore it into thin strips to use for binding the strange concoction to the wound. He congratulated himself on his cleverness. "Unwrap the mummy. Remove some flesh. Add some water. Mash it up. Pack it on the wound. Wrap it up like the mummy." He repeated this over and over as he worked. Maybe if he changed the dressing more often, it would heal faster. It certainly couldn't get much worse. But for now, they had to start moving before any more of those savages showed up.

Helping Sir Billingsley to his feet, Richard led him off into the desert. He wasn't sure which way to go, so he simply followed some tracks that were heading away from the river and were most likely going in the direction of the fort.

As they labored slowly along, Richard was unaware that underneath the dressing he had fashioned, the wound was already teeming with life. The toxic concoction in which the ancient Nubian witch had long ago treated the Egyptian general's body had consisted of chemicals, as well as viruses, bacteria, and spores. Some of the chemicals had killed off selected microlife subsisting in the liquid, but not all. Some had merely survived, but the strongest ones had thrived by adapting through mutation. Due to the life cycle of such small organisms and their speed of reproduction, and nourished by some of the chemicals as well as the dead flesh, the general's mummified body had become a flourishing breeding ground for new life. The Egyptian method of burial had put a temporary end to that cycle of life, or rather it caused a state of suspended animation. The unintended consequence of a burial in the desert served to preserve the strongest of these organisms.

Sir Billingsley's veins now carried and nourished these super strains that had lain dormant for so long. Aided by the unknown properties of the chemicals created from the mold in the bread, the diseases that were reawakened and mutating within Sir Billingsley had little to inhibit their growth. Some of the cells in his body became weak and died, but some others underwent changes in themselves. Some cells even began to create steroids, enzymes, and adrenalin. It was as if his body was being transformed into a miniature self-sustaining chemical plant. While parts of him wasted away, other parts actually became stronger. Unfortunately, this massive invasive attack inside of his physical being, also wreaked havoc on his mind.

Even as his body was wasting away to nothing, his mind was bustling with activity. His thoughts and memories would come and go almost without any will on his part, and he had little control over his thought processes. When Richard told him to eat, he ate. When he told him to walk, he did so.

Lilly was often in the forefront of his dreams, if that was what they were. The images and memories were so clear in detail he felt like he was actually reliving them. They appeared to be so real; he believed all he had to do was reach out and touch her.

He remembered her asking about her bloodline containing any Egyptian blood. If there *was* Egyptian ancestry in their family, that would mean he too must have the same blood. Could he have been related to that mummified general? Could he even have been the man himself in a past life? Was he the one who was cursed and damned for all eternity?

He wanted to cry out, to stop these bizarre thoughts. He wanted this living nightmare to end, and he prayed to break through this mental fog he was trapped in. But he could not speak nor resist the promptings of Richard. Whatever the younger man told him to do, he had no choice but to obey.

The two men struggled through the sand, each step after exhausting step, taken without thought. They were now just mindlessly putting one foot in front of the other and hoping they were headed in the right direction. The sun was growing hotter than Richard ever remembered it being before. He was so thirsty.

Sir Billingsley trudged along steadily and stoically. Even though he didn't appear to be aware of his surroundings, his physical strength seemed to be outlasting Richard's own. Richard proudly attributed this to the healing potion he had made. The next time they stopped to rest, he would apply more.

The scorching sun was so oppressive it felt like they were slowly and torturously being suffocated. Rounding a dune, they came upon a rock overhang, which was just large enough to cast a shadow on the ground. They took shelter in that tiny oasis of shade that felt so much cooler. It did much to revive Richard, and he broke out the last of their bread and shared it with his glassy-eyed companion, who didn't speak, but only automatically chewed the bread when small pieces of it were put into his mouth. He looked to be in a daze.

"Here, have a sip of water," Richard said hoarsely as he held the canteen to Sir Billingsley's cracked lips. The injured man managed to swallow a small amount but most of the precious liquid dribbled out the side of his mouth.

Setting the remainder of the bread aside, Richard pulled out his healing materials and prepared more. Removing the bandage, he froze and just stared at the gaping gash, transfixed by the colors swirling before his eyes. He squinted to see more clearly. Was that something moving? He rubbed his eyes and shook his head. "Don't be ridiculous!" he admonished himself. He repacked and covered it as fast as he could.

"Here, eat some more bread," he said, forcing a little into Sir Billingsley's mouth, but after a brief attempt at chewing, he stopped and leaned back against the rock wall. He didn't chew, he didn't swallow, he didn't even blink—he didn't react at all. He simply labored to breathe.

Richard suddenly lost interest in his charge. He was distracted by something he heard in the distance. Leaving the shade of the overhang, he shielded his eyes with his hand and looked about. Maybe if he climbed to the top of a dune, he would be able to see better. He clawed his way up the nearest mound and listened intently. Was that a woman's voice? Lilly?

He slid down the other side of the dune and started up the next one. She sounded so close maybe she was right on the other side. When he made it to the top, he was frustrated to see no one was there either. He strained to hear something, anything. There it was again. Definitely a woman's laughter. Not Lilly's though... Maggie? Yes, that was his mistress's voice! She was toying with him like that time she made him chase her around the garden maze searching for her. No matter, he would catch her, and when he did... Sweat was soaking his shirt, and the sun and sand were wickedly hot, but he didn't feel it at all. He was unaware of anything except the urgent need to reach Maggie and take her home. He never noticed the deadly wall of sand coming his way.

Farther south, Lilly's group had broken camp and started on their trek back to the original ambush site. They had salvaged what they could from their slain enemies, cleaned themselves up the best that they could, and Lilly had even found a Mahdist garment without the signature markings for Bala to wear. Bala seemed quite comfortable in her half naked state of dress, but Lilly preferred her to be more covered.

Reclaiming some of their camels, they mounted the wounded Corporal Smith on one and some supplies on another. The third camel was kept free to carry Sir Billingsley once they reached him.

"That was some fine shooting you did back there, miss," Corporal Smith said from atop his camel.

Lilly unconsciously repositioned the rifle she had slung over her shoulder. She didn't want to talk about the bloody battle they had just been through so she simple said, "Many women back in England know how to shoot." Now that it was over, she was feeling the effects from the trauma of having taken the lives of so many, even of men who deserved it.

"That may be, but how many of them do their shooting with a Lee-Metford?" It was evident she had received training.

"I had the good fortune to be instructed on the operation of the Lee-Metford by Sergeant Major MacDonald, and my friends of the 10th Regiment of Foot." Lilly answered shortly. She missed those men from the 10th and wished they were here now.

He thought about that and then asked with a wicked grin, "And is that all they taught you?"

Lilly caught his hidden meaning and was annoyed. Those were happy times for her, so exciting and carefree. How she missed it! And here was this man trying to sully her memories by insinuating there was unsavory business going on just because she was a woman.

Angrily, she retorted, "Those fine men taught me how to peel potatoes for fifty men, how to regulate steam pressure to propel a ship faster, how to splice rope to lengthen it." As an afterthought, she added, "And how to kill with a Maxim!"

Corporal Smith opened his mouth to apologize for upsetting her, when Bala suddenly called out, pointing toward a swiftly approaching swirling cloud of sand. Bala and the mounted soldier had seen these destructive storms before.

"Quick, Private Bey, we need to find shelter immediately!" Smith yelled, watching the oncoming threat.

"What's wrong? What is happening?" Lilly asked in confusion.

"There is a sand storm coming our way! We have to find somewhere safe to wait it out," yelled the corporal.

"But what about my father!" Lilly cried.

"We haven't any choice! We'll never find our way in the storm!"

Picking a good spot among a cluster of trees, they secured their camels; and gathering under some quickly rigged tent canvas, they settled down to wait. Once the storm passed, they would continue on, but even so, the soldiers had a tough time convincing Lilly that it was necessary to take refuge.

The storm hit them with tremendous force. The tiny grains of sand and debris pelted them mercilessly, stinging like thousands of ants, and working its way into their eyes, mouths, and nostrils. They all huddled under blankets to protect themselves from the worst of it, but the deafening roar was unnerving.

Witnessing firsthand the ferocity of the storm made Lilly even more frightened for her father's safety. Was he out in this storm unable to get to shelter? Injured, helpless, and all alone? Bala could sense that Lilly's fear was not for herself, but for her father. She scooted closer to the worried young girl and reaching out, grasped the light-skinned hand in her darker one in an effort to offer her comfort and strength. The two men cautiously moved in closer and sandwiched the women between them, pulling the blankets more snugly around them all. It wasn't much, but it was the best they could do.

Sir Billingsley dreamed he was standing in the midst of a battlefield. There were white-robed figures running everywhere killing soldiers. It was as if he was invisible. No one seemed to take notice of him; everyone ran right past him and at times, even *through* him. He could see Richard curled up on the ground, crying and pleading to be spared. One warrior stopped and was about to run the sobbing man through with his sword, but then he was distracted and ran off to fight a more worthy opponent. Sir Billingsley watched all of this in helpless horror. He wanted to participate in the battle but was unable to speak or move from his spot. All he could do was witness the terrible scene unfolding as it was replayed in his brain.

He could see his Lilly struggling with two warriors. She looked directly at him and screamed, "Father, help me!"

"Lilly!" As he tried to speak her name, he awoke from the nightmare. Something was in his mouth, and he spit it out... bread? He gagged as he realized there was sand blowing into his face. The granules felt gritty between his teeth, and he turned his head away from the wind so he could breathe. Although he wasn't feeling the sting of the tiny particles hitting his nerve-deadened face, he somehow knew that this was real and not part of his dreams or imaginings.

He shielded himself as best he could under the overhang. How he had gotten here, he couldn't remember, nor for that matter did he even know where he was. He could not do anything other than wait for the storm to end and just take one thing at a time. He would get through this and then he would worry about what came next.

He should have been feeling tired, severely wounded as he was, yet he did not feel weak. His heart was beating so fast. How strange!

His thoughts turned back to his daughter. She needed him; he could just feel it. Wherever she was, whatever was happening to her was his fault, and she was counting on him to save her. And save her he would as long as he had breath in his body!

Somehow it became clear to his confused mind that the dream of a battle and the attack on his daughter was something that had really happened, and a rage began to build up inside of him. He would tear their heads off with his bare hands! He suddenly had a taste for blood—literally. The anger and hatred rising up in him was enough to make him want to rip out their hearts and lick their blood from his fingers. He never knew such hate before. Adrenalin surged through him, and he was about to run off blindly into the storm, when reason unexpectedly returned. For that few moments of lucidity, he was able to think clearly enough to prevent him from acting on his reckless impulse.

A soft voice in the distance called out his name. He tried to see into the thick, massive cloud of blowing sand and caught a glimpse of movement. Who was it? A figure was taking form and moving nearer until it stood just a few feet away. It spoke his name again, and that is when he knew it was his wife! The confused man rubbed his eyes and looked again. This was assuredly a figment of his imagination, for he remembered that she had died some years past.

"Arthur, where is our daughter?"

This was but an apparition, yet he answered it.

"My dear wife, is it really you?" He knew it wasn't, yet...did he actually speak the words aloud, or had he simply thought them?

"Where is our daughter? You are supposed to be watching over her. You promised me you would."

"I don't know where she is! But I swear to you, I will find her, and I won't rest until she is safe! I swear it!" With that, the ghostly form faded away.

As his tenuous grip on reality came and went in waves, he struggled to make his plans. The first priority would be to reach the fort to enlist their help in finding his daughter. If the soldiers could not help him, then he would appeal to England for help. If *they* refused him, he would turn to the German Prince of Hanover, then to the Russian Nobility at St. Petersburg, the godless Turks at Constantinople, Wild West gunslingers on the American continent, or anyone else he had to. Even if it was necessary to sell every bit of the family estate to raise his own private army, he would search to the ends of the earth to find his Lilly.

26

The treacherous blinding storm had blotted out the daylight. Although they had no sense of the amount of time passing, it had seemed to last half the day; but when it was finally over, the sun was only a little lower in the sky. Even so, they scrambled to be on their way again since they had a lot of ground to cover before dark, so the four started moving immediately.

The sooner they reached her father, the better chance he had, for all kinds of frightening scenarios were playing out in her head. Her imagination was running wild as she thought of what might, or could be happening to her father. Back in England, such thoughts would never even have occurred to her. But now, after all she had been through, she knew that anything was possible.

She was also worried about her father being left in Richard's care. The last time she saw Richard, he had looked to have lost his mind. How could the soldiers have left her helpless father with a madman? She tried pushing those thoughts away. She had to, or she felt she might go mad from worry herself.

The blowing sand had made it more difficult to find the ambush site, but Bala was determined to push on until finally, they made it. Lilly was frightened to the point of panic when after a quick look around, her father and Richard were nowhere to be found. This was definitely the place where they had been left. Dead bodies were still strewn about, half buried now from the ravages of the storm. They searched around, even turning over bodies to ensure none of them were the two they sought.

Lilly came upon the partially buried mummy and took a few hesitant steps toward it. Even though she had grown to fear it, for some reason, she was still drawn to it like a magnet to metal. The busted coffin lay where it had fallen. She brushed some of the sand away with her foot, uncovering the arm that had been scraped at and shredded as if something or someone had been clawing at it. Part of the hand was missing, as was a portion of its face. It looked like the mummy had been trying to free itself of its wrappings, tearing at the bandages that bound its arm and head. Lilly forced herself to turn her back on the macabre sight and walk away. She was being silly!

"If they aren't here, could they have boarded a ship already?" she suggested. It was unlikely, but she was grasping at straws now. "Or perhaps, they headed back to the safety of the fort?" She didn't think her father was in any condition to be moved, but if he wasn't here, he had to be somewhere! "Please can we search one more time to make certain he is nowhere around?" Though she didn't say it, she wondered if Richard may have gone off and left him behind.

They spread out and searched once more, but it was clear neither of them were there. If they had set off to find the fort, their tracks were no longer visible, having been covered by the blowing sands. Lilly was secretly beginning to believe her father may have perished after all. She shook off that thought and continued on bravely.

"Well, if they're not here, then they must either have headed to the river to find a ship, or else they decided to make it back to the fort. If they are heading down river, they are out of harm's way. If they are going to the encampment, then we need to find them. If they're on foot, we may be able to overtake them if we leave immediately, and since you men will wish to rejoin your command at the fort, we may as well all travel together."

Corporal Smith exchanged glances with Private Bey and said carefully, "You know I sympathize with all you have been through, but there is one thing you seem to have overlooked. Somewhere in between the fort and us is a war party. If we stumble into them, we are done for. Two against fifty or more are not good odds, and one of us is wounded." Now that the corporal had done his good deed in rescuing the young lady, it was time he looked to his own survival.

She couldn't believe what she was hearing! Her initial surprise quickly turned to frustration and anger. Are these men cowards and deserters? "It is *not* two against fifty! I see *four* people here, damn you! Even with a bum leg, you can still shoot, can't you? And as handicapped as you may think *I* am by my gender, I believe that I have already proven myself with a gun. We are armed with rapid fire rifles and plenty of ammunition. Maybe Bala cannot shoot yet, but she can bloody well handle a sword, which will give us time to reload. *And* furthermore, with Bala leading us, I don't think we will be stumbling into anyone, but rather *we* will have the advantage of sneaking up on *them*. So I ask you one more time. Are you coming with us or not?"

The shock on Corporal Smith's face was almost comical. Such talk coming from a genteel lady! She too was surprised at her own audacity at speaking to a person of authority in such a way, only she dared not let it show and have it be taken as a sign of weakness.

Exchanging looks again with the private, there seemed to be an unspoken agreement between them. Corporal Smith felt ashamed. As the highest ranking soldier, he was the one in charge of looking after the welfare of those under him, including the civilians who had been entrusted to his care. "Yes, of course we will stick together and find your father. I apologize for my temporary lapse of judgment." At that, he stood a bit straighter and began organizing to move out.

Lilly spoke to Bala in words and signs about what they needed her to do. She had to make sure the girl understood their plans.

Surprisingly, she had already figured everything out for herself. She obviously understood much more than she had let on in the past. Night was closing in, but this didn't worry her since there were no trails or markings to follow anyway since the storm. She would do her best to find Lilly's father.

And so, armed with rifles, a sword, and plenty of ammunition and determination, the peculiar mismatched foursome headed off into the unknown.

Most of the fort had taken refuge from the storm inside the empty tomb. As soon as it was over, they shoveled most of the sand away from the entrance. Captain Lewis stepped out, removed his gloves, and beat them against his pant leg to get rid of some of the gritty particles that seemed to be everywhere. He could feel it on his scalp, under his collar, and even inside his puttee-wrapped boots. He unfolded a small lightly oiled bundle, revealing his service pistol. When he was satisfied that it was sand free, he was pleased that it had been his idea to use this method of protecting their weapons.

Not much damage had occurred to the fort except for some deep sand drifts lying against parts of the fortification, negating to some extent the effectiveness of the ramparts. The captain had some of his men completely re-seal the entrance to the cave with dirt, sand, and rocks in the hopes that at some point in the future, he could return to salvage something that might yet be of value.

The contaminated grain was left behind for the enemy along with a few odds and ends, including some erected shelters in order to make it appear that the fort was abandoned in haste. This would hopefully keep the natives from suspecting the grain had intentionally been left behind and could possibly be poisoned. Finally, all was ready for the column to assemble and move out. They had been forced to waste part of the day when the storm hit, so now they would probably not get far before it started to get dark.

As they put the security of the fort behind them, Charles wondered about the whereabouts of the others but most especially Lilly. Thankfully, she was well on her way down river by now and well away from all danger. He prayed he would make it home again, and he swore if he made it through this, he would no longer hesitate to tell her his true feelings. He knew now that he was in love with her, and he no longer cared about any obstacles in their way. That would be nothing compared to what he had gone through and the peril he was now facing. He would certainly have some exciting stories to tell her when next they met!

The soldiers pressed on in the direction indicated from the orders delivered by the dispatch rider. Along this route, they were to join with another column before marching toward a third one that would be approaching from the north. Out in front, and off to the flanks, Lieutenant Prescott had positioned his best men. They would be the first to warn of danger should it appear, as they were forced to travel slower than usual because of the need to carry the stretchers of the sick.

One of the afflicted men started screaming and thrashing so violently they had to stop for fear he would fling himself off the litter. As the professor tended to him, Charles checked on the other ill soldiers. Aside from the look of fear on their faces, they seemed to be holding their own. The professor had some men hold up a blanket to shield the poor man from the direct rays of the sun, and he wiped the clammy forehead with a wet towel. This seemed to soothe him somewhat, but then he unexpectedly let out an agonizing scream, and just like that he expired.

Captain Lewis organized a detail for a quick burial to be led by a reluctant Lieutenant Miles. The lieutenant didn't think it was a good idea to leave men behind for such an unnecessary task. After all, the dead man was just an Egyptian. When he made the mistake of questioning the captain's orders, he received a stern reprimand. Any hint of disrespect or questioning of authority at this point would not be tolerated as it could wreak havoc in the ranks.

"What would you have me do?" Captain Lewis growled in a hushed tone. "Should I leave the body behind to rot for his fellow soldiers to see? Or perhaps we should simply abandon everyone and everything that is slowing us down so we can run. Do you realize how quickly my command would disintegrate if that happened? Two headless Bedouins on a lame camel would have no trouble destroying us. The only things keeping this unit together are a fear of punishment, and/or, respect for us as officers. I suggest you pull yourself together and remember who you are—an officer in Her Majesty's service! Now keep a cool head and obey my orders, and hopefully your men will follow your example and do the same for you."

In an instant, the captain's countenance switched from one of harsh disciplinarian to one of fatherly benevolence. "Let's hear no more of that kind of talk, shall we?" he said kindly. "Go on now, see to your men."

Shamed by the rebuke, Lieutenant Miles saluted and went to assemble his detail. He knew the captain was right. An attitude of superiority on behalf of the officers was permitted and even encouraged in order to uphold the status quo. But on the other hand, British officers were expected to be exceptionally fearless in the face of adversity. Questioning orders was not to be tolerated and smacked of cowardice. There was also the danger of an uprising or revolt from the ranks stemming from a lack of confidence in their commanding officer if it became known the lieutenant didn't even have faith in his own superior's decisions. Thoughts of The Mutiny in India always lurked in the backs of many of their minds.

A mere half an hour later, Lieutenant Miles and his burial detail caught up with the main body of soldiers without incident. Shortly thereafter, the rear guard reported they were being followed. Until they knew for certain, they had to assume their trackers were hostile. The captain had the safety of the three British subjects, as well as the camp followers to consider, and so he pulled the professor aside to speak to him privately.

"The rear guard reports we are being followed by scouts who may very well turn out to be Mahdists. Should they decide to attack, we have no choice but to deploy to meet them. Unfortunately, our soldiers are not of the Crown and though they are of the 'new' Egyptian Army, as raised by the Khedive, this particular unit is much of the same ilk as those beaten repeatedly over and over again by the Mahdists in the past. In fact, some of them may have even been present at their great defeats at Kassala and Sennar in '85. If we do end up in a fight and should my men begin to waver, I fear it will cause a ripple effect, which may cause them to break ranks, and the break will become a rout, and a rout will result in a bloody free for all. Should that happen, it will necessarily come down to every man for himself. In that case, the fastest to flee the area may be able to escape, for at some point the pursuit will slacken off as more and more of the victors stop to partake of the spoils.

"If such a situation develops, your only chance is to keep heading north until you meet up with British troops of the North Staffordshire Regiment who are at this moment moving south to relieve us."

"What about you? Where will you be?" The professor thought he knew, but he felt obligated to ask.

"My place is with my men for it is there that I will finally find either my glory or my demise. Come what may, I will stand with them to ultimately share their fate. I may have made mistakes along the way in seeing to their welfare, but I aim to make things right from here on out. You can be assured I will not fail them this time."

After a pause, he added, "But we must think positive since we won't know the outcome until it happens." This last was said with a humorless smile, indicating he was resigned to his fate whatever it may be.

"Should I order you to, you, your nephew, and Mr. Brown must immediately go off on your own and do not look back."

They had not gone very far when Lieutenant Prescott's men at the front of the column held up their rifles to halt the march once again. These frequent starts and stops were bringing frustration and anxiety to the soldiers, and it was beginning to show. The captain, Sergeant Wright, and Mr. Brown came forward to investigate, and using their binoculars, they could clearly see a rider-less horse grazing up ahead in the distance. From the colors of the shabraque under the saddle, they deduced it most likely belonged to the earlier dispatch rider. If this was so, it was quite disheartening as there was no way of knowing whether their urgent messages had been delivered before the horse lost its rider.

The sun was sinking, so Captain Lewis knew they needed to make camp. It would be difficult, if not downright impossible to hold his command together as hungry, tired, and skittish as they were. Most of the men were not used to spending the night outside of their fortifications, so he decided it would be best to keep them too busy to think. He made sure to post reliable guards, and once that was done, he put everyone to work, cutting and stacking thorn bushes. Everyone and everything was to bed down for the night inside a circle protected by of a wall of thorns. Only the cooks would be exempt from this detail. At least the troops could anticipate a good meal at the end of their labor, and keeping them busy negated the detrimental effects of the idle chatter born of boredom and anxiety.

Thorn bushes grew abundantly in some areas of the desert and were very wicked indeed. Making a barricade of them would provide a great advantage for repelling an assault by Dervish tribesmen who may come charging out of the night. Such a barricade, known as a *zareba*, had been used from time immemorial and had been utilized in the ill-fated Khartoum relief expedition.

They didn't know how many Mahdist warriors might be out there, but they had become certain they were there. No doubt the natives were waiting for reinforcements or watching for an opportunity to do some mischief after dark and take them by surprise. By showing the enemy that they were aware of their presence by setting up a defense against the potential threat, the soldiers were hoping to make them think twice about attacking.

27

The Mahdist chieftain, Osman Abu Kru, could not believe his good fortune. Leading his men at a run, they halted just short of the unfinished walls of the abandoned military fortification. It was just as his scouts had said—the soldiers must have deserted the camp in haste. Waving his men forward, they let out a triumphant yell and swarmed over the low walls like a small army of ants in search of anything useful that may have been left behind. Though their religion may have frowned upon it, like fighting men throughout history, they set off to collect the spoils of war.

Favorable reports came back to Osman one after the other. There was no sign of the enemy, and the well was still intact with the water untainted. There were some tents and other usable odds and ends lying around, and there was even a rather large cache of grain and some other foodstuffs. The news of the water and the grain was especially welcome due to the severe drought that had left much of the Sudan parched and barren.

While the natives searched the site, another larger tribe of Mahdists was approaching from the southeast. It was they who had been sent to attack the fort and annihilate the enemy forces encamped there. The leader of this group would no doubt be surprised and maybe a little angry to hear the fort had already been taken by a lesser force than his own.

As Osman Abu Kru watched them approach, his chest swelled with pride to know that his small raiding party had accomplished what this larger group of warriors had been charged to do. Maybe now he would be rewarded with a bigger army of his own to lead. He possessively touched the handle of the beautiful silver dagger he had tucked into the belt under his robe. He would keep it for himself. It was a fine piece of craftsmanship, and it reminded him of the other prize he had waiting for him back at camp. The white woman with the fire in her hair and in her spirit would fetch a grand price from the slave traders. Maybe he should have taken the white male too, but that one would probably have been more trouble than he was worth. Having lost his senses, he would have been too hard to keep under control with so few men.

Ahmed Mohamed approached the fort with caution. He could see their flag had been raised but was still suspicious of walking into a trap. Inside the fort, Osman mounted the low wall and made a show of strutting back and forth as he awaited their arrival. Ignoring the skirmishers leading the way, he greeted the chieftain proudly as he crossed the rampart and proudly delivered the fort and its contents into his hands.

Corporal Smith and Private Bey had come to trust in Bala's tracking skills. Even though they had been thoroughly trained in this area, Bala displayed a natural talent and instinct when it came to tactical situations. Even now, she seemed to sense something undetected by the others. She slowed to a stop and held her head up, nose in the air as though she could actually smell danger. Handing the reins of her camel to Lilly, she scurried up the side of a large dune and dropped to her stomach, inching the rest of the way to the top.

When she didn't come back down, Lilly gave the reins to Private Bey and made her way up to join her. Climbing the huge mound of sand was quite difficult. She was tired from all she had been through, but she felt driven and somehow found the strength to make it.

As she neared the crest, Bala signaled for her to keep low, but Lilly was already lying flat against the sand. Bala realized it was she herself who had taught her this, and she was pleased to see it had been remembered. Lilly wriggled forward until she could see but was totally unprepared for what lay before her. The garrison, their safe haven, was gone! And in place of the British and Anglo-Egyptian soldiers, the fort was crawling with native warriors!

Bala traced a trail in the sand with her finger and then raised it to point off into the distance. From their vantage point, Lilly could see the line of tracks, leading her to believe the fort's prior occupants had gone off to the north. For a while, they watched the movements of the Mahdists, unable to decide what to do next. Should they steer clear of the camp and try to catch up to the soldiers? But they had counted on being able to replenish their dwindling water supply from the fort's well. As they lay there observing, some of the Mahdist horde began to scale the low lying walls and race off into the desert, following the tracks Bala had just pointed out.

Lilly watched this for a few minutes more and then started to back away. "Watch them, Bala," she said as she pointed to her own eyes and then at the activity below. She then turned and half slid back down to the bottom.

Corporal Smith and Private Bey watched Lilly's descent, feeling somewhat embarrassed at hanging back holding the camels while the women scouted ahead for the enemy. What a strange and unconventional scene this was!

As Lilly drew closer, Corporal Smith could discern the tense look on her face, which spoke volumes. There was trouble ahead.

She came up and reported to him like one of his soldiers would have done.

"It looks like the soldiers have abandoned the area and moved off north. A rather large tribe of Mahdists have overrun and occupied the fort, but many of them have just left in pursuit of the soldiers. Only a few have been left behind."

Corporal Smith was trying to decide what their next move should be. He knew for a certainty they wouldn't be able to do anything at all unless they could sneak into the camp to refill their canteens first. Only then might they try to catch up to his unit.

It took a little persuasive arguing on her part before Lilly convinced the soldiers to agree for her and Bala to be incorporated in their quickly formulated plan. They would necessarily leave Corporal Smith behind since he was wounded. The three of them would gain access to the well, and with a little luck and some cunning, they would hopefully remain undetected. Once they had their water and maybe even some food, they would meet back up at the dune.

When Private Bey conceded to the plan, Corporal Smith finally relented somewhat reluctantly. He knew by now that Bala had the skills necessary for such an undertaking, and Private Bey was also trained in this area. But his main concern was for the English girl. Did she have what it took to carry out something so dangerous? It would be his hide if anything happened to her, but with his leg injury putting him out of commission, they had to use the only three able-bodied people they had available.

And so the corporal had given in, but with one strongly stated stipulation. If they were discovered, the two girls, with no argument or hesitation, were to run away while Private Bey covered their retreat. With a large force of tribesmen still so nearby, they necessarily had to avoid the noise of shooting at all costs. Lilly consented to these terms, fully intending to comply with his wishes.

Fortunately, the few warriors left behind as guards were more interested in looting than in maintaining any form of discipline. They were clearly not worried about anyone taking them by surprise, and they laughed at the thought of the soldiers running away like frightened children.

Lilly marveled at the skill in which Bala guided them through blind spots and hollows in the terrain that served to hide them from view. All those times she had gazed out over these walls, she would have never imagined there were so many places where people could have been laying out here watching them without her even knowing. Now here *they* were, peeping over the wall on the outside looking in. No one was in sight.

Bala understood what they were there for, and she knew where to find it. She had made the trip to the well many times in the past. Slithering along the length of the wall to find just the right spot, she took one last peek before disappearing over an unfinished section closest to the well. Lilly quickly followed suit with Bey close behind, covering her back. Staying low to the ground, the three of them made it with still no sign of anyone around.

Bala carefully lowered the bucket to draw the first of the water. Hand over hand, she pulled the bucket back up again. The sinking sun was casting shadows around them, and working quickly, she poured the contents into the canteen held in Lilly's shaking hands. Three times she lowered and raised the bucket. Just one more time, and they would be done.

Just when they were beginning to think they were successful, a native emerged from one of the tents and started walking in their direction with his arms full of loot. He was so focused on not dropping any of his stolen items that he almost passed right by them. When he glanced up, he did a double take of surprise, and dropping everything, he immediately started shouting to alert the others. Bey sprang up and silenced the warrior with a single thrust of his bayonet, but unfortunately, it was too late. The dying man had already sounded the alarm.

Two more natives came running. One was armed with a sword, and the other with a spear. Bey moved forward to engage them, but his first thought was to protect the women. "Run!" he yelled.

Lilly automatically grabbed a couple of canteens and called for Bala to run. Bala grabbed the remaining containers, and they both started back over the wall.

A warrior was coming up on their flank brandishing his sword, but he hesitated while trying to decide whether to help his friends, or give chase and try to cut off the women's retreat. The longer he took to make up his mind increased the chances they would get away. He decided to stay back to help just in case there were other soldiers about.

When it became clear they weren't being pursued, Lilly slowed down, looked back, and then stopped completely. Bala slowed her pace, looking back to see what the problem was. They had a good chance to make it now, so why was she stopping?

The third native was advancing on Private Bey as he fought furiously against the other two. Lilly knew he wouldn't stand a chance against three of them, and she couldn't abandon him to a certain death. He had come to rescue her when she had been captured, and though the thought of being taken again terrified her, she owed him her life. She dropped the canteens and headed back with her rifle, bayonet leveled.

Bala felt no such loyalty for the soldier and would never have given a thought to helping him, but after all they had been through together, she would never hesitate to help Lilly. Without even taking the time to make a conscious decision, she followed her into battle.

"Hey, you!" Lilly yelled, hoping to take the third man's attention away from Bey. Much of her bravado instantly evaporated when the fierce warrior turned to face her. He raised his sword and came charging at her with a look of amusement at being challenged by a woman. Amused he might be, but he was a seasoned fighter and suffered no misgivings about killing a woman.

Her finger automatically curled around the trigger, but even though her rifle was loaded, she forced herself to remember that this was only to be used as a last resort. The report of a gun would only bring enemy reinforcements down upon them. Releasing the trigger, Lilly braced herself to receive the attack armed with only the very basics of bayonet usage. "Parry and thrust. Parry and thrust," she kept repeating to herself. Unsure of what to expect, she raised the bayonet-tipped firearm menacingly as she tried to block the blow of the heavy sword.

She was not prepared for the force of the impact, which vibrated through the length of the barrel, up through her hands and into her arms, nearly tearing the weapon from her tight grasp. She staggered back, somehow managing to hang onto the gun with her right hand, dragging the tip of the bayonet in the dust.

As he raised his arm to strike again, Bala flew past, smashing her blade downward with a savage scream. He easily parried the unexpected blow, but the sheer force of it briefly checked his advance. When he countered with a sweeping slash of his own, Bala was able to nimbly avoid being hit. Regaining control of the rifle, Lilly moved in again. Even with the warrior now between them, she didn't really think they had a chance. She only hoped they could keep this one occupied until Bey was free to take him on himself.

The humiliation of facing off against two women filled the arrogant warrior with rage. The fact that he had not cut them down on the first attempt was an embarrassment. He swelled with confidence and determination. He would chop these infidels into pieces and feed them to the dogs! He then realized that the white woman was the captive who had been taken the day before. How had she managed to escape? This time, he would make sure she didn't get away.

He knocked the bayonet aside with a vicious swipe, almost forcing the weapon out of Lilly's hands again. He then turned sharply and slashed at the dark-skinned girl who dared to oppose him using a sword of his own people. He would hack this insolent thief to death! One, two, three strikes on her sword in quick succession managed to drive her back several feet. Bala was becoming fatigued, and her arms were trembling from the effort of blocking the solid blows. Suddenly, the expression on her attacker's face altered as he felt a hot burning pain in his lower back. He turned as Lilly pulled her bayonet free of skin and muscle. The warrior screamed at her, enraged as he saw his own blood dripping from the blade.

He raised his sword for a strike, but that distraction was all Bala needed. Once again, he had misjudged this one's speed and strength. With one downward swipe, she severed his sword hand at the wrist. He grabbed his arm and stared in disbelief at the amputated hand lying at his feet still futilely clutching the sword hilt.

Determined to put an end to him once and for all, Lilly gave one final lunge with the bayonet. A guttural grunt escaped his lips as he tried to pull free of the penetrating blade. With a bit of savagery, which had replaced her fear, she gave the rifle a violent twist, opening a still larger hole in his ravaged gut. He screamed in agony and dropped. Before he even hit the ground, they had turned to help Private Bey who, thankfully, was still holding his own with the other two.

Seeing their fierce companion fall so quickly under the blades of these young women unnerved the two natives who only a few moments before felt they held the advantage. The one with the sword maneuvered around in order to engage the women who were closing in on them. Private Bey had been feeling overwhelmed and hopeless when fighting two, but now with only one opponent to worry about, he felt a rush of hope and a renewed strength surged through him. He parried a spear thrust and with surprising speed, stepped forward and countered with the upward swing of his rifle butt, catching the warrior under the chin and snapping his head back. The blow itself was enough to incapacitate his foe, but the bayonet Bey rammed into his chest finished him off.

With the odds now turned against him, the last warrior tried to escape only to be cut down by three blades stabbing and slashing in rapid succession.

With the battle over, the three weary victors sank down against the wall to rest. In the short time she had been in Egypt, Lilly had learned more about the world around her than she ever had during her whole life up to this point. She had matured in ways she could have never imagined. Like a finely crafted Spanish blade, she had been thrust into the fiery furnace of adversity until her whole being was wracked red hot in fear and anguish, and then was quickly quenched in the cool water of victory, which had hardened her like tempered steel, and toughened her character without blemishing the outer beauty thereof. Lilly never lost her angelic countenance or her love for her fellow man, but she could become a hardened force to be reckoned with in order to shield those of whom she chose to protect.

When they were satisfied there was no one left in the encampment, they brought Corporal Smith and the camels in. In the waning light, they gathered what provisions they could find to help them along their way. It was becoming evident that they were in the middle of an uprising and would have to fend for themselves as they tried to escape the war zone. Private Bey was elated to find plenty of grain and bread. As hungry as they all were, they uncomplainingly ate their fill of the unappetizing food. Now that they had provisions and water, they decided it would be best to leave immediately. With some luck and cunning, they might be able to avoid running into any other Mahdists.

As Lilly tied the sack of grain to one of the camels, she remembered the story of her friend and his devilish camel. "If only you were here now, my dear sergeant major."

She longed for the security she once felt among her friends of the 10th. A wave of sadness hit her, and she laid her head against the side of the animal, fighting the urge to just break down and cry. Clenching her teeth and taking a deep breath, she exhaled loudly. Consciously pushing the feelings of weakness away, she finished tying the last knot and determined she would *not* feel sorry for herself!

It was growing late, which meant they needed to leave soon. The men they had killed had obviously been left behind as guards until the others could return. And with an abundant water supply and the large store of grain, they definitely would be returning. Lilly was hoping her father and Richard had somehow managed to reach safety, or that they had been rescued by English troops. She had to believe her father was waiting for her somewhere. Perhaps he was just as worried about her as she was about him. This was the only hope she had left.

They were all so tired and sore, a rest was badly needed, but they would be taking a terrible risk to stay where they were any longer. The decision was made to get as far away from the fort as possible before stopping to spend the remainder of the night. It would be too dangerous to travel the whole night through, with the risk of inadvertently meeting the enemy in the dark.

Lilly walked over to where Corporal Smith sat, leaning against a pile of bricks. He looked pale, and sweat was beaded on his upper lip. "It's time we got on our way corporal," she said. When she didn't receive a response, she nudged his shoulder, saying, "Corporal Smith?" He continued staring straight ahead without seeming to even notice her presence. She crouched directly in front of him, shaking his shoulder, and she shouted his name again.

Finally, he muttered something that sounded like, "Pretty," before he slipped back into his dreamlike state.

Lilly stared at him in disbelief. What was wrong with him? Was he delirious from his injury?

Private Bey came over to ask what was going on, but when he opened his mouth, all that came out was, "I think I'm going to be sick!" As Lilly stood gaping at him in open mouthed surprise, he turned and ran off with one hand clenched to his stomach and the other held tightly over his mouth.

Bala wandered over to see what all the commotion was about, and she too stared as Bey raced past her, and she turned to Lilly with a furrowed brow. She glanced down at the catatonic corporal and grew even more bewildered. These white people were certainly acting strangely. *As strange as a band of drunken monkeys*, she thought with amusement.

Monkeys—she could picture them as such. Lilly would surely make a fine little monkey, running around getting into mischief, chattering, and ordering all the other monkeys about. Her father would be the great silver backed gorilla, sitting proudly with his arms folded across his great chest, very quiet and regal, with a piece of fruit grasped between his toes. And that other one, Richard, she could picture as a baboon, thinking himself all high and mighty and wise. He flashes his teeth threateningly, but when there is real danger about, all you will see of him is his big red behind! And then there is Charles, like a curious little chimp forever trying to figure things out. And all the while what he really wanted to be doing was showing his affection for the Lilly monkey by picking bugs off of her and eating them, but he was too afraid of raising the wrath of her mighty father.

A silly grin spread over Bala's face.

"What is so funny, Bala? Do you think our situation is funny? I have never seen you grin like that before." Then she remembered something she had once read and said, "I have often seen a Bala without a grin, but never a grin without a Bala." With that, she started to laugh at her own wit as she compared Bala to the Cheshire cat in *Alice's Adventures in Wonderland*.

"No, I take that back! I have too seen a grin without a Bala! That night you came to rescue me. The way your dark skin made you blend into the night and all I could see of you was your white teeth." She laughed harder, picturing a big white smile floating around the enemy campsite, scaring those brave, ferocious warriors to death.

Bala started laughing along with Lilly, when suddenly, she unexpectedly leaned forward and vomited on the ground. She looked up into Lilly's surprised face, and wiping her mouth with the back of her hand, she continued laughing as though nothing had happened. Every once in a while, Bala would hold her stomach and groan in pain, which only made them both laugh all the harder.

Lilly realized she was starting to feel dizzy, and a stabbing pain shot through her eyes. She sat on the ground and squeezed her eyes closed, and when she opened them again, Bala was wandering away still holding her middle and giggling to herself. She then remembered Corporal Smith, but he was no longer sitting nearby. Where could he have gone to all on his own with an injured leg? He *had* been there, hadn't he? Or had she just imagined it all? Her brain was foggy, and she felt confused. She was all alone now. Where had everybody gone?

28

Sir Billingsley hadn't walked very far before he began feeling extremely weak. Strangely enough, he couldn't even feel the burning heat of the scorching sun. The strength that had surged through him so strongly only a short time before had now left him like air escaping from a pricked balloon. Feeling drained and exhausted, he only wanted to lie down and sleep. Dropping to his knees, he fell forward and laid his head on the burning sand, but he could feel no heat from the sand on his skin. Closing his eyes, he imagined himself to be back at home in his own comfortable bed. He burrowed his hands into the sand as he would have caressed the silky, sweet smelling sheets. As he lay there thinking of home, he slowly drifted away until he completely blacked out. He probably would have stayed so until the life had drained out of him, had not the shepherd come along and discovered him.

It's hard to say whether providence was smiling upon Sir Billingsley, or if it was pulling a cruel joke. It may have been kinder had he never been found and had simply been allowed to die peacefully in his sleep. But this particular shepherd was sympathetic to his plight, for this shepherd was a leper who was used to being shunned by his society. When he found the half dead old man, he felt compassion for him when he saw the ghastly physical condition he was in. Sir Billingsley had grayish white patches on his skin, and there were unsightly red bumps and oozing brown pustules covering his body and deforming his face. Facial paralysis was evident on one side from the downward pull of skin and muscle, which distorted the symmetry of his features, and much of his hair had fallen out, leaving small tufts of gray amid the bald patches.

The only way the leper knew there was still life in this disfigured body was by the rise and fall of the unconscious man's chest. Looking him over, he could see that his hands were misshapen, the left one having a claw-like appearance, and there was seepage of blood coming from his travel worn boots. Regardless of this man's origins, his background or beliefs, the shepherd viewed him as a kindred spirit, for this unfortunate appeared to be suffering from the advanced stages of leprosy. And this was the worst and most horrific case he had ever seen.

The leper somehow found the strength to get the stranger back to his hut, which mercifully, was nearby. Sir Billingsley had lost so much weight that this wasn't difficult to accomplish. In the late stages of leprosy, there wasn't much that could be done, but the shepherd knew it was just a matter of time before *he* might be the one needing the mercy of a stranger, and so he felt duty bound to try to help. Lepers shared a bond that was thicker than blood or religion. Shunned by society throughout the ages, these stricken outcasts learned to live together and care for themselves as best they could, mainly because no one else would.

He himself was a young man in the prime of his life when he was stricken. Being gifted with intelligence and from a well-to-do family, he had pursued his dream of becoming a doctor in earnest before he was devastated by that dream-crushing diagnosis. Overnight, he went from a physician to a herder of sheep, a wandering nomad without home or family. This was the only means of living left to him where he could be kept separated from others who were deathly afraid of catching his disease. In the course of his wanderings over the years, he had observed his own body slowly deteriorating, rotting away as his disorder advanced in its normal progression, an agonizingly slow process that sometimes took over a decade.

Cast off from their family and friends, lepers were forced to form their own communities in an attempt to have a somewhat normal existence. No one really knew what caused this disease. Many believed it was contagious, though how it was spread was a mystery to all. This particular illness was unpredictable in that no one seemed to suffer to the same degree. But some individuals were hit hard with the telltale ulcers and sores covering their skin, while others had symptoms that progressed much more slowly. Because of the panic and paranoia of the people, many other ailments were simply lumped under the same name just to be safe. The former doctor had seen many outcasts like himself over the years, and had even treated some, but what he saw here unnerved even him.

To be truthful, his first reaction on seeing the gruesome appearance of the stranger was revulsion, but he had seen and experienced firsthand, lepers being beaten and ostracized by others who were afraid of them and their affliction.

Like it or not, he would care for this man as best he could. Considering the advanced state of the disease, this poor soul must have been suffering for decades, and it looked as though he was mercifully near the end.

In the fading light, he tore a clean tunic into strips and began wrapping these bandages around the man's rotting flesh. He would have been extremely shocked to know that this disease had originated from a neck wound only the day before. Even in the short time since he had been discovered, the disease had progressed from the bumps, which ulcerated and oozed fluids, to the bluish lumps that fissured and cracked. He could almost see the poor soul's face being ravaged before his very eyes as new nodules formed as though they were being infused with blood with every beat of his heart. Something that should have taken years to reach this advanced stage was bubbling up through this man's skin like a boiling pot. What began as a simple wrapping to cover his sores, turned into almost an entire head covering. Care was taken to leave the eyes and mouth exposed as he would need to see and breathe.

The former doctor was unaware that what he was witnessing was no ordinary case of leprosy but was caused by a most virulent strain of mycobacterium that had lain dormant for centuries. Sir Billingsley was actually infected with a host of microorganisms transmitted through the poultice Richard had packed into his open wound, which allowed the mummy's diseased contamination to wreak havoc throughout his body. There was no hope of a normal immune system being able to successfully fight off this invasion. Even before its deep slumber, the microorganisms had mutated, in no small part thanks to that vindictive Nubian witch, and were preserved under the hot dry sands of the desert much like the professor's Egyptian seeds. Using the dead body of the general as a scientist would a Petri dish, she had unknowingly cultivated a new form of disease that would have stumped men of science well into the twenty-first century. Now that it was unleashed on a human host, its morphology was synthesized into yet a new form due to the fungus-produced chemicals generated from the contaminated grain, which was still in Sir Billingsley's system. Mercifully, the disease attacked the nervous system in a way that would have been incomprehensible to the shepherd. Nerve damage had deadened any normal sensations of being able to feel hot, cold, or even pain. Sir Billingsley's immune system had shut down. Nothing more could be done aside from covering his exposed skin to protect him from the insects and the blowing sand.

From the looks of the unconscious man and his tattered clothing, it was apparent that he was a foreigner. The clothes appeared to be British, so the shepherd decided to take him to the place where he knew soldiers were building a fort. He had heard there were British officers there. Hopefully, he could leave him in their care. But how had an Englishman in this condition ended up here in the middle of the desert to begin with? Had they turned him out because of his disease? It didn't make any sense. He must have had this illness for a very long time. He knew this man would definitely die out here by himself, so he needed to be looked after by, and even die among his own kind. But that is *if* they would even take him.

He would let the poor old man rest for the night before he tried to awaken and move him.

It seemed like only a few minutes, when actually a couple of hours had passed where Lilly had sat alone before she went in search of the others. She discovered the two soldiers sound asleep in one of the tents. Perhaps Private Bey had helped the corporal there, and Lilly hadn't imagined her confrontation with him after all. She found Bala sitting in front of a campfire deep in thought, staring raptly into the fire. Sitting down beside her, Lilly also became entranced by the beautiful colored flames. She wondered what Bala was thinking about so intently.

In fact, Bala previously had many thoughts racing through her head, but at the moment, she was in a trancelike state where her spiritual being had separated from her physical body. She had been thinking about the young men of her village who believed they were superior to her and all women in general. The men spent their whole young lives training and mentally preparing to become hunters and warriors. They were puffed with pride when telling the stories of their first experiences at fighting even though for her tribe this was usually limited to small scale cattle raids where a victory was often decided by insignificant conflicts. Rarely were there any casualties. Why, she had already been involved in more fighting than most of them probably ever would!

Twice already, she had been locked in combat to the death, and both times she had emerged victorious. If anybody was entitled to the esteemed title of warrior, it was her!

She had also thought derisively about how proud and smug they were when receiving their first markings and scarifications commemorating their success in battle. Some of these skin markings were awarded for acts of bravery, and some were given simply because a boy had become a man. *Did they think having their skin pricked and scarred was such a brave undertaking? Let them try giving birth*, she had thought with satisfaction, *then we would see who was braver, man or woman.*

As the fire started to die down, Bala began to chant in a monotone voice. Lilly wasn't able to understand the words, but between staring at the fire and listening to Bala's voice, she began to fall into a trance of her own, similar to experiences she had with Charles in the past. After a while, Lilly even joined with Bala, chanting in unison as the same series of words was repeated over and over again. The chanting reached a crescendo as the native girl wrapped a rag around her hand and reaching into the fire, pulled out a large metal three-tined meat fork. Its prongs glowed red with the heat and as Lilly watched, Bala exposed the skin above her left breast. Before Lilly's disbelieving eyes, Bala pressed the hot glowing prongs into her tender skin. Lilly could hear the sizzle of burning flesh and smell the acrid odor of the smoke. Bala grimaced in pain, but no sound escaped her lips. Lilly scooted over to her friend and cradled her in her arms, wondering why she had done such a foolish thing.

Bala could see Lilly's concern, but she looked down at her angry blisters with pride. She laid her hand over the three blistering marks, which resembled the horizontal scratch of a tiger's claws, and then placed her hand above Lilly's left breast. Lilly then remembered reading about these types of rituals among the native tribes. Different tribes had different methods and different markings, but they were bestowed as a rite of passage and were a great source of vanity and superiority for the bearers.

If these markings were some sign of recognition and meant so much to Bala, then maybe Lilly should honor her by doing the same. They had been through so much together, and she had grown to trust Bala like she had never trusted anyone else in her life, except her own father.

Bala admired her burn again and said something to Lilly in her native tongue. Staring into Bala's eyes, Lilly pulled back the left side of her shirt exposing the bare skin over her own heart. When Bala didn't respond right away, Lilly pointed to Bala's mark and then indicated the same spot on her own chest. Bala could see Lilly was serious, so she placed the fork back amongst the hot coals.

As the tines began to glow, Lilly stared at them and began to chant as she had earlier. When fear began to rise inside of her, she shifted her gaze away from the red hot fork, to focus on the flames. Blocking everything from her mind, she closed her eyes and repeated the incomprehensible words louder and faster. She was vaguely aware that Bala had taken up the chant too.

Searing pain brought her abruptly back to reality. Lilly gasped and flinched slightly, determined not to pull away, but Bala was already finished. Somehow her mind had blocked out the initial pain. Lilly looked down at her three blisters and then back at Bala's. The two matched perfectly. Now that it was all over, she was glad she had done it, for it seemed to have made quite the impression on her companion. Facing each other, Bala laid her cupped right hand reverently over Lilly's fresh wound, and Lilly, mimicking the gesture, cupped her right hand over Bala's twin marking. A strong wave of love and unity surged through them both as they saw their own reflections in each other's eyes as though they had entered the body and soul of the other. They knew this was an important turning point in their relationship, binding them together forever.

29

The soldiers within the thorny circle of the zareba were up before sunrise. Except for the expected enemy scouts prowling the perimeter in search of a breach in their hastily constructed barrier, it had been a fairly quiet night. Had the soldiers not taken this precaution, they most likely would have been attacked in the dark; but by erecting this primitive obstruction, they had made it clear to the hostile natives that they were aware of their presence and wouldn't be caught off guard. For this reason, the Mahdists thought it wiser to wait for additional members of their tribe who were already en route to join them. Hopefully with the coming of the morning light, they would have the manpower necessary to annihilate the hated Egyptians.

At dawn, the men filed out of their protective enclosure. As they marched away, Lieutenant Prescott noticed many of them looking longingly back at the perceived safety of the thorn ringed encampment. He seriously wondered if they had the courage to rise to the occasion in the event of an attack, or if the Mahdists would gain yet another victory over them.

Almost immediately, the skirmishers were exchanging shots with those of the enemy who had firearms. Fortunately, the natives lacked the training that the soldiers had all received and their accuracy left much to be desired due to the native's cutting down and shortening their rifle barrels. But even so, there were still casualties on both sides due to the short distance between the two. Gradually, fresh Egyptian skirmishers began having to replace the wounded who were helped back to the main column.

Soon it became apparent that the soldiers at the front of the lines were gradually quickening their pace. This was causing a separation in the previously tight ranks, which encouraged the Mahdists to become even bolder. They moved in closer, and the ones who were armed began exchanging shots with the soldiers at the rear.

As always, the orders were for no man to be left behind. However, in the heat of battle, even though there are admirable individuals who rise to the occasion by performing feats of great heroism, there are always others who disgrace themselves and their uniform by their acts of cowardice. It was in such an instance as the latter, that a wounded man was abandoned by his comrades and taken alive by the enemy.

The Mahdist leader sent some of his men ahead in hopes of cutting off the soldiers and boxing them in. Whether they were attempting to join up with other soldiers, or simply fleeing from the frontier, by heading them off he could force them to stand and fight, thus destroying them to a man once and for all. These puling Egyptians were no match for his warriors!

Captain Lewis traversed the length of the column, encouraging his men with his commands as well as reassuring them with his presence. The racial and cultural superiority that he and other British officers presented to their troops could either work to their benefit or backfire on them. In this case, at least for the moment, it seemed to be working *for* him. Fearing for their lives, they looked to him as their only hope for their salvation.

Fortunately, the soldiers were better shots; and the number of rifles in the hands of the natives was limited, as was the ammunition available to them. Most of them were being driven off or killed by the soldiers.

A runner sought out the captain informing him about a large group of Mahdists who were seen advancing around on their left and right flanks, most likely with the intention of cutting them off to force a confrontation and to keep them from reaching any potential reinforcements. The nervous troops were looking worried and began picking up their pace again, which spread the soldiers out even more. The captain knew he had to retain order and keep everyone in formation or his men might panic and start to run. That would be disastrous and would seal the fate of every last one of them.

"Halt the men, and have them form square!" the captain bellowed. This was their last hope. If this didn't work, then they were all done for, but he couldn't let his hopelessness show. His men were looking to him, and he would not let them down. If they were doomed, then so be it. They would not go down without a fight! It was up to him, their leader, to instill confidence, and that is what he meant to do.

"Yes, sir! Form square it is, sir!" With that, the officers started yelling orders to the uneasy men around them. *This was it!*

With everyone rushing around attempting to make order out of the confusion, the professor, Charles, and Mr. Brown were feeling out of sorts and apprehensive themselves. The soldiers had been looking more fearful with every step they took, and now they were stopping? What hope did they have if they didn't press on? Both Charles and the professor still had their pistols even though they had never expected to have to use them. Charles prayed they all made it out of this alive and in one piece. He couldn't bear to think that something could happen to his uncle.

As the troops began to form their square, a huge flaw in the captain's order was revealed. Due to the number of casualties, and the nonmilitary camp followers, Lieutenant Miles realized there were not enough soldiers to form a proper square! Under normal, ideal conditions, each of the four sides would be composed of three or four rows of men with the first one or two rows kneeling and the others standing behind them. Those kneeling would either participate in volley fire or hold their rifles in such a way as to present the tips of their bayonets to the enemy. All the while, the rows standing behind them would continue firing over their heads.

As the men also began to realize there were not enough of them, disorder began to reign. Some tried to form two rows, while others formed a single line but were unsure as to whether they should kneel or stand. Fear showed on their faces, for they knew they were about to die.

When Captain Lewis saw what was happening, he knew he had to act fast before he lost control of the situation. It would be disastrous if the enemy were to see their predicament and attack while the soldiers were still forming up.

"Lieutenants!" he shouted.

They responded immediately, for they were both concerned about what could be done to maintain order. "Yes, sir!" they answered in unison.

"Have the men form square a single rank deep. Any additional men are to assemble in the center along with the civilians and the wounded."

"Yes, sir," they answered, with less enthusiasm than a few seconds before. This was clearly not the solution they were hoping for, but whether they trusted his judgment or not, it was their duty to obey.

When all the men had formed up, the captain gave them a quick pep talk in an attempt to raise their spirits and instill confidence. When this did little to inspire them, he decided it might be more effective if he were to use himself as an example for them to follow. Knowing all eyes were fixed on him, he surveyed the ground over which the enemy horde would shortly swarm. With forced calm, he passed through the edge of the square and began to walk the outside perimeter as he inspected his deployed men. Every so often, he would stop and calmly tell or show someone to, "hold your weapon as such," or "spread the ranks," or some other little bit of military know-how he seemed to have in abundance, and that would shortly come in handy. He pointedly ignored the occasional stray bullet, one of which he heard buzz past his head. Even when the soldier directly in front of him was struck by one of those bullets, he fought to keep his cool and carried on with his inspection.

This informal perusal of his troops under the nose of the enemy served its intended purpose. He could see respect and determination replacing the apprehension as he passed before them. He successfully made it around the entire outside of the square, and reaching his starting point, he gave another quick speech with the interpreters echoing his every word.

"About fifty years ago, a war was fought to the north in a land called the Crimea. The 93rd Sutherland Highlanders found themselves in a predicament much like this one that you now face. They were all that stood between a charging mass of enemy cavalry and their defenseless fellow soldiers to the rear. Only, in that instance, it was not feasible for them to form square, for the enemy would simply have ridden around them and butchered all of those behind. And so their commander spread them out in a long line two men deep. He then told them, 'There is no retreat from here, men. You must die where you stand.' *You must die where you stand!* Those are powerful words. Yet those courageous soldiers stood their ground, and some did die, but although some of them were doubtful, they successfully repelled the enemy. Watching from a hilltop, a journalist witnessed their bravery. Looking down on that scene, he saw stretched out across the valley floor, the thin red line that was the Highlanders in their red jackets. He witnessed the waves of Russian cavalry crashing mercilessly into them as they tried in vain to break through. Forever after, this stand was referred to as The Thin Red Line. Well, men, I ask no less of you. Are you ready to show these savages how brave an Egyptian soldier can be? Are you ready to die heroically where you stand in order to protect your brothers? Will you be *my* Thin Red Line?"

When the voices of the interpreters died down, Captain Lewis added, "Those fearless soldiers of The Thin Red Line were armed with muzzle loading single shot muskets. The rifles you men carry are equipped with ten round magazines. Your single rank has more firepower than four ranks armed with muskets! Stand your ground, and we will be victorious!" He then raised his pistol above his head, and yelled, "Men, prepare to engage!"

"Hurrah!" The cheers came from all sides. Captain Lewis was inwardly ecstatic and relieved. He really hadn't known whether his efforts would make a difference in the morale of his men, but thankfully their cheers told him more than words. These soldiers would give it their all and were now mentally ready for battle.

They didn't have long to wait. With a hair-raising war cry, the Mahdist warriors charged from all sides at once, like a great wave bent on crashing into and washing away the flimsy human barrier. The thin line of infantry, disconcerted by the aggressive attack, visibly wavered as the deafening war cries split the air. The officers started barking orders that were relayed from the captain. *Let them listen, and focus on that!* the captain thought to himself. Even *he* was rattled by the din of the combined voices of the horde as they surged closer at a run.

"On my command, one shot only!" the captain bellowed.

"Fire!"

The first volley rolled forth from all four sides of the human square, cutting down many of the charging natives who only moments earlier believed they were invincible. The devastating effect their first round of fire had on the enemy instilled hope in the soldiers, and the men quickly chambered a fresh round.

"Ready…fire!"

There was a thunderous roar from the second volley as more of the warriors were mowed down, but still they came on. And so it went, volley after volley, with lead smashing into solid flesh, dropping the attackers like cut stalks of wheat. A few of the Mahdists managed to make it as far as the defending lines of soldiers where they were met with the sharp blades of bayonets.

"Rapid fire! Ready!"

"Fire!"

Upon the execution of that command, the near continuous roar of the Lee-Metfords reminded Charles of the sound of the Maxim gun. Oh, if only they had one here now! But the rapid fire had done its job well, stopping many of the aggressive warriors before they could even reach the defensive line.

Whenever a soldier went down, a gap would appear, which the captain immediately filled with the last remaining men of his reserve. When another of his men went down, he realized there were no more able soldiers to take his place; so when the professor and Charles volunteered their services, the captain accepted gratefully.

"God save the Queen!" shouted the professor. "Let's go, Charles. Things are about to get a bit more exciting!" And they raced off, eager to do their part.

As Sergeant Wright saw them run past, thoughts of Lilly flashed through his mind. It was too bad she wasn't here. They could certainly use the extra fire power, and he had no doubt she would put up as good of a fight as any one of his men.

Mr. Brown was quickly schooled in the rudiments of loading a rifle, so he could help the wounded with reloading their weapons. Finally satisfied that the reporter would know what to do, Captain Lewis drew his pistol and decided there was nothing left for him to do now other than join in the fight. He saw a dangerous empty space where three soldiers had fallen, so he charged over to the spot firing his pistol along the way, cutting four warriors down in quick succession. Returning the empty revolver to its holster, he drew his sword and began viciously hacking at any who dared to challenge him.

Up and down the line, the soldiers courageously fought against their enemy using guns, bayonets, and swords. Some of them were successful, but some were injured or killed. Wherever a breach in the defense appeared, someone automatically stepped up to fill the hole without being told.

Finally, the Mahdists began falling back, leaving behind many of their dead and wounded. The Egyptian infantry cheered wildly as the enemy ran away. The captain let his men bask in their moment of glory before issuing new orders. They needed to take advantage of this brief respite to attend to the wounded and replenish ammunition, all while retaining their positions in the formation.

"Well that seems to have gone rather well," the captain said as he came upon the professor and Charles, checking and reloading their weapons. "I'm very grateful to you both for volunteering to help." He noticed blood spattered on them and a minor cut on the professor's arm.

"Don't mention it, my friend. It was actually rather exciting. It appears you had your own little Waterloo today, captain!"

"Ah yes, it would appear that way, wouldn't it?" The thought brought a look of pleasure to his face. What officer in the British Army would not want to duplicate what Lord Wellington did on that field in Belgium? On that day, the crème de la crème of the French Cavalry sealed its fate by charging the British Infantry in square formation, much like what had just happened here.

Charles had questions to ask of the captain but didn't want it to seem like he was doubting his decisions. But then as this was a life and death situation, he decided to bite the bullet, so to speak.

"It seems that as long as we stay in this formation, we have a chance, but we can't hold out indefinitely. There's no telling how many of them are out there. How will we ever make it to the other company? Or will we wait for them to come to us?"

The captain had been asking himself the very same questions and as yet was unable to come up with a viable solution. "Ah, those are very good observations, young man," answered the captain. "I am, of course, currently working on our next move. Never fear."

"It's too bad the men can't just continue to march while they're squared up," said Charles jokingly.

The professor and the captain looked at each other in surprise. "What a clever idea!" the captain exclaimed. "By Jove, I do believe that could work!"

30

Ahmed Mohamed fumed as his men were successfully repelled by the soldiers. And when the defeated warriors returned to him, bringing many wounded fellow tribesmen, he was furious. And now some of his best fighters were acting strangely, and some were falling ill. His force should have been more than strong enough to overrun these soldiers on the first attack but something was wrong. While it was true the soldiers were armed with new rifles, the bravery and fierceness of his warriors should have made them more than a match for these weak Egyptians. He would have to take stock of the situation and plan his next move very carefully.

Two of his men dragged a captured prisoner over to him. With very little persuasion, the terrified captive divulged the intention of his company to meet up with British reinforcements. Ahmed pondered this information thoughtfully. Should he take a chance on losing more men by continuing their attack here, or should they return to finish looting the fort? This was supposed to have been a simple raid, not a full scale war. He was not equipped with enough warriors for an invasion, and he had already lost more than he expected, and now this prisoner says there are British soldiers on the way. Those British fighting men were made of stronger stuff than these Egyptians, yet the Egyptians were the ones who had just successfully fought off his attack. What would happen when the English showed up to strengthen their forces, and he was outmanned?

He summoned Osman Abu Kru. "Take your men, and return to the fort with the prisoner. Gather up the store of grain, replenish water supplies, and head south."

Osman made a grand show of disappointment, but that's all it was—a show. He had no real desire to be the one chosen to stay and continue this fight. The battle was clearly already lost, so he was relieved to retreat with what was left of his men.

The prisoner understood some of what the chief was saying. He fell to his knees and begged them not to take him back to the fort. He frantically told them of the events that had transpired there because of a curse being placed on them all as punishment for the desecration of a grave site. He related how the soldiers suffered strange sickness and endured great hardships while there, but shortly after leaving, their fortunes had begun to change for the better. The prisoner was glad they gave up the fort, and he begged the chieftain to kill him rather than take him back.

Ahmed, being able to understand the Egyptian language, saw true fear in the face of the hysterical, pleading man. It was possible he was lying in order to keep them away from that area, or maybe he really believed in these things he had said. Either way, they were going back. It would be foolish to pass up this prime opportunity to loot an empty fort for goods and supplies. This man would not get his wish of dying on this day. He would go to the fort with the others, and then when the time was right, he would be sold or traded as a slave.

One of his tribesmen alerted Ahmed to some strange activity exhibited by the enemy. Sneaking up to get a better look, Ahmed could hardly believe what he was seeing. The army was moving slowly away, only they were still keeping their lines intact all the way around their giant square. He had hoped to launch repeated small attacks on them as they moved off in their standard formation. Now they would just have to watch them from a distance, and should the opportunity present itself, they would attack. In the meantime, he could make things more difficult for the travelers by having his warriors keep them on edge with sporadic assaults with bullets or spears.

Captain Lewis estimated there was another hour of daylight remaining when he halted his men to prepare camp. Progress had been slow due to the number of wounded, and it was becoming obvious they would not reach help before dark. Thorn bushes were sparse in this section of the desert, so there was concern about their vulnerability to enemy attack. After some thought, he decided to send Lieutenant Prescott on ahead to slip through under cover of darkness and lead the relief unit back to them. The wounded needed to rest, and he thought they would have a better chance of defending themselves if they were not expending so much energy on walking. This time, they would hold their ground until help arrived. Hopefully, they would not have long to wait.

As they were all trying to settle in, Charles pulled the captain aside to speak to him privately. "My uncle and I were wondering what plans you have for fortifying the camp. We noticed there isn't much in the way of brush available in this area."

"This is true," replied the captain. "In cases such as this, we will need to post extra guards and keep more alert as a whole."

"Might I make a suggestion?" inquired Charles, a bit fearful of overstepping his bounds. He didn't want to offend anyone, yet what he had to offer could make a difference in whether they lived through the night or not.

"Certainly," the captain answered a little abruptly, or so Charles thought.

"My uncle and I were discussing this very problem, and I remembered something from studying about the Roman Army. The Roman Army would always carry tools and building materials with them in order to build a fortified camp every time they stopped. This gave me the idea that we could do something similar."

As Charles explained his idea in more detail, the captain began to listen with growing interest. He had been ready to dismiss this inexperienced young man's suggestions and was impatient to get on with making camp, but the more he heard, the more he thought this was actually a good idea.

Using Charles's suggestions, they would make their camp in the manner of an ancient Roman Legion on the march. Studying history certainly had its benefits, the professor noted. Too bad Lilly wasn't here to see this. She would have been proud of Charles as he issued orders and instructions to the soldiers. He hoped with all of his heart that she was safe, and they would all be reunited soon.

All able-bodied men set to work. They began by digging a shallow continuous trench completely around the camp. It was most fortunate they had brought some of the entrenching tools with them instead of leaving them all at the fort. Although it wasn't deep, it was still a ditch. The dirt had been thrown up on the inner side of the hollowed out ground, so there was a small earthen rampart about two feet high for the soldiers to crouch behind. That, along with the depth of the trench meant the defenders, would have a height advantage of about four feet over their attackers. Because the enemy was armed mainly with handheld weapons, this was the perfect plan. Into the trench were thrown whatever bushes, thorn or otherwise, they could find. This increased the effectiveness of the dugout barrier. By nightfall, all had been completed. The digging and chopping had been hard work for the infantry especially after all they had been through that day, but now they could feel more secure and rest easier as they settled down for the long hours until morning. There was nothing left to do but wait.

Throughout the night, the sentries traded intermittent gunshots with the Mahdist skirmishers, but the expected full force attack never came. Unbeknownst to the wary men, Ahmed had given up on the idea of conquering this band of soldiers. He had already lost too many valuable men of his own, and his mission had not been to chase down the enemy, but rather to simply take possession of their encampment and kill or capture all those within. They would withdraw back to the Sudan. Since the Sudan was suffering a great famine, the grain was extremely valuable, and Ahmed would be greeted as a hero. He would have to be content with this.

Just before the sun rose, the remaining warriors slipped away undetected while at the same time, a rather large company of British troops were advancing toward the exhausted, entrenched men. Relief had finally arrived!

This regiment of British regulars, with cavalry and artillery, would succeed in holding the frontier and be part of a force that would begin to mount the general offensive aimed at retaking the Sudan.

31

Sir Billingsley dozed restlessly off and on. It was difficult for him discern when he was dreaming and when he was awake. He could see how sick and frail his poisoned body had become, but in the haze of half sleep, he wasn't really bothered by his physical state. He felt like he was in a sort of limbo. Not fully awake, yet not asleep; not yet dead but not really alive. He knew he lay in a tent but had no recollection of how he had gotten there. It was difficult to focus. His mind flitted from thought to thought like an impatient bee landing on flower after flower but never able to settle on one for long before moving on to the next. He had to find Lilly. Where was she? He couldn't remember when he saw her last. Would she even recognize him when he did find her? His spirit was trapped in this sickly, repulsive shell. He needed to find his true body. It was out there somewhere, but he couldn't remember where he had left it. Sir Billingsley remembered the fort, but try as he might, he could not recall anything after that. He just knew he had to get back to the tomb.

Now what had made him think that? Not the tomb, the fort! He had to get back to the fort! Lilly would be worried about him. He would return to the tomb to regain his strength. He needed to read the instructions on the walls to learn the secret of reclaiming his body.

No, that's not right! What was wrong with his brain!? He didn't seem to be able to control his thoughts. It was the *fort* he had to get back to, not the *tomb*! He struggled to remember why he had to make it to the fort, but the facts were already hazy. He just knew that he would remember everything once he was back in the familiar surroundings of his tomb.

Sir Billingsley awoke, slowly becoming aware of where he was. What strange thoughts and dreams he had! Now that he was fully awake, he tried to make sense out of everything. He raised his hands to the bandages on his face. It felt so strange. Half of his face was numb, as were his fingertips. He tried to speak but was unable to form a coherent word. Then he became aware of the white-robed figure hunched over in the corner tearing cloth into strips.

Hearing noises coming from the heavily bandaged man, the shepherd came over to him, saying something in his native tongue and motioning for him to not get up. Sir Billingsley tried to speak again, but his tongue felt funny, and all that came out was another series of grunts. He wanted to know why his head was wrapped up and why he couldn't breathe through his nose. Where was he and how did he get here? What was wrong with him? He needed answers but could not ask the questions.

His eyes followed the movements of the shepherd through the slits in his bandages. He could see that the stranger had some kind of deformity of the face, and his skin appeared thicker than normal, almost like leather. There was a large growth on his ear, and his nose and upper lip were badly misshapen. One of his eyes had a milky white coating over the iris that he was obviously unable to see through. The other eye was a beautiful golden brown, bright and alert and looked very out of place in that otherwise damaged face. There were sores on his hairless head, and his left hand was wrapped in cloth. Even through the wrappings, you could see that his fingers were bent in an unnatural way.

The shepherd worked steadily, anxious to start on the trek to return this man to his people. He only hoped the Englishman's condition did not get any worse. The disease that had spread at an alarming rate during the day seemed to have slowed down with the setting of the sun. Is it possible, he wondered, that the sun somehow accelerated the progression of the disease? This seemed to be the case here. The unusual rapid advancement of this poor soul's symptoms was beyond the scope of his knowledge. The sooner he got back to his own kind, the better. Let him die with the comfort of knowing he was among his own people.

Using some of the cloth, he wrapped the old man's sore-covered hands. He then had to cut the bloody boots off of his feet with a worn dull knife. Both feet were swollen to twice their normal size, and the pressure of his boots had caused many of the bumpy growths to crack open and bleed. He wrapped them both, using the remainder of the clean bandages. They needed more cloth. The way this disease was progressing, he almost needed to be wrapped completely from head to toe.

All the while he was being cared for, Sir Billingsley just watched with silent detached interest. Where another man might have reacted in panic or fright, he had remained disconnected and quite calm. It was as though he was observing a process that was happening to someone else and didn't involve him at all.

Finally finished with his ministrations, the stranger helped the weakened man hobble to his feet, but just as they were preparing to leave for the fort, three natives appeared. They had very dark skin, and their wild black hair was tied up on top of their heads. They were dressed in the traditional white, decorated with an intricate patchwork of bright colors; and gold earrings, neck chains, and colored head bands richly framed their faces. Their full bellies bulged, which was in stark contrast to other warriors who were lean and muscular. They were armed for battle, but these men were obviously nothing but bandits masquerading as warriors.

The two surprised men were recognized for what they were—lepers! The natives began yelling and jabbing their spears at them in an attempt to drive the diseased men off. Sir Billingsley backed away slowly and clumsily on his wrapped swollen feet, but it was the shepherd who stumbled and fell. They continued to jab at the fallen man, pricking him with their spears just enough to torment and draw blood. Sir Billingsley felt the anger welling up inside of him. If not for this stranger's help, he would still be dying or dead, alone out in the desert with no chance of finding his daughter. Now this good man was being tortured and robbed of his meager belongings, which were probably all he had left in the world. Without these possessions, the poor fellow would surely not be able to survive. He could not just stand here and watch it happen. Something about the colored patches on their white linen robes was tugging at his memory. He had seen this clothing before! He started to shake as his anger turned to a rage so intense; it suddenly exploded in a violence he did not know he was capable of.

Snatching up a long staff that had been dropped in the assault, Sir Billingsley struck one of the attackers across the face with it. The strength and speed of the blow surprised even himself. The impact had whipped the native's head back so violently that it crushed bone and snapped the staff in two. With a quick lunge, he then drove the pointed broken end of the stick deep into the stomach of the largest man. This time, the driving force lifted the bandit off his feet. The third attacker was stunned by such unbelievable feats of strength by someone so frail and sick. Such massive strength was extraordinary, and even surpassed that of most seasoned warriors.

When this last native saw the bloody staff protruding out of his brother's back, he was shocked into action and moved to draw his sword to exact his revenge. The crazed, wrapped figure quickly leapt in front of him, grabbing the wrist of his sword hand. The native had never felt such a strong grip. It felt like his wrist was being crushed, and it caused his hand to go limp on the hilt of his sword. In an instant, he was being knocked senseless as blow after pounding blow was delivered to his face. Finally, the viselike grip was loosened, causing him to stumble and fall. Before he had even hit the ground, his sword was snatched from its sheath, and with one quick slash, his chest was laid open.

The blinding violent rage that taken hold of Sir Billingsley suddenly vanished like a wave that washes up on the beach and just as quickly recedes again. He stood there bewildered, unable to believe what he had just done. In all of his life, he had never learned to fight like that! He dropped the sword distractedly, suddenly forgetting he had been holding on to it.

The fallen shepherd didn't know how to react. His initial fright had turned to a feeling of justice being served, but as he witnessed the strength and brutality of this strange, fragile-looking man, that feeling of fear returned. Although he was thankful the old man had saved his life, he was also alarmed. Where had that massive strength come from all of a sudden? Something was very peculiar here. Whatever was affecting this man was definitely not normal!

As the shepherd nervously started to gather their belongings, Sir Billingsley began to salvage whatever he could from those he had slain. The shepherd quickly glanced in all four directions with his one good eye. He was anxious to leave this scene of bloody carnage before other warriors happened upon them, and now this man was stopping to steal from the dead! He motioned that they must hurry and leave immediately.

Taking what little food, water, and weapons the dead men had carried, Sir Billingsley was finally ready to go. He handed the shepherd a small knife taken from one of the fallen. This was accepted with some trepidation. Hopefully, if they were confronted by other Mahdists, the knife would not be traced to its previous owner.

At the last minute before they left, Sir Billingsley stripped the robe from the least bloody corpse, thinking it would come in handy for bandages; but his companion adamantly shook his head, indicating that he wanted nothing to do with it. He didn't want to be caught with any evidence of what had happened here. Sir Billingsley refused to leave it behind, and since they didn't have time to nonverbally debate the matter, they gave up the disagreement and started walking.

As they neared the fort, the shepherd pointed in the direction for Sir Billingsley to follow and then turned to leave. He had hidden his sheep in a secluded area and was anxious to get back to them before they were discovered and stolen. Sir Billingsley thanked him as best he could by laying his bandaged hand on his savior's shoulder. He wished he could speak the words, but this would have to suffice. Knowing food and water would be available at the fort, he gave the shepherd all that he had.

As he slowly shuffled through the sand, Sir Billingsley labored to breathe through his mouth. He was deteriorating fast, and he now realized that whatever was crippling his body was too far advanced for a cure. All he could hope for now was to find his daughter in order to make sure she was safe before he died.

At the fort, he sensed that something was terribly wrong. The area was eerily quiet and still. Where had everybody gone? As he struggled to make sense of the situation, he suddenly remembered being attacked by natives and Lilly being taken. Had that really happened? If it had, that meant she would not be here waiting for him. And if so, how on earth would he ever be able to find her?

He wandered sluggishly through the camp with a sinking heart. Coming across the three dead natives, he started looking for somewhere safe and secluded where he could rest and decide what to do. There might be more of those natives around, or possibly others could come looking for them. Without any conscious thought of his destination, he found himself standing in front of a barrier of sand, and it came to him that he had reached the site of the tomb. This would be a good place to hide for a while, but why was the entrance covered?

Sir Billingsley started scratching and digging with his bandaged hands until he had managed to make a hole at chest level big enough to climb through. Once inside, he let his eyes become accustomed to what little light there was shining through the opening.

Blood had begun seeping through the wrappings on his damaged hands, so he used the Mahdist tunic to change his own dressings. He tore the cloth into rags and clumsily re-bound his hands and feet. Blood had started seeping from different parts of his body so that he was leaving a trail of red. He couldn't understand what was happening to him. In spite of his body oozing blood, he felt no pain. He ended up using every bit of the material to wrap the worst areas of his arms, legs, and torso.

He suddenly felt extremely weary and defeated. He made his way into the dark recesses of the cave, curled up against the back wall, and fell into a deep dreamless sleep.

32

By the time Lilly finally stirred from her slumber, it was already midmorning. She was still so groggy she had to fight the urge to drift off back to sleep. The camels were restless, and she could hear them stamping their feet and lowing to each other. Her whole body ached, and there was a burning sensation on her upper left chest. She touched the tender spot and was startled to feel the skin was raised under her fingertips. Pulling the neck of her shirt aside, she saw an angry-looking burn above her breast. Now she was fully awake and remembering the night before. Bala! Where was Bala?

The camels started snorting and bawling to each other. Then Lilly heard men speaking, but it took few moments to realize the voices were not that of Smith and Bey. A small rogue band of Arabs had sneaked into the fort and were in the process of stripping it of everything in sight. Had it had not been for the noises made by the camels, she might have still been sleeping, and they may have gotten away with everything.

She jumped up, yelling, "Get! You! Get out of here!" She looked frantically around for her rifle but couldn't remember where she had left it.

The looters started to work faster, and it was clear they didn't seem to think this girl was much of a threat, but when Bala appeared brandishing her sword, they were a little more concerned. Just the way she held the weapon was an indication that she knew how to use it. But this particular group was not interested in fighting. These were cowardly thieves who only survived by cheating and stealing, and they typically avoided physical confrontation whenever possible. They began scattering off into the desert, managing to make off with whatever they were able to carry. One of them was slowed down by his greed, and not willing to drop any of the items that filled his arms, he was intercepted by a fast moving Lilly. Among the things he was carrying were the two soldier's packs, and a rifle. Her rifle! She knew it was hers by the initials, LB, she had scratched into the stock with a penknife.

"Where are you going with that? Give it to me. It's mine!" she yelled menacingly as she grabbed onto the butt of the gun with both hands.

He started to resist her, for he had no intention of giving up such a fine rifle. As they struggled, Bala came charging forward with sword upraised. When he saw her coming, he instantly decided to drop everything and run, but in doing so, Lilly's gun was accidentally discharged with a loud boom! The Arab screamed in fright and ran away as fast as his legs would carry him. Lilly retrieved her firearm and the packs, but the Arabs had already managed to make off with the camels.

She was very upset. After all they had been through, they had now lost their only mode of transportation and most of their supplies. "Well, it looks like we have to change our plans, Bala. If anyone was in hearing range of that gunshot, it won't take them long to get here. We can't stay here any longer."

Bala listened with intelligent eyes. Lilly again wondered how much she could understand, probably much more than she let on.

"I better go look for Private Bey and Corporal Smith. If nothing else, that gunshot should have gotten *their* attention."

Bala followed her to the tent where she had last seen the men. Private Bey lay just outside of it, unconscious, with a bleeding gash to the back of his head. Corporal Smith was still inside asleep, but he was tossing and turning in semi-delirium caused by his festering thigh wound. With some effort, Lilly was able to rouse Bey, but try as she might, Corporal Smith could not be awoken from his slumber. She then explained their present situation to a confused Bey.

Private Bey sheepishly kept repeating that he didn't know what had happened. They had been sleeping when he woke up to noises. He had stepped outside to investigate, and that's the last thing he remembered. He appeared out of sorts and couldn't seem to comprehend what had taken place. Lilly gave him a cloth to hold on his head injury. She had to keep repeating herself to the private as he asked the same questions over and over again. She saw an angry red rash covered his face that he kept scratching at, causing some spots to bleed.

Both of the soldiers looked ill, but Corporal Smith appeared to be in very bad shape. He had lost so much blood that he was extremely weak, and as white as a ghost.

Lilly was trying hard to focus, but she was feeling dizzy and lightheaded. Maybe she just needed to eat something…but then maybe that was the problem! The only thing they had eaten in the last two days was old bread and raw grain. Could it have been spoiled? Was that what was making them all sick and causing their other symptoms and unusual behavior?

"Lilly!" It was Bala calling her name. She ran over to the wall where Bala stood pointing into the distance. She climbed up beside her and shaded her eyes but couldn't at first make out what the native girl was pointing at. When she squinted, she could just make out a dark mass that gradually grew larger and was obviously moving toward them. "What is that, Bala?"

Bala jumped down and motioned for Lilly to do the same. She seemed to be urging Lilly to run. Whatever or whomever was approaching, must be a threat. She trusted Bala's instincts, but where was there to go? The first thought was to run away off into the desert, but there were the others to think about who were unable to escape on their own. It was unconscionable to her to even consider leaving anyone behind.

Bala was pushing at Lilly to get her to hurry, and so she ran back to the tent trying to decide what to do. Confused and scared, all she could think of was that they had to hide. Supporting Corporal Smith between them, the two girls led the way, with a weakened Private Bey following with a backpack and the gun. They ended up at the only place Lilly could think of where they might be safe and possibly remain undiscovered.

When they reached the tomb, she was dismayed to find the entrance had been blocked except for a hole near the top where it looked like someone, or possibly an animal had burrowed it's way in or out.

Turning to Bala, she said, "Bala, help me," and they scrabbled to widen the opening, pushing the sand aside with their hands. Lilly's head was pounding with pain, but she knew she couldn't rest until they were safely inside. With the corporal's arm draped over her shoulder, she told Bala to climb inside and pull. As she and Bey pushed the limp injured man from behind, Bala grabbed his arms and pulled steadily until he finally slid through the hole and landed inside with a dull thud. They then handed the pack and the rifle through before climbing in themselves.

They dragged the corporal's body over to one side. The exertion had them all out of breath, but Private Bey's head wound was causing his whole skull to throb, and he started gasping as though he was unable to get enough air into his lungs, until he finally succumbed to the agonizing pain and fell over unconscious.

Once they were organized, Lilly noticed Bala darting anxious looks around their dim sanctuary. It was only then that she remembered Bala's aversion to being in this place. Come to think of it, the only time Lilly had ever seen her show fear was when they were here. Thinking back to when she first laid eyes on Bala being sold like a piece of furniture, it was defiance rather than fear that had blazed in her eyes. And the night when Bala had crawled into the tent to rescue her, it was determination. Even during the ensuing battle, there was no sign of fear, only anger as she swung her sword against their enemy. For the first time, Lilly was seeing the vulnerable side of this strong woman, but she knew instinctively that it wouldn't do for her to let Bala know she could see this weakness, so she decided to try to distract her from her worries.

Lilly took a drink from the canteen and handed it to her friend. As their eyes adjusted to the dim interior, she exposed her blister and showed it to Bala with an exaggerated proud look on her face. Then for some reason, she remembered the time her father took her to see the Kinetoscope. Stepping up on a footstool, she had peeked through the slot in the top and saw the moving pictures of the strongman, Eugen Sandow, flexing his muscles and performing a feat of strength by breaking a heavy chain wrapped around his chest by merely inflating his lungs and expanding his muscles to their limit. Imitating him now, she curled her arm up and squeezed her fist causing her muscles to harden and grunted through clenched teeth. This got Bala's attention. She then did the same with the other arm. This reminded Bala of the antics performed by the men of her tribe— the way they would strut around and flex their muscles showing off in front of the women and each other. Only, seeing a girl do with her smaller form, what the men do with their large bodies and bulging muscles, was comical.

Lilly brought her fists together in front of her, hunched her shoulders, and flexed her diminutive muscles. She was shaking with the effort, and her face turned red while she grimaced and grunted again. This brought forth a genuine smile from Bala, who then stood up and imitated her friend. This made them both laugh, lightening the mood considerably. They took another drink of water and then sat companionably together to wait for whatever might come next.

After a short while, Bala rose to her feet and started swaying to and fro while softly chanting. Taking her cue from Bala, Lilly did the same. Amazingly, she could feel, first a calmness and then an invigorating rush throughout her body making her feel invincible, like she could take on the world. Regaining her confidence, Bala started pacing with pent up energy, swinging her sword at an imaginary opponent. Following suit, Lilly took up her rifle and jabbed the bayonet at the air.

Private Bey was finally starting to come around but was having a hard time focusing and processing what he was seeing. The two women, one light and one dark, were stamping their feet and quietly murmuring in unison, while brandishing their weapons as they threatened invisible foes. He tried to rise but overcome by vertigo, he eased himself back down and blacked out again.

Lilly and Bala suddenly froze as a lit torch flew in through the cave opening and landed at their feet.

Osman Abu Kru watched as one of his men threw in a burning torch to light the way and then started to worm his way in through the opening. As he was crawling in, the torch was unexpectedly extinguished, and no sooner was the warrior inside when he let out a scream of pain followed by an ominous silence. Osman immediately sent forward two more men, but only one person could fit through the hole at a time. Before the second warrior was even fully inside, they heard a great commotion coming from within. Being as their eyes were not accustomed to the dark recesses and not knowing what lay inside, the two Mahdists were at a disadvantage. Sword slashes and bayonet thrusts were coming at them before they could even get to their feet. Only the second man squirming frantically made it back out. He had only been halfway through the hole when he was cut and stabbed at repeatedly. Mortally wounded, he was able to wiggle his way back out to land at the feet of his angry leader. The injured man screamed of blood-stained she devils, one black and one white, avenging guardians of the tomb.

This babbling was spooking the other warriors who were gathered around the tomb entrance. With one swift chop of his sword, Osman quickly dispatched of the fool before his ranting could have an adverse effect on the rest of the tribe. This was unbelievable! First there was the talk of curses by their prisoner, and now this nonsense! Osman ordered his men to widen the entrance to the cave. Even though they had reservations about this, they knew to disobey would mean certain dishonorable death at the hands of their own leader.

Inside, the women knew that once the entrance was opened, they would be trapped and overpowered. Lilly lifted her rifle and fired at a human form as soon as it appeared in the patch of light. Inside the cave, the report was deafening. The digging warrior clenched his throat and fell over backward. The bullet had passed through his neck and had hit the man behind him in the chest. The natives all stopped digging, shocked into immobility. That sounded like a gunshot, but it was only one shot, and yet it had killed two men!

The women's ears were ringing from the deafening reverberation, and the muzzle flash had temporarily blinded them. As Lilly's eyes tried to readjust to the darkness, she thought she detected a movement. Thinking it was one of the injured soldiers, she strained to get a better look. A form was shuffling slowly out of the darkness. It couldn't be but it was! *It was the mummy!*

She tried to scream, but her voice stuck in her throat, and she stumbled stiffly back, almost paralyzed with terror. She still gripped her rifle, but she could do no more than hold it protectively clutched to her chest. The mummy stopped and gazed at her intently. Then, ever so slowly, he turned his head to look at Bala. She also backed away, too frightened to react.

Out in the safety of the sunshine, and with no clue of what was happening inside, the chief was furious. He had enough of this! That was definitely a gunshot, and spirits did not use firearms. Drawing his pistol, he fired three times blindly through the opening, then he grabbed two more warriors and shoved them roughly through the widened entrance. Drawing his sword, he prepared to follow in after them.

Two of the Mahdist chief's bullets had slammed into the mummy, but the impact didn't seem to faze it in the least. As the girls watched in stunned fascination, the creature began fighting against their attackers. As the first warrior came stumbling through the entrance, he was greeted by a terrifying sight. The cloth-wrapped specter rushed at him, slamming him back against the stone wall with such force, he was stunned senseless. Moving on to the second warrior, the mummy wrenched the sword from his hand and used it to chop and slash at the native until he was unrecognizable as a human being.

Osman entered the tomb with a loud yell, and swinging his sword, he slashed at the monstrous figure's head. The sharply honed blade caught the creature on the face, slicing off some bandages along with part of its cheek. It hadn't even flinched and didn't seem to be affected in any way by the awful wound, which made one side of its face look like raw meat. Fear started to take hold of Osman. This thing was not human! Osman swung his sword blindly at the figure but missed his intended target completely. Before he could strike again, the mummy lunged at him, causing the sword to fly out of his hands.

As the two grappled, other warriors who were entering the tomb stopped, petrified by the bizarre scene unfolding inside. Their leader was in mortal combat with the undead, and they could see the fear on Osman's face. The creature seemed to be infused with super human strength, and everyone was stunned when he was able to pin the much larger, muscular man to the wall with no obvious effort or strain.

Osman's eyes were bulging in his terror. The bloody and disfigured face drew closer so that the chieftain could actually see maggots writhing within the open facial wound, and the putrid smell made him gag and turn his face away. At the instant he twisted his head to the side the mummy took a bite out of his exposed neck. Osman screamed in agony, and holding onto his bleeding neck, he could only watch as with lightening speed the creature recovered the dropped sword and with one mighty swoop, severed the warrior chief's head along with the hand that had been grasping the bloody bite mark.

The first tribesman, who had only been stunned, pushed and struck at the natives who were blocking his only escape. They all scrambled over each other trying to be the first to get outside to safety. Picking up the severed head, the mummy casually tossed it out through the entrance where it rolled to a stop amongst the terrified warriors. To a man, they all turned and ran without looking back.

The frightening blood-soaked monster then turned his attention back to a terrified and shaking Lilly who was huddled against a just as frightened Bala. He started to advance toward her, but noting her fear, he stopped and reached out his hand to her in supplication. After a few attempts at speech, he finally got out the words, "Yi Yi."

Lilly was still unable to move, but Bala hesitantly took a step closer to him, ignoring the other girl's attempt to hold her back. She was staring so intently into the bandaged slits over the eyes that she jumped when the mummy abruptly dropped to his knees and fell face first at their feet. Bala moved closer, knelt down, and gently rolled him over. There was still some life in those eyes—those kind eyes that she remembered looking deeply into once before. Bala turned sadly to Lilly. "Lilly," she said, pointing to the prone figure. "Father."

It took a minute for Lilly to process what Bala was trying to tell her. She sank to her knees at the creature's side. It was then that she knew it was true. This was her father! "Father!" she cried in anguish. He gazed back at her with the light of love shining through his eyes and reaching up a bandaged hand, touched her face gently before the life slowly drained from his body, leaving just the shell of a monstrous creature who was once a much beloved and handsome man. He had saved their lives, but it was too late to save his. Lilly held his lifeless hand to her chest and cried brokenheartedly. She never saw the single tear that slid down Bala's cheek.

This was the scene the soldiers came upon when they found them.

33

The leaderless Mahdists were fleeing the fort when the cavalry arrived. Many had escaped, but some were captured and taken prisoner. A few of those prisoners were showing the effects of having eaten the bad grain. This made Major Geoffrey Bader of the 21st Lancers wonder if it might not be put to good use by somehow delivering it up to the Mahdists in the Sudan.

Professor Buller convinced him that this would cause more problems than it solved. Whatever had caused the contamination was a powerful poison, and should it be spread throughout Egypt, and maybe even Europe, the results would be catastrophic. As the professor explained, there had previously been such outbreaks in the past with great loss of life, therefore, the wisest thing to do would be to burn it. *And this time, he would personally make sure it was destroyed!*

As the grain burned, a small group of mourners stood by with bowed heads and heavy hearts. Although it had pained her to do so, Lilly had taken the advice of the professor to have her father's disease ridden body cremated lest she or anyone else become infected. The thing that finally convinced her to consent to it was when he had reminded her that if she were to fall ill from contact with her father's body, his last acts to save her life would have been in vain. And so, they carefully laid his body upon the pile of grain that would serve as his funeral pyre.

Lilly walked away, unable to watch her father's body burn. Charles followed her to try and comfort her as best he could. She was too delicate, too fragile for all she had been through. "There, there, Lilly. I'm so sorry for the loss of your father. I know how much he meant to you. I just want to let you know that you don't have to worry about who will take care of you now. I am here for you, and I will always be here to look after you from now on."

Lilly thought about those words and was surprised to find they stirred up an anger in her. Just where was he during the crocodile attack when she was forced to kill for the first time? Where was he when she was attacked and taken by the Mahdists? Where was he when she had to fight her way out of the enemy camp? And where was he when she was under attack in the tomb? All those times she was forced to step up and take care of herself. And then at the end of it all, it was her father who had saved her, in spite of his horrible wounds and sickness. He was gone now, but he would always be in her heart. Not as the monster he had become, but as the loving father and the only man she could ever count on. No other man could ever measure up to him, and she would never put her trust in another. Charles meant well, and she didn't doubt his sincerity, but she realized she no longer needed anyone to "look after her."

Lilly looked at Charles, realizing that in some ways, he was still just a boy. He had spoken from the heart, and if he had offended her, it was only through his naive ignorance. Her experiences in this land had forced her to mature quickly, but Charles still saw the world through the eyes of an innocent. No, she couldn't be mad at him. He really did mean well, so she simply looked away without speaking.

Once the fire had burned itself out, the professor found Lilly to let her know it was over with and to have a word with her.

"Lilly, I feel the need to tell you how sorry I am. If it had not been for my planning this expedition to begin with, and then talking everyone into deviating from our original course, this never would have happened. I carry the burden of knowing all of the misfortune that has befallen you is my fault. I sincerely hope someday you can find it in your heart to forgive me. I never meant to harm you or anyone else." He wanted to hug her as a daughter, but unsure of his reception, he held back.

She could see how truly upset he was, and even though the words he spoke were true, Lilly realized that no one could have foreseen things would turn out this way. She knew him to be a good man.

"My dear professor, there is nothing to forgive," she assured him sadly as she stepped closer, taking his hand in hers. "Had it not been for this expedition, I most likely would now be unhappily married to a man who was not right for me. As it is, I got to see the world, and by sharing this adventure with my dear father, it brought us back to a closeness that has been lacking since I became a young woman. For that gift, I can never thank you enough. And as for the change of plans and coming down here to this place, I know you meant well. But had it not been for this diversion from our course, I would never have met Bala, whom has grown to be like a sister to me. So you see, professor, in some ways I will always be grateful for this experience. Although I will never get over the death of my father, I will now always remember him as the true hero he was."

The professor was so grateful for her kind words that tears threatened to spill over onto his cheeks. He heard the sincerity in her voice and felt it in the heartfelt hug she gave him. To him, it was a much-needed symbol of acceptance and forgiveness.

Lilly sat next to Bala amid their small pile of luggage, which consisted mostly of donated garments given up by sympathetic British officers. While the clothing lacked the femininity that Lilly had grown up being accustomed to, she now found them not only comfortable but practical. What good would a prize gown from the House of Worth do her out here? The loose fitting khaki jacket and breeches suited her just fine, thank you. No black veiled satin bonnet of mourning for her. Monsieur Worth could keep that as well!

Her only concession to mourning was to wear her father's ring on a black velvet ribbon around her neck. She felt her deep anguish over her father's death was something personal, and so she would honor him by wearing this symbol of the life he had lived. She would not dwell on his painful and premature death by wearing the traditional black from head to toe. She wanted to remember him as the wonderful man, friend, and father he was, and she could not do that by wearing clothing that every day would remind her of the circumstances and the sadness of his passing.

And so she sat, bravely stoic and dry eyed, in her men's attire. After everything she had been through, she would feel too vulnerable outfitted in a skirt and dainty slippers out here. She would just as soon dress as a man, complete with Sam Brown belt and holster, with a loaded .455 Webley service revolver. Nestled snugly in her belt was her silver dagger, which had been recovered and kindly returned to her. Across her lap lay her Lee-Metford rifle. Government-issue or not, no one had dared try to take it from her.

She glanced at Bala, who, other than being barefoot, was also dressed in khaki. Bala too preferred the clothes of a warrior over that of a woman. She had taken a special fancy to a pair of goggles that had been given to them, and she was wearing them proudly, like a badge of honor, Lilly thought. Bala's captured sword lay across her lap.

340

The two women sat side by side, solemnly watching the troops pass by. What everyone thought of the two women, the professor could only imagine. The soldiers couldn't help but notice them and stories of what these two women had been through, and their heroic deeds had spread through the ranks. Between the two of them, they had probably killed more Mahdists than most of these men ever would. And with each retelling of the tale, the body count grew larger, and the battle scenes bloodier.

The Anglo-Egyptian invasion of the Sudan had begun. Not content with leaving the Sudan a part of the Turkish Empire to be divided up and conquered by one of the other various European powers that were scrambling for the riches of Africa, Her Majesty's government decided it was finally time to rid the region of the Mahdist movement once and for all. And so they marched south with their regiments of Fusiliers, Grenadier Guards, and Highlanders, along with their British-led Egyptian and Sudanese battalions, supported by their Lancers, Maxim batteries, and Royal Horse Artillery. Many battles would be fought and many lives taken, before the Mahdist hold in the Sudan would be severed forever, culminating with the great battle of Omdurman.

Major Geoffrey Bader and his 21st Lancers would be there at that great battle, and would ride to glory in a charge reminiscent of that of Tennyson's Light Brigade at Balaclava in the Crimea. The charge would be witnessed and recorded by a young correspondent by the name of Winston Churchill, who would be reporting it firsthand as he accompanied the charge. He would then have to fight his way out when he himself got cut off and surrounded by Dervish warriors. But that was yet to come.

As for Lilly, Charles, and the professor, each had mixed feelings about their adventure in the land of the pharaohs. Each felt like they had gotten something out of it, both good and bad. By the same token, each was secretly relieved their ordeal was over.

Of all of them, Lilly had gained and lost the most. She had developed a deep bond with Bala, whom she trusted with her life, yet she had forever lost another, which devastated her and broke her heart. The times she and her father had shared on their ill-fated expedition had brought them closer together. Of course, she had always loved him, but only now did she realize the depth of his love and commitment to her. It was a true, totally unselfish, and committed father's unconditional love for his child, no matter what her age. Looking back on all of their times together, she knew she had never been happier, yet the fact that they were only memories, never to be repeated, pained her deeply.

Lilly was also saddened by the disappearance of Richard. Regardless of how he had turned his back on her when it mattered the most, she still begged Captain Lewis to send out a search party to find out what had happened to him. It just wasn't in her to be so callous as to not care about him at all. After all that was said and done, she couldn't condemn him for his moment of weakness.

Captain Lewis did in fact send out a search patrol; however, he really didn't believe there was any hope of finding the man alive. From the little he had seen of Richard, he could tell he wasn't the type to have the wits to be able to survive on his own. He was too used to having others take care of his every need without ever having had to do anything for himself.

By chance, months later, the missing man's signet ring was found on the finger of a captured Mahdist chieftain, but no one could get him to say where he had gotten it, or whether he knew what had happened to the man himself. They never did find any sign of Richard. The only conclusion that could be reached was to assume he had most likely been killed, or had perished in the desert. Word was sent to Sir and Lady Elliot, informing them of their son's disappearance and probable death, and later when the ring was recovered, that had been sent along to them also.

And now Lilly was afraid she was going to lose Bala as well. Although she had grown to love her, Lilly knew at some point she had to let Bala decide for herself what she wanted, and she had to do this soon. Should she take her back home with her to England, or should she leave her here to return to her own home? What would become of her, this intelligent, yet savage girl from the darkest regions of Africa?

Captain Lewis had had his own ulterior motives for sending his men out to search for Richard. They found the mummy right where it had been left at the ambush site, just as the captain had hoped it would be. Unbeknownst to Lilly, this was where the "search" had ended. Since the captain didn't hold out any hope that the missing man could have survived, he didn't have any qualms in making Lilly believe they had done all they could. The mummy was secretly transported to its original tomb for safekeeping until the time when the captain could secure a buyer. There was a demand on the black market for mummies to be used by the medical community. He should receive an excellent price for this one.

34

Bala could tell that Lilly and the others were about to go on a long journey, which would probably take them to whatever far-off land they had come from. But where did that leave her? Was she to continue on her life's journey with Lilly, or would she be left behind to fend for herself? Bala had grown accustomed to simply going where circumstances took her and doing what needed to be done at the time. This, however, was different. A trip was being planned, and for the first time, she didn't know if she was a part of those plans. The native girl longed to have a say in this decision. She had grown close to Lilly, and in a like manner, she felt Lilly shared similar feelings for her. But now that this adventure was over, perhaps there was no place for Bala in the other girl's life any longer.

Lilly, Charles, and the professor gathered together in a deserted public eatery to discuss last-minute details with Mr. Brown. Bala, in her boredom, wandered around unnoticed, when suddenly she saw that Mr. Brown had left his leather bag just inside the doorway. Bala remembered her curiosity at the markings that this man was forever scratching in his little books. At first she thought he might be helping Lilly by offering up prayers for her safety, but he also followed others around doing the same thing. Maybe he was helping them, but then maybe he was up to no good. It did seem that wherever he went, bad things ended up happening. Looking across the room, no one was paying any attention to her, so she casually reached into the bag and pulled out one of the secret books. *She* wouldn't be able to decipher the markings, but Lilly would surely be able to figure out what he had been doing.

Mr. Brown retrieved his belongings and bid farewell to them all, and then with a brief nod to Bala, he took his leave. He would be going on ahead alone. This had indeed been quite an adventure, and he was anxious to get home with his story. What had started out as an interesting article had blossomed into a full blown riveting story. He was sure to receive a bonus and maybe even a promotion with this assignment. The trip back to America would provide him with more than enough time to spice it up even more. He had a good idea of what his publisher wanted, so he had already begun taking notes to "liven it up a bit." As he hurried back to the hotel, he mentally went over some of his ideas. Although he might be "stretching the truth," he wasn't really hurting anyone. It was after all, just a matter of artistic license. For all he knew, the people involved might never even read it. It was a long way from San Francisco to London.

When he reached the lobby, he began rummaging through his bag. He still had some time before his train arrived, so he thought he would make good use of it and work on his story. As he dug through the contents, he stopped short in surprise. The notebook containing his latest notes was missing. Where was it? All of his hard work! He started searching through his pile of luggage, as well as another stack next to his. In his agitation, he was making a mess of things. He forced himself to calm down and think logically. He remembered having the book just before he had stopped to bid farewell to his traveling companions. He smacked himself in the forehead with the heel of his hand. It must have fallen out! He quickly turned and rushed back out the door.

As soon as Mr. Brown had left, Bala motioned for Lilly to follow her.

"What is it, Bala?" Lilly asked as they entered an adjoining room.

Bala waited until she was sure they were alone before she handed the book to her.

"What is this?" Lilly asked with surprise. One could never tell what Bala was up to, but whatever she did, it was always for a good reason. As Lilly perused the random notes, she realized to whom they belonged. "Bala, where did you get this? Did Mr. Brown give this to you?"

She did not answer at first, and Lilly detected a look of guilt on her face. She suspected that Bala knew right from wrong, and as if confirming what she was thinking, Bala lowered her gaze to the floor and slowly shook her head no.

"Oh, Bala! We had better return these to him right away, you naughty girl!"

Lilly was unable to resist flipping quickly through the pages, feeling like quite the naughty girl herself, when something caught her interest. Her brow furrowed in a deep frown as she paused to read more. "I can't believe he would do this! I thought Mr. Brown was our friend," she said as she hurried off to show Charles and the professor.

The two men looked up as she strutted angrily into the room. "You will never guess what our good friend Mr. Brown has been writing about us for his newspaper!"

They both scanned a few pages. Charles was upset about what he read, but the professor didn't seem to be surprised at all. He had dealt with unsavory reporters in the past, and he knew they would do or say just about anything to get a juicy story, even if it meant making parts of it up themselves and twisting the truth.

"That Mr. Brown has not painted a very accurate picture of our characters," she fumed. "And the things he says about my father's illness! Why, that is not anyone's business but mine! And he calls him a...a monster!" She almost choked on the word. "How could he be so insensitive?"

The professor tried to calm her down by saying, "My dear, unfortunately we have to deal with these things when working with reporters. There are some who are honest and up front, and then there are others who are unscrupulous and don't care who is hurt in the process. My advice to you would be to confront the man and find out directly from him which type of reporter he truly is."

"Confronting him is exactly what I intend to do! Come along, Bala, we need to pay Mr. Harry Brown a little visit."

Lilly and Bala had not gone very far before they ran into him coming their way. When he saw them, he was relieved to see his notebook in Lilly's hand; and assuming her mission was to restore his missing property, he held out his hand to receive it. That was when he noticed the angry spark in Lilly's eyes.

She ripped a few pages from the book and waved them under his nose. "Mr. Brown, I demand to know the meaning of this!"

Playing for time, he stated indignantly, "I believe those are mine. Thank you for returning them, but I am in a bit of a rush. I've a train to catch as you know."

What had she read? How much did she know? He desperately searched his memory for what information this particular journal contained.

"How could you have done this to me...to all of us?" she scolded angrily, trying to hold back tears. "We welcomed you on this trip as a friend! And my father! Why, he couldn't have been kinder to you, and you repay that kindness by writing things about him that have no basis in fact. He was not a monster! He was a living, breathing, loving man, Mr. Brown! Have you no sense of decency and loyalty?" Lilly was breathing hard and fought to control her angry trembling. "Is it really your intention to give this fabricated story to your publisher?"

Mr. Brown at least had the good grace to look embarrassed. He tried not to meet her eye because he was ashamed now that she had confronted him. But as ashamed and embarrassed as he might feel, he had a job to do and an assignment to fulfill. Finally, he remembered what his colleagues back home would say when looking for justification for whatever story they had published. "Freedom of the press is..." But Lilly didn't let him finish.

"Don't you speak to me about freedom of the bloody press! That is not what we are talking about here. We are talking about common decency. We are talking about our good names. Why, this is nothing more than slander!"

That may be true, he thought, but he had seen his publisher, the great Randolph Hearst get away with saying things that upset and offended many. Mr. Hearst certainly didn't get to his elevated position by being a nice guy. If Lilly wanted to go all the way to America to challenge his side of the story in court, then so be it. She had the money to be able to do that, but the case would be extremely time-consuming, so he doubted she would take it so far as that. A story such as this came along once in a lifetime, and it had the potential to make him a rich man. He hoped to stretch it into a serial, or maybe even write a book. Regardless of his personal feelings of guilt, he had to stand firm on this decision.

"I'm just doing my job, Lilly. This is a profession where you can't please everyone no matter what you do. I'm sorry, but I fully intend to submit my story whether you are happy about it or not."

Without another word, Lilly threw the loose pages in his face and dropped the book at his feet, before storming off in a rage. Her actions were not very ladylike, but he should just be glad she had refrained from throwing the book at his lying head!

Bala paused to give him a piercing glare and then turned to follow after Lilly. So she had been right! This witchdoctor in the straw hat was conjuring up bad magic after all. It was a good thing she had uncovered his true intentions before anyone else got hurt. This just confirmed the fact that Lilly needed her around. Whatever happened, Bala had to make sure that she and Lilly stayed together.

Mr. Brown thoughtfully watched them stalk away. He really did feel bad, for he had liked them all very much. Ever so slowly, he gathered up the loose pages, tucking them safely back inside of his notebook before walking back to the hotel. He had to shake off these negative feelings and move on, so he shrugged his shoulders and made his decision. He was not pleased with himself, but he did have an obligation to his employer.

Little did he suspect, this iron-willed girl was not going to give up so easily. If she had learned one thing, it was that she was strong enough to stand her ground for those she loved.

Lilly had regained her composure by the time she reached the steps of the small mud brick building, which housed the government office. With some detective work, she had been successful in obtaining the name of a member of the British Foreign Service who was located in the same town as her lodgings. She was glad she had taken the time to change into a proper dress, which had been given to her by a soldier's sympathetic young wife. It was a little snug and plain, but she wore it like a princess would wear a rich bejeweled ball gown, with her head held high as though she was the belle of the ball. She had a feeling that looking like a proper lady might help her to get what she wanted. And she was not above using feminine wiles if needed, although it seemed ages since she had put them to use.

As she was about to enter, she stopped to tug at the low-cut neckline of her dress but then changed her mind and decided to leave it as low as decently possible. Then turning to Bala, she said, "I really don't know how long I will be, so why don't you sit here and wait for me," and she indicated a small wooden bench against the outer wall.

Lilly smothered a smile when Bala went over and sat down. Bala obviously had a good understanding of the Queen's English when she chose to. When she had more time, Lilly would work on expanding Bala's vocabulary, and then she would teach her to read and write. As for now, she straightened her bonnet, threw back her shoulders, and stepped inside.

Centered in the small foyer facing the door was a plain wooden table. A rather young clerk of European extraction was sitting there, making entries in a ledger of some kind. As soon as he noticed her, he jumped to his feet, knocking his chair askew, bowed gallantly, and said, "My name is Robert Cratchit. How may I be of service to you, miss?"

Had it been under any other circumstances, Lilly would have found humor in the irony of his name; but at the moment, she was not in the mood to engage in friendly banter. "My name is Miss Lilly Billingsley, daughter of the late Sir Arthur Billingsley. I do not have an appointment, but it is imperative that I speak to Sir Philip Moran immediately on quite an urgent matter."

"Please have a seat, miss," he said as he gestured to a sturdy but worn-looking wooden chair on the opposite side of the table. "I will see if he is available to meet with you." With that, he quickly knocked, paused, and then disappeared through a door.

Lilly could hear muffled voices. They were no doubt discussing her. When the door finally opened, an older gentleman emerged wearing tan pants and matching vest. His white shirt sleeves were rolled up, his tie was loosened, and his dark hair showed streaks of white and was slightly ruffled. His shirt was sweat stained, and there was a coating of dust on his black shoes. He gave the appearance of a very busy man who spent a fair amount of time in the field.

Sir Moran was pleasantly surprised at the beautiful young woman waiting to see him. The simple dress did nothing to detract from her beauty, and on the contrary, he had to fight to keep his eyes from straying to the tight-fitting neckline of the gown. Her green eyes were framed by thick black lashes, and a becoming dimple flashed appealingly in one smooth tanned cheek. Her bonnet was unable to completely hide the reddish gold highlighted curls that had defied any attempt at taming them. This was an unexpected pleasure indeed.

"Welcome, my dear. If you will follow me, we shall have more privacy in my office."

She offered him her hand on which he bestowed a little kiss, and then used it to help her to her feet. She allowed him to take the lead and assume the role of the gentleman. If that was what it took, she would play along, she thought to herself remembering what the professor once said about having to pay the price to get things done. She let him gallantly lead her into the next room.

There was not much difference between this room and the foyer they had just stepped out of except for the ceiling fan, and the fact that this room contained a proper desk. The fan was actually a large rug hung from a bar, which swung back and forth stirring the air enough to create a slight relief from the stifling heat. A rope was attached to it that was being pulled and released, no doubt by some unseen native hand on the other side of the wall.

Sir Moran ordered some tea and settled in behind his desk. They made small talk while waiting for a servant to bring the brew, and after it was served, they got down to business.

"So, Miss Billingsley, what can I do for you?" He actually already knew her story, but after meeting her, he couldn't believe even half of it was true.

Lilly started from the beginning. "My father and I came out here on an expedition...."

Ten minutes into her narrative, Sir Moran began to realize this would take a while. He had indulged in a few sips of tea, when he decided he might do better with something stronger. Excusing himself, he produced a bottle of whiskey from a cabinet, held it up to Lilly, and politely asked, "Do you mind if I…?"

Lilly shook her head and replied, "Not at all, please feel free." And she took up her story where she had left off. He poured himself a small glass of the liquor and sat down again. Tea was a Crown drink, but whiskey was more to his liking.

When Lilly had finished relating her tale of woe and had explained the newspaperman's plan to exploit her suffering for his own personal profit, she asked Sir Moran for his help in preventing this injustice from happening.

After a moment of consideration, he replied, "I am truly sorry for your misfortune, Miss Billingsley, as well as your dilemma with Mr. Brown, but I am afraid there is really nothing I can do. Mr. Brown is a citizen of the United States, which is also where he intends to publish his article, so you see, my hands are tied. Perhaps you could seek legal recourse from an American attorney. But even then, you don't really have a case against him until he actually carries through with his plan. I am sorry I cannot help you, but I wish you the best of good luck."

He stood up in an effort to end the meeting, and Lilly stood as well. She knew he could help if he chose to. She had to hold herself back from throwing her cup of tea in his politely smiling face, but she forced herself to remain calm.

She thanked him for his hospitality and the tea and as she extended her hand, and as he reached for hers, she noticed something that was very familiar to her. He looked confused as she withdrew her hand before they had even made contact, and instead released something from around her neck. She then clasped his hand in hers, and when she let go, Sir Moran was left with something in his palm. It was a Masonic ring—the very same type of ring he wore on his own finger. He looked at her quizzically and waited for an explanation.

"My dear late father was a devoted Mason. He always told me that if there was ever a time when I was in dire need of help, all I would have to do is ask a fellow Mason. That is a Masonic ring, is it not?" When he nodded in affirmation, she said, "Well, then I ask you one more time. Sir Philip Moran, will you help me?"

Caught off guard by her plea, and knowing that it was his duty to assist her under the circumstances, he smiled in recognition of her determination and audacity. He then said, "I will look into the matter, miss, but that is all I can promise you. If there is indeed anything I can do, you may rest assured I will do it."

"That is all I ask. Thank you, Sir Moran, may the Great Architect smile favorably on you." She hoped he was a man of his word. He had better be. She also hoped that she did not appear too fragile and helpless, as she wanted him to know she would not be easily dismissed. She came here for a reason, expecting to get help, and she didn't intend to give up until she received it.

After he returned her ring, Lilly took a couple of steps to leave and then stopped, turned, and strode back to the desk. She picked up his glass, which still held some whiskey, raised it ever so slightly as she had seen others do to toast to companions, threw back her head, and swallowed the contents in one gulp. She did not like the strong smell of it, and it burned like liquid fire on the way down, but she refused to choke or even make a wry face. She set the glass down with a bang, smiled sweetly, curtsied, and walked out into the foyer trying not to laugh at Sir Moran's gaping mouthed expression, which had quickly turned into a silly grin.

Robert Cratchit rose to his feet as she left the inner office and reentered the foyer. He hurried over to open the outer door like a gentleman. "Good day, Miss Billingsley."

"Why thank you, Mr. Bob Cratchit, and a good day to you too!" she said with a big smile. *Now* she was in the mood to find the humor in his name!

Mr. Brown was sitting in the depot waiting for his train to arrive when a strange man approached him. "Mr. Harry Brown?"

Even though he wore civilian clothes, Mr. Brown could guess from his bearing that he was either a distinguished gentleman or possibly a military man. "Yes, I am he." What could he possibly want?

He sat down next to the curious reporter and leaned closer to him as though he wished to share a confidence. Mr. Brown's interest was instantly peaked. Did this person have a scoop for him? He leaned forward in anticipation to hear what he hoped would be a juicy story.

"It has come to the attention of Her Majesty's government that you have recorded certain information concerning the events which transpired at a military fortification on the frontier."

Suddenly, the reporter's guard came up. Oh no, they were after his story!

"The events in question deal with sensitive information involving important members of government, and possibly royalty. Some of these details are confidential. We must therefore ask you to refrain from submitting, and or, publishing the said information and request that you turn over all of your notes concerning these events."

Mr. Brown was thinking fast, quickly trying to figure out his options. Unfortunately, he was at a disadvantage being such a long way from home.

Receiving no response, the mysterious stranger continued, "In return for your cooperation, I have been authorized to present you with this packet of information, which you can submit to your publisher. In addition, I am to offer you this bank draft to compensate you for your labors and expenses thus far." With that, the young man handed Mr. Brown a large thick packet and an envelope.

Inside were maps of the African continent with the movements of German troops marked in. From what he could see, there were also telegraph cables of a diplomatic nature and official stamped documents concerning these movements. If these were genuine, which he had no doubt they were, his boss would most assuredly be interested.

The bank draft was indeed quite generous. Even without selling his story, this money would make his stay in Egypt worthwhile. Regardless, he decided to test his options by asking, "And what if I choose to decline your generous offer?"

The gentleman's expression hardened as he realized the reporter was fishing to get a better deal. "This is my one and only offer, Mr. Brown. You may take it or leave it, but I strongly suggest you take it."

The information offered in exchange was clearly genuine, and most likely valuable. By giving it to him for publication, it probably served some purpose that was beneficial to the British. That means they would *want* him to get home safely with it, and no unfortunate "accident" was likely to befall him along the way. The bank draft was an extra incentive to close the deal. If they were going through so much trouble to stop him from writing his story, he hated to think what they would do to him if he refused to comply.

The reporter reluctantly handed over his case containing all of his long hard work, with mixed feelings. "Everything you seek is inside."

"Thank you, Mr. Brown, and good day to you." With that, the man rose to his feet and walked away.

Mr. Brown sat and just stared at the packet. He had been looking forward to publishing his story about the curse, Lilly, the fighting, and the strange circumstances of her father's transformation from man to beast. It was all he had been thinking about for these past few weeks. Now he had been asked, no, he had been commanded to just forget all about it. His chance at wealth and notoriety was snatched from him in an instant.

One bit of consolation was that he no longer had to struggle with his conscience over the dilemma of his story, verses what distress it would cause Lilly. He had really grown to like and admire her, so maybe taking the decision out of his hands was for the best after all.

He looked through the papers in the packet more carefully. Some of them were written in German, which meant he would need to obtain an interpreter. A grin spread over his face as he remembered a cute little blond he knew back home who could both read and speak German. It seemed things might be looking up for him already.

35

Lilly, back in men's khaki, and Bala, in the more comfortable Egyptian attire, stood on the dock with Charles. He didn't quite know how to act or what to say, so much had transpired since they had started on this trip. Lilly had been through so much that he wasn't sure she was even the same girl he used to be so close to. Because of his uncertainty, his old shyness and clumsiness had resurfaced. How could they ever be normal again after all they had been through? Summoning his courage, and remembering what his uncle had told him of his own true love, he decided not to waste this opportunity. It was now or never.

"I am begging you to reconsider, Lilly. Please return home with us. After all you have been through, you need your friends and family close by." The professor too had done all he could to persuade, cajole, and even threaten her in order to get her to agree to go back with them. He finally gave up when she wouldn't budge, but he made her promise to return home soon. All he could do was provide her with funds and hope she was being truthful when she said she would follow them shortly.

Charles boldly took her small hands in his. "I love you, Lilly! I see now what I was too blind to see all along. I think I have always loved you." She looked deeply into his eyes and saw what she never really noticed before—the sincere look of true love.

Lilly smiled back at him. "I love you too, Charles. You will always hold a special place in my heart, my dear friend. I know that we will be seeing each other again one day, only I am not ready to leave this place just yet."

Dear friend? He wanted to be more than that, but he would have to accept what she had to give for now. Perhaps she wasn't ready to commit to more. "But who will look after you? A girl needs her family and friends at a time like this. You need to go home."

"No, Charles, I'm past needing someone to take care of me. I am a grown woman." Lilly glanced away from him as a shocking thought occurred to her. She looked back at him with a sad smile. "Why, Charles, do you realize my birthday has passed without my even realizing it? I am eighteen years old! I truly am officially a grown woman, which means that I no longer have to account to anybody for anything I do." Then her smile faded as she said, "Besides, I have no family to go back to. I have given your uncle power of attorney to see to my affairs and to send me money when I need it. Besides, my father's ashes are here." Looking off into the distance, she continued, "Maybe it was best that he was cremated, for whenever I think of him, I can simply close my eyes and imagine the breeze that is caressing my cheek is actually my father's gentle touch of love."

Charles didn't know what else to say. What *can* you say to that?

Lilly leaned forward and gave him a light kiss on the lips. "Have a safe trip, Charles, and try not to worry about me."

He stood paralyzed by the totally unexpected gesture, until Lilly finally said, "You had better get on your ship. It seems they are about to leave without you."

He picked up his bag and a stack of books and started to run, but he had only taken a few steps when some of them slid off the top of the pile and onto the ground. He bent to pick them up but then abandoned the task as he ran back and kissed Lilly again on the mouth. This kiss lasted longer than the first, and then with a big smile plastered on his face, he turned to go, paused, came back, and hugged a startled Bala. He grinned mischievously and ran over to retrieve his books. As he did so, he yelled happily over his shoulder, "Write me!" He finally gathered the unwieldy tomes into his arms and then nearly dropped everything again as he juggled his belongings while attempting to wave while crossing the gangplank.

Lilly waved to Charles with an unexpected lump in her throat and a tightness in her chest. She lightly touched her lips, which still tingled from their last kiss. She wanted to call him back to her, but it was too late, the ship was leaving. Was this more than just love for a friend she was feeling? Suddenly, Lilly realized that although she would miss both Charles and the professor, it was Charles that she was already yearning for.

Sensing the feeling of heartbreak and loss, Bala stepped up next to Lilly on the dock. The two women, so different yet in many ways so similar, stood shoulder to shoulder, solemnly watching the ship depart. They didn't know what the future held; they only knew they would face it together.